INCHOATIO

INCHOATIO

IVO Q.C

Inchoatio

by Ivo Q.C

Published by TecnoTur Publishing

Editing: GM Par

Internal layout: Allan Tépper

Cover design: Karla Herrera

ISBN of the paperback:

979-8-9925106-0-7

ISBN of the electronic version (ebook):

979-8-9925106-1-4

For all the heroes out there, those that don't wear capes; the ones that were remembered and the ones that have been forgotten; those that are cheered on and those that go unnoticed.

Keep fighting, you're making a better world.

INCHOATIO

Adj. /ɪnˈkoʊ.t.i.əʊ/

Word used when something is at the very edge of existing; just the very beginning. Can be used for expressions like 'the tip of the iceberg' or 'the first layer of the onion'.

PROLOGUE

Every place has its ways, its traditions, its fables, and especially its myths. In Latin America grandparents tell the story of a lady who lost her son, yet she called him every night: *La Llorona*. In Scotland, there's the tale of a mysterious and horrible creature that lives in a nearby lake: the Loch Ness monster. And in ancient Greece they had an extensive list of myths with bad-tempered gods that played with life as they wished.

As you can see, a myth is rarely a good thing, a concept mostly used to keep the word *curse* out of children's mouths.

All I'm about to tell you has something to do with a myth. Not one you have probably heard of, but certainly an interesting one. Not many know about it, or actually acknowledge it. The few who do, either love it, or hate it.

Do you remember all those movies you ever saw as a child? All those books you read? All those heroes you followed? What if I told you they aren't heroes, not all of them anyway.

Being a hero is far more complicated than putting a cape on and soaring through the skies. Being a hero is not all about the battles they fight on the outside or the victories the news gets to film. It is more about the battles we fight within ourselves. The battles humanity has been cursed to lose forever.

Today, finally, I have gotten tired of this strange version history has been telling you: the heroes they're trying to sell and the villains they're trying to make you hate. There is far more in these stories than what they want you to know. There is love, hate, betrayal, tears, smiles, pain, kindness, strength, and most importantly, perseverance. And it all came from a small group of people that had no idea what they could do. They just tried to live, and on the way, they realized they would have to fight for it. Some lives were lost, some backs were stabbed, some people misjudged, some pains were shared, and some families were broken. But maybe it's all worth it if people get to know the story. Don't you agree?

THE MYTH

I guess if I'm going to play narrator and tell you this story properly, I also must share with you the myth I have talked about so much. There are thousands of versions out there, not counting those that are far from reality of course. I have done my job, researched for hours and finally I have found a way I can explain it and keep all my Christmas gifts.

Iroes, that's what they all call them, the one thing they all agree on. The world whispers it around, using it as an insult. As a sickness. I don't know who started it or when it will end. I just know it has been around for so long for it not to have a meaning.

The "sickness" started in the north, far from the rest of the world, in a small village. When kids turned eight, they were brought to a teller, a man with the duty of reading the children's future. Yet it was done more out of tradition than actual belief in the man's abilities.

One day, decades ago, so far in the past that their houses were still being lit by candles, a couple brought their kid. The teller did with him as he did with all others. He brought his tea leaves, his books, his cards, everything as routinely as clockwork. But he found something outrageous, the kid was stronger than normal, and he never got sick. He was different. It was then that the teller knew he was the bringer of a curse.

The teller tried to take the kid away from his parents, attempting to save the village. The parents didn't let him. Instead, they took their son back and ran to their house, shutting the door and all windows. As they ran, the teller screamed at them, begging them to get rid of the kid and save their people.

A week after visiting the teller, the story says, at night, screams came from the kid's house, atrocious screams.

The next morning there was nothing left of the village, but ashes and blood. It had all burned down. There was just one survivor: the teller.

After having watched his home burn, he ran to the neighboring villages and told the story again and again. Soon they had been given a name: Íroes, the cursed children.

The tale from the northern village stuck to some cities more than others. People grew more scared every day; everybody asked the teller to visit their kids. It wasn't much time afterward when parents decided to take matters into their own hands. For years babies were tested, left in the cold snow or in the deep waters for seconds, minutes or hours. If the child survived miraculously unharmed or recovered extraordinarily, they were abandoned, left to die in the hands of nature.

Nobody knows how many lives were taken this way, how many kids were robbed of their futures, how many great minds were lost or how many more could have been unjustified if it had not been for Lester Eslinger.

Lester Eslinger appeared in history books half a century after the northern village had been burned, and he came up with the solution. He founded The Superiors, an organization designed to help free humanity from the curses of genetics, or that's what they offered, and everybody bought.

Eventually, all the cities that had been ruled by fear for nearly fifty years gave their power to The Superiors, old monarchies and democracies long forgotten or ignored, forced into the corners of their own territory. Meanwhile, Lester Eslinger and his people kept their promises, they cleansed the genetics of any curse, seeding an immense fear of anyone who dared to be a bit different. Yet there's still the belief that one day the Íroes will return and bring their curse all over humanity as revenge for all the pain that has been hidden away.

1

HOW IT ALL STARTED

Hally swore the glass had shattered before it had even touched the ground. Just as she swore Ms. Knox had screamed before the glass had shattered.

"Hally Black Sols!"

None of the other students moved, they'd witnessed this scenario enough times the last semester to know one thing: they had to let it take its course, just like a hurricane or a tornado.

Hally looked at the transparent liquid spreading across the floor, no one restraining it. The classmates beside her had already learned not to put their bags anywhere near unless they wanted to take glass and chemicals back home.

"Yes ma'am?" Hally asked as she raised her innocent eyes,

she knew what Ms. Knox was going to say, she just needed her to say it.

"Out of my class," Ms. Knox demanded, pointing at the door.

Hally kept her smile hidden behind the best scared and sad look she could maintain. She organized her notebooks, grabbed her backpack and gave a slight look to her right. Tom returned the slight nod and tapped his notebook; he would take extra notes for her.

The whole class stayed quiet as Hally moved past the desks and reached the front.

She clutched her notebooks closer to her chest as she walked in front of Ms. Knox, as always, she looked at the lady's right arm before meeting her eyes. The white tattooed rose was the only reminder she needed to want to get out of that class. When Hally finally looked at Ms. Knox's eyes, she realized her teacher had been looking at her right arm, where no tattoo decorated her skin, instead, a scar tried to hide.

Then the moment came, it was shorter than a second, but it meant everything to Hally. To the rest of the world, it was a simple look shared between a clumsy student and an angry teacher. To Hally it was the 'truth look'. For that split second, she was able to shove into Ms. Knox's face, what they both knew, the beaker hadn't fallen by accident and that tattoo had no power there.

The door was closed behind Hally's back. She looked at the empty hall and she heard Ms. Knox restart the class where she had left off. A smile crossed her face from ear to ear. She took a deep breath; the joy strengthened inside her. She loved that moment, the moment school ended, and her afternoon started.

We could start at the real beginning with the iconic "in the beginning there was nothing" and build the story from there to make you understand why Hally hated her chemistry class. But frankly, I don't think we have to go back that far. If you don't know basic history by this page, that's a problem you have to deal with yourself, not me. Also, it would take much too long, a lot of things had passed in the last three years since the Black-Sols had moved from Costa Rica to the small town of Tirabia in the northeastern side of Florida. There was just one thing needed to be known: Hally had soon learned the white roses didn't like Latins.

Needless to say, this doesn't explain why Hally dumped her bag outside school and headed east when her house was west. The answer to where she was going depended on who you asked. If you asked her parents, she never left her school. If you asked the teachers, she stayed behind and helped Tom. And if you asked Tom, she was off to a book club near Miso. All these excuses were as true as Hally calling every lab accident an accident.

I guess if you wanted the truth you would have to ask her directly, and still there was a big possibility of not getting it. After all, Hally knew it for a fact, she was playing with fire. But no one ever asked, so she never told.

Hally looked at the colorful houses on the sides of the street as she untied the sweater that hung from her waist. In a couple of blocks, those houses would be replaced by the half-destroyed buildings that had been once someone's home. A few blocks after that, she would be in Miso. She never walked that far, of course, she may have been reckless, but she wasn't stupid, she knew where she lived.

Hally considered this side of town as a sick community that was slowly dying. The news called the sickness a rare case of restitution. She liked the word chaos.

Tirabia was divided in two: Miso, the eastern side and Flikos, the western side. Hally lived in Flikos, as far away from all the mess as possible. Flikos was a nice town if you didn't mind the silence and boredom. It had lots of cafes with incredible pastry, a decent library, a small museum and a set of incredibly ignorant people who neglected to talk about the mess that just a couple of blocks away ended tens of lives prematurely. Miso, as the evil twin, was horrible. Hally's scar said that in itself.

The young girl covered her face with the hood before the beautiful houses changed. The closer she got, the more she had to go unnoticed. That's why she left her bag behind: no student came this way, much less one that didn't wear a white rose, the sign of purity.

Hally discovered the Superiors' existence back in Costa Rica a few months before her sixth birthday. Her grandmother had told her and Tom the myth, the beginning of the 'cleansing group'. Back then it had seemed to be nothing more than a fable away from all of reality, out of reach like the sun or the moon. Reality had struck when she'd gotten to Tirabia.

A few years back, long before the Black-Sols family had ever set foot in Tirabia, the Gang had appeared, wearing their Superiors badge like a medal and their new ideas like commandments. The rest of the world had been so used to the blood spilling that no one had given a second look. After all, around the world, The Superiors, the Gang, or whatever name the locals had given them, had one goal: purity. An intense genetic purity. And, as you may have guessed, purity doesn't come violence free.

The burnt houses. Or the marked doorways of the 'impures'. Or the twenty odd victims of gunshot wounds. This all was Hally's evidence: sometimes fighting back was as painful as giving in.

One hundred and fifty nine... That was the number of people Hally had stood by as she saw them take their last breath, the number of hands she had held until their last heartbeat. For 158 of them, she had sat there, not able to change anything to prevent their deaths. But there was one she could have avoided, one life she didn't save.

The refuge used to be just that, a refuge: a home for the lost, a shelter for the unsafe, and a hospital for the sick. Now it served another purpose, it was the Back-Fighters head-quarters.

There wasn't anything pretty about the building that lay on the border between Miso and Flikos. It was an old cement building with small windows on the sides. The walls were covered by moss and cracks forming small holes all around, just like scars. The building was in such decay that it raised the question whether it or the refugees needed the most help.

Hally walked to the backside of the building. Since the Gang had realized it was the rebels headquarters, they sat posted at the entrance day and night. They rarely attacked, they weren't that stupid either, but what they did worked. The guns and the black vans up front were enough to scare away any person who sought help, the underground tunnels still a secret few knew.

The Latin girl walked to the left corner where the biggest cracks and holes were. The first time she'd seen them they had been just about the same size as the others, after all these months the cement had worn off and the holes were slightly bigger and round shaped.

Carefully she placed her feet in the first holes, and just as she'd been doing all the time before, she climbed her way to the top.

Once on the roof, Hally looked at the sky and took a deep breath. There, she stood meters from the ground, the cold air hit her face and for a second everything in her life disappeared. For a second she was as free as the chemicals inside the beaker she had broken in class.

"Afternoon," a deep voice interrupted Hally's peace.

"You're early," another voice added.

Hally rolled her eyes.

"I'm always on time, and you always say I'm early," she replied with a soft chuckle.

She crouched down and crawled to the border, between Milo and Barbara. These two had been part of the police department before the Gang had taken over, now they stood watch all afternoon until another officer took over by midnight. They were just an example of the many people, just like Hally, with a growing need to do something against the Gang.

Hally poked her head barely enough to see what was going on in front of the old wooden doors. As always there were two black vans parked alongside the road. Beside them stood two Gang members with their improvised armor, their weird face paint, guns hanging by their sides and the white rose shining on their arms.

"Got what I asked for, sunshine?" Milo asked.

Hally smiled at the nickname. She took a plastic bag out of her pocket.

"I love you," Milo thanked her and poured a few sunflower seeds in his mouth.

The first time Hally had been in the refuge she had babbled something about sunflowers being her favorite flower. Milo had snapped back, arguing they were the ugliest, meant to eat. Hally had replied saying she didn't care; she could love ugly. The next day he had gotten her a couple to cheer her up. Since then, as an ongoing joke, he called her sunshine, and she got him sunflower seeds, not seen in Miso for years now. Sometimes they even exchanged sunflowers.

"How are they doing?" Hally asked, ignoring the sound of Milo's chewing.

"Same as always," Barbara replied, her usual red hair tucked behind her ears in a ponytail. "They stand there for a while, wait a few minutes for the bathroom and complain."

"We're betting on how many complaints we'll hear today, you in?" Milo asked.

"Nope, my mom taught me not to take money from poor people."

"Hey! I'm not poor."

"No, but you will be, if I bet," Hally ventured.

Barbara laughed at her partner's offended expression.

"Oh yeah, yeah. Laugh all you want, we'll see who wins," Milo warned Barbara.

"Sure-"

"That one's new," Hally interrupted Barbara. A third black van had just pulled between the other two.

"What do we have here?" Barbara muttered to herself.

From the new van two people came out, one adult man and a boy.

"We'll be ready in a while," the man said. There was no need for him to speak loudly, ever since the first shot had been fired years ago silence ruled the streets.

"Ye-ee-ss, sir," the boy stuttered, his voice echoing through the street.

Sure, Hally wasn't friends with the Gang, but with time she'd grown to recognize some of them. On Wednesdays there was a tall guy allergic to peanuts, who complained all afternoon to his partner, mostly about the weather. On Fridays there was a girl near her mid-twenties, she had just broken up with her boyfriend and had spent many of the last weeks planning her revenge although it was clear she still loved him. And on Mondays there was a much older guy who always fell asleep from three to five with a picture of his granddaughter in his hand.

But this time, there was that fourth member, a kid similar to Hally's age, not one day beyond his sixteen years, who she'd never seen. He had two identical bandages on each arm. Hally knew what they meant; he was a new member. The right bandage stood for his new tattoo and the left bandage for the test he had to endure to prove his purity. A combination of those two could only mean one thing, and it wasn't a good thing.

"Damn it, they're having an initiation today," Milo grumbled under his breath.

"I'll tell Jess," Hally hurried to say.

"You do that, we'll get our snipers ready," Barbara added.

Hally stared at her for a second, eyebrows slightly raised.

"Relax. We won't use them unless it's necessary."

"He's just a kid, remember that, please," Hally begged them.

"We will, now go tell Jess," Milo assured her.

Hally made her way back, away from the edge. She walked to the corner, where a loose skylight awaited her. Then she removed the loose glass and went through the hole. She landed on the top of a cupboard from the lab. From there, Hally made a small jump over to the table and then to the ground. She was instantly greeted by the sounds of life.

She rushed and grabbed her white coat from the hangers. Hally had worked there as a medical aid for a while now, and the first thing she'd learned: it didn't matter how much you'd studied or if you'd studied at all, if you didn't wear a white coat, none of the refugees would let you treat them. Then, she went through the doors to the open room.

The refuge hadn't changed much when it had started to be called the Back-Fighters headquarters, aside from the occasional meetings and lots of 'fragile' marked boxes it was still the same: a big open room filled with people laying around, some in improvised beds and the rest on top of whatever they could find to keep themselves warm, a wooden floor that creaked with each step and the old walls patched with different colors to hide whatever blood couldn't be cleaned off.

As soon as she made it through the doors Hally's eyes fell on the first bed. There wasn't anybody on it. The sheets had been cleaned and were well organized. The pillowcases had been replaced and a thin blanket had been folded into a square and put on the corner. In front of the pillow, in the middle of the bed, there was a white paper, in it was written the name "Galo Mez." the period at the end burning through Hally's eyes into her heart.

Whenever a person's life was lost, they had the tradition to leave their bed empty for a day and write their name. The period indicated another story had reached its end.

Hally sniffled.

"She died at night, in her sleep. She went in peace," Rory said by her side. He was one of the three nurses that worked alongside Jess, Lisa, the other doctor and Hally. They were the ones that made sure the Gang's victims were given the best care until a hospital in Flikos was able to take them.

"She was a good lady. I talked to her yesterday. She was fine. She even talked about the possibility of going to meet her new grandchild in LA," Hally said, there was always a part of someone's death that was too hard to grasp.

"Yeah... Her heart just stopped. We don't know why."

Hally cleaned off the one tear that fell from her right cheek, she had to talk to Jess, it was an emergency. The mourning would have to wait.

"Are Monica and Maxwell still here? I saw the coffee stains on the table."

Rory shook his head.

"You just missed them by a couple of minutes."

"Dang it," Hally muttered. "Where's Jess?"

"Down by Ms. Wang. What's wrong?"

"There's a new recruit out there."

"Oh," Rory whispered. "I'll start moving the patients. We don't need more deaths, this one has already hit pretty hard."

Hally nodded in agreement.

The famous bosses were the perfect trio: Monica, Maxwell and Jess. Jess was the doctor; he was the one that made sure the refuge kept running. Monica was what the nurses and Hally called the Ambassador. She was the one that kept contact with the Gang, got information on where they were going to attack, and called out to Miso and other cities for help. And Maxwell, he was the head of the police department of Miso, which had now been dismantled by the Gang.

Each of these three had their own territory. The refuge was Jess', although it was considered the headquarters. Monica had secured the town hall when the restitution had started. And Maxwell had recently recovered power over the police station. Yet nothing caused as much drama as hitting where the weak felt safe.

"Jess," Hally called before she had reached him.

The doctor had his long black hair combed backwards, and in his hands, he held what Hally assumed to be Ms. Wang's information.

"Hally! I'm glad you're here. I need four bandages on beds six, eighteen, twenty-five, and eleven. Mr. Chia needs his medication. The girl on the end needs a suture. And could you check if the blond guy's signs have returned to normal? They were a bit fussy the last time I saw them."

"Doctor Shellow!" Ms. Wang snapped. "Manners! You didn't even ask the girl how she was doing!"

Jess cringed at the scolding.

"I'm fine, *thank you for asking Ms. Wang*," Hally smiled. "Sometimes it's nice to be appreciated," she added.

"We appreciate you!" Jess defended himself.

"Sure." Hally pulled him to the side for a second.

"What was that about? She already thinks I'm a monster without manners!"

"There's a new recruit out there," Hally interrupted what would have been a funny chat.

Jess' eyes darkened. He was young, and he looked young, but whenever bad news reached him, which was pretty often, wrinkles and huge bags under his eyes seemed to appear out of nowhere.

Jess started to walk towards the entrance, Hally followed him close behind.

"We got a code black people! Code black!" he announced as he walked.

"Rory has already started to hide patients," Hally informed Jess.

"Great. Help him move the mild conditions to the back and when they are there hide with them."

"Jess!" Hally whined.

"Hally! We're not having this conversation again. Unlike what you just told Ms. Wang, we do appreciate you. Alive! You're hiding with the patients," Jess said, there was no question mark in his voice, it was an order.

"He's my age."

"Who?"

"The new recruit! He's my age. You know what that means! The Gang is growing, wildly. Once the younger ones join, we can give the place up for lost. The Back Fighters are going to need all the help they can get. I am the help!"

Jess stopped; they had reached the doors.

"I know you want to help. And I know you can help, that's why we let you come here and deal with the patients. But you're fifteen, your parents don't even know you come, and you're Latin, they don't need another reason to want you dead and we don't need one to keep you alive."

"I can help," Hally insisted. In past years she had learned all she could about medicine. Then she learned all she could about Miso's culture, people: their myths, economics, politics, dreams and fears. Sometimes the refugees didn't need a doctor, only a friend. But that wasn't enough, she knew she could still do more.

Jess looked at Hally's right arm. He had been the one to save her life, the one to attend to that open wound.

"That was years ago, a lot has changed. I can help," she repeated.

Jess licked his lips, he was thinking.

"Help Rory hide the rest of the patients, and then come back. You're on door duty."

"Door duty?"

"That or you hide."

"Fine," Hally mumbled. "Door duty it is."

She ran down to the back where she pulled the vault door wide open for the patients to hide. There, her hands started to sweat, her wrist started to itch, and her heartbeat sped up. Things were about to become more real now. And she could mess them up, like always.

Not now. Please not now. Hally thought

The air wasn't finding its way to her lungs. Her throat was closing.

Okay, you know what to do. Deep breaths. Hally's brain ordered herself.

Hally took a deep breath, held it in, and exhaled. She did it again. And again. And again.

Everything is going to be okay. Everything is going to be okay.

I'm not gonna mess it up. I'm not gonna mess it up.

Hally closed her eyes. She cleared her mind, focused on breathing and...

"Hally! You okay?" Rory asked.

"Of course," she responded, opening her eyes immediately, the breathing back to normal.

Hally was back at the entrance, standing beside Jess, her white coat had now been replaced by a bulletproof vest. Behind her, Rory and Lisa stood looking straight at the door, guns in their hands. Behind those two the place was empty, all patients had been moved to secret vaults on the backside of the building, vaults that had been built after the first attack. They were waiting. She hated that feeling, the peace before the storm. She hated the dreadful silence that filled the refuge waiting to be interrupted by the inevitable initiation. And she hated that fear that made her legs tremble and her palms sweat.

Jess stared at the door; he had already made the phone call. Maxwell was on his way back from the police department with ten other police officers, whether they were going to get there in time for the initiation was a question only time would answer.

Bang! The door was knocked. The answer came rather quickly.

The Gang's initiation was simple, the new member had to make his way into the refuge and leave his painted hand on the back wall. Once the new member made his way back outside, they were given the pleasure to direct their first attack.

The new members got to choose how to make their way into the refuge, some chose a sneak attack covered by the darkness of night. When they chose to do it in daylight it meant one thing: they were planning to shoot their way in, the highest honor within the Gang.

Jess grabbed the small, silver gun in his hands firmly, he looked at Hally and nodded. The old members of the Gang wouldn't intervene until the new one made his way into the refuge and came back out. They would however intervene if the refuge door wasn't opened. By then there were only two options, discourage the new member from continuing the initiation or stop them at any cost, usually by taking life.

Hally took a deep breath and opened the doors letting the sunlight hit the big open room.

"Step away now and no one will be hurt," Jess ordered.

The first rule of door duty: always stay behind the door.

Hally rushed to the small crack between the wall and the door.

"I repeat step away and no one will be hurt!"

The kid, the new member, looked nervously behind him; a lot more people had appeared since Hally had been on the roof. There were four more vans and perhaps twenty more people.

The man with whom the kid had appeared looked at him and to another man behind him: Cloak Guy. Hally recognized him. He was always there wearing a long black coat; his face was never seen, and he was always playing with rocks that he took from his pockets. He was respected and more importantly, feared.

Cloak Guy shook his head, the kid had to do this on his own.

The kid's eyes returned to Jess, neither of their guns had been aimed, but he could see that Rory's and Lisa's were. Just like Barbara's and Milo's.

"Step away," Jess repeated, his voice was firm but still warm with empathy.

The kid looked at his hands, in one hand he held a gun, the other was covered in red paint.

He didn't move for a few seconds, he was thinking. Then his head went back up and his eyes landed on Jess. Hally recognized that look, he'd made up his mind, he was completing the initiation.

Things may have gone differently if the new member was an adult. Then, Hally could have closed her eyes, covered her ears and dealt with the nightmares later. And perhaps, just maybe, she could have gotten over it years later. But he wasn't an adult, he was a kid, just like her. She knew what it was to be young and stupid. She couldn't let that happen. The second that boy raised his gun a bullet would be put through his brain, and that life, that young life would be Hally's fault.

The boy tightened his grip on the gun.

"Wait!" Hally exclaimed; she came out from behind the doors, who would say one single rule would be so hard to keep?

"Hally! It was one fricking rule! What are you doing?" Jess whispered to her.

"Saving his life," Hally whispered back.

Slowly she walked outside, her hands up by her sides showing she was unarmed.

"What's your name?" Hally asked, every set of eyes on her, the sunlight bathing her. She wasn't behind the safety of the door anymore; she was exposed to the world.

"I-I can't tell you my name," the boy answered, his eyes having shifted back from Jess to the gun in his hand.

"That's alright, just tell me a name I can call you," Hally replied.

The man (the one that had arrived with the boy) looked at Cloak Guy, he once again shook his head. This was the boy's thing.

"Bob, you... can call me Bob," the boy, 'Bob', said, regaining Hally's attention.

"Okay Bob. My name is Hally. That's my real name."

The boy kept looking at the gun.

"You know that the gun you're holding is capable of taking a life?"

Bob nodded slightly.

"You don't want to do that. It'll haunt you forever. It'll drag your life to the ground. Pierce your soul. Break your mind."

Hally made a small pause before continuing.

"You have options here, even if you don't feel like you do. If you take this choice, there's no going back. You'll be a killer and that title will never go away. People might not call you that, but you will. Every day you wake up your heart will scream it."

"I ha-ve to do-o i-i-i-t. I have to do it."

"No, you don't. You *can* do it, but you don't have to. If you do it I promise your life will be over. You might not be dead, but your life will be over. You're young, you still have a lot to live for, don't give that away now. Don't." Hally's voice had shifted, she was no longer saying things, she was begging him.

"They'll kill me," Bob said.

"This is a refuge; we'll protect you. I promise. You'll be okay."

There was silence.

"Look at me," Hally asked.

'Bob' doubted. Then he slowly raised his head. His eyes met Hally's. He was scared.

"Put the gun down."

Bob nodded and slowly he put the gun on the floor.

"Ty, that's my real name," he admitted.

"That's great Ty," Hally said with a smile. "Now carefully walk slowly inside," she said as she took slow, small steps backwards.

Ty nodded and took one step.

"No!" the man exclaimed.

A huge explosion ripped Hally and Ty apart. Ty was thrown into the street, Hally into the refuge.

"Hally!" Jess exclaimed, he ran to her, and Rory and Lisa ran to close the doors.

"I'm fine, I'm fine," Hally said without looking at Jess, her head was ringing, and she had scratched her elbows from the hit, but she was okay. She looked at the weird white smoke coming inside the cracks of the doors. "Where's Ty?"

"Hally..."

"Where's Ty?" Hally asked again. "They'll kill him, and it'll be my fault."

"We'll get him, if not today, tomorrow. I promise. Get out of here," Jess rushed her.

"I'll go hide with the others," Hally accepted.

"No Hally, I mean go home. Your eyes are glowing; you were lucky enough they didn't see it once, don't try your luck again. They won't be happy you talked one of them down, and it will be worse once they find out about the rest. They'll hunt you till they find you."

"Jess…"

"Run Hally. And don't come back."

"What about Ty?" Hally cried.

"Hally, I mean it. We'll get him. Go home!"

Hally nodded. She picked herself up from the ground and ran to the back. She climbed onto the table, then the cupboards and onto the roof.

"That was awesome, stupid and incredible," Milo exclaimed when he saw her.

Hally smiled back.

"Hey, what's with your eyes?" Barbara asked.

Hally looked at her reflection on the skylight, just like she feared, her eyes were glowing silver.

"They're coming out!" Milo announced before Hally could answer. "Get away," he said.

Hally didn't need to be told a second time, she pulled her hood on and she climbed down rapidly. When her feet touched the ground, she ran and ran. When the shots started to sound, she just ran faster. She knew what that meant, Ty was gone.

Hally didn't stop running until she arrived at the alley behind her school. There she let herself fall to the ground. She had tried to save his life, instead she'd been his doom.

Hally looked at her reflection in one of the shattered pieces of glass on the floor. She was still wearing the bulletproof vest, her eyes still glowing with that faint silver light she hated. She took the vest and threw it as far inside the alley as she could. Then she rubbed her eyes. The glow wasn't leaving. She closed them over and over and over again, every time she opened them the silver light was still there.

Finally, she knew she would have to let them be. She buried her face between her knees, she was a curse, that's why she wasn't able to save lives. Wherever she went she caused chaos.

"I'm not built for this. If I was, my list of mistakes would be getting smaller, not larger," she sobbed to herself.

Eventually, when there were no more tears to cry and Hally raised her head, the glow was gone. Good, it was already late.

She cleaned her cheeks and smiled at her reflection, the smile had to be believable, or it wouldn't work. She smiled again; it was good enough.

The walk to her house was silent, too silent to mean anything good. Hally hated that feeling as well, the peace after the storm, it was only a reminder that there were a lot of things left to clean up.

A block before she reached her house she saw Tom in the corner, he wasn't happy.

"You're late," he said.

"Sorry," Hally apologized and smiled. "It was the last chapter of the book, and the discussion was very interesting," she said. Tom had offered to cover for 'her unapproved book club' every afternoon with the condition that she was always on time, a condition she rarely kept.

"What happened to your elbow?"

Hally looked at it, she had completely forgotten it was still bleeding.

"I fell on the sidewalk. There was a hole I didn't see, and I fell," she answered without missing a beat, the lie was good enough for her brother.

"Fine, just clean it. Let's go." Together they walked to their house.

Tom looked just like Hally, after all, they were twins. They shared their dark brown hair, Tom's perfectly combed backwards, Hally's long and curvy. They shared their tanned skin color and their dark brown eyes, Hally's slightly shinier than Tom's. The only big difference, excluding the five centimeters that made Tom taller, were their facial features. While Hally's were hidden by her chubby cheeks, Tom's were marked by the serious look he held most of the time.

Quickly, the twins reached their house, a small two floor house, painted white, with a small porch in front.

The kids stepped onto the porch and Tom opened the door.

"We're home," he announced as he went in.

Hally hesitated before following him. One hundred and sixty lives she could have saved. One hundred and sixty lives she had seen fade away in the last three years, two were her fault. It was definite, she was a curse, nothing could change that.

She took a quick look at her reflection on the window, her normal brown eyes stared back at her. Those 160 lives stayed outside that door, inside that house she had to be the normal fifteen-year-old teenager her parents thought she was.

Hally practiced her smile once again; it was much better than before.

Satisfied, she entered the house.

2

CURSES DON'T EXIST

Tom's day had been terrible even before his sleep had been interrupted.

He had reached school like he did every day; he'd taken notes for Hally in chemistry class and when the bell marking three o'clock rang, he had picked his things up and walked between the rest of the teenagers to the small classroom that had become his home for the last years.

There weren't many things that made Tom happy, he liked not having to deal with people, staying inside, dealing with numbers and having his things well organized. The Classroom was no exception to these rules, it was small, there was no doubt, (that's why they let Tom use it), but it was well organized, up to every single pen that fell within its borders.

Tom made his way inside the Classroom. He placed his color-coded books within five centimeters of the upper corner of the wooden table he called a desk. Softly he hung his bag on a hook in the wall behind the door and he sat down in the hundred-year-old chair. There, he sat waiting, looking firmly at the only other small desk that stood in front of him, Classroom was so small that there was no place for anything else. Still, Tom had made it possible for the small bookcase in the corner holding the best edition of the classics he'd been able to find in the school's library.

"Everything's in place," Tom mumbled to himself.

The door flung open. A young boy, no older than twelve, came in running, covered with sweat and breathless. He forced the door closed behind him and fell against it.

Tom looked at the boy speechless. His blond hair had been stained with blood, his eyes were filled with fear, all his clothes were wet with sweat and Tom could perfectly see a giant purple circle start to appear around his right eye.

"Carlos!" Tom exclaimed.

The kid looked up at him and gave him a half smile.

"Sorry Teach, got a little bit entertained on the way," he said.

"What? Why? What happened?" Tom asked.

Carlos stood up sloppily and let himself fall on the only desk there was left. He was a sixth grader and he'd been Tom's student for over a year now.

"Oh, you know, the usual," Carlos replied as he cleaned his face with the end of his shirt. "The Jilsons found me in the hallway, and they looked pretty bored. Pretty sure they lost an English exam or something and needed to blow some steam."

"Are you serious?" Tom asked. "Isn't this the third time this month?"

Carlos clicked his tongue.

"You know how these kids are. They come from Miso and my parents are Latin, why else do they need to hit me? Anyway, they'll forget about me in a month or so."

"Until they come back again," Tom exclaimed.

Carlos shrugged.

"Then, I'll deal with them again, Teach. The trick is not letting them see how they break your spirit, if they see it, then they'll do it more. The more you show that it doesn't affect you the less they like to do it."

A bang came from the door.

"Come out you little filthy scumbag, we aren't done with you," an angry voice said from outside.

"Sorry, maybe later. I'm in the middle of a class," Carlos responded.

They banged the door even harder.

Tom's heart raced as the bang's became louder.

"It's alright Teach, they won't break down the door, then they would have to explain that to the principal and it would be a mess. They won't get into such a mess just for me, I assure you that," Carlos said.

Tom looked at the twelve-year-old, the fear was long gone from his eyes and the sweat was almost completely dried up. He was sitting comfortably with his feet on the desk while there were possibly three or four guys waiting outside to beat him until they got tired. How could he do it? How wasn't he afraid?

Tom grabbed the edge of his chair until he felt the wood was about to cut into his skin. He didn't even know what he would do if they broke in.

Eventually, like Carlos had said, the banging stopped, and Tom and the sixth grader were once again left in silence.

"So Teach, I'mma need some help with today's Math homework. The teacher never attended the lecture to explain concepts in a clear way," Carlos said with a laugh as soon as the last bang came.

Tom looked at him, his heart still beating rapidly. He studied Carlos, his eyes now completely covered by an awful looking purple.

He shook his head.

"This isn't right," he said and stood up.

"Wait, wait, wait," Carlos stopped him. "What are you doing?"

"This isn't right," Tom said pointing at the closed door. "Somebody has to do something."

"Yeah Teach, I agree. But we're in their territory, they have the power here. Going out there and getting yourself a beating won't change a thing. You'll just make their afternoon better."

"You're right," Tom said. He took his seat once again.

"There you go, that's much better," Carlos said, and he resumed searching for his homework in his backpack. "I mean nothing against you or anything, but you're just a teacher, it's better if you leave war for the warriors."

The words weighed heavily on Tom's brain.

"Yeah," he said. "You're right."

But he didn't want Carlos to be right. Tom didn't want to be a teacher. He didn't know what he wanted to be; he just knew he didn't want to be a teacher. He wanted to be somebody else. He wanted to be in charge, to be a leader, to have power, but he didn't know in what way or how. He just knew one thing for sure, he didn't want to be 'just a teacher'.

For the rest of the afternoon that ruled his mind, 'I'm just a teacher'. While he taught Carlos, while he packed up and locked Classroom, while he walked back home, while he waited for Hally, while he ate with his family, while he organized his room, while he got ready to sleep... And finally, it had been his last thought before falling asleep, 'he was just a teacher'. He knew he was meant for something greater, but what that was, was a mystery for him to solve.

"Mmmmm," Tom said as he pulled the pillow from under his head and covered his ears with it.

Just one door down he could hear Hally's steps circling her room. Something was bothering her, or she couldn't sleep for a reason. Either way, Tom was not interested, he just wanted to sleep.

The steps kept going. Tom squeezed the pillow over his ears. It didn't matter, he could still hear the faint 'clack, clack'. Then, for a second, they stopped, and there was quiet.

The door opened, and a small figure came in from outside.

Tom remained still, if he didn't move maybe he would be left alone.

"Tom," Hally whispered, he didn't answer.

"Tom," Hally whispered again.

"Tom, are you awake?"

"No."

"Ja, ja," Hally replied sarcastically, and she stepped closer to the bed. It was certain now, she wasn't going anywhere.

"What do you want?" Tom asked.

"My eyes glowed again today," Hally said.

Tom sighed. He just wanted to sleep; he was tired. Why couldn't he just sleep?

Tom opened his eyes and looked at his sister. She was serious.

"What were you doing?" he asked.

"Nothing much," his sister replied. "I was at the reading club, and they started glowing."

Tom looked at her.

"I'm serious," she babbled. "I'm not a fool. I know your rules. No sports, no feelings, no friends..."

"Hey! We both know those rules have a purpose and it's to keep us away from a science lab for the rest of our lives. Stop saying them as if they were a curse."

"But they are! The rules are a curse! And we're a curse too!"

"Oh Hally, don't start this again. We are not cursed! Curses don't exist!"

"Then how do you explain all of this? My eyes glow like a mythical creature from a fable. And you can't get too excited about anything, because then, you overpower every outlet of the house and every electronic device fries up. If that isn't a curse, then what is it?"

"I don't know. But curses don't exist! All of this has a scientific explanation, you'll see."

"Yeah, when? When we are cornered by the CIA and sold internationally to the highest bidder? Accept it Tom, we are cursed, and we are a curse. Grandma knew it, why do you think she told us the myth the way she did. She knew we were a curse!"

"For the last time Hally, curses don't exist!"

Hally remained quiet for a second. Tom was scared he had been too mean to her.

"Did someone see you today?" he asked, changing the topic.

"I don't know… Maybe. I won't be going back to the book club anymore, just in case," Hally said, there was a true sadness from the words she said .

"So, someone could have seen you."

"I suppose," she answered.

"We have to tell mom."

"No!" Hally barked right back.

"Hally, unlike the weird version of mom you get in those weird dreams of yours, our mom is good. We can trust her. She won't sell us to the CIA."

"I wouldn't be so sure about that," Hally answered.

"Then…" Tom took a deep breath," If you don't want any help from mom you must really commit yourself to the rules. You live a crazy life-"

"I live a life," Hally interrupted Tom.

"Well, we can't do that, not here, not ever. We are Latin, we have an accent when we speak, our skin is brown, and we live in Tirabia. Things are bad enough for us as they are, we can't add glowing eyes and human battery to the mix."

"You're right," Hally sighed.

"I haven't had an attack for over two years now. You get one every six months."

"They're not my fault; you know that we can't control them."

"I know, but you can do your best to prevent them."

There was silence once again.

"I promise, someday I'll find the scientific reason on why your eyes glow, or why I fry up things. Then, I promise, you won't ever have to doubt again that we're a curse."

Hally smacked her lips together.

"Maybe I'll find the reason first."

Tom laughed.

"You can always try."

"I mean it Tom, I could discover it before you do," Hally proposed.

"Again, you can try," he scoffed.

Hally walked towards the door but stopped before leaving the room.

"Tom."

"Yes?"

"Are you sure curses don't exist?"

"Yes, Hally. Curses don't exist. Why do you ask?"

"I don't know. I guess, sometimes life does feel like we are cursed."

Tom didn't answer. He couldn't argue that with her.

"But anyway, nothing we can't fight back, right? Good night," she said, the sadness was now obvious.

"Hey, but close the doo-"

It was too late; Hally was long gone.

Tom stood up and closed the door before throwing himself onto the bed. He truly couldn't argue with Hally, sometimes his life did feel like he was cursed or even worse, he was the curse.

He couldn't remember the first time he had had an attack; in fact he didn't remember much of his life up to when he was six years old like any other human being. He did, however, remember the last time he had had an attack. It had been a normal Wednesday. He and Hally had just gotten a new TV to share like an early birthday present from their parents.

Then, sometime that afternoon Hally had done something. It had been so silly that Tom couldn't even remember what it had been. He just remembered that he'd been very, very angry. So angry, that his eyesight had blurred, his arms had been covered by goosebumps and the lights had started to flicker.

The next thing he remembered was falling over and fainting.

When he had woken up the room had been cleaned. Whatever he'd done had caused the new TV to explode, along with the light bulbs. Hally had cleaned everything to make it look like nothing had happened and she'd taken the blame for it. She had also nursed him for the next four days when he could barely walk. Up to the present Tom knew his parents thought he had gotten a terrible flu instead of the truth.

Since then, Tom had thought much about that attack. He didn't like them; he couldn't control them. He longed for a little bit of control in his life and the attacks were just more proof that he had none. But he liked how they made him feel. For that second, he felt like the world was at his feet and he could overcome anything.

3

THE JILSONS

The usual ticking came at five thirty exactly.

Tom woke up without any problem. He never dreamt, not ever since he could remember anyway. He wasn't so sure whether that was good or not. Hally had been haunted by dreams ever since they had moved to Tirabia. The same nightmares had haunted her long enough that Tom knew she'd started taking them more like memories than actual dreams. At times he wondered if maybe he was the problem, and he'd forgotten something he shouldn't have. But then, he thought about all of Hally's sleepless nights, and he remembered that at least he could control when to fall asleep and when not to.

Unlike the night before, that morning went on as usual. The twins had breakfast with their mom at six thirty, like most days their dad had gone out before they had even woken. After breakfast Hally got the lunches ready and Tom helped their mom in the kitchen. And later, they resumed their usual morning quarrel.

"Hally, I'm begging you."

"I'll be down in a second," Hally said.

Tom looked up the stairs from the first floor, he knew for a fact his sister was no closer to being ready than the last time he had asked her to come down.

"We'll be late!" Tom exclaimed.

"No, we won't," Hally shouted back.

"We're already late!"

"I'm coming!"

"You have said that five times in the last ten minutes."

"It's because I'm coming, eventually."

"Before I get old it would be great!"

"You're already old!"

"We're the same age!"

`That's debatable."

"No it's not, it's-"

"Kids!" their mom's voice echoed from the kitchen. "If you don't quit yelling, I swear I'm going to..."

The sentence was left for the wind and the twin's imagination to finish it.

"Technically," Hally started to say.

"Here we go," Tom mumbled.

"I wasn't yelling, I was just exclaiming with a loud tone," Hally said.

Gia, the twin's mom, appeared from the kitchen and came beside Tom at the bottom of the stairs.

"I'm going to show you what exclaiming with a loud tone is if you don't get down here before your brother gets a heart attack young lady."

Tom looked at the stairs, waiting for a response. It didn't come, in its place Hally appeared ready to leave the house.

"Well, I guess we'll see you Mom," Tom said, turning to his mom.

Gia looked at him, there was shock in her eyes.

"I can't believe that worked," she whispered.

Tom laughed.

"Have a nice day Mom," Hally said. "See you later."

Tom copied his sister with his goodbyes and together they closed the door behind them as they began walking to school.

"How's your elbow doing?" Tom asked as they turned around the corner of Mrs. Maddison's pink house, she was one of the few neighbors the kids had gotten to know. She made some killer brownies and always made sure to give them a few whenever she baked some.

"Has it healed yet?" Tom continued.

Hally looked at him through the corner of her eye.

"You know it has," she responded harshly.

"Why the bandage then?"

"Mom saw it yesterday. So now I have to wear it for a few days. A little bit of eyeshadow and glue should do the trick. In a few days I should be able to appear with my healed elbow without her noticing a difference."

"It seems like a lot of trouble we could avoid."

"I thought there were rules," Hally replied.

She was right, they shouldn't have been talking about that in the middle of the street. That was a rule, one Tom had created.

"Since when do you care about rules?"

"Since I benefit from them. Besides, I'm not a rule breaker, I know you think I'm one. But I'm not. I'm a rule bender."

"And that means?"

"Every rule has some limit where it can be bent and adjusted for you to use it how you wish without breaking it. I work within that limit," Hally explained.

"You know for someone who worries about being cursed you could definitely try to act more normal."

"And *why* would I change myself just to fit your definition of normal? I might have to hide the fact I'm not normal at all, but I'm certainly not one of those boring copy and paste human shells!" She moved her hands from side to side. "No sir, not happening."

"You're doing the grandma talking again," Tom complained.

Hally turned.

"At least I don't organize my desk five times in a row frantically."

"Hey!" Tom fought back. "Organization is the foundation of success."

"Sure, who told you that? The detergent ad?"

Tom opened his mouth ready to reply, but nothing came.

"Hate to break it to you Tommy, but they're just trying to sell the lemon scented liquid for a higher price than their competition."

The teacher arrived two minutes after the bell had rung, about the same time Hally'd noticed she'd lost her notebook and her pencil case and had asked Tom for a spare of both. Tom hated it when they did that, but there wasn't anything he could do that he hadn't done before. He would just have to accept it, his education system and his sister both sucked.

Their first class was English, (the only class except science in which the twins were together) which Tom had always found ironic. English was his second tongue, and yet there were days he knew for a fact that he spoke better English than half the native speakers in the classroom. It hadn't been like that before. Years ago, when Tom had first set foot in Tirabia his English had sucked, worse than anybody could imagine. But then he had learned in a way Hally described as forced learning. Let's just say it didn't take long for their whole family to understand that being heard talking Spanish was like asking for trouble. So, they'd dropped it, inside and outside the house, forever. Of course, Tom could still speak it, yet he knew it wasn't the same.

Sixty minutes and fifteen language torturing presentations later, the class was over. The bell rang and everybody got their things ready and prepared to go to their next class. Tom did just that, he organized his notebooks, put away his perfectly sharpened pencil and was just about to stand up when Hally tugged his arm.

"Wait," she said.

"What? I'm going to be late for history."

"Discreetly look behind me," Hally asked.

Tom moved his head a few centimeters to the side and looked.

"What am I looking for?"

"Is Drey Jilson still staring?"

Tom's eyes fell on a blond-haired boy sitting three desks away from his sister. As he looked at him, a shiver ran up his spine to his neck. Tom could still remember the smell of blood coming from Carlos the afternoon before. Looking at those freakish eyes he knew, that boy enjoyed that smell.

"Yes-" Tom answered.

"Why is Drey Jilson staring?" Hally asked.

Tom thought about it. He didn't like it for a second, but they two had never had any problem with the Jilsons ever. There was no way that Drey had woken up that Wednesday and decided that he was going to mess with the Black-Sols kids, right?

"Maybe he has a crush on you," Tom proposed.

Hally's shiny brown eyes turned to Tom's and glared at him, no sign of a slight laugh coming.

"Oh c'mon! It's funny when you do it, but not when I do?"

"I'm funny, you aren't. And I don't tease you with Jilsons. They hate everybody. We are part of everybody!"

Tom looked at the boy again, he was still staring just like before. He couldn't argue with Hally, something was wrong. Why had he suddenly acknowledged their existence?

"Get moving, your next class starts in a minute," the teacher said.

"Come," Hally said and pulled Tom from his desk to the door before he could argue.

Once in the hallway Tom turned to his sister.

"What are we doing about the Jilsons?"

"Nothing," Hally answered. "Let's just hope that he's just being his normal weird self and he isn't following us because he wants trouble."

"What? He's following us?"

Tom turned and looked behind him.

Hally slapped his arm.

"What part of act natural didn't you understand?"

Tom rubbed his arm; Hally certainly knew how to slap.

"You didn't say to act natural," Tom complained.

"No, because it comes implicitly!" Hally exclaimed in a whisper. "*¡Agh! No puede ser posible!*" she mumbled to herself.

She grabbed Tom's arm and pulled him to the side of the hallway, against the lockers.

"Okay, listen closely and carefully. Do you remember what we talked about last night?"

Tom's eyes opened widely; he hadn't even thought about it.

"You don't think that he-"

"No. I don't, but we have to be careful. So listen-"

"I'm listening," Tom assured her.

Hally took a deep breath.

"I'm going to economics, Drey comes with me to economics. Be on the lookout for the rest of the Jilsons, but I don't think any of them go to history with you. If by the next period they're still following us, then we play sick and go home."

"Skip school?"

"Yes Tom! Skip school and keep our lives!" she retorted.

Hally turned to her locker and started to put her English books inside.

"We'll see how it goes," she continued. "If they persist, we will deal with them then," she nodded.

The bell rang one more time, they were officially late for the next class.

Hally turned one last time to Tom.

"If-"

"Hally!" Tom exclaimed as he tried to cover her from the rest of the kids in the hallway.

"What?"

"Stop it!"

"Stop what?"

"The glowing. Your eyes are glowing!" Tom exclaimed.

Hally looked at the small mirror that hung inside her locker.

"It can't be," she said and hid her head inside the metal box.

"C'mon Hally, you can't be seen like that," Tom said, the hallway grew emptier by the second, they couldn't be the last ones there, it would bring too much attention. "Stop it. Breathe. Calm your mind."

"I know, I know. But- Tom this isn't me. I'm not doing it."

"What do you mean? Who else would it-"

The words were cut by the feeling; the feeling Tom loved. He felt the electricity move through his veins. The lights started to flicker. His hair spiked.

"Oh no... What's going on?" Tom asked.

"See, I told you it wasn't me," Hally said.

"I can't control it Hally, please do something," Tom said, standing frozen. He'd forgotten what it felt like, he'd forgotten how powerful he could feel, and how scared he was at the same time.

"Okay, okay, okay," Hally mumbled.

She looked for something inside her locker, and when her head finally emerged from the metal box, she was carrying the darkest shade of sunglasses Tom had ever seen.

"I'm always prepared," she told him and handed him a cap. "Cover your hair we're going-"

"What is it Hally?" Tom asked.

Hally didn't answer.

He turned. There were seven figures waiting for them. They were in trouble, real trouble. The Jilsons had found them.

4

THE RUN

The scene would have looked hilarious to anyone from afar. Hally knew she would have laughed if it was a scene in a TV show and she was able to stand in the sideline with popcorn. That wasn't the case. It wasn't even close.

"Oh rayos!" Tom let out under his breath.

"It could be worse," Hally said.

"How's that?" Tom asked, he was barely opening his mouth to speak and the flickering lights gave him a pale look.

"We could not have legs," Hally said. "Then we wouldn't be able to do this," she said before grabbing his arm and running as fast and as far away as she could.

It didn't take long before the heavy footsteps of the Jilsons echoed behind them.

Hally dragged her brother through the corridors, turning sharply at every corner. First left, then right, then another left and another right. The Jilsons kept coming. She went through the first door she saw.

"Hally, that's the li-" Tom tried to warn her, it was of no use, Hally had no care for the silent students that were preparing themselves for their next exams or simply enjoying the journey of a good book, she still ran through the wooden floors.

They went through another door, ending up once again in an empty corridor. There they ran through several corners, taking turns here and there. Hally had spent way too many hours in recent years in that place for her not to know where every room, every door and every class was.

At the last turn, she found the tall metallic door she'd been waiting to see. Before Tom could argue with her, she grabbed his arm tightly and dragged him into the sunlight, right into the parking lot. They sprinted by the guard so fast that he'd no chance to stop them.

Luckily, they would have lost the Jilsons inside the building, probably in the library considering most of them had never seen a book.

Hally looked over her shoulder just as five of the seven figures exited the metallic doors. They were not that lucky.

The adrenaline coursed through her veins, and she quickened her pace .

"Come on," she said to Tom.

"Hally-" Tom tried to say.

We need an alley, or somewhere to hide.

"Hally-" Tom tried to say one more time.

Hally's eyes fell on an alley, the same one she used to hide her stuff when she went to the refuge. *That can work.*

"Hally."

She paid no attention to her brother and ran into the shadow of the school walls.

"Hally!"

A burning sensation spread from the tips of her fingers to her neck.

"Ahhhh!" Hally exclaimed in pain. She looked at her right hand through the dark glasses. She didn't need to take them off to see the white bubbles forming around the black spots on her flesh. Nor focus to sense the smell of burning flesh.

"Oh!" Tom's voice broke. "I'm so sorry. Really Hally. It wasn't my intention. I'm so, so, so, so sorry," he cried, the words mumbling into each other.

"It's alright," Hally muttered through her teeth as she held her hand tightly trying to make the pain stop. It hadn't been Tom's fault, she knew it, but that didn't make it any less painful.

With her left hand, the good hand, she untangled the bandage she'd used to wrap her already healed elbow in the morning and managed to wrap her right hand.

"I'm really sorry, I really am. Please, please, please, please, forgive me-"

"Tom, it's alright," Hally interrupted her brother's emotional breakdown that would have certainly ended up in tears they didn't have time to dry. "It will heal in a couple of hours," she continued, although she didn't even know if that was true. She'd never been so badly hurt in a single place, not that she remembered, and she didn't have any idea of how her healing actually worked.

"How are we going to explain it to Mom?" Tom cried. "This is the end. We're done. I'm done. We're dead."

"We'll figure out something," she assured him. She, too, wanted to freak out. She didn't know why her eyes were glowing or how to stop them. And the Jilsons were coming after them. This could absolutely be the end, the very end. If she even started thinking about what the Gang could do, what they *would* do if they found them out. She had once seen an old man who had been burned almost to death because of rumors. These weren't just rumors. They would be held hostage, shamed, skinned alive, their teeth would be removed one by one and... Their parents.... They would suffer as well... Hally could almost hear their agonizing screams...

No. She told herself when the familiar feeling started to fill her stomach. *One of us needs to keep their head clear. I can have my own breakdown later.*

Hally took a deep breath and her mind cleared.

She turned to Tom, grabbed his shoulder with her unburned hand and forced him to look in her eyes.

"We'll figure this out," she assured him, she was swearing it.

Tom nodded gently; he had believed her half-truth.

"We need to go home," he said looking around at the walls that stood at each side and then at the street the alley opened to. "Where are we?" he asked himself. "I think home is... that way?" he continued.

Immediately Hally forced his hand down.

"Don't point, don't ever point," she scolded him. "Not until we are sure they aren't anywhere close. If they found out where we live-" the words were left hanging. Once again, Hally could swear she could hear her parents' screams from afar.

Tom looked at her, his eyes studying her.

"Hally, have you had problems with them before?" he asked.

Hally thought about it for a second, she could use this moment and tell Tom the whole truth. How she had spent every afternoon, the truth that there were other people who knew who she was besideshim, the non-existence of the book club, the many dangers she'd faced and how she'd ended up in the refuge in the first place.

No. It's not the time, nor the place. He'll just freak out even harder and I need to keep my head clear.

Before she could answer, Tom's eyes fell on something behind her. Hally turned to see what he was staring at just to find more proof this was not her lucky day. There against the wall, where she had forgotten them the afternoon before, lay her notebook and her pencil case.

"Hally-"

"I promise I'll explain later, I promise," she said. "But first, we need to get home."

Tom accepted her answer.

"Come here," she said and walked deeper into the alley to a half-rusted ladder that made its way up to the school's roof.

"Are you sure we can't just walk away, I think we have lost thcm," Tom said, frowning at the ladder.

"The guard said they came through here," Drey's voice echoed from afar.

Tom didn't wait for another clue and started climbing. Five steps behind, Hally followed him. Climbing had never been hard for her, not when she could use both her hands. When she could only use one it was another story.

"Here, I'll help you," Tom said once he reached the top.

Without thinking Hally moved her right hand and without thinking either, Tom took it.

"Ahh!" Hally screamed from the top of her lungs as his fingers touched her burnt flesh.

"Here they are," one of the Jilsons said. They had found them.

Hally winced. She would've loved to wait for the pain to lessen or even better yet, for her hand to heal. There wasn't time. She pulled herself awkwardly to the top and her body fell against the warm roof.

"Hally, they're coming," Tom warned.

Hally closed her eyes tightly; she couldn't think through the pain.

"Hally," Tom called again.

Dang it Tom and your stupid electrical things.

An idea surged.

"Touch the ladder, a slight touch," she mumbled.

Tom doubted.

"Do it."

He did. Just one finger, barely touching it. From the floor the complaints came as the electricity reached them.

"Freak," one of them said.

She turned to her side and turned the threads at each side of the ladder until it was so loose it fell, cutting the path for the Jilsons.

"Ha, you think that's going to stop us?" Drey asked.

"Drey, it's done. How are we going to get there?" one of his minions, one of the Jilsons, told him.

"Idiot," another minion said. "If we can't get there, they can't come down, we only have to figure out how to get up there."

"I think I know where they keep a ladder here," Drey said. "Don't worry, we'll be back here in a sec, and we'll do as we must with Latin scum like you," he added and after spitting on the floor by their feet he and his crew went to find a ladder.

Hally threw herself once again on her back and she poked through the bandage. The black spots were turning a bit pink, all the blood had dried, and the white bubbles weren't bubbles anymore. It was healing, that was for sure, not fast enough though.

"Hally, please tell me there is another way down," Tom begged her.

Hally chuckled and sat up.

"Do you seriously think I would get us up here without a way down. I'm not that stupid, not all the time anyway," she said. "Come on, follow me, we're going home" she said and stood up.

Tom followed her along the roof, to another corner, where another ladder stood, hidden behind garbage.

"You gotta be kidding me," Tom blurted out.

"Not today, not right now Tommy."

Holding their breaths and pinching their noses, (Tom, at least, who could use both his hands), the twins made their way back to the ground. After ensuring the ladder was hidden even better than before, they quietly made their way onto quiet streets around the school. At first Hally forced Tom to take wrong turns and make a whole round trip to a block that wasn't even close to their home to make sure that the Jilsons weren't even close. Once she was completely (mostly) sure and Tom refused to take another step in the wrong direction, they quietly made their way home.

By the time they reached the house they were covered in sweat and gasping for a cold drink, but they were breathing and that was what mattered.

As soon as Tom closed the door behind him, he let himself fall onto the couch and Hally threw her dark glasses on the table. She walked to the kitchen, put some ice and water in a bowl and enjoyed the numbing feeling when she put her hand in it.

"What do you think they'll do when they don't find us?" Tom asked from the living room.

Hally grabbed the bowl and sat beside her brother.

"I'd rather not think about it. We'll have to move, get out of the country, probably. Maybe we can go back to Costa Rica."

"You know all of this means we'll have to tell Mom, right?"

"Tell Mom what?" a voice asked from the stairs.

Hally and Tom turned; they'd never heard that voice. On the stairs, someone awaited them, a lady they had never seen.

"I'm afraid your mom won't hear any about it," the lady replied with a smile.

A bag went over their heads, and everything went black.

5

HOSTAGES

When the bag finally came off Hally looked around. They were on a bus. It could be said that it was a nice bus. The seats were covered with velvet cushions, there was AC keeping the right temperature for the tropical kids, it was tall enough for the ride to be smooth and prevent Hally from getting car sick and the windows were pitch black. The only thing Hally disliked was the lady holding a gun at her back.

Aside from the twins, the lady and the driver, there were five other kids. None of them spoke. Clearly some of them had fought their kidnappers, the bruises were proof. They all seemed around the twins' age: between fifteen and sixteen with a few exceptions.

The oldest looking was a dark-skinned girl sitting in the front row just behind the driver's seat. She was gorgeous, with a pair of emerald eyes capable of freezing anyone with a look. Her face was surrounded by beautiful long, black hair made messy by a bag similar to the one Hally had just taken off, yet she still pulled it off. She was well dressed, as if attending a bar exam to become a lawyer, a quality that suited her face. She was very elegant, sitting with perfect posture, both hands laying gracefully on her knees and focused on a single spot in front of her, without blinking too much or too little.

Three seats behind the fancy girl, sat the total opposite. Not only was this boy the youngest looking of all, by far, (Hally estimated he could have been close to twelve years old), he was also a mess. Unlike the fancy girl up front who had made sure to dress to impress, this guy had certainly pulled on the first thing he had found: a gray wool sweater. Paired with the sweater, his messy blond hair and his tired blue eyes tried to hide the fear that came over him every time the lady moved her gun.

On the other side of the bus there were kids Hally considered mediocre, kids that fell between the two, the elegant girl and the blond, drooling guy.

In the second row on the right side sat an Asian girl. She looked a little older than them. From a distance anybody could tell she was angry, although Hally had a slight suspicion that that was just her natural expression. She had long dark brown hair and fiery dark brown eyes. On top of her eyes lay a frown causing her eyebrows to almost touch each other, only making it easier to see the bruise that was starting to cover the left side of her face. Her mouth seemed not to have smiled in years and her hands appeared permanently clenched in fists. There was something that didn't fit, though, while her face shone with the most grayish of personalities, her overall look was filled with splashed paint all over the fabric of any imaginable color. She was an artist, that was for sure.

Behind the angry artist sat *her* total opposite, another girl. This third girl had slightly tanned skin as if she lived at a beach, a wave of red hair fell on her shoulders and her light brown eyes studied the bus. Her eyes were big, and where they used to be filled with happiness there was only fear. Horrifying, soul breaking fear.

Sitting behind the kind face girl there was another pale boy closer to Hally's age than the blond one. He sat there, his brown hair a mess, as if this weird, small, hostage blue bus was the same bus he rode to school every day. If he was scared, he wasn't going to give his kidnapper the privilege of seeing it. However, his bored look was not enough to hide his feelings, not from a person like Hally. There was a shine in his brown eyes that was enough to show his fear, the anxiety and all the questions that were huddling up inside his brain.

Across from Mr. Bored, the twins sat in silence, hands intertwined. At least the kidnappers had not forced them to sit apart.

Hally looked at the driver and at the gun lady. This was a bad situation, a terribly bad situation, but it wasn't the worst. There was only a gun, and seven kids. The driver was on his own and considering they couldn't have left Tirabia yet. She just needed…

A cold thing touched her head.

"Don't even think about it," the lady warned her. "You think we don't know about you and your trouble making? Believe me, I will keep an eye on you, especially you," the lady came closer and whispered into Hally's ear. "You escaped me once. It won't happen again."

A shiver crossed Hally's back. She knew she recognized that voice. It was one of the many that haunted her sleep.

"As for the others," the lady turned to the rest of the kids, all of them hiding their heads at the sight of the gun, "worry not, we're almost there."

"I want to go home," the kind girl sobbed.

"Nobody's going home. You freaks belong to the boss now."

The lady returned to her original position, giving one final tap to Hally's head with her gun. When Hally looked up, the other kids were looking at her. They were all begging with their eyes for her to do something, for someone to do something. For goodness' sake! They were being held hostage at gunpoint and taken to who knows where! They needed help, they did. But for now, there was nothing she could do to save them.

"Listen up," the lady yelled minutes later. "Tie your hands." She threw a bunch of rope at the kids. "Do it now!" she ordered.

Hally picked two pieces of rope and gave one to Tom.

Tom looked at the rope, his eyes trembled with the tears he was trying to hold back. Hally nodded, assuring him it was okay.

It took him several tries to get the knot right. Once he'd done it, the lady came and undid it.

"Tighter," she ordered.

Tom did it again, crossing the rope through his shaking fingers

When he was done, Hally grabbed the second one and did the same to him. The other kids copied them, quietly helping each other tie the ropes around their wrists. By the time they had finished the bus had stopped.

Once the lady checked all of them and made sure no rope was looser than it had to be, she looked at the driver and nodded.

The doors were opened, and the bus was filled with people dressed in black with their weird paint and improvised armor. The Gang members came like a storm, they ran in, pulled the kids to their feet and covered their heads one more time.

"Hally!" Tom yelled.

"Tom!" Hally cried back, she tried to push the guy off her. She couldn't let them take her brother away. She couldn't.

"Tom!" she yelled back.

"Get off me," she struggled.

"Behave," a voice stroke.

They tightened the grip around her arms and pulled her. She was moved through hallways, turning left and right.

"Ah," a man exclaimed from the front. "This one burns."

"Move him," another yelled back.

In the front Hally heard the other kids struggle as well, some more than others. They were keeping them together.

"Here." The soldiers stopped.

From the front a few voices argued.

"What do you mean he isn't here? We used the remaining powder to get them!" the lady from the bus screeched.

"You sure it's them? The seven?"

"I followed the signals!"

"You'll have to wait."

She growled.

"I want to be the first, you hear me. I put in the work. I want the glory for it."

"You'll have it."

"Take them to the cells."

The improvised soldiers grumbled.

"You'll have your fun later idiots. Move!"

Hally was grabbed again and pushed. She wanted to call for Tom, if she was where she thought they were, separation was a death sentence.

She was pulled through more hallways, their footsteps echoing across the walls.

"Lock them," the lady ordered.

By her side Hally could hear the other kids struggling against the soldiers, fighting off the bags over their heads. It was of no use.

Hally was thrown against the floor, the door locked behind her.

"Hey! You alright?" the bored guy asked Hally as he helped her get the bag off her face, his hair messier than before.

Hally sat up and cleaned the blood off her mouth.

"We need to get out of here," she said as she pulled the rope off her wrists.

The lady on the bus, she was from the Gang. Which meant they were somewhere in Miso, probably far from the refuge, far from anybody that could help her. She would have to do this on her own.

Hally looked at the other six kids, all young minds frightened, stolen from their homes. None of them had her knowledge. Most of the time she would consider that a blessing. Right now, it was a curse. They had no idea what would happen if they stayed, and therefore, they didn't have the urgency Hally had to get away.

She stood up. She gently touched her scar, she'd been here before, she'd gotten out once, she could do it again. Sure, last time she had had help, and she had been held as a Latin, not as a... whatever she was now. She had no idea how that could backfire on her, but... Potato, potatoe.

Tom handed her a piece of cloth and whispered in her ear: "for your hand."

Hally looked down, she had lost the bandage somewhere along the way, her wound was visible for anyone to see.

"Oh my go-aish!" the blond kid exclaimed. "What happened to you?"

Hally looked up and smiled slightly, hoping that would be enough to compensate for the sight of the half-burned skin.

"It's nothing," she assured.

"Nothing? Nothing my grandma, *that* is something," he continued.

Hally chuckled.

"It's alright, actually it was done by him," escaped her mouth before she thought well about what she was about to say.

"You burned her?" asked the other boy, Mr Bored, joining the conversation along with the blond boy.

Tom's eyes opened widely at the accusation. His mouth fell open as he tried to find the words to defend himself. There weren't any, maybe, because it was the truth.

"It wasn't my fault, I promise," he managed to mumble.

"He's right, it wasn't his fault," Hally jumped in to support her brother.

"Then how did it happen?" the blond boy asked.

Oh no.

"Well, he actually..." Hally struggled to explain, for the first time in a while she didn't know what to say.

"Was it because of any weird abilities?" the blond boy continued.

"Abilities?" Tom and Hally asked, trying to sound as if they didn't exactly know what he was talking about.

"Yeah. And don't worry about us, we're all freaks."

"Pardon?" a voice exclaimed from behind.

Hally turned just to find the fancy girl looking at them, her hair still messy but beautiful.

"I don't consider myself a freak. Nor will I let myself be called one either," she continued, even her way of speaking was elegant.

"I'm sorry Ilma but it is what we are," the blond boy said.

"It's Isla. Is-la," the fancy girl said as if she was talking to a three-year-old. "And what I did was miraculous, not freakish. There isn't anything freakish about making plants grow rapidly."

"Well, I do have to be honest, I actually considered this was a circus until you guys joined," Mr. Bored said to Hally.

Hally let out a snort before she covered her mouth to hide her smile.

"That's so mean," she sighed.

"But you laughed, so who's really the mean one?" the boy asked.

Hally chuckled again.

"Lukai," the boy extended his left hand, "not a freak, just a boy who got control of light for a few minutes."

Hally extended her good hand and shook his.

"My name is Hally, and I have glowing eyes," she said, not managing to say the words without a laugh escaping her lips. Every time she said it aloud it sounded so ridiculous not even she could take herself seriously.

This sounds like an AA meeting.

"The name's Piet. I turn objects into rocks," the blond boy said with a wink.

"Didn't you say it only happened once?" the angry artist asked, the bruise had turned black by now.

"He did, nice seeing you were paying attention... What was your name?" kind face asked.

"Pam," the angry artist answered harshly. "And I wasn't paying attention. I just like correcting people."

"I *was,* paying attention, I mean. I'm Ayala, I turned into an otter for a while," kind face said with, obviously, a kind smile. "Nice meeting you all."

"So, it seems everybody has been introduced except you. What may your name be?" Isla asked Tom.

"Ummmm, I'm Tom," he answered.

"And what do you do Tom? Fire?" Pam asked.

Tom licked his lips.

"Nope, I... Kind of..." Tom's filled with panic. He didn't know what he was. He couldn't explain it even if he wanted to. And that killed him, every day.

"He's electrical, of some sort," Hally jumped in.

"That's what happened," Piet exclaimed pointing at Hally's palm.

Hally finished the bandage, and her burnt skin was no longer visible.

"I wouldn't worry too much, I'm a fast healer, it should be gone before tomorrow," she mumbled.

Hally gave a second look to the walls. They were in a small

black room, the only door locked. The only visible door, anyway.

"I think I can get us out of here," she added.

All the laughs disappeared, everyone remembered where they were.

"Yeah, about that. What the heck is going on? And where the heck are we?" Pam asked.

"Language!" Isla exclaimed.

Pam turned to her.

"Who are you? Fricking Captain America? Besides, I said heck," Pam replied, getting a rolling eye in response.

"It's hard to explain," Hally said. "I used to work with some people at a refuge and... I got in trouble some time ago. I ended up here." Hally tried not to look at Tom, he shouldn't have found out like that.

She started to search for something in the walls.

"Which is exactly where?" Piet asked.

"A made-up prison the Gang set up. The Gang are a subset of the Superiors," she mumbled.

"The Superiors?" Lukai exclaimed; his muscles tensed all the way up to his face.

"We're with the Superiors?" Ayala asked. "It's the worst place we can be right now!" she cried.

"That's why," Hally found the crack and pulled at its edges, "we're getting out of here."

She gave a second pull and uncovered a hole in the wall. One thing she could rely on in times like this, no one bothered fixing things.

"C'mon, one by one," she said, no one moved. "Wanna get out of here? It's this way," she added.

Ayala looked at the hole, it was barely big enough.

"Fine." She went in. One by one the rest started to follow Until only Hally and Tom were left.

"Don't think you're going to save yourself from this conversation. You have some explaining to do," he threatened her.

"I know."

"Do you know what you're doing?"

"I think so."

Tom nodded, that was a good enough answer for him. He followed the rest of the kids, behind him went Hally.

The hole brought them to a big white empty office.

"Now what?" Isla asked.

"Follow me, quietly," Hally said.

The Gang members, the ones who liked to be called soldiers, were always far too busy sleeping or eating to look at the hallways, unless there was noise.

Slowly, Hally opened the door and poked her head into the hallway. The wall still hadn't been painted and the floor hadn't been changed since the last time she had been there.

She walked out, the six followed. She walked down the corridor, looked both ways, made sure there was no one and sprinted to the other side. One left, one right, through the red door and they would be out.

They turned left, they turned right.

The place was way too quiet and way too lonely for it to be normal. Yet, there wasn't enough time to figure out why.

The place creeped her out, especially the way everything was exactly how she had left it. The floor tile was still broken where a missed bullet had hit. The small table in the corner was still missing the leg Hally had ripped off. And in the very end of the corridor the wall was still stained with red, her blood.

Hally opened the red door.

"Hey!" a painted face man exclaimed.

Second door! Not first!

Hally closed the door as fast as she could.

"Wait a second," the man exclaimed.

I am stupid.

"Come here," she called the other kids and ran for the second door.

It was too late; the man came out followed by three others.

Hally opened the second door as fast as she could.

"Block the entrance behind you," she ordered the other kids as she ran across the last room for the door with the exit sign.

She pulled it. It didn't open. She pulled again. It stayed just like it was.

"Hally- they're coming," Pam grumbled.

Hally looked back, they were close, fighting their way through the chairs and the table the other kids had put there. She looked back at the exit, it wasn't opening. Why?

Her wrists started to itch, her legs to tremble. The air didn't find its way to her lungs.

Not now, please, not now.

She started to fight for oxygen. All she wanted to do was to curl up in the corner and cry. The smell of her own blood was still vivid in her memory. The sound of her screams. The bullets coming, hitting the wall around her. Why couldn't she just forget it all? She just wanted to be normal. Live a normal life. Why was the world so desperate to prevent her from having it?

"Hey," Lukai grabbed her shoulder and looked at her. "Breathe. I'll open the door. You keep them occupied."

Hally took a deep breath and the memories went back to where they belonged, the past.

She nodded.

She looked over at her right.

Yep, that'll keep them occupied.

She ran to the kitchen. Behind her Lukai exclaimed: "Piet, Ayala go help her. Pam, Isla and Tom, come with me."

Piet and Ayala followed her to the kitchen.

"What are we looking for?" Piet asked.

"Oil. And matches, or something," Hally answered.

"Are you sure?" Ayala questioned.

"Yes!"

"Does this work?"

Hally looked; Piet was holding a gallon of cooking oil.

A smile crossed her face.

"I don't know if I should be worried about that face," Piet admitted.

"It just means that it will be helpful," she replied, taking the gallon off his hands.

"Will a candle work?" Ayala asked.

Hally looked at the small flame in the candle.

"It will. Bring it here," she said and ran back to the room.

Lukai, Tom, Pam and Isla were still working on the door.

"How are things going?" Hally asked.

"Not past this door," Pam exclaimed.

Hally turned to the red door. The soldiers were about to come through it.

"Hurry up," she cried. She prepared a line of oil separating them from the crazy painted faces. Once she was done, she took the candle in her hands and looked at the red door. She tapped her front pocket where a small knife she'd found in the kitchen was hidden. Hally didn't like violence, she despised it. But she had to be prepared, if things didn't turn out well and Tom's life was in jeopardy, she was willing to fight.

The red door flung open, and the painted faces started to pour in.

Hally let the candle fall. The flames rose up from the floor. The Gang wasn't coming anywhere near them, not today.

"Hey," Lukai called the others, they had opened the door.

Hally gave one last look at the flames and followed the rest.

Outside it was raining. Even though it couldn't be past noon, the sun was nowhere to be seen, while dark clouds filled the sky.

There, a lady was waiting for them. She was an old lady. Behind her stood seven figures.

She smiled when she saw the kids.

"Great, I didn't have to look for you," she turned to the figures. "Generation, round them up, they are coming with us."

As the words came the ground parted and a hole swallowed the kids.

6

THE WESTERN GUARDERS

Tom was supposed to be in a history lesson, sitting in the first row and taking notes as his teacher spoke. Instead, everything was out of control, out of *his* control. And he hated it, he despised it with every fiber of his being.

There was only one moment when that silent anger disappeared for a second: when they got themselves up from the ground.

"What the heck is this place?" Pam asked.

"Language!" Isla exclaimed. "Where are your manners, young lady?"

"Seriously?" Pam snapped back, turning to see Isla. "I used heck."

Tom looked up; he too was wondering what the heck that was.

There were no words. Not enough words to describe it, at least.

The place was *'maestoso'*, in all aspects. They were in the middle of the forest, trees surrounded on all sides the small, medieval civilization formed by the hundred houses built into round rings, like an onion.

If Tom hadn't been attached to scientific proofs and he had been told that these cottages had come from the Grimm's tales, he would have believed it.

Each house (cottage) was different, even though they all shared certain similarities. They were made of gray rock or trees, most of them having plants as part of their construction or decoration. They all had the palace-like windows and pointy towers or roofs. The doors were all beautiful, some were made of rock and almost looked like they could be transported to another era, some were made of wood and had such patterns that not even the most skilled artisan could make, and some had some many flowers around them that looked as colorful as a rainbow.

Yet the place was empty, completely empty aside from those seven kids, the lady and the other angry looking group behind her.

"Welcome to the Western Guarders," the white-haired lady said, a proud smile ruled her face.

"Western Guarders?" Hally asked, in the name of all the rest of the kids. She'd just pushed herself off the ground, her face stained with dirt, her burnt hand clutched against her stomach.

The lady forced a smile. She turned to the kids behind her, seven teenagers the same age as Tom.

"Generation, please make our guests as comfortable as they need to be for the explanation."

The angry teens didn't move.

"Move!" the lady screamed at them. The teens crawled like cockroaches.

The lady turned back to the hostages and forced another smile.

Reluctantly, the Generation, as she called them, brought a golden chair for each of the kids and forced them to sit side by side. A few even gave a fruit basket (Piet and Ayala received a basket) while the others got flowers and food.

Tom looked at the very confused Hally sitting beside him. She was holding a blue cupcake, not knowing if to eat it or to put it in the ground and run. He looked at the sunflowers in his own hand and wondered if he had the same expression on his face.

"My name is Elowen, and I am the Director of the Western Guarders," the lady continued, she opened her mouth wide and pronounced her words completely, as if she was expecting the kids not to understand her English.

She was a tall woman. Her head filled with gray highlights glowing between her long black hair. There was a big nose in the very center of her face, just in the middle of a pair of eyes that seemed to have adapted permanently to give the impression that she was judging you. She was wearing a long, light green dress filled with floral patterns and leaf forms on her skirt.

Neither of the seven moved or said a word at the introduction.

"How many of you heard about the Íroes?" Elowen asked, or was it Director Elowen?

They remained frozen like statues.

Elowen forced another smile.

"C'mon now children, don't be shy," she grunted, kindness wasn't her native tongue.

Slowly all the hands were raised in the air.

"How many of you have heard it as a myth?" she asked.

All hands remained where they were.

"Well, it isn't a myth-" she continued.

"See, curses do exist," Hally whispered to Tom.

"Actually, curses don't exist," Elowen corrected Hally, her smile fighting it's way to stay up, she wasn't happy about the interruption.

"Ha!" Tom couldn't contain himself from saying it.

"So, curses don't exist but Íroes do? Aren't Íroes curses?" Piet asked.

"No! Absolutely not! That's the myth," Elowen corrected him.

"Excuse me, but you just said it wasn't a myth," Isla added to the confusion.

"What are you trying to say?" Lukai asked.

Elowen looked at the confused kids. She massaged her temples.

"Oh," she sighed, "this is going to be way harder than I thought."

"Alright," she continued. "I'm going to explain to you what really happened and what is true. Some things may be similar to the myths you have heard, and some others might be extremely different. Just try to stay as focused as you can."

She paused.

"To start, we must go to the past-"

"You mean 150 years ago?" Piet asked.

Elowen forced another smile.

"Would you please stop with the interruptions?" she muttered, except it didn't really sound like a question.

The seven answered with silence and the teens behind her laughed at their scolding.

"Even more to the past," Elowen continued. "Half a millennium ago, Íroes wandered across the earth. They were free and somewhat normal."

"When you say Íroes, you mean-?" Hally asked.

Elowen took another deep breath that seemed to keep her from screaming.

"Humans with powers, abilities each unique in its own way, inherent since birth," she clarified.

She continued.

"Then the earth was ruled by kings and queens, all with their own kingdoms and armies. There was a set of kingdoms, stronger than all the others, known as the five kingdoms of the north. Out of those five kingdoms, the biggest was Queen Sila's. Before she took the throne her father reigned. He was the first to claim sovereignty over the Íroes, accept them into society, helped them grow their powers and even made a special place for them in the army. Sadly, the king wasn't able to finish this mission when he passed away. And Queen Sila assumed the throne, at just ten years of age."

"As she became queen her reign helped the Íroes become the strongest foundation for society in history. Years passed, a war broke out, and by its end, the five kingdoms were long gone. With them, the Íroes were forced back into hiding. Nevertheless, Íroes were never forgotten within the true bloodline. In the time of war, Queen Sila and some of the other rulers, provided several places for the Íroes to hide. Places like the Guarders. Since they have disappeared, these same places have dedicated themselves to keeping the legacy's purity for when they appear once again. Despite the many obstacles and lies history has tried to inflict, that day has finally arrived."

She spread her hands and pointed at them, at the seven kidnapped kids.

"Oh heck nah!" Tom exclaimed. "You expect me to believe that we are some kind of magic creatures with powers? How are you so sure we are the ones? And if that was the case, why are we just getting to know this?" He wanted answers. These were the answers he was getting. Why wasn't he satisfied?

"You're right boy, you're right," Elowen said, getting angrier each time with the interruptions. "You see, there's this tree..."

"A tree?" Lukai asked.

"As I was saying there's this tree... called Megalo Dentro. This tree grows a flower for every Íroe. For centuries it has been flowerless, until you were born. That day, a flower appeared. Slowly, it was followed by six more flowers. I was tasked to find the Íroes and bring them over here, to the Western Guarders, the rightful place for them to grow up. But I couldn't. Some people, bad people, people who are also seeking your power, realized they were new flowers in Megalo Dentro and they were ready to hunt you down. It was then that I realized that bringing light into who you were at that moment would only give you a life of danger and I decided to wait until you were old enough to make decisions on your own. I was going to wait until you were eighteen."

"What happened then? We're certainly not even close to being eighteen?" Isla asked.

Elowen smiled, this time from true joy.

"Fate," she said. "Fate has allowed me to figure out your true identities before time. But, I wasn't the only one. Not that you should worry about that, for I have saved you from all the others and brought you to your wonderful new home."

There was silence for a moment.

"Are you saying... Are you saying that we're being... hunted by more?" Hally asked.

"I'm afraid so," Elowen finally admitted and renewed her smile. "There's nothing to fear here, there's no way anyone is going to find you in my territory."

"What!" Lukai asked.

"I don't like this," Tom mumbled through his teeth. He didn't like to hunt, much less the idea of being hunted.

"Like hunted, hunted? As in danger?" Ayala asked.

"Is there another type of hunted?" Piet asked in return.

"Calm down, children. Calm down."

Between the commotion a calm voice grasped everyone's attention.

"I'm sorry to ask, but... How are we so sure you're not part of the ones that are hunting us? How can we be so sure that you mean well?" Hally asked.

Elowen laughed.

"Oh," she said. "You're funny." She realized it was a real question. "These are the Western Guarders, we're the best of the best. This is your new home, you're staying. I'll soon give a tour, once we're done, if you don't want to stay, which I don't see how that could happen, we'll talk about it. Later."

There was something in her voice, a sense of threat. Tom had the feeling they were as much prisoners, as in the Gang.

"Okay, great, you're not hunting us. What are we doing here?" Lukai asked.

"The Guarders, the others, are crazy. They have lost their way and what they were created for. Here, under my wing, you can learn what your abilities are, how they work, and together we can regain the power that the Western Guarders once held."

A masked, short, green soldier appeared from behind a cottage pushing a little young kid with a broken nose towards Elowen.

Elowen's face turned red with embarrassment and then anger.

"What is this?"

The masked soldier whispered something, as the kid stared at Elowen, trembling.

"A night out should be enough," she answered.

"No, no, please," the kid begged.

Elowen kneeled over and slapped him.

The kid fought the tears back.

She stood up. "Take him away."

The soldier nodded. The kid sobbed as he was dragged.

The crazy lady turned to the kidnapped. She smiled.

The kids tried to stay emotionless. All mouths dropped open, a few eyebrows raised.

"You must excuse the interruption."

She gave a signal to the Generation behind her and two of them disappeared.

Tom turned and saw Hally. She was thinking. Tom looked up, birds flew through the sky.

Minutes later, finally ending the torturous silence that reigned over the place, the two teens Elowen had sent out reappeared with a young lady and five soldiers around her. The soldiers, wearing the same green uniform as the first one, stomped their feet, their entire faces covered by black masks.

Elowen gave one final forced smile.

"This here is Pepper, she'll be your guide. She will explain to you our rules, our traditions. She will help you understand your power. And she will keep an eye on you at all times to ensure you're having nothing but the best time."

That was another threat.

"As for now," Elowen continued. "She will prepare you for the ceremony."

"About the ceremony-" Pepper tried to say.

"There *will* be a ceremony," Elowen demanded. She waited for a second, when she was sure Pepper was not going to fight her, she continued.

"Generation," Elowen said to the teens behind her. "Tell all the Villagers that after lunch no one will be allowed outside of the cottages, we must make sure they don't bother our guests."

The teens nodded with disgust and disappeared, each to a different cottage and then to another and another, until all doors had been knocked and everyone had been told what Elowen had said. Along with them, Elowen disappeared inside the biggest cottage.

Pepper cleared her throat.

"Nice meeting all of you, my dears. I'm Pepper, although I think you already know that." She smiled, she too seemed to force her smile in a way. She was short, dark skinned, dark eyes and braided hair.

"Follow me," she ordered. The kids looked at each other, confused. "Please don't make me repeat it."

She started walking. Tom looked at Hally. Hally shrugged, eyes on the soldiers beside Pepper. She wasn't sure about how much of that was optional either. The kids grabbed the things they had just been given and followed her.

Tom liked the place, he wouldn't lie. The grass was well cut. The cottages were organized. Everything was clean…. Even the soldiers that walked around the kids as dogs keeping the sheep from getting lost, walked in perfect formation. There wasn't a leaf out of place.

"What's that?" Hally asked.

Tom looked at where his sister was pointing, so did everyone else. Behind one of the many cottages, in a failed attempt to be hidden, there was a wooden stage. Above it hung a branch, a rope fell from it. Tom had seen some of those earlier, in his history books, as part of the medieval torturing ways.

"Oh," Pepper stuttered, the color had left her face. "Historical value," she mumbled.

"Get moving," one of the soldiers ordered behind his mask and pushed them far from the interesting apparatus into a cottage. Tom analyzed it. It was made mostly of rock and wasn't as covered with flowers as the one beside it. Yet it had a door, a beautiful door whose lines told a million stories. The twins shared another look, that wasn't seen in history class either.

"In here," Pepper said. The soldiers pushed them all inside before locking the door behind them.

Inside the cottage the fairy tale likeness was left behind and the kids found a modern living room. The floor was made of shiny wood, there were comfy green couches surrounding a small wooden coffee table. The whole room was illuminated by both windows and an enormous crystal chandelier hung from the roof.

Hally came closer.

"I don't like this," she mouthed.

Tom looked at her. They were siblings, they were used to not being on the same page in a lot of things. Actually, most of the time they were never on the same page. Yet, Tom couldn't help being astounded by her lack of scientific curiosity. Why wasn't she looking for answers? Just one night ago she was crying about being a curse, and now it had been proven that there wasn't any curse. What was she doing? Why did she want to run away? The Guarders could hold everything they needed. All the information they had; he'd been longing for.

Pepper pulled Hally's arm and looked at her.

"Ok, you have to start behaving," she said, her tone, her eyes and her expression all changed. She was no longer the smiley helpful assistant.

Hally frowned.

"What?"

"You think I can't see it on your face? This place is crazy. And dangerous. Crazy dangerous. But you're here now. And there's no way out. I had the bad luck to be born here, you guys were brought, that changes things a lot," she turned to face all the rest of the kids. "So listen closely, from now on, if Elowen laughs, you laugh. If she cries, you cry. What she defends, you defend and what she hurts, you hurt."

"Like I'm doing that," Pam growled.

"Yeah, that ain't living, man," Piet added.

"Well dear, this is no longer about living, it's about surviving. Right now, she believes you're the Íroes, after tonight we'll know for sure. If you are what they say you are, she's going to do anything in her power to win you over, on the bright side. If you resist, she will break your spirit and every bone in your body that it takes for you to work for her. Outside these walls, you don't complain and don't resist. You don't say anything to anyone outside and don't even think about making a comment about the atrocity of this place, Elowen has spies everywhere and she isn't one of those to give second chances. Do you understand?"

The kids nodded.

"Are we ever going to get out of here?" Lukai asked.

Pepper looked at the ground.

"Native Villagers can't leave here without her permission. But as I said, you aren't from here. Still, the soldiers will follow you everywhere, and the barriers that separate us from outside are almost unbreakable."

"Almost," Hally repeated.

Pepper looked at her, in her eyes she was begging.

"Don't do something stupid, please. Right now, I know there are no good options. If you don't make it through the ceremony, she'll kill you. If you make it, you'll live here. But if you live here, at least you get the chance to learn a little, let the rest of the trail go cold and then once you have her trust run the hell out of this place. Maybe in a few months-"

"A few months?" Isla asked.

"I'm afraid so..."

"What will we do until then? I'm sorry but I don't want to live here. No offense, it's a lovely place, but it really isn't my vibe," Ayala admitted, her high-pitched voice echoing in the living room.

"Didn't you hear? We survive," Pam answered.

Morale plummeted. A day before they were all normal kids, living their separate lives. Now, no matter how much they blinked, pinched themselves or ran, this wasn't a dream. They were there and they had to make it through.

"I'm sorry it had to be this way," Pepper apologized once more. "If I could, I would let you go, take you elsewhere. But you might be a living myth and Elowen loves the Myth."

"Do you think she can actually teach us something?" Tom asked.

Pepper smiled.

"Oh she can, and she will. But there's a price that comes with her teachings. The question you should be asking is, are you willing to pay for it?"

Tom looked at the ground thinking. What was the price he was willing to pay for knowledge? It couldn't be that bad.

Everyone was just exaggerating things a little bit, right? Either way he could finally get some answers, he wasn't throwing that opportunity away.

"And now? What do we do now?" Isla asked.

"Get settled, I'll get you some clothes to change into. If you make it through tonight Elowen will have the Villagers build you a cottage, until then you'll stay here, in the guest rooms."

"Can we at least choose our rooms?" Pam asked.

Pepper smiled, but that didn't prevent her mouth from curling downward and the few tears she had came out of her eyes shining against the light.

"Yes, that's one thing I can give you."

7

LUNCH AND GRWM

When Hally went back downstairs the living room was empty except for the one couch and the small wooden table in the middle. The boys were upstairs trying to make the last couch fit into their room. Pepper was helping them. The rest of the girls were tidying up their own room.

Hally looked around, the loneliness and silence were just perfect. She left the pillows by the stairs.

Pepper seems like a good person, a star in the darkness she thought as she studied the pictures around the unused fireplace.

Truth be told, she didn't like the control she saw outside. Whenever people were refused their freedom, the outcome was never good. She had seen it. Firsthand. Not second handed, not third handed, not as a rumor of the wind, but firsthand. So she knew it. More than she would ever admit to herself. More than she would ever be able to tell anyone. She knew what bad people did once they wanted power. She didn't want to stick around and see what the Guarders would do with theirs. After all, that was what this place looked like: people seeking more power, the *wrong people* seeking power. The kind of people that only wanted more, the same ones that had already crossed so many lines that a new one wasn't even a deal.

She saw it in Elowen, clear as day. Her with her smile. Oh! Hally had learned, a long time ago, that people didn't like her as much when she wasn't smiling all the time and actually opened her mouth. She remembered a day in school when she'd just gotten to Tirabia. She'd been paired with a horrible girl.

"Why don't you let your brain think before you speak?" the girl had snorted after Hally had proposed an idea for their project.

Back then Hally had endured week after week of horrible comments, only responding with a smile, fearing that the second she spoke up they would stop liking her.

"Why don't I punch your empty head before I speak?" It had been the first time she had fought back, laying her ground. She was too tired of being ignored and played with.

Tom had jumped in.

"We don't hit people."

"We nothing! Speak in I. The only thing I'm interested in is the ay, ay, ay, she is going to say-"

She then had learned that there were just some types of love that were overrated, not worth biting her tongue.

Hally left Pepper's pictures alone.

She had to figure out how to get out of here, soon. Before her cheeks drooped and she couldn't smile anymore. Before they started asking for her blood. And before they won Tom over.

Meanwhile the only thing left was to make sure Pepper was trustworthy.

She moved silently across the room analyzing everything her eyes fell on. She found a pile of handwritten essays.

She's smart.

Lots of pictures but no parents. Where are they?

Hally left the essays where they were.

There are many books. Lots of psychology.

She didn't study psychology.

Maybe English. Or literature.

She does see literary material.

Look! A degree? Some kind of Guarder Degree.

History and literature? Does make sense.

Hally scanned the room with her eyes. She kind of liked Pepper, she was a nice girl, neat, smart, kind, and she had a great collection of board games. Seemed to be trustworthy, but then again, the ones that aren't trustworthy always appear to be, at the beginning.

She walked to the window and gently pushed the curtain to the side, barely enough to create a small hole for her to see through. In front of the cottage the masked soldiers stood stationary, ready to keep anyone from getting close to the cottage, and anyone from getting out.

How am I going to get Tom out of this one?

"Hally, you lost or something? Need me to draw you a map to find the pillows or what?" Pam's voice echoed from the second floor.

"Coming. Got them right here," Hally replied, leaving the window behind and most of her thoughts with it.

The second floor was mostly rooms and bathrooms, three rooms and four bathrooms in total. On the further side of the hallway there was the main room, Pepper's room. Beside it there was a bathroom, the only bathroom in the hallway. By the bathroom there was another room, the boys room. When Hally had gone for the pillows, they'd been doing their best to make a couch fit through the door. Now that the door was shut Hally could just assume they'd managed it. The last room was in front of the stairs, temporarily the girls' room.

Hally went in, into the mess. All the original furniture had been pushed to a corner to make place for the extra mattresses and couches, the bags Pepper had lent them with new, colorless clothes were laying on the floor and Pam was still fighting to inflate the mattress Pepper had lent them.

"Shoot! Are we missing a mattress?" Hally asked, there was only one bed, a couch and the mattress Pam was still fighting with.

"Oh no," Ayala responded. "I'd rather sleep on the floor, that's just the way I do it in Tuvalu. Mattresses are way too hot and uncomfortable. I have my mat just here." She showed the girls a brown mat Pepper had brought.

"If you say so," Pam accepted. "While we're on the topic of traditions, would you all mind not using shoes inside the room? They're too dirty," she said.

"Who says you have some sense of cleanliness?" Isla snorted.

"Don't be mean now girls you wouldn't want Director Elowen come and scold you," Hally said mimicking Elowen's horrid voice.

"Please no. I *do not* like her," Isla grunted.

"Generation," Pam mocked.

The girls laughed; it was the only thing they could do about it inside the safety of the cottage walls.

"Seriously, would you mind the shoes?" Pam insisted after the laughter was gone.

"We wouldn't have a problem," Ayala accepted as she took

her shoes off and placed them beside the door. The other two copied her.

"I guess now we must decide who gets the bed," Isla said.

"I have no problem. I can sleep anywhere, anytime, that's my real superpower," Hally chuckled, it would often end up with some motherly scolding about personal appearances, but it was useful. "It's up to you both to fight for it."

Pam and Isla looked at each other.

"Fine, I'll sleep on the mattress. I'm fighting so much for it to work that I should be the one to enjoy it," Pam accepted.

"Thank you so much," Isla cheered, and she threw herself onto the bed.

Hally laid down on the couch and looked at the roof. At least in the middle of the chaos the girls were nice.

It was a few minutes past noon when Pepper came back to take the kids for their lunch.

The seven of them walked slowly and quietly down the stairs, six of them hiding behind Hally.

When they reached the first floor, Pepper looked at them.

"Let me see your smiles."

The kids smiled, bright ear to ear smiles. Even Pam did, as unnatural as it looked.

"Great, just stay that way all the time," she ordered and knocked twice on the door.

The masked soldiers opened it. Together, followed by the soldiers, Pepper took them to where all the people were: the dining hall.

The dining hall was the biggest cottage of all, placed in the very center and made entirely of wood. Against the walls, people made lines across the food filled tables serving their own dishes, buffet style. The rest of the room was filled with long wooden tables surrounded by chairs and benches. The place was filled with people, everyone in the village.

Hally looked at them. It was weird to believe all these people lived there yet they had seen none when they had arrived. The people looked normal, this was normal to them, even the masked soldiers guarding the whole place.

The kids were welcomed by a big table filled with pots of bubbling, green soup.

"Uf," Lukai complained quietly enough to make sure no one else heard, visibly resisting pinching his nose. "What's that?"

"Is that supposed to smell like that? I don't mean to complain," Isla asked louder.

"Oh gosh!" Pepper exclaimed as she got between the table and the kids, trying to get them as far away from it as possible. "Elowen would kill me if she saw you here," she mumbled.

"Do you eat that?" Piet asked.

"Yes. No! I mean yeah... not you. It's for the Lowers," Pepper explained.

"Does that mean something in English or...? I just don't remember learning it in school," Hally whispered to Tom.

"I have no idea," Tom replied.

"Pardon me, the what?" Isla asked.

Pepper sighed and stopped trying to push the kids away.

"The village people, the Villagers, are separated into groups according to their achievements. The smartest students, the best workers, the prettiest people, the first in everything, have more benefits than the others. There are the Lowers, Mediums, and the Ringers, although I don't know why they call them that..."

I can think of a reason.

"Anyway, as you can see, everything they do has to do with where the Villagers stand. The Lowers live in the outer circles and smaller cottages, while the Ringers live in the inner circle, in the best place. The only time and place Lowers, Mediums and Ringers share a space is when they eat," Pepper said and turned to the dining hall. "Lowers on the right, Mediums in the center and Ringers on the left."

Hally looked around the room. The difference between the 'classes' (if that's what they could be called) was noticeable. Even if Pepper hadn't said anything it wouldn't have been hard to figure it out. On the right side of the hall the people wore worn out clothes, not damaged, but clearly old. They were sitting down at an unfinished-looking table, sipping the bubbling green soup. Meanwhile, as one moved to the left, the tables presented more choices of nourishments, better looking food. Ending up where there was a literal feast for the few glamorous people sitting down at their shiny mahogany table.

"Come," Pepper pulled them. "You're the Íroes. Makes sense you eat at the Ringers' side."

As the kids moved every single pair of eyes followed them.

"Why are they watching us?" Tom asked.

"I don't know, but I kind of like it," Piet said. He turned and winked his eye to a nice girl he walked by.

"Focus superman," Hally called to him as she pulled him away from her. "They don't seem to like that," she said looking at a soldier who was ready to intervene.

"She's right. Why do you think there are soldiers every-where? To keep everything at bay. You're Ringers, and even more importantly, you're the Íroes. You're above all these people. They don't get to touch you, talk to you or even smell you. They only get to see you from afar. Can you imagine, if the Íroes mixed with Lowers? The whole system would be ruined," Pepper declared, then her eyes fell on the table on the farthest left, where fifteen angry looking teenagers stared.

The kids looked at Pepper, their eyes said more than their mouths would ever be able to.

Pepper took a step closer to the seven.

"Their game, their rules. Play by them," she whispered before taking the step back and smiling. "Look, the fact that you're here. The fact that we have real Íroes walking among us is a miracle."

"We're just humans," Ayala said. "Just like every-

"Don't!" Pepper exclaimed. "Don't talk like that, not here," she whispered. "Go get your food and meet me at that empty table there. And stay far from the Lowers and the Mediums. In fact, stay away from everybody."

"Where are you going?" Lukai asked.

"I'm not a Ringer, I'm a Medium. I can't take food from your table," Pepper replied and walked down to a table in the middle of the room.

Hally turned to the table beside them and her mouth turned into water. There wasn't a centimeter that wasn't covered by a dish, all of them depicting such a smell...

Hally, just like the others, picked up an empty plate and started filling it as she wished . Not even the Guarders were going to ruin food for her. When they had selected all the food and drink they wanted, one by one the kids started to sit at the table where Pepper was already waiting for them.

Hally grabbed a piece of chicken and sniffed it.

"Is this rosemary?" she asked to her left where Tom had just been standing.

"Nope, that's oregano," Lukai answered.

Hally turned.

"Sorry, I thought you were Tom," she apologized.

"It's alright," Lukai laughed. "Do you want any help?" he asked.

Hally looked at her bandaged hand and the cup she had to bring to the table.

"I would appreciate it," she said.

"Are you really a rapid healer or did you just say it to sound cool?" Lukai asked as they walked to the table.

"I am," Hally responded. "A rapid healer I mean," she cleared. "I'm just not used to talking about it with others that aren't Tom."

"That's alright," Lukai chuckled. "You guys are-?"

"Twins. He's older by nine minutes," Hally answered as they sat.

"Tonight, at the ceremony, you all must behave. Not one thing may go wrong," Pepper said to them as she put a spoon of rice to her mouth.

"What's that about a ceremony? What does it actually mean?" Ayala asked.

"The ceremony is to prove you are Íroes and then to demonstrate what kind of Íroes we've been blessed with. They'll bring everyone, decorate this place and prepare you for introduction as they would have done when the Guarders were founded. They'll give you a little bit of powder, and it will change color. If it turns green, you're Naturae. If it turns gold, you're Bellator. If it turns brown, you're Veteris. And if it turns blue, you're Woldier."

She paused momentarily to have another spoonful of rice.

"Naturaes usually have a power revolving around fauna and flora. Bellators have very specific powers. Veteris have specific powers as well, about one or two though, and they need an object to use it. And Woldiers have one power with many uses."

"I thought there were five categories," Tom said. The myth he and Hally had heard talked about five sections.

Pepper let out a laugh.

"That's the actual mythical part of the story. There are no such records except of Queen Sila. Although many believe she was just a powerful Woldier. And others even say she had no powers at all... Anyway, the chances of one of you being a Magister, the fifth you talk about, are impossible, they might not even exist! Having said that, if Magisters were really a thing, and just for the sake of the explanation, if one of you was a Magister, the powder would turn silver. Magisters allegedly have simple powers with complex uses. There are also other myths saying that each category represents a different kind of soldier. Don't believe in that, most of it is considered lies, even here."

"Then why do they have the categories?" Piet asked, mouth full of fish.

"Tradition. Technically, in the myths, there are different ways to help each Íroe to use their powers and different rules each one has to follow."

"When you say powder, what do you mean? Dirt?" Lukai asked.

"No, Unicorn Powder."

All mouths dropped open.

"You crush unicorns?" Piet exclaimed.

"Unicorns exist?" Ayala asked at the same time.

Pepper chuckled, covering her mouth with one hand.

"Yes, there are unicorns in the south, but they live in a refuge. You won't see them running around. And no, we don't crush them. The unicorn's horns shed like snakes do, we grab the shedding and crush it to create the powder. Unicorn Powder is known to absorb a small amount of the powers of Íroes, a lot can neutralize their powers temporarily, but a small amount will change colors to allow us to see your category," Pepper answered. "Only Guarders are supposed to have the powder, although they lost a shipment a while back."

Hally looked at her plate, it had already been emptied several minutes ago.

"What was that you said about soldiers?" she asked.

"That's just rubbish people have invented," Pepper mumbled.

"What did they say?" Isla insisted.

Pepper licked her lips.

"They proposed that Veteris are soldiers, meant to keep information intact and make new discoveries. Naturae are nature's soldiers, meant to fight for the flora and fauna of our world. Bellators are society's soldiers, fighting when humans turn against each other. And Woldiers are humanity's soldiers, in charge of protecting humanity from any outside source, like dragons or giants."

"Dragons and giants?" Ayala asked bewildered.

"Later," Pepper responded.

"And Magisters? What are they soldiers of?" Pam asked.

"Magisters, who I keep saying might not exist, are said to appear only when a problem is near. They are the bringers of war. Some would even say a curse."

Suddenly the air turned cold and the silence heavy. All the spoons and forks were left alone at the same time, all dishes were put down and every head raised up.

The sound of a bell filled the dining hall. Everybody stood up synchronized, as programmed robots would do. The kids copied them as fast as they could and followed Pepper when she started to walk along with the rest.

"Come, it's time to prepare you for the ceremony," she said.

The walk back to Pepper's cottage was just like before, the eight of them rounded up like sheep while the soldiers made sure none of them moved a centimeter more than they had to. As they walked, Hally looked to her right. Where the wooden stage had been visible before there was only a white fabric covering everything. A shiver went down her spine, that place only kept getting creepier.

In the cottage, Elowen was waiting for them, to make matters worse.

"Director Elowen," Pepper saluted her with a smile and a small head bow. The soldiers closed the door behind the kids, and locked it.

"Pepper, I see you have done great with the Íroes," she congratulated her. "And you, my beloved kids. Are you enjoying the place?"

"It's incredibly congruous," Tom said.

"Tom's right, it's lovely," Isla backed him up with a smile.

"And the people are great," Piet added.

"I'm so happy to hear that," Elowen cheered. "I have brought the clothing for the ceremony and the Generation will be here any minute to help you. Now, I expect Pepper to have already said this to you, but remember, even though you want to explore out there, you must be accompanied by one of the soldiers. It's for your own good," she said.

"Don't worry, they understand," Pepper assured her.

Elowen smiled one last time before making her way out the door.

It's for your own good.

I don't like her.

"What does she mean that the Generation will be helping us? Who are they?" Ayala asked.

Pepper massaged her temples.

"The Generation used to be represented as the 'Íroes', or that's how Elowen pitched them. She insisted everybody should treat them like heroes, because she needed the Villagers to believe in someone, and if she didn't have them, then she invented them. Then the rumors started to fly, that the real ones, the real Íroes, were somewhere out there. If the word had gotten out to the rest of the Villagers it would have been a disaster, a real one for sure. But Elowen always has a plan. She hunted you down and beat everybody else in the race towards power."

"Towards us you mean?" Lukai asked.

"I'm afraid-" Pepper's words were interrupted as the door was almost kicked down and a set of seven teenagers entered the cottage, a mean faced girl leading them.

"Excuse me," Isla said cordially. "Have you no manners? What about knocking?"

The guy who stood behind the first girl snorted out a laugh.

"Manners? As if your people had enough education," he blurted out with a laugh joined by several of the other kids. The first girl, however, did not join them. She was too above them to even share their laugh, although it was clear it amused her.

"My people?" Isla asked. "I beg your pardon, but have you seen yourself lately? A pig's showcase has more hygiene than you," she replied.

Before the boy snapped back, Pepper put herself between them.

"Gunner, Isla, this conversation ends here. Are you out of your mind Ulyssa?"

The first girl, Ulyssa, scoffed.

"Certainly not enough to let a Medium speak to me that way."

Pepper pulled her arm, just like she had done to Hally hours ago.

"You and I both know that I'm not any Medium. I'm the one you always ran to when you messed up, like you always do. Don't make me take your dirty laundry out for everyone to see now."

A couple of the other kids laughed at the threat.

"I'm serious," Pepper continued. "They've been here a day, but you? You know how this works. Elowen's hand won't get any softer just because of who you are and who she told you you were. She cares about one thing, and right now that thing moves around these kids. Either you play with her rules or you're out of the game and you know it."

All the smirks disappeared. They knew what Pepper was talking about.

"Now stay here," she ordered before turning to the others. "Come kids," she called them and guided them towards the stairs.

"I really really want to punch them," Pam muttered when they reached the second floor.

"Who?" Piet asked.

"Any of them," she replied.

"They're just bullies, you give them no attention, they dry out. Like weed," Lukai declared.

"Weed?" Ayala exclaimed flabbergasted.

Lukai rushed to clarify himself.

"Not *that* kind of weed," he explained.

"You know, back in Costa Rica when someone bothered either Hally or me, we used to play a game we called 'crazy Hally'," Tom proposed.

Hally laughed.

"I love that game!" she exclaimed, she had so many great memories with it.

"I hear the idea, no 'crazy Hally'," Pepper turned them down. "I know they're impossible, but no good will come from getting on their bad side from today. They may not be Elowen, but they still have power. Do you understand?"

The fun 'crazy Hally' memories were drowned.

"We do."

"Go off then, to your rooms, I'll get your traditional clothes," Pepper said and went back downstairs. When she came back, she brought the cardboard box to the girls' room and four of the Generation girls.

"Aidden, you will be helping Isla. Shafi, Ayala. Ulyssa, Hally. And Magaera, stay with Pam. I already laid it clear as day for you, you're here to help. As for you girls, the ceremony will be soon enough, so get ready," Pepper announced and closed the door leaving the eight girls alone.

Hally picked the box off the floor and looked through it until she found the most wearable dress.

"Oh Hally, that will look beautiful on you," Isla cheered.

"I guess that's a first, having a whole dress only for yourself," Magaera hissed at Hally, opening her eyes and blinking as innocently as possible. "Sure, it's a little dusty, but you must be used to dirt living on the street."

Shafi and Aideen joined her in laughter.

Guests, we are guests.

Hally took a deep breath.

"Let's just get this over with." She picked up her dress and hid herself inside the bathroom. There she did her best in getting inside the hundred-year-old fabric and took the bandage of her burned hand away, it was almost healed by now, there was no need of it anymore. Once she was ready, she opened the door.

What she found when she opened the door was three times as much chaos as she had left behind. The bags laid open widely. All the things had been thrown around the room, as if someone had searched for something. Then, on one side of the room, Ayala was doing her best to be nice to the Generation girls while getting her things back. And on the other side Isla was doing *her* best to hold a very angry Pam who kept muttering words in Mandarin that Hally recognized from the 'not-to-say-words-list' her teacher had once created.

Isla turned to Hally.

"Forget what Pepper said. We need crazy Hally, if not Pam will kill them, or worse Ayala will end up without any of her things," she begged.

Hally couldn't help smiling slightly, this was going to be fun. She turned to Ulyssa who kept taunting Ayala, pulling her hair, shoving clothes in her face, pinching and pushing her.

Hally set her face, the first step for 'crazy Hally' was the emotionless crazy eyes and the serious expression. She walked towards them.

"You have pretty hair," Hally said. Not the brightest start.

The Generation girls turned to her.

"What?" Ulyssa asked.

Hally gave a step closer to her.

"You have such pretty hair. I just... I wonder how it would look in a bag."

"What?" Ulyssa asked once again.

Hally gave a step closer. Ulyssa took a step backwards just to realize there was nowhere else she could go, and her friends had no intention to help her.

Hally looked at her dead in the eye.

"Oh you could be Goldilocks, beautiful locks you have. Would be a shame to lose them. Shame for you of course. Me? I would have such fun."

"You wouldn't... dare," Ulyssa struggled to say, grabbing her hair.

Hally laughed internally. There was always a feeling stronger than any other... Stronger than even superiority, jealousy and even anger. It was fear. And although it usually played against her, there were days it was on her side.

"That's the beauty of it. You have no idea of who I am. Not. One. Small. Idea. Of. How. Crazy. I. Am. Witch," Hally smiled. "Hand over the picture and sit your butt on the couch. Don't talk. Don't move. And if you even breathe loudly, you'll pay." The smile dropped.

Ulyssa swallowed hard and did just as Hally had asked. The other girls didn't even wait for Hally to blink when they were already sitting down beside her, as frozen as dolls.

Hally made sure Ayala was okay and she turned to find Isla and Pam smiling.

"I love crazy Hally," Pam whispered.

Hally chuckled.

"Well, crazy Hally doesn't want to have crazy hair later, do any of you know how to do hair?"

"I do," Isla said. "And after that stunt you just pulled, you deserve the best-looking hair of all," she said.

And now it was them who shared a laugh.

Right at sundown the kids were ready and waiting all dressed up in a line in the living room. They all looked, well... nice. Much like they were lifted from a fairytale. The girls were wearing dresses. Ayala's dress was long sleeved. It was white and red with golden stitches and patterns all around. Around her neck the dress had beautiful, lace decorations and the skirt was filled with flowers made of golden fabric.

Pam's dress was long-sleeved, too, but it was quite different. It wasn't as decorated or as fancy as the last one, instead it was a plain, light blue long dress with long, loose sleeves that fell from her arms and touched the ground.

Isla's dress, on the other hand, had no sleeves. It was a long, pinkish dress. The entire fabric was covered with some butterflies that seemed like they were about to fly any time now and with every step she took, they seemed to come alive.

Lastly, there was Hally's dress. Hally's dress had short, puffy sleeves. It was a beautiful green, an emerald green. The whole dress was made of several layers and the top one was a sort of veil like fabric. On the skirt there were some flowers stitched with silver thread.

The boys too were well dressed.

Lukai was wearing dark pants with a long-sleeved shirt under a long, sleeveless, green shirt with the crest of a half-moon, a sunflower and rainwater in the middle of it. He looked like a knight, only missing the shining armor.

Tom was wearing a loose, long, blue shirt under a brown belt, a pair of brown pants and tall loose boots. His brown hair had been combed back and his serious face forced into a smiled

And finally, Piet was dressed in a plain white shirt tucked into his pants all topped with an old looking, red cape.

They didn't look bad, on the contrary, they looked perfectly well considering the place. The only problem Hally had was that she couldn't decide if Tom looked more like Peter Pan's lost siblings or Jack Sparrow's crew and that bothered her a lot.

8

THE CEREMONY

The second Elowen's eyes saw them, they opened wide, and a smile grew across her ugly face.

"You look like royalty, the way you're supposed to," she cheered. "Generation, cover your eyes, this is greatness only Pepper and I can look at this spectacle ."

The Generation covered their eyes without hesitating. Their lack of independent thinking worried Hally. They didn't even question Elowen's request, it made no sense covering their eyes now, they had seen them get ready! But now again, this was a different type of world they lived in, one where questioning someone like Elowen could just cost their lives.

Elowen gave them a last look, she smiled. She opened the front door.

Outside, the village was almost unrecognizable. In the few hours it had taken the kids to get ready, the Villagers had produced their finest work. If the place was almost impossible to describe before, now it was more than impossible. Lights had been hung between the cottages simulating thousands of stars. The air filled with the smells of the greatest and biggest feast of all. And a bright golden path had been built to connect Pepper's cottage and the dining hall.

"Villagers!" Elowen announced. "The Íroes."

The air filled with cheers.

"Go, follow her, and remember to smile," Pepper whispered to them as she shoved Lukai gently out the door.

One after the other, they left the privacy of Pepper's four walls and walked out unto the crazy screams and may I say, the crazy Villagers.

The path, although it could also be called a bridge, had been built with enthusiasm in mind. A few meters above the ground, the kids could watch the crowd organized in perfect lines according to their rank. None of the Villagers dared to step out of line, especially not with the no-face-soldiers observing everything from the side. But there was something not even the soldiers could control, nor Elowen, it was the excitement.

"I can't believe it, look at all of these people," Piet exclaimed. He waved at a group of girls and their cheers doubled.

"It's different, I'll give you that. But not worth dressing up for" Tom managed to say, keeping his smile. "Right Hally? Hally?"

"What's wrong? Where's your smile?" Isla asked, she was stuck behind the frozen Hally.

"That kid is bleeding," Hally said.

"What?" Pam asked.

"There's a kid bleeding over there," Hally repeated.

Pam stepped closer and looked. There, in the middle of the crowd, forced into the queues was a two-year-old, hands over his small ears. His cheeks were covered in tears and a small drop of blood falling from his nose.

"Why isn't anybody helping him?" Pam asked.

"Where are his parents?"

"I bet Elowen can fix it," Tom said.

"No," Hally tried to stop him, it was too late.

"Ms. Elowen," Tom called her. "There seems to be a bleeding child over there," he said.

Elowen turned over her shoulder, the cold eyes fell upon the child.

"You must forgive us, there are some of us that aren't as clean as others," she said and made a signal to the soldiers.

"Clean? He's two!" Hally muttered.

"Honey just walk, smile and walk," Isla ushered her as the soldiers came and ripped the child from the ground, his crying muffled by the cheers.

Step after step Hally did that. She smiled even though she could hear the screams of that little boy as he was beaten between all the cheers. She walked even though she wanted to run into the woods and forget that place.

Their game. Their rules.

Their game. Their rules.

Their game. Their rules.

She repeated to herself until all other thoughts were silenced.

Inside the dining hall everything had been changed. One big table had been placed in the middle of the room, seven chairs behind it facing the roaring crowd. The big wooden table had been covered by a long white cloth; small diamonds stitched into it. On top of it seven places were prepared for the feast, all of them arranged with three plates of different sizes, a bowl, and an elegant set of cups. The plates shone of pure gold, rubies, emeralds, and diamonds encrusted at its borders.

Keeping the crowd in line, the hall was surrounded by the masked soldiers. No one was allowed inside, except Elowen and a few Villagers dressed as waiters.

Before they reached the entrance, Elowen stopped, beside her was Pepper hiding in the shadow, barely visible enough for the kids to notice her.

"How did she get there?" Hally heard Piet ask from the front, his question was answered by a shush from Tom.

Elowen raised her hand; the cheers went quiet.

"My people, my village, my protegees, my sons and daughters," the idea of Elowen being a mother sent a shiver down Hally's spine, "today we shall receive our duty. Our honor. And especially, our power." The bridge shook from the cheers. "But before, these young humans must prove their lineage and the power they bring inside their veins. Or face the consequences of lying." She smacked her lips. "Let the ceremony begin!"

Cheers and roars arose, the improvised bridge shook again.

"Come," Elowen called Ayala, the first in line.

Ayala looked at Pepper. Once Pepper had confirmed the command, Ayala walked towards her.

"First," Elowen said, and the crowd calmed, they all wanted to hear every word. "The Unicorn Powder will show your true color."

Elowen retrieved a small bottle from one of the waiters.

"Put your hand up girl, let everyone see," she commanded and opened the small bottle.

Elowen smelled the cloud of smoke that came out of it.

"May the Unicorn Powder show you veracity," she announced and poured the powder into Ayala's hand.

And then, the world froze. The wind stopped roaring. The trees stopped moving. There were no cheers, no sound at all.

No one drew a breath, no one dared to. And no one dared to blink and miss what was going to happen.

The white powder turned green, and the previous steadiness was replaced by such excitement that the soldiers tightened their grips on their weapons. A crowd like that was not going to be manageable.

"Dear Naturae," said Elowen, her white teeth shining through her smile. "Show us your voice."

Ayala looked at her and then at the crowd. All of them waiting for her. She opened her mouth but what came wasn't a normal song. It was actual music. Pure. Sweet. Beautiful. It felt like the taste of your favorite candy. Suddenly Hally wasn't there, she was on the beach enjoying life, the sea roaring by her side, the sun warming up her body.

Then the water grew, and a giant wave hit her. She couldn't breathe.

She covered her ears, there was no more music, just a thousand needles being pushed inside her ears. She looked at the crowd, all of them consumed by the beauty of Ayala's singing, tears coming down their cheeks. Was she the only one that could hear the screeching noise?

"Glorious," Elowen congratulated Ayala, the singing ceased.

The air returned , and Hally could breathe once again. She touched her ear; a single drop of blood was falling from it. She rushed and cleaned it doing her best not to look where the kid had been just minutes before.

"Not all of us are clean." The memory of Elowen's voice sent another shiver down her spine.

"Are you alright?" Isla asked.

Hally nodded.

"Are we all going to have to sing? I don't have a great voice," Piet admitted.

His comment was once again met by a shush.

"Today, it's my honor to crown you with this," Elowen showed a small half crooked wooden circle, "a branch of Megalo Dentro. Ayala Homasi from Funafuti, Tuvalu. Naturae of Animals, salute your people." The Villagers went crazy, throwing flowers, cheering, laughing and even crying. Now they had proof, the myth was real.

The crooked circle turned magically into a crown as it touched Ayala's head, the wood transformed into a green, shiny material without explanation.

"You may take your seat," Elowen said. "Come," she called Lukai.

"May the Unicorn Powder show you veracity," Elowen repeated as with Ayala and dropped the sugar-like powder into Lukai's palm.

Once again came the steadiness... The calmness... The silence...

This time the powder turned blue.

"Oh," Elowen let out, even she was not able to keep her astonishment hidden. "A Woldier between us, the most powerful type-" she mumbled, her words lost. "Dear Woldier, show us your power," she asked as a waiter brought a bright blue rock the size of a mango. Hally had never seen that type of rock, not that she was a rock expert. It certainly didn't look like something she would find wandering around.

"Go ahead, touch the great Revelateur, the first form of identification in history."

"Do I just touch it?" Lukai asked.

Elowen nodded.

Lukai frowned at the rock, the few freckles of his face gathering in his forehead. Gently, he touched the rock and it turned into light. Then, it disappeared just as it had appeared. Hally lowered the hand from her face. She looked at Mr. Bored, he didn't seem so bored after all.

Elowen took another crooked wooden circle.

"I crown you, Lukai Woostar, from Quebec Canada, Woldier of light. My troops are your troops. Salute your people!"

Lukai gave the crowd an awkward smile, it was enough for them.

The wooden circle turned into a crown.

"You may take your seat at our noble table." Elowen announced.

Piet stepped up.

"May the Unicorn Powder show you veracity."

Unlike Lukai or Ayala, Piet showed no sign of fear. Either he truly felt comfortable in front of that crowd with the cheers and the eyes. Or he was just a better actor than everybody else. At this point it was almost impossible to pick which one was correct.

Piet smiled eagerly as the powder fell into his pale palm and even got the smile through the intense silence that came as the crowd waited for the switch of color.

But it didn't come.

One thousand. Two thousand. Three thousand.

The powder kept its normal color.

Piet's smile dropped. Pepper had been extremely clear about what was going to happen if they weren't who Elowen was trying to prove them to be. Even worse, Elowen had not made things easier when she had specified, 'face the consequences for lying'.

"Wha- wha– I can–," Piet stumbled through the words.

The powder changed to brown. A sign of relief came from everybody.

Piet chuckled nervously.

"You know what they say, better late than never," he said.

"You're quite right," Elowen maliciously responded. She called for a waiter. "May the stick of Megalo Dentro show your power," she handed the stick to Piet.

Piet looked at the plain tree branch and grabbed it. He wasn't sure if he had to throw it for a dog to catch it or use it as fire-wood. Again, nothing happened. Until it did. The wood changed to rock and as if Piet was a superstar the crowd went wild.

"If they keep it up this way, they will destroy the bridge only with noise," Pam muttered under her breath while keeping an incredibly fake smile.

"Maybe they can be called Woldier of noise," Hally muttered back.

Isla dazzled them with her eyes. "Shut it."

"I crown you," Elowen put a stop to Isla's scolding. "Piet Ívarson, from Akureyri, Iceland, Veteris of rock. May we take leverage of your great wisdom, knowledge warrior. Salute your people and take a seat at our noble table."

"What wisdom is she talking about? Has she heard the kid?" Pam asked.

"Maybe on how to win over high school girls," Hally added as Piet gave a final wink to the crowd before stepping inside the dining hall and joining Lukai and Ayala at the table.

"Girls," Isla growled. "Don't," she advised and looked at her right.

Even between the cheers and the enthusiasm there were soldiers focusing only on them. Watching their moves, their words, their actions.

They are not here for the crowd; they are here for us.

"May the Unicorn Powder show you veracity."

Tom answered the statement with a nervous smile. Hally could have sworn his hair had spiked as he heard the words, leaving his combed look in the past. And that it spiked even more as he looked at the powder fall into his hand.

Please switch colors. Please. I am begging you.

Hally looked at the soldiers, she noticed that they tensed their grip as they waited for the colors to switch.

"Marvelous!" Hally relaxed; the powder had turned golden. "Bring in the water," Elowen called.

A new waiter came from the dining hall carrying a big bowl filled with water. It looked like normal water, until it got within a meter from Tom, then it started to glow.

"May the warrior water show us your true self, brave Bellator," Elowen cheered.

Tom looked at the water. He hesitated. Slowly he touched it. It was then that the water shone brighter than ever. From the bowl a small storm appeared and a small lighting bolt shot out in every direction.

The crowd screamed and hid their faces, even the soldiers.

"Sorry," Tom mumbled, eyes open wide.

Elowen looked at him, she was marveled.

"Don't be," she said. "I have the honor to crown you, Tom Black Sols, from San José, Costa Rica. Bellator of electricity! Salute your people."

The crowd cheered.

"Go ahead and take your rightful place at our noble table, beside your partners."

Tom gave a small head bow to Elowen and threw Hally one last encouraging look before joining the rest.

My turn. Yay!

"May the Unicorn Powder show you veracity," Elowen said just as she had to everybody else before her. Hally's heart gave a turn. The words had seemed so distant when they had been said to Ayala, or even to Tom. They were now being told to her.

"Hope so," Hally whispered to herself.

She raised her hand, even though it felt as if she was trembling, even though her legs were shaking, even though she wanted to cry out for the fear she had, none of it was visible, and that was what mattered.

Elowen flipped the jar.

The white powder felt like flour and looked like sugar. In a way it was fascinating. Hally could've stood there and watched it fall forever, grain after grain. But once again, this is no fairy tale. We don't do that kind of thing here.

The powder didn't turn blue like Lukai's or green as Ayala's. Nor brown like Piet's. Much less gold as Tom's. It turned silver, the only color it wasn't supposed to turn into.

There were a few seconds of silence.

The crowd cheered even stronger than they had all the time.

Hally looked at Elowen, something had changed , something behind her smile. It was no longer real.

The air turned cold, even colder than what it was before. And it all came from Elowen's eyes. She wasn't happy, not anymore. She was angry. She was upset. And it was Hally's fault.

"May I present Hally Black Sols, from San José Costa Rica, a Magister!" Elowen announced.

A crooked wooden circle came to her head and Hally felt it as it changed into something light.

"Salute your people! And take your seat at our noble table," Elowen rushed Hally.

Hally looked at Pepper, this hadn't been like the ceremony for the others. There was something wrong. Pepper had said being a Magister was almost impossible, and there she was. That couldn't be the problem, right? That couldn't be the thing that got her killed?

"Later. Inside," Pepper mouthed at Hally's looks.

"A Magister huh?" Lukai asked Hally, she was sitting between him and Tom in the exact middle of the table.

"You could say it a thousand times and still it wouldn't mean a thing to me," Hally replied.

Lukai shrugged.

"The myth was pretty big back home, I had to move five times because the Superiors got too close," he said.

"Is it a good thing being a Magister?" Hally asked.

The second her powder had turned silver the whole place had changed. To Elowen it was not good, the look she had given her and tension made it clear. She was not happy. To the crowd it had been a miracle, cheering on and on even after Hally had already taken her seat at the table. For the waiters it was like an honor, repeating those exact words over and over again as they got close to her. And to the rest at the table, it meant nothing but the fact that they were one person closer to ending that horrid ceremony.

"Mmmm," Lukai insinuated. "I'm not sure."

Hally swallowed her doubts.

"Hey!" She turned to Tom. "Brave warrior, huh? Suits you well," she congratulated him.

Tom chuckled.

"What's wrong?" Hally asked.

Tom looked at her.

"Hally. What if this is our place? I mean Costa Rica was home, but never our *place*. Then, Tirabia was a mess. What if this is where our purpose lies?"

"Tom, what are you talking about?" Hally exclaimed, this couldn't be their place, it couldn't be.

"They gave us crowns!" Tom argued.

Hally looked at Tom's crown. It was made of gold, tall with small pearls at the tips and diamonds surrounding the base. Across it there was small lighting imprinted.

"Tom just because-"

"Shhhh," Ayala alerted them, the waiters were just behind them hearing every word.

"We'll discuss this later," Hally whispered.

In the front, Isla's powder had turned green.

"Let us hear your voice," Elowen asked.

Isla turned to the crowd. The music came back. It was so beautiful that Hally could feel like floating in the sea, with no worries and no fears. With every note she brought joy, peace, and warmth.

Hally covered her ears, there wasn't any more music now, just needles. Those horrid needles were back.

"Hally. Hally!" Tom called her. "It's over," he removed her hands from her ears. "See, it's over."

Hally looked up at him.

"Am I the only one who feels that?"

"No, we all do. But for a reason it only hurts you," Tom replied. Lukai, from the other side, nodded in agreement.

"Villagers, may I crown Isla Raveloson from Antananarivo Madagascar, Naturae of Flora. Salute your people." Elowen cheered. "You may take a seat at our noble table."

Isla smiled, relieved, and stepped inside, leaving a very tired Pam out alone.

"Finally, we reach our last one. May the Unicorn Powder show you veracity."

Pam extended her hand and Elowen poured the powder. In no less than five seconds it switched to gold.

"My people, we have been blessed with a second Bellator!" Elowen announced. "Bring the water."

One more time that shining water was brought out. At the sight of it a few Villagers covered their faces, after Tom's incident they couldn't be too careful. Soon enough the soldiers forced them to stand straight and watch as Pam touched it.

Instantly, it grew out of the bowl, dancing around like a living thing. Then, it froze in midair just to disappear into smoke.

The crowd and Pam turned to Elowen waiting for her to explain what it meant.

Elowen remained quiet, her smile fading as every one of her few brain cells did their best to work.

She has no idea.

Gently, she inclined to Pepper who whispered something in her ear and the smile returned.

"I crown you Pam Tang from Taipei Taiwan, Bellator of matter. My army is yours. Salute your people!"

Pam smiled, another fake one.

"You may take your place at our noble table," Elowen cheered.

Pam entered and dropped her smile, just to realize that the waiters still had their eyes on her and she forced her teeth to show again.

"My beloved Íroes, I am blessed and honored that fate has brought you to our humble home. The simple sight of your crowns is unbearable and majestic. I ask you to take off your crowns and place them in front of you."

Behind Elowen, Pepper mimicked what the kids had to do. They did it.

When the crown was placed in front of them it dissolved into a glittery serpent and changed into a new object, just as before each unique in its own way. Hally's turned into a silver ring, Tom's into a golden pin, Pam's into a beautiful golden earring, Piet's into a brown bracelet, Isla's into a green choker,

Ayala's into a green seashell necklace and Lukai's into a set of blue dog tags.

"With these symbols," Elowen continued, "may all the Guarders of every corner of the earth know your true identity and respect the power you have brought us. May the feast begin," she declared.

At that instant the dining hall was flooded with even more waiters and the Ringers started to set down for dinner.

Minutes later, when they weren't being watched by everyone, Isla turned to Pam and from the other side of the table called for her attention.

"Pam, do you need me to ask for some ice?" she joked. "For your cheeks I mean, I don't think you're used to smiling that much," she continued.

"Ha ha ha," Pam fake laughed and turned her attention to the newly placed bread in front of her. Hally copied her.

"What are you doing?" Lukai asked her not long after.

"What?" Hally asked, confused.

"Why are you mutilating your bread?" he hissed.

Hally looked at her plate where she had been meticulously taking out every single raisin of her bread.

"Taking out the raisins, duh."

"Yeah but why?"

"Why?" Hally exclaimed. "Why would they put them there in the first place? This is a type of violence. Bread is perfect on its own, why add weird wannabe grapes to it?"

"Because it's incredible, the taste the raisins add to the bread is unimaginable, the sweet and salty mixture they create are so melodic that it just melts in your mouth," Lukai argued.

"It's horrible."

"No it's not and you can't ruin the plate by taking them out."

Hally looked at him and smiled as she pulled another raisin out.

"You didn't dare-"

"Shush," Hally said. "Pepper!" she called.

Pepper walked to her.

"Yes?"

"Come closer," Hally asked and waited until she was close enough to keep the conversation between them. "What was all that about before?"

"You're the Magister, Hally," Pepper smiled as she said that word.

"People keep saying that. I don't know what it means," Hally replied.

Pepper took a step closer and lowered her voice.

"Hally, the second that powder turned silver you proved a miracle. Now everybody who witnessed that, any Guarders that sees that silver ring on your finger, will know that it's pure power that moves through your veins. And they, the other Guarders and this crowd, will follow you to the ends of the earth if you ask it, even if Elowen or any other Director disagrees. Hally, the color of your powder just told Elowen one thing, either she gets you on her side or she will have to break you, if not, all her power will be gone."

9

F.R.I.E.N.D.S

Hally's sleep didn't last long. As hard as she tried, her eyes just didn't want to stay shut. She couldn't stop thinking about Jess and the refuge. She wondered how they were doing. How everything had ended up. She knew Jess would have laughed if he could see her now. He had always said there was going to be a day when she wouldn't be able to run from herself. The funny thing is he'd never asked many questions. One day he had just said 'I have seen enough to know you're an extraordinary human being.' When Hally had asked if he meant about her glowing eyes, he had responded he hadn't even thought about that.

"Ps," Hally whispered, doing her best not to wake the sleeping Piet and the snoring Lukai behind her.

"Ps," she repeated, this time adding a poke to Tom's cheek.

"Mmmm," Tom mumbled.

"Tom!"

"What do you want, Hally? Can't I have one night's sleep?"

"Come," Hally pulled his arm softly.

"Where to?" he moaned.

"Come on, come," she repeated.

Tom sighed.

"Alright, alright," he accepted. "Give me a second," he said.

He sat up, looked for his slippers, rubbed his eyes, stretched his arms out and looked at Hally.

"Where we going?" he asked as she pulled him.

Hally didn't answer.

"To the bathroom? Why are you...?"

"Shut up."

Hally pushed Tom inside the bathroom. As soon as she closed the door behind her she turned to him.

"I don't like this place."

Tom massaged his temples as he sat at the edge of the tub.

"It's a bathroom Hally, there's not much you can do about it except keep it clean-"

"Not that, moron," Hally interrupted him. "I don't like *this*. *All* of this. The place, the people, the ceremony... It's like a sect."

"Ugh," Tom growled. "You gotta be kidding me-"

"I know you want answers but-"

"Hally! Listen to me. Just last night you were moaning about being a curse-"

"I am a curse!" Hally exclaimed. "I am the Magister, whatever that means. Pepper said it, the bringer of war."

"Oh gosh," Tom moaned. "Hally, I take back what I said. Don't listen to me, listen to yourself. Listen to the nonsense you're saying!"

"Nonsense? Have you seen what's going on out there? People are crazy in this place. Everything is crazy. And I'm the one talking nonsense?"

"Yes! They are crazy! But they have the answers to the questions you and I both have. They could teach us," Hally rolled her eyes. Tom snorted. "I'm the oldest. You're my responsibility. If I say we stay, we stay!"

"Oh please! You've never been responsible for me, not once in your life! I was there when you couldn't sleep because you were sick. It was I who waited at the bus station by your side when you were afraid. It was I who never doubted to risk my life for you. And what have you done for me? You don't even know my favorite color! I've never asked for anything in return for all I have done. But don't you dare come and say such a thing!" Hally exclaimed. It wasn't after the words had flooded the air that she realized what she had said.

Tom had always wanted to be the stronger one, the one Hally looked up to. She knew it. He tried it. Over and over again. When the time came, he always froze. So Hally stepped up. She did the work, covered up the disasters, attended their wounds, made up the lies, and she got away with it because she had to. She'd to start reading people to know where the first punch was coming from and prepare for it. She'd clean the dirt off her clothes whenever she fell and managed to keep a smile. She never had anyone to protect her. Her parents were too busy, her sister too far, and Tom... poor Tom had always lived in his own world, leaving her alone in this one, defenseless. And he knew it, he knew it every time Hally couldn't sleep, every time she appeared with a new bandage. Every time he saw her, the only thing he saw was another thing he'd fail at. He hadn't protected her, he hadn't been able to, and that scorched his heart.

"I'm... I'm sorry..." Hally mumbled.

"It's purple," Tom replied. "Your favorite color is purple."

Hally closed her eyes and sighed.

Something died inside her.

"It's green," she corrected. "Tom, my favorite color is green."

Something died inside of Tom now. How had they reached this point?

Tom shook his head.

"Nah... You're right. Of the two of us, you're the responsible one, you're the boss." He took a deep breath. "Still, where would we go if not here? You don't trust mom-"

"We would put them in danger either way. We can't go back home."

"Then, where?"

Hally scratched the back of her head, doing her best for one more minute to hold back the tears she had wanted to let out all day long.

"Hally, this time I'm taking responsibility. I'm keeping us safe. I promise," Tom declared. "Let's do this, we'll stay another day, maybe two. Let's see what they really have to teach us," Tom proposed.

"What do we do if I don't like it after a few days?"

"I'm sure you'll love it by then. Hally this place is magical. The order, the organization, the neatness surrounding it... It has a sense of harmony," Tom said with a smile.

"And if I don't."

Tom licked his lips.

"Then we talk about it."

Hally moaned.

"I hate that phrase."

"Fine," she finally accepted. "We will talk about it."

Tom rubbed his eyes one more time.

"Not every candy tastes sweet at first. This place might end up being the best for us."

"Or not."

Tom managed to get a chuckle through.

"Just let me sleep, *please,*" he begged.

"This time I'm taking responsibility," Hally mimicked her brother. She loved Tom, utterly. It was because of that that she knew, better than anyone, that taking responsibility was not his thing.

The forest was cold, colder than what she had expected. By the time she was far enough from the cottages she was freezing. Getting by the soldiers without being caught had proved easier than expected. After eluding the ones posted at the front of the cottage by taking the unguarded back door (clearly someone hadn't thought about the posts adequately), other soldiers were scattered around the cottages leaving more than enough room for a quiet and small Hally to get through. From then on, she had just kept walking forward.

"There has to be a frontier of some kind, if not, all the unhappy Villagers, like Pepper, would run away. And runaways would show the rest that Elowen doesn't have the control she claims."

Control. A similarity between Tom and Elowen that caused shivers down Hally's spine.

No, he's never going to become like her. He's better, he's a good person. He's Tom, he won't lose his way. Never.

"But then again," Hally continued whispering to herself, it was only in her solitude that she could savor the pleasure of speaking her thoughts as they came. "Elowen could have done enough coco wash for all these people to not worry about runaways."

"Pero... If I was her, I wouldn't take the risk."

"If by sunrise I haven't found it, I'll start heading back. If they ask, 'I lost my way while I took a refreshing walk to meditate on my new title of Magister'."

Hally laughed at her own nonsense. It was stupid enough for them to believe it.

"What are you doing out here young lady?" she mimicked Elowen.

"Oh, I'm walking to clear my mind and set goals for my new power as Magister," she responded to herself in a higher pitched faked voice.

She managed to get one chuckle out before it was drained.

"Magister," she repeated to herself as she raised her hand and looked at her brand-new silver ring. "Bringer of war. Pure power. A curse...," her voice broke. "I don't want any of them... Why is it always me? Why can't it be someone else for once that carries the flag and leads them out?"

She sighed.

"Maybe I should be sitting quietly in the corner of Pepper's living room. Perhaps that would save all of us a lot of trouble.

Elowen doesn't like me already. I don't see why. I'm such a delightful and obedient human being-"

Hally's eyes widened.

"Ha, I was right," she babbled.

Before her stood what can only be described as a giant curtain, like one of those white cloudy ones people use in the bathrooms. It extended up into the sky until it disappeared between the clouds, wider at the side than what Hally could see.

Hally touched it, gently. A set of ripples moved until they were too far to be seen. It was as hard as a wall. No matter what she did there was no way she was going to go through it.

Her eyes fell. There, on the other side, was a beautiful deer. It was noticeably young. His dark eyes shone like the stars, his white spots looked like paint and his small nose moved from one side to the other,

"Hi," Hally said.

The deer lifted his head to smell Hally's hand.

"You can smell me, huh? But you can't see me, or hear me..."

She was baffled.

"Getting out of here is going to be hard, isn't it buddy?"

The deer kept trying to find the source of the smell.

"What I would give to be one of you-"

"Checking the northern perimeter, over," a male voice said from behind somewhere between the trees.

Hally didn't need a second warning. She had seen what she needed to see; it was time to go back before someone caught her.

Skipping over branches and jogging by the trees as quietly as she could, Hally made it back to the village. Everything was as still as before, if not even more. No leaf had been moved, no soldier had changed, no light had been turned on. She could almost imagine the stone-cold Villagers sleeping like frozen statues in their beds.

Only the thought of it gave her a chill. Jess had once said, 'life is like a bike. If you don't keep moving, you'll fall.'

Hally made her way to the back door of Pepper's cottage and stepped inside just to be pushed to the ground.

"Leave us alone!" Piet demanded.

"It's me!" Hally cried. "Put your- milk and powdered chocolate? You're expecting me to be threatened by milk and chocolate? What am I? A lactose intolerant dog?"

Piet lowered the food.

"It was all I had in hand," he explained as a pretext.

Hally laughed.

"Why are you attacking people through the door anyways?" She stood up.

"We thought you were a soldier," Pam replied from the other side of the kitchen. "I doubt they would be happy to know that we are not currently sleeping in our beds."

"We were actually just talking about one of them breaking in and forcing us to sleep when you came in... Anyway, sorry for the push. Hot cocoa?"

Hally nodded, with a faint smile.

"What were you doing out there?" Pam asked.

"Taking a look at the frontier. I wanted to see what kind of barrier we were dealing with, in case we want out of here," she added, assuming the rest wanted to go, what would she do if they all thought like Tom?

"Is it bad?" Pam asked. Hally was relieved, she wanted out too.

"A little bit. The whole border is like an invincible, iron curtain. Only odors get through, nothing else. Even if someone comes looking for us, they'll never find us."

Piet handed over two cups with hot cocoa, one for Pam and one for Hally. Then he sat down on the other side of the counter. The kitchen was so modern and normal looking that if it wasn't because of the tense air, the kids could have easily pretended they were in their homes.

"Maybe that's good. I mean, where we were before, the place you broke us out of," he said to Hally, "it didn't seem as welcoming as this one."

Hally's mind filled with the picture of the wall that still had traces of her. She pushed the memory to the back of her mind.

"They weren't," she assured. "Maybe you're right. We are Íroes now, whatever that means, it's just another label. Maybe this is the best we are going to get and there's nothing for us out there."

"No!" Pam slammed her cup against the counter. "You're getting us out of this."

"Me? Why?" Hally asked.

Pam stared at her, eyebrows raised, nostrils wide.

"Because you saved us from the first crazy people, you'll get us away from the second. And in case you have not noticed, you're the Magister, therefore you're the best of us. The strongest and clearly the cleverest. I don't trust people, it is when you give trust that you give someone power against you, but I do trust *you* enough to get us out of here."

"You're expecting too much," Hally snorted, sipping her cocoa.

"Pam's right," Piet replied. "We are all fighters, but we need a leader."

"Tom's smarter than me."

"Hally!" Pam exclaimed. "You're not getting it. We're never going back to our old lives, whether they were good or not. Even if we tried, things are different since this morning and there's no changing that. In this new chapter, everyone has to step up and fulfill their role, even you. We have all seen it. There's something in you, something that burns anything standing in its way, you just have to let it grow. "

"Nah."

"Yes!"

"No…"

"YES!"

"Fine." She agreed, to shut them up. Yet it felt right. That was what she had to do. "I'm gonna try. Not the whole head, leader, thing. We'll see how that goes later. I'm going to try to get us out of here even if I have to convince Tom. And," Hally added a new spark of hope shining through her eyes, "you know what? I take back what I said. There must be a place where we can all just live in peace, without fear, together."

"All of us?" Piet asked. "The seven?"

"Of course!" Hally responded. "We're family now. Someone has to help this one with her trust issues. And someone has to take care of you, after all how old are you? Twelve?"

"Hey," both Piet and Pam complained, they weren't really offended.

"I'm about to turn fourteen," Piet replied.

"Yeah, when? Three years from now?" Hally asked.

"Two months!" Piet exclaimed. "I'm not a baby!"

"Yeah, yeah, whatever," Pam pushed his words aside. "*I don't have trust issues.*"

"You see, your issue is not with the trust issues, your issue is in the issue that you won't accept your trust issues," Hally said, making her and Piet burst out in laughter.

Pam rolled her eyes.

"I think a few brain cells just killed themselves because of that sentence."

Piet and Hally looked at each other and burst out laughing even harder. Soon the laughter grew so loud they bit on napkins to maintain silence as they held their stomachs.

"This is awesome, I haven't laughed like this in years," Piet later said, holding his stomach and wiping his remaining tears with a napkin. Pam was trying to clean a mess she had accidentally caused, and Hally was sitting on the ground after falling from her chair.

"So what do you say? A toast?" Hally asked from the ground.

"A toast for what?" Pam asked.

"The very first day of our new lives, for better or for worse," she said.

"And for good company even in the scariest corner of the world," Piet added.

The three cocoas cups came together.

"Cheers!"

10

FIRST TRAINING?
YOU MEAN THE FIRST DISASTER

Tom awoke and stared at the ceiling. The wood cracks moved all the way through, forming lines and shapes. There was silence. He loved silence. There was no Mom squeezing orange juice on the first floor. There was no Dad filling the house with cologne. And there was no Hally running around trying to get her things together. There was just him. And of course, Piet and Lukai, but they were in such deep sleep not even a bomb could wake them.

Outside, the sun had barely set, the birds seemed too tired to sing and there was no wind to whistle through the trees. This was paradise, the Guarders order. There was control and people believed themselves not to be important enough to bother him. And finally, he would have the answers to all of his questions. There was one and only problem: Stupid Hally!

Aggghhh! Tom loved Hally; he loved her to death, so much that sometimes he just wanted to... Why couldn't she just be a normal teenage girl that brought bad boyfriends home for Tom to beat up, not that he would if that was the case, but the idea wasn't bad at all.

Tom and Hally had been raised side by side. They had received the same lectures, the same scoldings. They had seen the same shows and gone to the same parties. They had read the same books, heard the same fables and studied in the same classes. But, somewhere along the way Hally had grabbed her stuff and taken her own path.

Tom would have to be blind and deaf not to notice Hally's scar in her right arm. Or not know that most of the time she was running around in danger. Yet, there was nothing he could do to change it. He himself had no control and no power. And when he did have power, he got her hurt, just like he had done the day before. He needed this place; he needed this education. Maybe this way he could finally be on her same level. Maybe this way he could finally do his older brother's job. It had been years since he had been able to take care of Hally. Lately, no matter what happened, Hally always ended up helping him, saving him. He knew she was tired of playing the adult, he just wanted to help. He needed to help her.

Breakfast was served in the cottage. Pepper had gotten the kids ready to eat with everyone else when Elowen had come. That day she wore a bright red suit, lace coming out her neck and sleeves. She had said that she considered it better for everyone if the kids ate inside and just came out once they were ready for their first training. Which raised another question, if the Villagers were forced to eat in the dining hall together, why did the cottages have a kitchen?

"What are we supposed to do with the jars?" Pam asked Pepper while they were eating.

Pepper looked at the small jar filled with golden powder in her hand.

"You can all keep it there. The only one who is going to use it is Piet," Pepper turned to the young blond boy. "Veteris have been noted to have problems getting hold of their powers. They usually have an object to help them. The object can be any kind, but it must contain the first powder the Veteris in question ever touched."

Pepper took something out of his pocket: a brown leather bracelet made from three thin leather strips braided together. "I got you this, I think it is easy enough to manage and to hide. All you need to do is pour the powder and the object will absorb it."

Piet took the bracelet and studied it thoroughly.

"What if I want to change it later? Can I move the powder? And, why is it only me?" he complained.

"No. You can't change it later. If you wanted to use another object you would have to touch another portion of Unicorn Powder and put it on the object. But it would never be as strong as the first portion; each time you touch more powder it will be weaker. As for the uniqueness, I can't answer that. I'm afraid I don't know. It's how it is."

"Then, why don't I touch a lot of powder the first time and then just use a little bit with each object?" Piet asked.

"Because Veteris are more likely to lose energy with the Unicorn Powder. It's unhealthy for any Íroe to get in contact with a large quantity of powder, it could lead to a drastic loss of energy, but for Veteris the large quantity doesn't have to be that large for it to be dangerous."

Piet looked at the bracelet and nodded in understanding.

"You have to be careful when you touch Unicorn Powder again, it will be your second time. You might want to keep it in a jar in case something ever happens to the bracelet."

"Will do," Piet replied and poured the powder.

Tom watched curiously while the powder fell from the small glass jar to the bracelet. When it touched the bracelet at first, it looked like brown glitter, then it turned to a sugar like appearance and then it completely disappeared.

When it was done the bracelet remained the same. Piet picked it up and put it on his wrist next to the other bracelet he had received from his crown the night before.

"If we all poured powder into other objects, what would happen?" Hally asked.

Pepper licked her lips.

"I seriously don't know. I know they used to pour it in chains to control the powers. If you poured, let's say Wolider powder, I figure the object would momentarily get the abilities of said Woldier. Truth is, I don't know. Experiments have never been done or recorded. And it's been quite a few decades since Unicorns were seen. Nobody is wasting their powder like that."

"Shouldn't I be feeling a power source or something?" Piet asked, taking back the attention.

"Maybe if you spin around quickly you'll start glowing," Hally suggested.

"Ha ha ha, very funny Hally," Piet replied, although Tom could see in his eyes, he was actually considering it.

Pepper chuckled.

"I doubt it would work, you're welcome to try it. I don't think anything major it's going to happen until you uncork your powers for the first time though."

"How is that going to happen?" Isla asked.

"With your first training," Pepper responded.

"What's that first gonna look like?" Tom questioned.

Pepper opened her mouth. Closed it. And then opened it again.

"I'm afraid I don't know that either. I suppose we'll have to wait and see." Tom didn't like that answer.

A crowd was waiting for them at the front of the cottage once they had had their nutritional breakfast. Piet and Ayala enjoyed it, they greeted, smiled, and winked (the last one more Piet than Ayala). Pam and Tom hated it. And Lukai, Isla and Hally ignored it or tried their best to.

The Villagers were being held back by the same soldiers as the night before. Nothing seemed to have changed since then, except the attention each kid received. The smaller Villagers ran to try to talk to Ayala and Isla for the worst luck of the second one. The older Villagers wanted an eloquent conversation with Piet, who was wishing to run over to the pretty teenage girls. Pam and Tom were incredibly respected by the soldiers even getting a few winks and handshakes themselves. And finally, Lukai and Hally received the most utter respect and attention from most of the village and from Elowen, although that one seemed fake at times.

Far from the touch and words of the Villagers, Pepper guided them to the center, where the same seven golden chairs as yesterday, waited for them. Beside each one, one of the assistants stood. They had been groomed for their best appearance and they had been forced to hold out a golden platter with a cup of water and a towel.

After the Íroes had sat down, the Villagers had calmed down, and the assistants had taken a step backwards, Elowen came. Tom had to admit that it was impossible not to see her with that suit, and that wasn't a compliment.

"Villagers, after centuries of preparation, studying, and hiding, the Íroes, finally found their way back home yesterday. Since then, we have started our way to the top, to what the true power of the Western Guarders once were. This morning, all of you, have the honor to see with your own eyes the life changing experience of our heroes setting free their powers for the very first time."

Elowen pausedfor the Villagers to digest what they had been told.

"Magister, step up and let us see your power."

All eyes turned to Hally, even Tom's.

Hally cleaned the loose clothes she'd been given as best as she could and smiled at the crowd. Tom couldn't help but admit he was happy for her, all that power inside of her, all those opportunities. He could even say he was a pinch jealous, but she deserved it.

"In the earlier times Íroes were known for using their abilities to demonstrate their power over every other living creature. From our best Villagers we have chosen a few that have been honored to serve their duty in such traditions."

Seven badly dressed and severely underfed Villagers were pushed up front by two soldiers. Tom looked at them, they had to be the lowest of the Lowers or maybe even prisoners of some kind. Whoever they were, they were surely not the best Villagers as Elowen had promised.

The crowd received them with a boo.

"What?" Hally asked.

The crowd were left in silence and Elowen's smile went from happiness to fakeness one more time.

"The Íroes are creatures superior to all others, it make sense the first thing you have to do to unset your powers is remind them of that. So please, if you may-"

"You want me to hurt them?" Hally asked.

Oh no, Tom thought.

The crowd's eyes went from Hally to Elowen. Maybe it had been her tone, or maybe the choice of words, but they were all looking for the response of their Director, even the soldiers.

"In a manner of speaking, to unleash your power you do-"

Hally had the audacity to interrupt the ugly mad lady one more time.

"I won't do it. If it involves hurting innocent people, I won't do it."

The air filled with tension. Pepper covered her mouth with her hands. The rest of the kids didn't dare breathe. The Guarders certainly had not prepared for Hally. The worst was that Tom knew it, even if they had received a year's notice, an intensive course and a capacitation, they still wouldn't have been ready for her.

"It's the way-"

"Find another one, one that doesn't involve hurting."

Elowen clenched her fists.

"Stupid girl, this has been our way for centuries. It's tradition!"

"Maybe that's why I'm an Íroe and you're not."

The crowd held a breath as Elowen turned visibly red.

What are you doing Hally? Tom thought. This was her moment, the moment she had been longing for. Finally she would be able to say that she wasn't a curse, she was a miracle. Why was she playing now?

"How dare you-"

"Speak?" Hally continued. "Maybe that's another thing, you should stop talking and listen to me. Because I am an Íroe. Not any Íroe, but the Magister. And that can only mean that there's something in me that is the reason I have the power you so much want and will never have."

"I'll do it," Tom blurted out before the crowd, Elowen, the soldiers, the Generation or Pepper exploded. "I'll do the exercise, with one condition. I won't do it against these Villagers, I'll do it against one from the Generation." He turned to his side. "I'll unleash my power against Gunner."

Tom looked over at Gunner and had to resist the need to smile when he saw the realization in his eyes. He had never been a vengeful guy or even a scary guy, that was more of a Hally thing to do, a Crazy Hally thing to do. However, there were a few times he made exceptions. The night before, Gunner had taken the lead with the boys and said horrible things about the girls, things that Tom didn't even want to think about. Now those stupid, reckless comments were going to make him pay and the fear in his eyes was enough to satisfy him.

The crowd looked at him.

"Marvelous," Elowen said, truly fascinated.

Tom looked at Hally, her eyes were glued on him. "What are you doing?" she mouthed. He resisted the idea of yelling back "saving your butt."

"Villagers, we have a volunteer!" Elowen continued. "Follow me to the arena." She gave Hally a last warning look.

Elowen wrapped Tom with her skinny ugly arm and escorted (pulled) him, leaving a roaring crowd, confused Íroes, an angry Generation and occupied soldiers behind.

"This is incredible!" Elowen exclaimed to him; she was pushing him hard.

"What's happening?" Tom asked, he saw a small portion of the Villagers following them.

"We must get you ready for the fight, Bellator," Elowen said to him.

"A fight?" Tom asked, that wasn't what he had expected.

"Surely," Elowen replied. "You're a Bellator, a fighter by nature. There's no way you will learn if not with pain and scars." She gave him a last push behind a cottage.

Tom's heart dropped as he was indulged by tens of assistants, soldiers, 'fans', and Elowen.

The next time he was alone he was finally able to see what he had been forced into. Over his normal t-shirt and jeans, a heavy golden arm suit had been shoved. It was heavy, too big and too warm. If Tom was the owner, he'd have hung it in the wall and left it there as the decoration it was.

He remembered a play he'd done in Tirabia, where he'd acted like a conquistador that harmed Latins, his people. He'd been forced into a stupid custom and then forced to act. He'd felt as terrible then as he did now.

Tom took a deep breath, for the last ten minutes he had been surrounded by people all saying different things. "OMG, you're so brave." "Hit him hard, I like blood." "Marry me." "Don't touch the armor, I just cleaned it!" Now he was all alone, in peace, well as much peace as he could knowing he was about to fight the biggest guy of the Generation. Revenge wasn't tasting as sweet as he had hoped.

He looked at the other side of the cottage, Elowen had insisted on a few moments alone to 'clear his mind before the fight'.

The Villagers were arranged into organized lines and circles around the newly built arena, the wooden stage. The stage wasn't that big, barely covering half the ground of a normal soccer field, enough space for Tom to receive a good beating, though.

He looked over at the thrones that had been moved from the center of the village. The rest of the kids looked as bored as three-year-olds in a lecture, playing on the grass, looking at the clouds, smiling only when necessary. All of them were there, including the Generation. All except one.

"Pepper," Tom called.

The pair of brown eyes turned to him, she was worried about something or just contemplating the soldiers organizing the Villagers, impossible to tell.

"Where's Hally?" he asked, not seeing her he felt a hole in his stomach. What if his stunt had put her in trouble? He was a little bit happy that she wouldn't be there to see his defeat, but he needed to know she was okay. As insufferable as she was, she was still Hally.

"Elowen sent her to my cottage with a couple of soldiers," Pepper answered.

"Is she okay?"

"Sure, the soldiers were fangirling a little bit, nothing she can't handle as we saw this

morning," Pepper mentioned the morning as if a bomb had fallen.

"Is Elowen mad about that?" Tom asked.

"You think? She's been babbling about it nonstop. We'll have to wait and see what happens. The Villagers love your sister and it's not like she told a lie, she just.... said it." She shook her head trying to get the idea out. "Never mind that, focus on you right now. Elowen will give instructions as you go. Make sure- Is Pam painting the throne?"

Tom looked at the thrones. Pam had gotten a black marker out of who knows where and had started doodling on her arm rester.

"That's antique, more valuable than me," Pepper exclaimed. She looked over at the still raging Elowen, she hadn't noticed it yet. "I got to stop her."

"Wait," Tom called her as she walked away. "What about me?" Tom asked, she had left the advice halfway there.

"Just remember you're the one with the pin," she babbled back.

Tom looked at the barely visible pin underneath his armor. The sight of it didn't change a thing.

"Villagers, Villagers," Elowen called their attention. They all stopped what they were doing and raised their heads, programmed like robots. "Give a big applause for Gunner, from our very own Generation."

Gunner stepped up to the middle of the stage and saluted. The crowd returned the salute like a three-year-old does when forced by his parents.

"And now," Elowen made a dramatic pause, "receive our Bellator."

The real applause came.

Tom swallowed hard. He looked at Gunner, from up close he looked angry, real angry. Behind him, the rest of the Generation waited anxiously for the fight to begin and the other Íroes all sat at the verge of their seats with the same look on their faces, if something went wrong, they were ready to barge in. They were a group now, they had to cover their own backs.

However, after the morning, Elowen had learned normal teenagers weren't as tamable as she expected, and she had placed five soldiers beside the thrones, all ready to stop anyone who might interrupt her class.

At her signal a separated group of Villagers started to sing. Their voices filled the once quiet air, with the sound of a thousand warriors ready to say goodbye to their families and march into an endless war.

The melody flushed adrenaline into Tom's veins, maybe that was its purpose.

His eyes locked into Gunner's; this was what he had to do.

Gunner smiled and muttered an expression that I won't dare write on this page, one that he had used before to refer to Hally and one that Tom had promised to beat him for.

Tom thought of Carlos the day before, he had said, 'It's better if you leave the war for warriors.' He was a warrior now. He thought of the Jilsons and all the times he had wanted to fight them but had held back. He thought of everything that had ever hurt Hally and he had not been able to defeat.

His fists clenched. He only needed one word and the beast would be released.

"Fight."

In the first seconds Gunner analyzed Tom. He pulled his fists in front of his face. Tom copied him. Gunner, then, rapidly walked back to the Bellator and threw his punch. Tom copied him one more time and both fell to the ground.

Tom looked up at the sky, eyes watering.

Gunner's punch had hit him directly in the center of his forehead.

He put his hands on his forehead; he could almost feel the bruise appearing. That had to be it, the end, right? Gunner, pissed, stood up.

Before Tom could even blink, the big kid pulled out a small knife from his back.

Then, he understood why the rest of the kids were on the edge of their seats, they could see something that he didn't.

Tom pushed his body off the ground and gave a few steps back.

"This isn't fair, where's my weapon?" Tom complained a bit louder than what Elowen would have liked.

"You're a Bellator, the only weapon you need are your hands," Elowen declared.

Gunner threw himself into Tom knocking him back to the floor, flashing the small silver knife. The choir intensified.

Tom managed to hold Gunner's hand and knock the knife to the other side of the stage, but not before Gunner managed a small cut on his cheek.

Tom looked at the boy, the drops of blood falling to his mouth where he could taste them. It was not until this time that he realized what this was. There was no way that he was able to get out of this one without harming Gunner... Elowen wanted him to get his hands dirty, take a leap that he would never be able to change even if he ever wanted to.

Gunner managed to get his arm back and poured out his anger, one punch after another.

To this day, neither I nor Tom know whether the confusion came from that realization or the punches. We just know one thing, as the punches came, and Gunner dared to say that phrase one more time, Tom knew that he wasn't going to let him get away with this. HE was a Bellator! And HE was going to make him pay!

The fire inside him ignited and he set it free.

The hair of his head spiked, his stomach was filled with lighting and the emotion that shone around him was power.

A crack followed through the ground rising like a lion's growl and Gunner fell immediately in pain.

The voices shut up; no more music filled the air.

"Ahhh!" Gunner exclaimed; he moved around like a slug who had just been thrown salt.

"That's it! That's the power!" Elowen exclaimed with small leaps of joy.

This high-pitched scream jolted Tom from his shock and he realized he was digging his fingernails into the palms of his fists. He let go.

Gunner stopped moaning, but he stayed still on the ground, staring lost at the sky.

Tom sat up and looked at his hands, he had done that. He had gotten his hands dirty, and he had liked it. Elowen was right, this was power, real power. Once Hally experienced it she would not even consider the curse thing for one more second.

"Rise," Elowen said.

Tom stood up, behind him a couple of uniformed soldiers took Gunner off the stage and into the shadows.

"You have unleashed your power Bellator. Your kind are known for being strong and fierce in the face of threats. Today you have proved yourself."

The crowd cheered.

Tom smiled and waved.

"Come," Pepper whispered by his side, keeping a smile on her face.

"Why? This is amazing," Tom muttered the same way, for the first time he liked the crowd.

"This is the first time you used your powers. You'll be tired in a few minutes. You don't want to pass out in front of... everybody."

Tom looked at her. "Fine."

Pepper pushed him gently back to the dark side behind the cottage.

"Here, I'll help you get this off," Pepper said.

As the golden cover came off and a cold wind hit his sweaty clothes, Tom realized what Pepper had meant earlier. His eyesight blurred; his legs failed.

"Hey, hey, take it easy. You're obviously tired. Here, take a seat." She helped him to the ground; it wasn't of much help.

Tom closed his eyes; it didn't stop the world from turning.

"This is bad, really bad."

Pepper chuckled.

"It's part of the game, your body isn't used to that kind of energy drop. You'll get used to it-"

Tom didn't stay conscious enough to listen to the rest of the sentence.

11

WHAT ARE YOU DOING?
AND WHAT YOU HAVE TO DO

Elowen cleared her throat and Tom awoke.

"Don't worry Bellator, you're in our infirmary."

Tom looked to his sides. The place was just like Pepper's, with more beds. The walls were the same color. The furniture was made of the same wood. The floor had the same echo. And the decoration was exactly the same: a few paintings and a picture of the village.

"You did wonders out there my dear. You seem to have an incredible ability to heal rapidly despite a few bumps. Nothing to worry about."

Elowen chuckled.

"Where are the others?" Tom asked. "The rest of the Íroes."

"Pepper's taking care of them. They'll have to wait for tomorrow for their very own class."

"Why?"

Elowen's eyes darkened, between the many things she despised, being questioned seemed to be a pretty important one.

"To keep the Villagers happy. They loved your fight and enjoyed it so much that I decided to save the rest for another time. We wouldn't want to get rid of all the excitement in one day, would we?"

"No we would not," Tom answered. "The entertainment helps with control and control helps with the organization of this place."

Elowen smiled as if Tom had fallen into her trap.

"Exactly, control... What was your name again?"

"Tom, short for Thomas," he replied, people usually had no difficulties remembering his name, not with it being as simple as it was.

"Mmmm," she said. "Are you aware that the meaning of your name is the twin?"

"I am, yes."

Elowen smiled.

"Well, this is just perfect....," she made one of those dramatic pauses she loved doing. "I believe you, out of all the rest, understand the importance of the role that control and organization have in the world."

Tom frowned.

"I do." He wasn't quite sure of where this talk was going.

"And I suppose you comprehend what it would be to the world if there weren't any?"

"There would be chaos, anarchy.... Humanity. Unlike the rest of the animals, we don't thrive in the chaos of nature, or the nature of chaos. We need order, control, organization. Often it must come from a rightful leader."

"That's right," Elowen stated. "As one would normally think, as the leader you speak about, I have to deal with everything and everyone that presents a threat to organization and control."

Tom nodded.

"Even if they are supposedly worthy of all respect," she grunted.

"Of course," Tom assured her. Then he realized she was talking about Hally.

"I understand what your sister said this morning, I was once a rebellious teenage girl myself. And considering she was raised in the wild, outside world; it's considered a normal reaction. However, she can't keep questioning the bases of our traditions, it's the only thing the Villagers know! Imagine if she kept pulling the traditions apart, the whole system this people believe in would fall! Oh poor Villagers," she expressed. "I know you understand it. After all I am aware you have a lot of questions, questions to which *I* can provide the answers to. I can't do that if my control is challenged."

Tom gulped.

"Right."

Elowen recovered her smile.

"I have called the Magister for a meeting this afternoon, where I hope that we can settle these things that you and I both understand. I would like you to give her this gift." Elowen handed Tom a box filled with blue tea bags.

Tom grabbed them, they had a weird smell.

Elowen knocked on the wall and the doors opened. "These soldiers will accompany you to your cottage."

Tom realized his time in the infirmary had ended, even if he was not fully recovered. He stepped off the bed and walked towards the door. His muscles still ached. He was still bruised. Elowen didn't care.

"Thomas," Elowen stopped him before he crossed the door, "make sure the Magister drinks that tea before our meeting," she warned.

"Will do" Tom assured.

"There you are champ," Piet received Tom as he stepped inside.

The door was closed behind his back. Pam, Piet, Lukai, Isla and Ayala stood frozen. Whether they were scared, amazed or had just not expected someone to interrupt their game of UNO, he didn't know.

"Hey," Tom saluted.

"Hey," the rest responded by command.

"Where's Hally?" he asked.

"Up- upstairs," Isla stuttered.

Tom looked at them awkwardly for a second. Then smiled as a thanks and walked to the stairs feeling all eyes following him.

"You were totally checking him out!" he heard Ayala whisper to Isla on his way to the stairs.

"I was not!" Isla defended herself.

"You totally were, even I noticed. And I'm a guy!" Piet whispered to her.

"Well what if I were, we all saw what we saw back there-"

Once on the second floor the conversation quickly faded.

Tom opened the girl's room. There Hally sat in the middle of the floor surrounded by books.

The twins' eyes crossed for a second.

"What are you doing?" he frowned.

"Close the door," Hally said as she sprang up and forced the door shut. "*Gosh.*"

"Is everything alright?" Tom asked.

"What am I doing? Seriously? Me? *What are you doing Tom!*"

Tom took a step backwards.

"What do you mean?"

"We don't hurt innocent people Tom!" Hally argued.

Tom chuckled.

"Is this what that is about? Ha!" he laughed. "I thought you were serious... He wasn't that innocent Hally, if you had heard the things he said... Besides, I wanted to show you what we are capable of. Oh, you should have seen it..." He stopped a second to remember the feeling. "We are not a curse Hally! We are powerful!" he cheered.

Hally's expression didn't change.

"Anyway, he had it coming, and I barely touched him," Tom defended himself.

"They had to resuscitate him, Tom," Hally clarified.

Something sunk in Tom's chest. He had wanted Gunner to pay for what he did, he wasn't expecting it to go that far.

Tom let himself fall on the closest bed as he looked at the floor.

"Do you see now Tom? We are not powerful, we are *dangerous!*" Hally insisted.

"Wha- Whe- How did you even see it? Pepper said soldiers accompanied you here."

Hally licked her lips.

"Come on Tom. Elowen sent soldiers to watch the door, a house has windows. Did you think I was going to leave you out there on your own?"

"Jeez Hally! Don't you seriously understand what it is to stay in one place?" he exclaimed. "And let me guess, these books are Pepper's,"

Hally's eyes opened widely.

"You have no idea what I have found. I was trying to find a way out of here, but I ended finding this drug the Directors created to control-"

"Jeez Hally!" Tom exclaimed one more time.

"What?" she asked, confused.

"This is what I mean. You have no respect! We are guests, you can't behave like that!"

Hally rolled her eyes.

"Oh please Tom. We are not guests, we are prisoners!" she declared.

She opened her mouth to add something but closed it and let herself fall into the bed beside her brother.

"Why are we fighting? We are the only family the other has

left. We should be growing together, not separating." She sighed. "I guess, maybe it's my fault-"

"No," Tom correctedher. "You're absolutely right, you always are. We are prisoners not guests," he finally accepted.

He placed his arm around her, and Hally let her head fall on his shoulder.

"I'm sorry, for the yelling, the insisting, the stupidness, everything," he apologized.

"I'm sorry too," Hally apologized.

They stayed there for a second, thinking of the life they had left behind the day before, all the moments, places, people they might never see again. Their parents, grandparents, May. Tom wondered if they were looking for them. He imagined their empty room. The tears in his mom's eyes. The police searching for them.

"Do you remember our tenth birthday when you went with me to buy a video game and we didn't get anything in the end?"

Hally straightened up.

"Sort of... You didn't buy anything because you said the guy's tone sounded like he didn't believe in what he was selling."

"I want answers Hally. And I truly think that we aren't dangerous or a curse. I believe we have power. I want to understand it and use it. There's nothing wrong about it. But Elowen doesn't even believe in what she's pitching."

"So?"

"You go to your meeting with Elowen, apologize and make peace. Meanwhile," he pointed at the books with his chin, "I'll figure a way out of this place."

Hally smiled.

"I can live with that."

Tom nodded and stood up.

"Well I'm going to get something to eat, I'm starving," he added as he left his sister the same way he had found her.

When he closed the door, he wrapped his hand around the tea bags that were inside his pocket. He wasn't going to fall for that one. No kind of power would make him turn against his sister. Maybe when he was younger and often asked his mom why he hadn't been born alone or why she had kept the other, ugly baby. Not now though, definitely, not now.

He went, determined, and one by one poured the contents of the tea bags down the drain. They would have to try harder than that to break him.

12

THE PERKS OF BEING A MAGISTER

Hally wasn't worried about her meeting with Elowen. If you saw it for what it was, it wasn't much different from a meeting with the principal. She was used to meeting with the principals back in Tirabia when the whole problem with the white roses and Ms. Knox had started. The science behind those wasn't difficult, all you had to do was to listen, speak only when asked, apologize and there was a big chance you would leave on good terms.

Hally turned the page even though she had stopped paying attention to the words a while back. She would give anything to be right back to her life in Tirabia. It was a mess, it was dangerous, certainly it was far from perfect and it had taken years for her to understand it, but finally she had managed to get a grip on it and found some kind of peace and balance.

She turned another page.

She couldn't help but think, if Tom had been able to 'kill' a guy without even trying, what was she capable of? If what they were saying was right, if she was indeed a powerful Magister, how powerful was she truly? And with her bad luck and clumsiness that could only be called a curse, how many lives would she ruin?

The next page was filled with pink highlighter bright enough to bring Hally's attention back to the books. She had grabbed them from the library Pepper kept on the first floor. At first they had seemed like the normal 'school' books used to educate the Villager kid of their ways. But once she focused on the notes and the colors, Hally had realized Pepper had used a code beside every text. There was a note of a possible fertilizer Elowen put in the food to make the Villagers more manageable, Pepper even proposed that in high doses could change a person's entire mind. The shield that protected the village was in complete control of Elowen and whoever had crossed it was under its protection. And finally, the possibilities of a man who had been chosen between the four Directors to handle the Íroes and avoid the exact same thing Elowen was doing.

Hally closed the book and put it in the pile with the others. She knew for a fact that Pepper had more books in her room, books which she had seen from afar the day before, yet Pepper had been nothing but good to them from the start. She had been there to receive them, protect them, teach them, advise them and guide them... Hally couldn't throw all of that away and steal her books. Even taking the books from the first floor had been heart wrenching.

The door was opened as if Hally had summoned it. Pepper looked at the books by Hally's feet and then at Hally before shutting the door and locking it.

"Pepper?" Hally mumbled, Pepper's eyes were dancing up and down with anger and her fists were clenched.

Pepper threw herself across the room towards Hally.

"Have you figured it out yet?" she asked.

Hally looked at her eyes again, they were inches away from her face. It wasn't anger that ruled them, it was fear.

"What?"

"Have you figured out how to get out yet?" Pepper repeated.

"No."

Pepper sighed and laid back against the bed.

"I tried, I'm sorry. You're clever, I hoped you would find a way by now but... I have called a friend either way, if anyone can get you out of here it will be him. Just avoid being trapped."

Hally stood up.

"What are you saying?"

Pepper imitated her and forced something into Hally's hands.

"You listen to me, Hally Black Sols. I tried, but I'm not a Ringer. We have little time. They're coming, I asked Lukai and Piet to stall them. You'll go with them, you have to. Don't let yourself be tied, or that will be your end. You use this, do you understand me? And you run and run and run into the forest. Whatever you do, don't let the soldiers get you or you won't get back. I'll take care of the rest. Tom will be okay. But you, Hally, you don't strike me as one who is easily broken and if Elowen can't break you, she will finish you. Do you hear me? What do you have to do?"

Hally stared at Pepper, what was going on?

"Hally! What do you have to do?"

"Run! I have to run."

Pepper gave a firm nod.

"Yes, you run."

Hally looked at the object inside her hand, a small silver knife.

"Hide it," Pepper ordered, Hally did.

From outside Hally heard a set of heavy footsteps coming up the stairs.

"You run Hally, you run," Pepper begged one more time before the door was knocked.

Hally nodded, that was the one thing she knew how to do.

Pepper opened the door revealing two of the biggest soldiers.

"Magister," their voices seemed robotic coming from underneath their helmets. "Director Elowen asks for your presence for a meeting."

"Fantastic!" Hally cheered. "It was about time."

She put a smile on her face and crossed the door.

"Where we going?" she asked in the same cheerful tone, she wasn't about to let them see her crumble with fear.

"Just follow us," the soldiers muttered.

"Alright."

They went down the stairs, a soldier in front of her and another behind. The rest of the kids stared at them as they crossed the living room, among them Tom. Their worried looks followed them from one end to the other. Hally responded to all of them with a smile, there was no reason for them to be scared for her. There wasn't anything they could do, none of them. This was Hally's problem and Hally's alone.

The town would have been called a ghost town by anyone who didn't yet understand the nature of the village: the Villagers got to live peacefully as long as they made sure to stay inside every time Elowen commanded them to.

The soldiers guided Hally across the whole village until they reached the outer circle.

Hally looked at the forest simply a few meters away. This would make running easier. But it could only mean one more thing, Elowen wanted pure privacy for this meeting.

The soldiers stopped.

"Right through there," they ordered.

Hally looked at where they were pointing.

Out of all the cottages she'd seen in the village this was the only one that was not being taken care of. The structure was small, the wood unleveled, the paint was of different tones and the roof was filled with leaves. It seemed as if the owner had died, it had been forgotten or the theory Hally liked the most, it hadn't gone as Elowen expected, so she had made sure to keep out of all eyes, just as a wrinkle in a dress or a seed in the juice. A disturbance in her perfect plan, just like her.

Hally took another look at the forest on her left.

"Over there," a soldier repeated.

Hally turned to them. They had noticed her staring at the trees and their hands were ready to pull their weapons if needed.

She smiled at them.

"Fabulous," she cheered and walked inside the den.

The den was a dark, very dark, room once the door was closed. Hally looked at her sides, it would take a while for her eyes to get adjusted and even then, she doubted she would get to see much.

"Excuse me," she cleared her throat, her very first mistake.

A blow came directly on her back dropping her to the floor.

"First rule. You speak only when you're supposed to," Elowen's voice echoed.

A bright white light filled the room.

Hally pushed herself off the ground and sat up. Besides her and Elowen, the room was filled with four other soldiers, one in each corner and each of them holding a wooden club in their left hand.

"I knew you were going to be trouble since the very start young lady," she sighed as if Hally's behavior was the heaviest of her burdens. She signed to the soldiers. Like robots, the four of them forced her off the ground and into a chair. They pulled four pieces of black string.

Pepper's words echoed in Hally's mind: *Don't let yourself be tied, or that will be your end.*

Hally fought the strings, pulling her arms against her chest and kicking the soldiers that tried to tie her legs. The soldiers struggled.

"Tie her up you idiots!" Elowen shouted.

"She's moving too much," a soldier whined.

Elowen growled. She picked up the wooden club a soldier had left and struck Hally across her face and hit two of the soldiers in its way.

Hally's vision blurred. Her mind froze and so did she. That would leave a mark, she was sure of that.

When her thoughts returned her hands and feet had been tied.

"Finally," Elowen said. "You didn't let yourself be trained properly, now you will be trained the other way, the way queens and kings did centuries ago when they found a powerful enemy soldier: breaking them and molding them the way they wished."

She paused and started to walk, her heavy footsteps dry against the floor.

"Who are you?" Elowen asked.

"I'm Hally Black Sols."

"No!"

She felt a whip on her shoulder and the skin underneath her shirt burned for a second.

"You're the Magister, *my* Magister. I'm going to ask again. Who are you?"

"I'm..." she thought about the answer for a second. "Hally Black Sols."

She felt the burn on her back, another whip. This time it was a hundred times stronger.

Hally bit her tongue to avoid saying something that gave away her pain.

The pain became worse. The scar on her right arm started to

burn. Her mind filled with images she had promised herself to never remember.

Not now.

Please not now.

"You don't seem to understand the exercise, perhaps a demonstration will help you." She turned to the soldiers. "Who are you?"

The soldiers answered loud and clear in unison.

"We're soldiers ma'am, your soldiers!"

Elowen smiled.

"Do you see? In here you are not who you are outside. You are who I want you to be."

"Why's that?" Hally asked, hopefully a question would save her from another beating.

The club struck once again against her face; she was mistaken.

"You will speak only when spoken to! Ill-bred child!" Elowen shouted.

Hally focused on the edge of her eyes through her pain. It was brief, almost unnoticeable but there was a flinch in every soldier. It made sense. Earlier Elowen had accidentally hit two of them when she had her tantrum. They knew that when she got mad, she would strike anyone around her, no matter who they were. And that's why they stepped away.

Hally wrapped her hand around the cold small silver knife she had managed to get out of her pocket. She was slowly and quietly trying to get rid of her hand ties, but even if she did she would need to get past her soldiers. However, if they were far from her... then things would change. All she had to do was to make Elowen angrier and that was easy.

Hally looked at Elowen and spit right on her shoes.

"Ah!" Elowen growled.

The club struck Hally's cheek, this time ripping her skin apart.

The soldiers took a small step far from the chair. Hally felt the warm thick blood faintly falling in drops on the right side of her face all the way to her hand.

Hally looked at the blood and memories mixed with the present. For a second she was not in that den, she was back at that dreadful dark room in Miso. Instead of Elowen standing in front of her there was a man holding a burning knife. He was laughing, it was about to begin...

"Who are you?" Elowen asked.

Hally shook her head.

Focus.

The whip made its burning contact against her back.

"Answer me," Elowen demanded. "Who are you?"

"Soy Hally Black Sols, bruja," Hally shouted.

Elowen smacked her face.

"Keep your filthy tongue to yourself!"

Another blood drop fell on her arm and the memories collided with reality.

"You stupid Latin trash rat, don't you know you're very far from home?" the man laughed.

"No, no," Hally had cried, she would have had better luck talking to the walls.

Focus.

She came back to the present. Her body was shivering, not from the blows. She could almost feel that knife both cutting and burning her skin. The pain was too much to ignore. Her eyesight had blurred, and her thoughts had faded for once.

"Who are you?" Elowen asked again, this time her voice was not enough to bring Hally to full consciousness.

Hally pulled on her restraints desperately. It was about to begin and once it did it was never going to leave her alone. She pulled harder, her left hand came free.

"Do not move!" Elowen roared and swung the club.

Hally covered her face waiting for the firm wood to hit her arm. Maybe a new pain would take the memory of the last away.

The blow never came.

She looked up, slowly. Elowen was frozen in mid swing. The club was in the air, her suit was in the move and the evil angry expression was still on her face, but she wasn't moving. She was like a statue

Hally looked at her eyes, the only part that was moving. They had no hatred, no anger, only fear. Fear of her.

She chuckled, she was doing that, just as she would walk or talk or even count. She was doing it! She didn't even have to think about it, it came naturally.

Before the soldiers realized what was going on, Hally thought about it while they were pushed against the wall and on the ground. She stood up, with a single swing getting rid of her restraints.

She ran to the door. It blew open, landing a few meters away.

And then, before Elowen unfroze, the soldiers stood up, and the one outside noticed her. She did what Pepper had told her and she ran, faster than she had ever done, inside the forest, the dark forest.

13

MEGALO DENTRO

"Over here," the blond-haired girl had called her. Her voice had been as sweet as her smile, as were her manners. She was great, kind and nice, the exact friend Hally had been looking for. She had even shaken her hand that first night.

Hally growled.

There were never my friends.

But they had been her friends, a long time ago they had been. They had shared classes, recesses, and even gone to the real book club of the town. Hally had been happy with them, the blond girl and the red headed one, and they had seemed happy with her. They did everything together, laughed and cried.

Stupid! That's what I was!

One day they had invited her to a sleepover.

"So neither your parents nor your brother will be in town?" they had asked.

"No, they'll be out," Hally assured them.

"You should come over," the blond girl had proposed.

"I would love it," Hally had cheered. She had never been invited to one of those and the feeling of a new adventure was so intoxicating she hadn't really thought about it. Not when she packed her backpack without anyone noticing and not when they had convinced her to cross over to Miso.

I should have never crossed! Never!

At first, Miso hadn't seemed worse than anything she had ever seen before. It wasn't long before she forgot she was on the other side of the railway.

"Are you sure it's here?" Hally had whispered to the redheaded girl.

"Yep, here's where I live, go in."

She had been so nice there was no reason to believe that on the other side there was a person waiting to put a bag over her face.

Hally's heart skipped a beat, she could still remember the bag against her mouth as she gasped for air. Or the first feeling of the handcuffs that would leave scars for weeks on her skin.

When the bag had finally been taken off, her 'friends' were behind the man that would become the main character of her nightmares. They were laughing with him as she screamed for help, tears pouring down

"We get ourselves branded righteous," the man had said, her 'friends' behind him had shown the white rose tattooed on their wrists. "We must brand the human waste as well," he'd explained as he pulled the knife out of the fire and then into her arm.

Stop it! Stop thinking about it.

Hally had thought the pain was never going to end, until the door had been blown open showing her saviors: Jess and Phil.

"Phil take her to the refuge," Jess ordered his best friend, he was far different from what he would do later as a doctor. The man and Hally's 'friends' were long gone.

"What about the plan?" Phil had asked him.

Jess glared at him.

"Yeah yeah," Phil agreed. "Keep moving or die, this one is a pessimist." Of course *he* was joking. The worst part is that Hally had laughed.

Outside, things had been chaotic. For her luck or demise, the day she had decided to stupidly go into Miso was the same day as one of the first attacks against the Gang.

Phil took Hally through soldiers, both Back-Fighters and the Gang. They crossed doors and hallways, fights and liberations. The Gang had been working, getting prisoners and using them as house slaves. Hally wondered if that would have been her fate if they hadn't saved her.

"C'mon," Phil had said. "Keep moving or-"

Just like that a single bullet flew through the air into his skull.

Maybe it was just bad luck. Maybe it was the wrong place and the wrong time. Or maybe it had been fate. Hally didn't care, she knew that if she hadn't crossed, he would have survived.

"Phil!" Jess had appeared minutes later, Hally hadn't moved, not one centimeter, her face splattered with tears and her clothes with blood.

He had taken one look at his friend, he was gone, long gone.

"Come," he had called to Hally, but she didn't move ha.

Jess had grabbed her by the shoulder.

"No! I can't leave him! No!" Hally fought holding on to the walls and leaving marks of blood that would stay on there for years to come.

Hally stopped running. She had been running for hours, or at least that's what it felt like. Her heart echoed through her ears, her legs burned, and she was sweaty.

She wondered when Elowen was going to come for her. She didn't think she was still frozen. No, she wasn't that powerful. But perhaps she was powerful enough to scare them a bit and make them wait to come after her. Either way she just had to hold on for Pepper's friend.

Hally followed the river's sound. There she cleaned off the blood of the half-healed wound on her cheek and did her best with her back. And then, she kept walking, as north as she could get.

The forest was way prettier at day than at night. The sunlight helped her appreciate the flowers, the birds, the big old trees and even some colorful butterflies.

Hally walked, not ran, for a while longer. Wandering in any direction, except the village.

"Maybe Pepper's friend won't be here on time," she sighed. "What will happen to Tom? It was stupid of me to leave him there."

"No," she added later. "Elowen likes Tom, she won't hurt him, probably."

She kept walking, doubting everything, step after step.

"And if she tries to hurt him then I'll get her." She chuckled at the idea, knowing full well she probably wasn't even going to do it even if the situation presented itself.

Hally froze, she had found it. She didn't even know she was looking for it, perhaps *it* was looking for her.

"Whoa."

In front of her was the tallest and biggest and most beautiful tree she had ever seen. The wood was a dark, so shiny brown that if someone ever dared to cut it and use it, it would be perfect for the most incredible and unimaginably expensive pieces of furniture. The leaves seemed as soft as clouds, letting off a soft melody every time the wind danced through them. They were of every color, purple, pink, brown, yellow and even the natural green seemed a surprise. Between the leaves, there were seven single white flowers like no other Hally had seen before. All she wanted to do was to climb the tree just to get a single sniff of its scent, a scent that seemed to be able to turn the most vicious criminal into a good person. However something kept her from it, she knew that tree and those flowers were too good for, too good to touch or to ruin with her luck.

Hally laughed, she knew what it was, surprisingly.

"Megalo Dentro."

"You're a smart girl," a voice said.

Hally raised the knife Pepper had given her and faced the voice. It was a young man in his early thirties. He was wearing a long, beige coat with a smile on his face. His head was covered in a tangle of black hair unsuccessfully combed back, and his nose was slightly crooked to one side adding a mischievous look.

The guy put his hands up. His eyes opened wide, whether it

was due to traces of blood or the surprise of the knife we'll never know.

"Wow," the guy said. "Elowen played a bad one on you, didn't she?" He spoke with a Britannic accent.

Hally didn't answer, neither did she lower her knife.

"Don't you think it's time to lower the knife. I am here, and you are there. Besides," he opened his hands, "I have no weapon."

Hally looked at him. He was right, perhaps she was a bit too paranoid. She gently lowered it but kept it between her fingers.

"I'm Blake," the guy said as if Hally was supposed to know him.

"Congratulations?"

"Pepper's friend," he clarified.

"Sorry?"

Blake chuckled.

"Didn't she tell you I was coming?" he asked.

"How do I know that you are actually him and not someone who just got the information from him before disposing of his body?" Hally asked.

Blake stared at her blankly.

"You've been watching too many movies."

"Tell me it has zero possibilities of happening, and I'll let it go," Hally replied.

Blake opened his mouth but closed it after thinking of what he was about to say. Then he opened it back again.

"Don't you remember me?"

Hally looked at him, there was something remotely weird in his crooked nose and his blue eyes, something familiar.

"You... you were in the refuge once," she remembered, he had gotten a sprained wrist and a few scratches. He'd been there for a night and then disappeared by the next afternoon. They had never spoken, but she remembered him.

"Yes-"

Suddenly a bunch of memories surfaced.

"And you were in Costa Rica, at the reading festival. And at my science fair in Tirabia, you asked a question and because of my explanation I won a place on the podium," she chimed and then it hit her. "Have you been stalking me? Who are you?"

Blake gave a small innocent smile.

"I told you, I'm Blake. A long time ago, I tried to prevent something like this from ever happening, the four Directors decided to put some people in charge to keep an eye on the Íroes without revealing their identities to the world. People around the globe have always been hunting the myth, not as much as now, but they did. My job was to make sure the seven of you were being taken care of and as far away from your pursuers as possible. Not interfering, just watching."

"So, you've been there? Always?" Hally asked, but it didn't make it any less creepy.

Blake looked at the ground ashamed of something.

"Yes... Hally, I have to apologize. I failed you. It was my job to keep you safe. When your parents moved to Tirabia I should have been nearer. Instead, I put my attention elsewhere. It was my fault the Gang got so close to you," he pointed with his chin to her arm. "It was my job and I failed."

Hally covered her scar with her hand.

"No it wasn't. I trusted them when I didn't have to. I let myself be manipulated. You didn't force me to cross the railway, I did it because I wanted to."

"But you didn't know, I did," Blake insisted. "And in truth I also failed yesterday. I knew they were getting closer, but I never expected them to attack the tree."

He pointed at a big scratch in the wood.

Hally looked at it, how had she not noticed it earlier?

"When the tree is in danger there is usually a war occurring or about to happen. So, it lets his warriors know that trouble is present. That's the reason for all the weird episodes of yesterday. By the time I realized what it was, the Gang had already used Wisatawan powder to travel to all the countries and get you. When Pepper called and told me you were here,

I thought maybe it was for the best. Elowen knows way more than I ever will, and I thought she could give you much better help than me. Then, she called me again saying that you weren't really going with the flow."

"Sorry," Hally apologized.

"Don't apologize, it was just a matter of time. If it wasn't you, then it was going to be Pam," he chuckled. "You actually helped me win a bet."

Hally managed to let out a quiet laugh.

"What are you doing here then? Rescuing us?"

"Sort of. I have two missions. One is going to happen and the second depends on what you decide. I would like to take you all to another place."

Hally raised her eyebrows.

"What for? To tell us who we are supposed to be? I should've known, you're like the rest. Everybody wants to tell me who I have to be, or who I have to become. Not gonna happen," she scoffed.

"No," Blake answered. "Definitely not. They," he pointed at the village, "might believe that you are the Magister by luck. I don't think it came by luck, Hally, or destiny gave it, nor that you gained it. I think it is written in your soul, your blood, your mind and heart. Frankly, I think we all have it, but you, the seven of you, have been the only people in centuries that have been brave enough to follow it. Brave enough to be heroes."

Hally scoffed, one more time.

"Us? Heroes? We are kids! Not heroes."

"But you are Hally," Blake corrected her. "Who told Tom he had to give tutories? No one. Yet he has always been patient with the so-called 'lost causes' and gave them a chance for a brighter future. Or Isla, she has never doubted once to use her money and time to make all the girls in her town feel as pretty as she has always wanted to feel. Or Lukai, he never thought twice before giving his lunch to the homeless or cooking something for them. And Ayala! She has never turned her back to an injured creature that came her way. And Pam has taken so many beatings for things she hasn't done so that other kids don't have to suffer the nightmares she has. Or Piet, he has been a pillar for many and walked them through feelings he does not allow himself to have! And finally, you, Hally. You have healed so many in the refuge and helped many more by just being there. And when they couldn't be healed you were the only one brave enough to stay there and wish them farewell."

"So yeah, you might not be heroes with capes and comic-book names. But you have been brave enough to act against all that society says and fight for what you stand for. And that, that makes you heroes." He took a deep breath.

"What I have to offer, the place I have to offer, is not much. I'm not an expert, at all. And my 'classes' will be filled with a lot of trial and error. But it's a big place; peaceful and beautiful. Since it is my fault that someone got this close to Megalo Dentro and your identities have been revealed, I believe there's nothing fairer than to give you a place where you can live a somewhat normal life, finish your education, learn to control your newly unlocked abilities and more importantly, be kids without a target on your backs."

"What if I say no?" Hally asked.

Blake looked disappointedly at the tree.

"I'll take you anywhere you want to go, out of here."

There was a pause of silence. Hally studied the tree. The wind kept moving through the flowers' petals.

"How should I know what's right?" she asked.

"Trust your gut, it's what gives you your powers. Makes sense, it would be what leads you to your future," Blake shrugged.

Hally closed her eyes, her thoughts quiet. She didn't make a pro and con list, neither did she play all the multiple outcomes in her mind. She just let the air come in and out of her lungs and let her internal compass show her where she had to go.

She opened up her eyes. She knew what to do.

"So?" Blake asked.

Hally opened her mouth to answer, before she could speak a scream echoed from inside the forest.

Blake and Hally turned bewildered. Blake had been taken by surprise and Hally... well she had heard that scream before. That was Tom's scream.

14

THE DROP THAT MADE
THE GLASS SHATTER

"Tom," Pam called him for the second time.

Tom still didn't answer.

"Thomas..." Pam threatened, she wasn't going to call him a fourth time.

Tom lifted his eyes from the amber colored pages Hally had left behind. She had been right to take these books from Pepper, they were filled with so much information and theories that made him realize more things than what he'd ever thought about. As for example how all the Villagers seemed to have perfect vision and teeth, using neither glasses nor braces. Apparently when the time came, and the kids started to show tendencies to certain health conditions Elowen would banish them off their land to ensure good genetics. Or the whole village had little knowledge about the outside world, one that they were taught to hate and to be disgusted by. And then, there were the books that spoke about all the things that were older than Elowen or any other Villager, such as how through every village, people could get to Megalo Dentro even though it wasn't on their land, yet it could be found only by a few. Or how the mysterious force field that was designed to protect the village was completely under the control of the leader, choosing who to let in and who to let out without any scientific explanation available.

"This is a crazy place," Tom confessed to Pam.

Pam looked at him and chuckled.

"Are you figuring that out just now, genius boy?" she asked.

"It seems so," Tom replied. He closed the last book and touched the cover gently, how messed up had he been to believe for a second that this could be a home. His hunt for an answer drew his common sense away; he couldn't let that happen, not ever again.

"Sorry, what is it that you need?"

"There's a Jerry... Jimmy... Gerard... I don't know his name. He's looking for you."

Tom frowned.

"I don't know any Jerrys, or Jimmys or Gerards."

"I would be worried if you knew him. He's a soldier, he says it's about Hally. "

Tom dropped the book.

"Yes, I think it's better if you follow me," Pam said and guided him to the first floor.

"Where's everybody?" Tom asked, he had been so submerged within the books he hadn't noticed the sudden disappearance of the screams calling each other a cheater every time someone dropped a plus four.

"Lukai and Piet are up in their room, and Ayala and Isla were helping Pepper with something. No, over here," she said to him when he walked towards the front.

"He came by the backdoor?" Tom asked.

"He did, they don't get more suspicious than this," Pam muttered.

The kids walked inside the empty kitchen and Pam opened the door. There, just as promised, a soldier waited for him without his helmet.

Tom stared at him, it was the first time he had seen one of those soldiers without their helmets, it almost felt illegal to do it, it probably was. And worst of all, he was barely an adult. Jerry, Jimmy or Gerard, couldn't have been older than twenty.

The soldier stared at Tom. There was a tinge of fear in his eyes, or was it hatred?

"Director Elowen is asking for you," he announced.

"Is she?" Pam asked.

The soldier had to make an effort not to roll his eyes.

"Not for *you*, for him," the soldier clarified.

"That was clear," Pam muttered back, showing she too could make a visible effort not to roll her eyes.

"What does she need me for?"

"Have no idea. You have to meet her to know," Gerard answered.

"Okay."

"Wait a second," Pam extended her arm to stop him. "I'm going with you."

The face of Jerry tensed.

"She doesn't need you, you weren't called."

"Yeah Pam, I'll be fine," Tom assured the angry girl.

"Nah Tom, I'll go. If it turns out she doesn't really need me then this delightful gentleman over here can escort me back."

"Pam," Tom insisted, he didn't want to get Elowen any madder than what she probably already was. "I'll be fine."

"I'll go Tom," Pam wasn't asking. "Believe me, I can smell a drop of alcohol a block away," she muttered.

The soldier rolled his eyes.

"Let's go," Pam stepped outside, behind her, the soldier. Tom closed the door.

The soldier led them through the cottages. Surprisingly, the rest of the village was as quiet as a dead valley, not even the wind daring to break the silence.

"Where are the rest of the soldiers?" Tom asked, all the normal sighting places lay abandoned.

"Off," Jimmy answered.

The soldier stopped at the unnaturally empty and quiet dining hall.

"On the other side."

"What?" Tom asked.

"They are waiting for us on the other side," Pam explained. "Don't dare to move," she threatened the soldier as she walked away.

"Wait," Tom called catching up.

Behind the dining hall a row of torches had been lit even though the light of day still shone brightly. Empty glass bottles laid in the smashed-up grass beside lots of candy wrappers. Someone had had a party.

"Elowen is not here, neither is Hally," Tom said.

"But we are," an inconsistent voice said, it was Ulyssa speaking. The Íroes looked up. Three of the Generation were there, sitting shoulder toshoulder, drunker than anyone Tom had ever seen.

"We were just leaving," Tom excused himself. "Right Pam?"

Pam stared at the bottles on the floor and then at the ones in the kids' hands, there was an air of pity around her.

"Yes," she finally replied.

"But the fun part is only about to start," another voice said behind them, three other kids had sneaked up behind them and now stood between them and the safety of Pepper's cottage.

Tom could smell the alcohol coming from their mouth.

"Have a good night," Tom whispered and tried to walk past them unsuccessfully, three of them easily picked him up from the ground and grabbed his arms. The other three did the same to Pam.

"We will, the party just got started," Ulyssa cheered, the rest copied her. "Let's see if you are so tough now."

Aiddeen picked Tom up and punched his face so hard he fell to the ground. Then again and again.

Tom tried to look up, his eyesight blurred and his ears ringing from the punches. He could see Pam trying to get the kids off, they were too many even for her.

They were both picked up off the ground, new blood falling down Tom's ear and neck.

"You think you can humiliate us?" Shaffi asked. "You'll pay for it now."

The drunken teenagers wrapped their hands tightly around Pam's and Tom's arms, ripping their skin as they dragged them through the mud.

"Let us go," Tom babbled as Pam swore the whole earth on her side, none of the words made a change.

Then the sound of running water started to appear.

They were finally released when they reached the river,

The three threw Tom to the ground, his face ended in the dirt, mud entered his mouth going all the way down his throat.

He tried to get up. Someone placed one foot on his back holding him down.

"Did you think you could shame one of us without having to pay the consequences?" Ulyssa asked.

Tom opened his mouth to answer, he could try to talk all of them down just like Hally would have done. Before any sound came from his mouth another kid shoved his head into the ground. His whole mouth was filled with dirt, and he could not breathe. He tried to push himself up, he couldn't. The panic took control of him.

Pam yelled for them to stop in all the languages she knew, one of the other kids covered her mouth until the sound was stifled.

"That's enough for now," Ulyssa said.

Tom gasped for air.

The kids laughed at the sight of his panic.

"What? You can't get yourself out of this precious Bellator?" Magaera asked and spit on Tom's forehead.

Tom moved trying to avoid the spit, it didn't work.

"Magaera!" Ulyssa said. "Don't be mean, he's our guest, remember? Let's give him something to wash his face," she boasted. The rest laughed even harder.

Between hiccups, swearing and mocking they pulled him to the edge of the river, his face centimeters away from the water.

"Have a nice swim," Magaera exclaimed and shoved his head in the water. For a second the world disappeared, all Tom could see was black, all he could feel was the water burning through the recent wounds and all he could hear was Pam still struggling against the punches of her captors. When the pain started, all Tom could do was to let the loudest scream out.

Tom's body was filled with pain, a kind of pain he had never experienced. Usually he tried to bite his tongue when he wanted to scream, he didn't consider screaming an appropriate way to handle anything. Any other time he would try to stop it. This wasn't the case, the first seconds he had tried that, he had only managed to fill his mouth with that horrible taste of his own blood. The pain was just too much; he was being poisoned by his own venom; he was electrifying himself with every single drop of water that stuck to his body.

"Don't touch my kids," one of them said, imitating Pepper's voice. "Now who's going to protect you little girl?" another said to Pam as they kicked her right in the ribs.

"Where's that mighty Bellator that we saw this morning? Waiting for that witch of your sister to come help you?" one of them asked Tom before dunking his head in the water.

Inside the water Tom let out another scream, burns were starting to spread all over his face and neck.

Once again, his head was brought out of the water.

"Answer me when I talk to you!" the same kid yelled with his alcohol filled breath and dunked Tom again.

Another scream. With a couple more dunks he was sure that he would pass out. After that, he feared what the Generation would do.

Tom's head was brought out again.

"If you're not going to answer me then I suppose there's no need for you to breathe," they said. His face met the water.

The burns in his face were worse than ever, his lungs wanted to explode, and the electricity that traveled through his entire body gave him the strongest need he had ever had to scream. He couldn't, there was no air left in his lungs.

For a moment, he forgot he needed to breathe to survive, and he just took a look at the surroundings. Deep down in the river, there were colorful fishes, swimming freely, full of life.

He closed his eyes, felt the adrenaline rushing through his veins and something stronger, his powers. He felt like he could kick a mountain out of place, run around the whole east coast of the United States and come back to have five chess matches at the same time without even breaking a sweat.

Finally, the time came, his body demanded air. He couldn't provide it. I have always heard that just as a person drowns, they feel peace when they let the water into their lungs. Tom started to feel that peace. He was about to give up, let the water come in.

His head was brought out with such strength that his whole body was thrown a few meters away from the river.

The moment air went inside his lungs his brain was reset. The peace disappeared and Tom's inner clock started to count seconds once again.

A huge guy with no hair, completely dressed in black, and with soulless eyes, came on top of him and pointed a gun at his face.

"Found the electric Bellator," he yelled. Another guy came

and poured a bucket of water on top making him burn once again as if it was acid.

The two men forced him to stand up in the middle of his pain.

Tom looked up, the scene was not the same as the one he had left behind the last dunk. Black dressed guys were running around. All of them were carrying guns. All pointing them at someone.

Three guys were keeping the Generation cornered against a couple of trees. Two were keeping guns pointed at Pam as she stood. She wouldn't let go of her ribs, and her arms and face were filled with bruises and blood. At least her face was still filled with her usual anger which meant that she was okay enough to continue to hate most people.

And the rest of the guys, apart from the two of them that were forcing Tom to walk towards Pam, formed a perfect circle pointing their guns to the woods as if they were expecting a monster to come out of nowhere.

Tom walked to Pam; the guns pointed at his head. He stood right beside her.

"Are you in a lot of pain?" Tom whispered, that was one of the only questions he remembered Hally had asked him when he got hurt.

Pam looked at Tom, she was shocked he was still breathing.

"Not enough to stop me from beating these dudes," Pam

muttered and cleaned the blood coming from her mouth spreading it all the way to her cheek.

Tom looked at the men with the guns, he didn't recognize any of them.

Behind the weapons and the chaos there were a couple of trees and between the trees something caught Tom's attention, a set of shiny brown eyes staring right at them. His heart stopped.

Tom shook his head slowly and pleaded that Hally didn't do anything stupid.

15

SUPERIORS

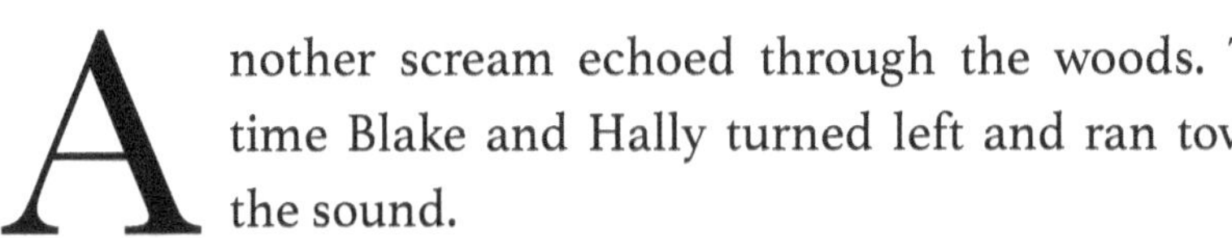

nother scream echoed through the woods. This time Blake and Hally turned left and ran toward the sound.

"Wait," Blake exclaimed, both of them stopped. "I think we went too far."

Hally looked around, the last scream still seemed to echo through the leaves, maybe it was her imagination.

They waited for a couple seconds. Another scream came. This time it led up the forest. Without hesitating, both ran. They were getting closer when a figure came out of nowhere. Hally stopped at once. It was Piet.

"Piet?" Hally exclaimed. "What are you doing here?"

Piet took a deep breath; he seemed to have been running for a while as well.

"I don't really know," he mumbled between breaths. "We all saw Pam and Tom following a soldier through the windows. When they didn't come back Lukai went out to search for them. I followed him and Isla followed all of us scolding that leaving the house without telling the rest was not respectful. By the time she finished scolding me and Lukai, we had lost Pam and Tom. We followed the noise of the Generation into the forest."

"The Generation?" Hally asked

One last scream came, as an answer.

From a meter away neither Tom nor Pam seemed to be alright. There was way too much blood, way too many wounds, way too many guns.

"Are you sure the Bellator won't be a problem?" one of the black dressed men asked the other without lowering the gun that was pointed at Tom's face.

"The boss said that as long as we keep him wet, he won't be able to electrocute us," the other responded and turned his eyes back at Pam and Tom. "Besides, he's not the one we're looking for."

She turned just in time to see Pam's eyes close, her body had given up. Tom grabbed her, stopping her from smashing to the ground. Immediately the guns were pointed at him.

"Put your hands behind your head," a guy said to Tom.

Tom lifted his head, the light shining against his burnt flesh.

"I'm going to put her gently on the ground, she has been severely beaten," Tom explained. The guy moved the gun closer to him.

"Behind your head I said!"

Tom looked at Pam, if he let her go, she would hit her head.

"What are we going to do?" Hally whispered to Blake.

"Right now, *we* aren't doing anything. The situation is too volatile. Help is on the way," Blake said.

Hally pointed at her brother.

"They're about to shoot him, we have to do something."

"Not right now," Blake replied. Hally lowered her hands pressing them into fists. She was not happy with that response.

"Either you put your hands on the back of your head, or I'll shoot you," the guy threatened.

"If I let her go, she'll hit her head," Tom repeated. "I'm going to lower her carefully and then put my hands behind my head." He spoke slowly and soothingly.

Without waiting for a response, he started to lower Pam.

The guy growled and pushed Tom against a tree. Pam fell making an awful sound as her head met the rocky ground, blood following the hit.

"When I say put your hands behind your head, I mean put

your damn hands against your head you stupid scum!" the guy screamed at Tom's face.

Tom's eyes stared back. A shine came from them. His hair spiked out of anger. The air got colder, preparing for the electricity.

His body was covered by water. Everything went back to normal.

Hally watched him fall to the ground and yell in pain.

She gave a step forward; Blake held her back.

"Not yet," he insisted.

The man pushed Tom, harder against the tree, elbow pressed against his neck. He laughed in his face. Tom was shivering and moaning. His face had no color, the burns were brighter.

"And you are a Bellator?" he laughed. "I can't believe one of the most powerful humans is stopped by a little bit of water."

The man raised his fists one more time. Tom's face met the ground again, his nose pouring red blood.

The grip on Hally's shoulders tightened.

"I was going to wait for that powerful and mighty Magister. He's surely hiding under a can. I guess that I'll have to deal with you," the man mocked. He raised his fist one last time.

"Don't touch him!" Elowen's voice roared from the other side of the forest.

All the guns shifted to her, the village soldiers stood behind her, their own guns pointed.

"Do as she says," another voice added.

All the black dressed men straightened at the sound of the voice, as a dog does as the sound of food. The man who was messing with Tom let him go, his eyes still shining with malice. For Tom's luck, whoever's voice it was, he was stronger and more powerful than his anger.

From the shadows the voice was revealed, a young pale man stepped into the moonlight. As if the world had been put in pause, no one dared take a breath as he walked, his wooden black cane hitting the ground beside his right foot. He was the evil one, the villain, Hally could almost smell it. His shadow seemed to change with the steps he took, his eyes were two dead orbs inside the bone cage that is usually called a head and his smile left nothing else to see than a set of shiny white teeth.

"Leave this place, at this moment!" Elowen squeaked. Who was she kidding? She was no one beside that man. She may have had power, but he had POWER.

"My dearest Elowen," the man clicked his tongue. "I'm not leaving this place until I get what I want."

Elowen tried to laugh; it sounded more like her body was failing.

"You? You won't get anywhere with my Bellators. Soldiers,

aim!" the masked soldiers behind her aimed their guns at the man.

The black dressed men prepared themselves to respond the same way. With a signal from their boss they stopped.

"I don't even think you are *that* stupid," the man said. "My men are better trained, stronger, faster. If it's really the Bellator that worries you, take your tea, he's merely the appetizer. I'm here for the big fish." He made a pause and scratched his chin. "People start to talk, they say things to others, who then say things to even more people who eventually end up with me. Rumor says that you have a Magister. A Magister is the power the Superiors need and therefore the one I'm getting."

Elowen tried to keep her calm; she was unable to. Her voice broke.

"Magister?" she laughed. "I would wish, James."

James, the man, smiled. "They say she's a girl and that this boy," he took a step towards Tom, "is her brother. Certainly, she's not letting me hurt him, not with all the power she has on her hands. How would she live with herself?" Why did he sound awfully similar to the voices in her head?

James turned to the forest; Elowen was no longer his interest.

"Where are you? Aren't you going to save your brother?" he mocked.

"Don't," Blake whispered to Hally. Hally's eyes met Tom's; he was begging her to stay put. She listened to him. James wanted her out there, inside his game, she couldn't fall for it.

James sighed at the silence.

"Guess you're not going to care for this," he said and pulled a silver gun from his belt.

"No!" Hally exclaimed.

James and the black dressed men flew across the air hitting the trees, knocking the masked soldiers to the ground, and splashing into the river.

This time not even Blake's tight grip made Hally stay in her place.

Her eyes glowing brighter than ever, Hally busted into the perfect circle of black dressed guys; guns flying out of their hands when she got close, pushed by an invisible force into the air meters off the ground.

She ran to Tom's aid. She could feel the strength rip the ground open, the ability to move every single grain of dirt under her feet, the force to push every single guy with a single move of her hand. She felt power soaring through her like oxygen.

"Are you okay?" Hally asked Tom.

Tom stared at her, his face was filled with burns, his mouth was swollen, and his right eye was nowhere to be seen.

Before he could answer, James came back like a cockroach.

"Find ya," he smiled.

Hally turned to him, with a single look his arms were pressed against his body, his neck twitched to one side. She wasn't angry at James or hated him, she was frightened and that made her a most dangerous mix: powerful and scared.

James tried to move, he couldn't.

"That," he laughed, his voice cracking as she tightened her grip, "that is power!"

Hally's head tilted, she knew she could keep squeezing him, the way she would squash a bug. At that moment, that man, as evil as he was, was nothing compared to her power, *no one was*. She was stronger, the *strongest*.

"That's it," James continued laughing. "Find the pleasure in it."

"Watch out!" Piet cried from the trees.

The cold hit came to Hally's head, and she fell to the floor.

"Ahhh," Piet yelled as he tackled her attacker, one of the black dressed men. Behind him Pam was gaining consciousness and at the sight of Piet tackling a guy she stood up and pushed her captors. From the trees by her side, Lukai appeared and helped her alongside Ayala and Isla.

"Don't use guns," James cried. "Get the kids. Get the kids!" he ordered.

Elowen took advantage of the chaos and her soldiers were free. "Attack them!"

Hally stood up; using the same club her head had just been hit with, she swung at the soldiers that got near her.

Then she placed her arm around Tom's shoulders and picked him up from the ground.

Around her, chaos unraveled. Lukai was punching the black dressed men. Piet was still dealing with the same first guy. Ayala and Isla kept trying to get Pam away, every time surrounded by even more men. And the village soldiers were getting the still drunk Generation into the woods.

"Forza!" James yelled from the ground; he had taken a look at the scene.

At the word, the air shifted. Piet's attacker gained on him. Ayala and Isla were grabbed off the ground. Pam was pinned to a tree. Lukai was given a bad hit. And Hally and Tom were separated by two men.

"Don't touch me!" Isla threatened her attacker.

A man grabbed Hally across the hip and swung her above his shoulder as one does a sack of potatoes.

Hally struggled, uselessly.

Beside her, Piet was in the same position.

"Leave us alone," he screamed.

As if the words had been an order from the highest authority the black dressed men let them go squealing and swearing.

"They burn!" one of them said. "Their skin burns!"

"What are you saying?" James growled. "Just-"

Blake silenced the scrawny guy with a clean punch.

"Megalo Dentro punk," he answered. "You're on its land. The tree will protect the Íroes while they are here and that means no one can do anything against their will except the Director, a title you do not possess." He spoke with satisfaction, relishing the act of putting him in his place t.

James looked up from the ground as he fixed his jaw.

"I wondered how long it would take for you to come out of your hole. Certainly, I didn't expect to see you in your long-lost home," he said.

"And I didn't expect you to not know the protection of Megalo Dentro." Blake's eyes opened as he realized. "You were not here to get them; you were here to make sure they existed."

James smiled as he stood up.

"One has to make sure rumors are true. Out of all people, you should know, Blake."

Blake lifted his fist.

"Break his jaw!" Pam encouraged from behind.

"Make him pay for the Superiors," Lukai added.

"Na-ah," James said. "I might not be taking them with me, but I don't care if they are seven, or six or five. I only need her alive," he pointed at Hally.

Blake looked at him, he was a disgrace, an honest disgrace. He dropped his arm.

"Good boy," James teased, he cleaned off his clothes and grabbed his cane. "Elowen, gentleman, ladies, Íroes, Magister, I hope we see each other soon enough. And thank you," he said to Ulyssa, "for the hole. Who would have said teenagers would be capable of putting their whole village in danger just to get alcohol and candy bars through?" He gave them all a last crooked smile and just as they had appeared, they disappeared into the shadows.

"Go after them," Elowen ordered.

"It's of no use," Blake muttered. "They are gone by now."

"We can still get them," she insisted.

"No, they are gone, Elowen. Wisatawan powder. You're no longer the only one who has it. And with that hole-"

Elowen's face flushed red.

"Go! Make sure they are not here, check the barrier and close any holes!" she ordered her soldiers, some scattering into the forest and others on the way to the village. She turned to Ulyssa. "You! Stupid girl! Wait for me in my office, you will pay."

Blake walked towards Hally and helped her stand up.

"Are you alright?"

"I'm better than they are," she looked at the rest.

"I'm Blake," he introduced himself to the other kids.

"You seem to have a very good punch," Tom greeted him and shook his hand. He was hurt, not dead, manners were still a thing.

The rest of the kids moved closer and greeted him as well.

"Blakelish," Elowen interrupted them, her tone having turned flirty. "We are eternally grateful for your help. I knew sooner or later you would come and visit us."

Blake looked at the lady like he had just tasted sour candy.

"I'm not here to visit Elowen, I'm here because Pepper called me. I'm getting the kids out."

Elowen's flirtatious smile dropped.

"Why?"

"Why?" Blake asked back. "You have had them one day and you already tried to brainwash one of them. Not to mention that you are already planning to get them to function like a machine. Or the fact that the leader of the Superiors just made his way through your barrier because some teenagers wanted to have fun. They are not safe here, not with you. You can't really be that blind that you don't see they'll be safer with me."

"But you can't take them! Surely you are trying to lure them away. Outside they won't have Megalo Dentro's protection," this time Elowen spoke almost as if she was talking to the kids. She was trying to paint Blake as the bad guy.

"You know far too well Megalo Dentro's protection isn't flawless. The Superiors and the rest of the hunters aren't going to take much time until they discover the inconsistencies, or they penetrate your barrier again. It might have been a long time ago but James will remember all the secrets. They'll be much safer in Platz."

"No!" Elowen cried.

"It's not even your choice, Elowen, it's theirs." Blake turned to the kids. "Kids, I have this place, it's big and nice. It's a little old and aging, but it's home to me. There you can live a somewhat normal life, finish your education, learn to control your powers... I'm not an Íroe. I have all the knowledge one can get about the subject. I know the myths, legends, history, places, and maps. However, there hasn't been an Íroe for the last nine hundred years. I can promise you that I will do my best to train you, teach you all I know, and give you my advice. Might not be the best. But it's your choice. You can stay here, you can leave with me, or I can take you anywhere you want, even if it's dangerous, but if that's what you want, I'll do it. The decision is in your hands."

The kids contemplated Blake, it was the first choice they'd been given.

There was silence.

"Hally, are you going?" Pam asked.

"What?" Hally replied.

"Are you going?" Pam repeated. "You have been our leader since the beginning. You got us out of that first jail, you stood up for the best before Elowen and even fought James. I said it, I trust you. If you go, then I'll go."

"Yeah," the rest backed her up.

Hally looked at Tom, then to the others. They shared the same expression.

"No... what are you saying? I'm not-"

"Yes you are, we'll follow you," Piet added.

Hally looked at their faces, they were certain. The choice was hers.

Just trust your gut.

"What do you say?" Blake asked, eyebrows raised, hands open by his side.

Hally raised her eyes to the sky. The decision came easily.

"I hope you have good food in Platz," Hally replied.

16

THE NEW PLACE

Tom woke up for the first time inside Pepper's cottage. His face had been bandaged, his wounds tended, and his clothes had dried. He was lying on one of the couches, in the middle of the living room. The last thing he remembered was Elowen yelling at the kids about the slim chance of survival without her.

Hally came down the stairs.

"Hally-" he tried to sit up.

"Oh no, Tom," Hally placed his head back. "Go to sleep again. You have to heal."

"Okay," he muttered, and his eyes had closed.

He was no longer inside Pepper's cottage. He was back at the river in the middle of the forest, with the sun up high. The wind swung delicately through the leaves, the air was slightly tinted with the smell of his grandma's food, and he could swear he could almost hear Dvorak playing in the background. Everything was in place, perfectly, peacefully.

"Not today Tommy boy," Ulyssa's voice whispered in his ear.

Tom turned around; the peace disappeared. The sun had been replaced by the moon. He looked at his arms, they were covered with bandages. He ripped them off revealing perfectly healthy skin, still he felt the pain. It didn't make sense, all his bruises had disappeared, yet he could still feel them every time he moved, like a ghost that had decided to haunt him.

"You're not that powerful now, right?" the same evil voice spoke.

Tom turned around one more time. There, one meter away from him, the Generation was looking at him. They all smiled wickedly. Their lips moved but no no sound came from them.

They walked towards him and picked him up.

Tom tried to fight them. It didn't matter how much he tried to move his arms and legs, they stayed frozen like ice.

The Generation placed him by the river.

Tom saw his reflection in the water, it was a younger version of himself, around the age he had first realized he had powers.

"Drink," Ulyssa laughed and pushed him into the water, burning his face.

He woke up.

"It's alright Tom," Hally calmed him. "We're here."

"Huh?" he asked.

"We're here," she repeated.

Tom realized where he was. His neck ached from the weird position. His back begged to be stretched.

"A van?" he asked Hally.

"Yep, to reach Platz we had to go through some magical road or something, Blake borrowed a van from Elowen," she explained.

"Kids," Blake called from the front. "Come on."

"Thank goodness we've arrived!" Isla cheered from the front seat.

"Yes," Pam added, she turned to Hally. "One more minute in here and I would have killed someone."

"Hey," Piet complained. "It wasn't me the one snoring the whole way."

"Go back to sleep, little baby," Pam replied.

Hally laughed.

"Come Tom," she jumped off the van. Tom followed her with difficulty.

Unlike all the other kids Tom wasn't relieved when his feet touched the ground. His body still ached the way it had when he had been pulled from the water the first time. Every time he closed his eyes, he felt his head being pushed underneath the water, all the electricity burning his face and neck one more time.

"Wow," escaped from his mouth, for a second all the pain had disappeared.

It was the view. It was... Stately... Magnificent... Grandiose...

"Where are we?" were the first words to fill the air after minutes of staring.

"This is Helden Platz, or Platz for short," Blake said, answering Hally's question.

"It is sublime," Tom said in a whisper as if he was scared that a loud noise would make all the beauty go away.

"What?" Piet asked.

"It means majestic," Hally said with the same tone as Tom.

"Then why didn't you say that?" Piet asked with a normal voice.

"Because it is more than majestic," Tom replied, no one argued with that.

I'll do my best to describe it. Although I've seen it a thousand times, I'm still amazed whenever I visit.

Platz was big, really big. It was a valley surrounded by mountains in every direction, except to the east, where a golden-sand-covered-beach received the dancing waves. The blue sky with the morning sun and the magnificent tree-covered-mountains created the perfect setting for a painting, if there's ever going to be a good enough painter able to replicate the scenery correctly. It all looked as if someone had taken years to make sure that every single flower and color was perfect.

In the middle of the valley there was a small 'city' (five buildings).

The buildings were quite unique, each of them beautiful in a different way. Four of them were forming a big square, each had what we can call a quadrant connected by shiny-rock-trails, black lamp posts at its sides. Each quadrant had an adornment far from all others; they almost seemed like different countries. There was only one building without its own quadrant, the one that was at the very front.

"What's this place?" Isla managed to ask.

"It was built hundreds of years ago during the time of Queen Sila. It's one of the protected Íroes places," Blake answered.

"Who's ready for the tour?" Pepper asked, she had decided to accompany them now that there was nothing left for her at the village. "This place has the best history ever," she added.

As they walked, Tom turned to Hally.

"Did Elowen, seriously, let us leave so easily?"

"After Blake threatened to get the Villagers against her, there weren't many options."

The first quadrant they visited was the one at the left rear, the one that was called Four.

It was a fairy-like place, there's no better way of saying it. Every inch was filled with flowers and colorful bushes grown to form incredible patterns, and in some cases, drawings. On the far-left corner there was a small pond. The smell there was unequal to any Tom had ever experienced: the scent of hundreds of sweet flowers, with a pinch of freshness coming from the wet grass.

The building of Four was the smallest building of all. It was made of an interesting rock and glass mixture. It had the domestic feeling of a cottage, similar to the ones seen in Elowen's village, but better. The color and light of a greenhouse's fullness and the elegance of a medieval palace was accompanied by all kinds of butterflies flying around and colorful birds singing gracefully on the roof.

"I think I can get used to living here," Isla said.

"This is the Naturae building, your building, actually" Pepper said as the kids continued with their expressions of amazement. "In the ancient times, they tried to build a kind school for the small kids that were born with powers. They created each building because each category of Íroes had different techniques of teaching and learning. In my opinion this is the most beautiful quadrant, just don't get into the pond," Pepper said with caution in her voice.

"Why?" Hally asked.

Pepper stared at her.

"It's really deep and has a lot of fish," Pepper said with disgust.

"Pepper has a weird disgust for any kind of underwater life," Blake clarified. "You may swim in the pond if you know how to swim and if you don't ever go alone," he added. "I can't have kids drowning."

They continued their way through the rock trails. They crossed the meadow and walked into the next quadrant: Three. Four had a peaceful look inspired by fables and spring, Three looked as if it had been taken out of a Greek myth, set for war.

Three didn't hold flowers or bushes on its grounds, instead it was plain, utterly covered by grass. A clear blue river of literally glowing water divided the quadrant diagonally in two. In its middle there was a gray-rock bridge that connected both halves.

The one storey building was indeed the result of a real fan of Greece. It was all made of white marble, surrounded by thick gray-marble columns. Drawings of warriors and heroes covered the walls and drops of gold shone through the glassless windows. It was open and fresh, allowing the kids to see through it to the other side. It didn't seem to have any roof in the center, letting the sun hit it beautifully and raising a single question.

"What happens when it rains?" Ayala asked. "It has no roof."

"It gets wet," Blake responded. "It's really not much of a problem. Snow on the other hand... Well let's just say we'll spend a good amount of time shoveling in the winter."

Lukai sighed. "And I thought I left my shoveling days in Canada."

Blake laughed.

"This is where you'll spend most of your training time," Blake continued.

"As you can see it is the safest. It has no trees or bushes you can bump into," Pepper said. "Although, for sure you don't want to swim in that river. According to the legend there used to be conflict between the Naturaes and the Bellators, so a Bellator decided they would make the river poisonous for any other Íroe of another quadrant. It was a mess. In fact the legend says that it almost caused a civil war. Then a Woldier came by and built the bridge to stop the war," Pepper finished up the story as if it was a fairy tale she had been told every night before going to sleep as a youngster.

"My people, of course, always fixing the problems," Lukai boasted.

"You didn't even know Woldiers existed three days ago," Isla replied.

Lukai smirked.

"Yet one knows when there is greatness in one's blood."

Pam and Isla rolled their eyes.

"Perhaps you'd like to go back to the van, I suppose you might find it there," Hally said.

"Find what?" Lukay asked.

"Your humility."

"Now that you mention war, Pepper," Blake said, "I won't tolerate any kind of physical fight between you guys if it's not part of the training. And never go into the mountains alone, or at all, the last thing I want is losing a kid or worse."

"That isn't very comforting," Lukai responded.

Blake thought about it and shrugged his shoulders.

"Does this mean this is my building?" Pam asked, her eyes shone with an idea.

"Yes and no. It *is* the Bellators building, however you will all be staying together elsewhere," Blake said and continued walking.

As they made their way over the bridge Tom looked at the water and felt as if his face was once again burning.

"Ahhh," he muttered under his breath

"You okay?" Hally asked.

"Sure."

She stared at him, studying every tiny expression on his face.

"What a big fat lie," she snapped. Tom remained quiet. "Look," she continued, putting her arm around his shoulders as their mom would. "I know it hurts and I know you doubt yourself, but you can't let what some drunk bullies did to you bring your whole life apart. There's no problem with feeling pain, it *is* okay to not be okay, no one will judge. The problem is when you stay there forever. The problem is when you let that doubt, fear or pain swallow you entirely and take your life second by second." She paused. "You don't have to get out of that hole on your own, that's what friends are for, what sisters are for, what ropes are for."

Tom let out a small chuckle, a real laugh.

"That's something I pity about only children, they don't have that friend that sticks to you like a tick, annoys you, and helps you forever. We've been together since birth, and we'll continue this adventure together as well and every adventure to come. Even if we aren't always physically close you need to know that I'm here for you."

Tom couldn't help but let out a smile. Hally was certainly good with words.

"You feeling better now?" she asked.

Tom looked at the water, this time the water did not cause any feeling. How did she do it? How did she manage to bring out his brave side?

"Yeah."

"Let's go then, it's been a while since a sassy comment, it's getting quite boring," Hally said. They both joined the group just as they entered the next quadrant: Two.

Two was mostly covered with grass and there was, in fact, what seemed to have been an old soccer field. The whole quadrant looked to Tom like what he considered typical high school grounds, nothing much to see, except the architecture. The building, or better said, the buildings, were worth every second. There were two buildings squeezed together, the one on the left, tall and thin, and the one on the right, short and wide. They both looked ancient, yet not Roman, nor Greek, like Three.

The buildings were made of a brown, colored cement, the walls consisted of beautiful carvings of flowers, leaves or simple geometric designs. However, what made the buildings look even more extraordinary were both roofs. The roof of the shorter one was very simple, a cement roof that reminded Tom of snow. The roof of the taller one, on the other side, had a weird cylinder shape, it ended up forming an antenna.

From the front there were not many windows, from the side, the walls were half covered by windows. It was similar to old Catholic churches. The weird thing was that the building was facing south, so the windows would never actually receive the light directly, making the building weirdly dark inside.

"This is the Woldier quadrant," Pepper said and contemplated her next words very carefully. "There's a lot of things we can say of the Woldier quadrant, I don't want to scare you though, not on your first day. Let's just say that you'll never train in this quadrant. And *never* let a drop of blood touch the grass."

"What?" Piet asked confusedly.

"*Never* let a drop of your blood touch this grass. The girl who created it wasn't very happy or supportive of war and decided that if war ever touched her grounds, then people would pay for it, gravely."

"What does that mean exactly?" Lukai asked.

Pepper and Blake remained quiet for some seconds.

"It means this place is ancient, we must respect its rules," Tom answered

"He's right," Blake boasted, a proud smile showing.

"Rules?" Piet complained. "I thought we were going to be free."

"Shush, or we'll send you to the shame corner," Hally snapped.

"I'm not a baby!" Piet wept.

"How old are you?" Isla asked.

"I'm not that young!" Piet insisted with a growl, the rest laughed.

They reached the last quadrant, the one that would eventually be known as One.

One was covered by trees, all of them with red, orange or yellow leaves. There weren't as many trees like a forest, yet enough to remind the kids of a real forest. With the trees also came the birds, sitting there, singing, and flying around.

The building that held this quadrant looked like a museum. Outside, it was built of red bricks. Unlike the last one, it had windows on every side, although they weren't very big, except for the ones on the back that covered the whole wall. Through the windows you could see the brown rugged floor and the walls made of a very shiny wood carved in intricate ways. Later, Hally would go to Tom and tell him that that place reminded her of the X-men school Professor Xavier had built, who knows what she meant.

"This is the Veteris building, it holds the best library you'll ever find," Pepper said.

These were magic words for several kids, Tom included.

"Before you ask, you'll be able to visit it later, once we get you properly settled in."

"Don't you have a gaming section for those of us that don't read?" Piet wondered.

"You don't like to read?" Isla asked.

Piet made a grimace.

"It's not my thing."

"Perhaps you have to learn how to read," Hally proposed.

"I know how to read."

"Seriously?" Lukai asked. "So young?"

"I'M NOT THAT YOUNG!"

They laughed, all except Piet.

"Come children," Blake called them. "They are waiting for us."

The kids walked over to the front, beside Blake.

"And this...," Blake said, although having seen the building many times before, he was having a hard time expressing his thoughts with words. "This is what we call Center. Here, you'll eat and sleep. Might as well call it your new house."

You know that expression of last but not least? I had heard it for most of my life, yet I didn't understand it until I had to write this part of the Íroes story.

At first I was considering writing and explaining how the fifth and last building looked, now I think not even a million words could actually be enough to give you an accurate image that assimilates a little of the beauty that once again took out every single sound and expression from the children's mouths. Also, I guess that in the end, it really doesn't make any sense for me to describe it.

"This is one heck of a house," Hally confessed, her eyes shining from all the astonishment that filled her being.

"One heck of a building," Tom agreed.

"All the colors remind me of home," Isla mumbled minutes later.

Piet and Ayala stared at her.

"What colors?" Ayala asked.

Isla looked back at them and pointed at the building as if it was the most obvious thing.

"All the colors. The blue, the orange, the yellow, the red!" Isla responded.

"There aren't any colors," Piet argued. "The whole building is made of bricks."

"Bricks?" Hally exclaimed. "It is made of glass and rock."

"No!" Pam contradicted. "It is made of cement with colors all around."

"Calm yourselves," Blake urged them with a soft voice, he let out a soft laugh. "This is why I wanted to leave this building for last."

He took a deep breath.

"The extraordinary thing from Center is that somehow it takes the form your mind wants. Whenever you see it or touch it, it will be different and unique to every single person."

"But what is it made of, originally?" Pam asked. She wanted to win the argument. Tom suppressed a laugh, she had the same look he assumed whenever he fought Hally about something neither of them knew anything about, except that the other was wrong.

"No one knows, it affects Ommons just like Íroes interestingly, unlike the river on Three," Pepper answered.

"Don't go to the river commanded Ms. Pepper," said a kind, childish voice no one had heard.

"Ohh, children," Blake said, as if he had just remembered something. "Meet our secretary, Bobby, and a good friend of mine and fellow ex-villager, Beira"

From out of Center came a figure, revealing the source of the strange childish voice.

The figure was a man, well a human being who for his age could be called man, but even from meters away Tom noticed that Bobby was almost like a five-year-old. He was tall, really tall, and his skin was a beautiful dark brown color. His eyes were as shiny as a puppy's eyes revealing his adorable persona. He was wearing loose clothes, the kind that looked like pajamas. In the front of his shirt there were some traces of mashed potatoes. He came with the biggest and brightest smile that even Pam could not resist smiling back.

"I am Bobby. Are you the Íroes?" he asked the kids.

"Yes, we are," Ayala answered kindly, perhaps they weren't so sure about it, but for him they could act like it.

"Yay!" Bobby said, he started applauding and giving small jumps of happiness.

Bobby was accompanied by who the kids assumed was Beira: the snow queen. Her skin was paler than paper and her hair was the purest blond Tom had ever seen. She was wearing a pair of big and dark sunglasses and with her right hand she held a long thin cane that she moved as she walked.

As she got closer to the kids Blake gave her his hand, she was near his age and it was obvious both of them knew each a long time and were close friends.

"You brought the Íroes?" she asked him, surprised.

"Yes, they chose to come."

Beira smiled.

"Say hi kids," Blake said.

"Hi."

"The Íroes," she pronounced the last words with difficulty. "I want to see them, please," she begged. Blake walked her to the closest kid.

"Here," he said once Beira was in front of Hally.

Beira extended her hand to Hally but didn't touch her.

"May I?" she asked.

"Yeah?" Hally's answered, although it was more of a question than a statement.

Beira took the 'Yeah' seriously and she ran her hand softly through Hally's hair and later carefully over her face.

"You are short, with long beautiful hair. And your chubby cheeks. I wish I had them. Where's your accent from?"

"Costa Rica," Hally responded.

"Oh," Beira sighed. "Sometimes I wish I lived in the tropics, someday you must take me there."

"I also want to go!" Bobby said excitedly.

Hally laughed.

"Maybe someday I'll take you both there."

Immediately Bobby started to jump up and down, joyful of the news.

"What kind of Íroe are you? Do you know yet?" Beira asked Hally.

Hally looked at Blake, wondering if it was alright to say. He nodded.

"Yes, I'm a Magister."

The words made Beira stumble back a few steps, Blake kept her from falling.

"A Ma-ma-gister?" she asked.

"A Magister," Blake affirmed.

Beira turned to Hally. She didn't have to show her eyes for all the kids, even Tom, to notice she was proud.

"Your powder turned silver?"

"My powder turned silver," Hally replied humbly with a smile.

A tear fell from behind the sunglasses on Beira's cheek and before she could clean it, it fell to the ground.

"In moments like this I wish I could see, so that I could have experienced the color change and the astoundment that everyone in the village must have had. Especially Elowen," she said with a chuckle. She then held Hally's cheek. "I have known you for minutes and only heard a few words from your mouth, yet I have no need to know you for decades, hear you give speeches or even see you to know that God made no mistake choosing you as our Magister. It is my honor meeting you, a new era began the second you were born" she said and let go of Hally's cheek. "It is my honor meeting you all," she said to the rest of the kids. "Take me to each of them, I want to see all our heroes," Beira commanded. Blake did as told with a smile.

17

ROOM, LUNCH (BREAKFAST?) AND YOU GUESSED IT, CLEANING

Beira met each one of the kids. With each greeting she made them feel inspired, loved and special. Hally could even see in Tom's eyes how his fear left temporarily. He wasn't the same he had been a week before; I mean how would he? He had suffered harm, if not torture. You don't get past something like that so easily, even if you are a miraculously, rapid healer.

After the greeting, Pepper took Bobby to finish his lunch inside Center. And the kids, guided by Blake's instructions, crossed the dining room, into a long hallway, up the first stairs they saw.

The stairs were made of a shiny dark brown wood. They went to an open and small living room with a hallway on each side: girls to the right, and boys to the left. The walls were light brown, of a material Hally couldn't really decipher. On the opposite side of the stairs there were a pair of big and shiny windows that gave a wonderful view of the other quadrants. Between the two windows there was a stone fireplace. In the middle of the room there was a small yet fancy oak coffee table. The coffee table was surrounded by three big and comfortable brown couches each of them with dark blue pillows at their sides.

"Wow," Hally said perhaps for the tenth time in an hour.

"I think I speak for everyone when I say we can get used to this," Lukai confessed.

"Absolutely," Ayala supported him.

"Finally, what I deserved! An enormous couch," Piet said as he jumped on the couch. He bounced against the fluffy cushions and landed on the floor.

"Manners!" Isla scolded him, but she wasn't angry, no one could be angry in that room.

"Are those mulberry silk?" Tom asked, rushing to feel the material of the cushions.

"Who cares? I want to see my bed," Pam exclaimed. "Come on Hally."

"Be right there," Hally replied. She stayed beside Tom.

Tom looked up from the cushions.

"I'm fine Hally, go."

"You sure?" It felt weird leaving his side, she couldn't stop wondering if she hadn't run, would things have been different for Tom?

"Yeah," he smiled, a good true smile that warmed its way into Hally's heart. "Go on."

"If you say so..." Hally followed Pam into the hallway and across a heavy light brown door.

The girl's room was pretty much what Hally had ever thought a room from a medieval palace would look like. The walls were an almond, almost yellowish color. The floor was made of a light brown ceramic, easy for Hally to step on quietly. At the very end, the sunlight and the beautiful view made its way through enormous glass windows.

The room was completely furnished. At the side of every window there were long, brown curtains behind white linen ones. There were four middle size beds covered with fancy red mattresses and white pillows. By each one's side there was a nightstand made of polished dark brown wood and on the other side of every bed there was a small, tall wood table with a comfortable brown, cushioned chair. By each bed there was a big wooden wardrobe, so beautiful that Hally wanted to try to get inside and search for Narnia.

"Mirror!" Isla exclaimed as she opened her wardrobe.

"And glitter," Ayala pointed at the faint shiny dust inside hers.

"Nice," Hally responded. "I call this a bed," she said before throwing herself on top of the second bed from left to right.

Pam imitated her and threw herself on the third bed from left to right.

Isla on the other hand sat elegantly on the other bed next to Hally's.

"You could at least try to have some manners and not make a mess of this room right away like you did with the last one," Isla accused.

For a second there was pride in her face as she thought she had finally talked some sense into the other girls. That was until her face was hit with a pillow.

A very angry Isla looked back at the three girls who were giggling, her green eyes opened widely.

"Who did it?" she asked.

The girls just kept giggling harder each time. When their giggles met the point of laughter Pam's face was hit with another pillow.

"HEY! It wasn't me, it was Hally," she fought.

"Oh really," Isla said as she threw a pillow to Hally's face. Hally ducked the pillow and it hit Ayala's kind face.

"Hey," Ayala replied with a pillow of her own, hitting Pam and declaring war.

A bell rang loud enough to stop the pillows. Then it rang over again and again, like an alarm. One by one, the girls went to the living room where they found the boys looking just as confused as they were.

"What was that?" Ayala asked.

"We've no idea," Lukai responded. "Maybe it means that lunch is ready."

"You mean breakfast? We didn't have dinner yesterday either, I think. I don't know what day it is anymore," Tom let himself admit.

"Maybe we'll get brunch," Piet added hopefully.

"Well I certainly hope so, I'm starving," Hally said.

In a few seconds they all reached the dining room.

The dining room was no exception to all the beauty the kids had seen throughout Platz. If it compared to something Hally had seen before in her life, she would compare it to a greenhouse. From the moment you stepped out of the hallway the floor was no longer ceramic but grass, and the brown walls turned into glass.

There were about seven wood tables scattered throughout the grass floor, at one of them Pepper and Bobby.

In the backside of the dining room was the kitchen. It was separated from the dining hall by a simple wooden bar. In front of the wooden bar there were several stools.

Piet walked over at the wooden bar.

"Did you call us?" he asked.

Inside the kitchen were Blake, cooking, and Beira organizing some newly harvested fruit.

“Ummmm, no?” Beira said, before turning to Blake. “Did you call the kids?”

“Nope,” Blake responded.

“Then what was that bell for?” Isla.

“That wasn't a bell. I just dropped some pots,” Blake said and gave Isla a small smile.

The kids looked at each other, their stomachs making more noise than a lion's roar.

“That means there's no food?” Hally whined.

“No dear, there's no lunch yet. Why? Are you hungry?” Beira asked.

Hally nodded before realizing that didn't work when talking to Beira.

“We didn't have breakfast or dinner or lunch,” Hally said.

“WHAT?” Beira exclaimed immediately; the glass walls seemed to shake. “You didn't feed the kids! What's wrong with you?”

Blake's face turned pale; his eyes opened as big as plates.

“We-e-e-e were coming here, I had no time,” Blake stuttered.

Beira mumbled in disapproval and came out of the kitchen pushing the waist-level-door on the left side with her cane.

“Here kids, grab some fruit while Blake finishes up with the lunch," she said. "Did you like your rooms; Bobby and I did our best to organize them just in case."

"They were beautiful. Thank you," Lukai said.

"Later I was thinking of going to town and getting some clothes, shoes or something. So, if you want or need anything, just tell me."

"Thank you," the kids said before she returned to the kitchen and continued scolding Blake.

The kids took the basket and sat beside Pepper and Bobby.

When they reached the table Bobby waved at each of them excitedly.

"Did you see the glitter in your wardrobe, I put it there, so you all looked brilliant like Pepper says," Bobby declared, taking a bite of a banana.

"It was very pretty," Ayala responded. "Everything in here is very pretty."

"Definitely. We don't have to deal with Villagers, the Generation or Elowen," Pam mumbled her way through an apple.

At the sound of the last name Bobby's smile faded and his eyes seemed to fill with tears.

"Elowen is evil," he sniffled.

"There, there," Pepper calmed him. "Why don't you go help Biera and Blake cooking, I bet they've no idea they need to add salt to the food," Pepper proposed. Bobby's face lit up again.

He nodded and skipped to the kitchen.

"What was that?" Pam asked when Bobby reached the kitchen. "Why is he so scared of Elowen?"

Pepper took a deep breath.

"Both Bobby and Beira were born in Elowen's village. Elowen wasn't very happy with them. They could 'dirty up the genetics of the village.' Blake saved them as soon as he realized what was happening. He took both from the village and brought them here to be their new home," Pepper said, keeping her voice down.

"What happened to Bobby?" Piet asked, he had noticed the multiple scars on his neck and arms.

"Bobby's situation was not as bad before. It worsened when he was ten years old. Elowen took him down to the river and tried to drown him. Somehow, he escaped and ran to Blake. Elowen tried to convince Blake that he needed to go to a special asylum, obviously he refused and kind of adopted him."

Tom shifted uncomfortably in his seat at the mention of the river.

"And Beira? What happened to her?" Isla asked.

Pepper tilted her head a little to the side and thought about the question for a few seconds.

"I don't really know. She was born with albinism, but I don't think she was born blind. Beira and Blake have always been friends, even from school. Whatever happened to her, whatever made her blind just made them closer and made Beira leave the Guarders, forever."

Hally turned to the kitchen, Beira was still scolding Blake, but Blake struggled to suppress the laughter it caused him. She wondered what kind of nightmares she suffered.

Minutes later lunch was finally done. The kids ate as if there was no tomorrow. Then remembering their manners, they thanked Beira and Blake, and kept eating.

Seven empty plates later Blake brought four buckets filled with cleaning supplies and four brooms.

"Who's ready to clean?"

"Clean?" Isla asked.

"Yes, clean," Blake said, handing her a broom. "It has been a long time since Platz has been in operation. Beira, Pepper and Bobby are going to town and we're going to need some things for your lessons. Unless of course you'd like to stay in your rooms with nothing to do."

"Please no, I don't do well with boredom," Pam begged.

Blake laughed. "You'll be working in groups. Pam, Piet and Tom will be helping me put some things out in Two for tomorrow's training. I also need some books from the library at One, I need to freshen my knowledge," he handed Ayala a piece of paper. "You and Isla can go there and search for the books, there are not many of them, but they are in a mess. In the meantime, you can see if you find something you'd like to read."

Isla and Ayala agreed.

"And finally, I will need some things from the storage room, I trust you two can handle it," he gave another paper to Lukai and Hally: a list of items.

"What do you need this for?" Hally asked, reading the list. "What are we going to do?"

"Ah, that's the surprise for tomorrow."

Hally and Lukai crossed the bridge and made it to Three in no time. Even though Hally had already seen the building, its beauty made her gasp once again. Inside, ceramics had been used to carve into the columns even more. The walls were covered with paintings that deserved a place in a museum. And the long round hallways echoed the two kids' steps.

"It really is a beautiful building," Lukai whispered to himself.

"It is quite a charming-breath-taking-gasp-inducing building," Hally responded.

They made their way into the hallway Blake had told them about, and into the open room that held thousands of boxes, shelves and antiquities.

"Do you always create such complicated nick names for things?" Lukai asked.

"When necessary. And not only things, you have to hear the nicknames I have given everybody, although those are not that complicated."

"What have you nicknamed Blake?"

"Mr. Uncle because he's like those uncles that are left with their nieces and nephews and have some idea of how to take care of them but in reality he is making everything up as he goes."

Lukai laughed. "I have a feeling from now on things will work that way, but the nickname is good though and so is Blake playing Uncle," Lukai responded while he looked for some of the objects on the other side of the room.

"What's Pepper's?" he asked.

"Ms. Gosip. She's our source of information," Hally explained.

"What about Bobby's?"

"Bobby has no need of a nickname, his name suits him perfectly."

"Make sense, what about... What about Beira's?"

"Ohhh, she's definitely Ms. Mom," Hally chuckled. This was easy.

"Pam's?"

"Ms. Anger."

Lukai laughed.

"She would get so angry about that," he chuckled.

"Hence the nickname," Hally replied.

"Hey. And Tom's?"

"Well Tom's my brother, I don't need a nickname for him."

"That's right," Lukai accepted. "Piet's?"

"Mr. Cool."

Lukai stopped moving the boxes for a second and looked at the other side of the room where Hally still searched for the first item.

"Why?"

Hally stared back.

"Because he's like a character taken from the Disney Channel, sometimes acting so 'cool'."

"Fair point," Lukai said and continued what he was doing.

"Ayala's?"

"She is Ms. Nice."

"Isla's."

"Ms. Manners all the way."

"Mine."

Hally stopped sweeping and there was silence for some seconds.

"You're the Chef," she replied finally.

Lukai laughed, "I like it. The only one missing is you."

"What nickname should I have?"

Lukai thought about it.

"First of all you're not a miss, you're a doctor."

"Alright."

"You'd be, Dr. Sass no-raisins-in-her-bread."

Hally laughed.

"Well, I'll change your Mr. Terrible nickname for sure."

"Why? That's a good and accurate nickname," Lukai replied.

"No, it is not. Well, maybe." Hally said, still laughing. "Who puts raisins in their bread anyway?"

"Good chefs do, they actually make the perfect combination."

"I think you have the definition of chefs and maniacs confused."

"I think you are the one who...," Lukai was interrupted by a glass jar breaking. "Are you alright?"

"It's okay, just a normal jar. I hope it wasn't important," Hally mumbled. Lukai appeared from behind some boxes. He looked at the mess, then at her.

"Sure you don't want to switch places?" he asked.

"Why do you ask?"

Lukai stared at Hally, then at the stool she was standing on.

"You are a meter point six max, that shelf is literally twice your height and you're standing on a stool that could actually be a hundred years old."

Hally stared at the broken glass on the floor and carefully got off the stool.

"Fine, I've never had a good relationship with glass anyway, it always jumps out of my hands," Hally said, grabbing the broom.

"You mean it's like what your power causes?" Lukai asked, looking through the shelf Hally had just been searching without the need of a stool.

"No, I'm just clumsy," Hally admitted. "Actually, I wished that was what my powers produced. You got something cool. You get to somehow play with light. I get glowing eyes and moving things with my mind, that's like the most basic power," Hally mumbled.

"But you get to be the Magister. You heard Pepper! And Blake, and Elowen, and James. You're literally a myth come true," Lukai said the 'myth' part with a funny voice.

Hally sighed.

"You could perfectly tell me that I am Queen of Silvironalia."

"That's not a real place," Lukai informed her.

"Exactly."

Lukai remained quiet for a few seconds.

"I got lost," he finally admitted.

"C'mon, I put up with your nicknames, you must suffer my analogies," Hally said.

"Okay, okay, okay. What you're saying is that you feel just as powerful being the Queen of a non-existent place as you feel having the title of Magister. Is that it?"

Hally nodded and took a deep breath.

"I don't understand what it means or what the world wants from me. Although I tend to think that maybe it is part of the job of being a Magister, you know, the not knowing part. There always has to be that first person that finds out how everything works before teaching it to others."

Lukai thought about it for a few seconds.

"Maybe that's it, maybe that's the answer you're looking for..."

Hally stayed quiet waiting for Lukai to finish his sentence. He never did.

"But?" she finally asked.

"Oh no, I wasn't going to say but. I was going to say that maybe that's the answer you're looking for Dr. Silvironalia's Wisdom."

Hally let out a genuine, pure laugh.

"THAT'S EVEN WORSE. How do you come up with such bad nicknames? It is not that hard, you just have to come up with a good idea," Hally exclaimed, wiping the tears covering her cheek from the laughter

"HEY!" Lukai complained, but it only made Hally laugh harder.

"By the way," he added later. "Your powers are amazing. Yesterday you were fighting off the Superiors like they were flies. You're awesome, don't think otherwise," he said.

"Thanks," Hally smiled. "I'll try."

The list was completed quite quickly once Hally and Lukai realized that all they were looking for was inside a set of boxes marked 'Later'. It was then that Lukai took the box to Center and Hally was set free to explore the place.

She made her way to admire One's paintings and sculptures. Two's long hallways, Three's historic monuments and Four's marvelous decorations. And then, just when the sun was setting, guided by the familiar sound of the waves, Hally ended up in a paradise of golden sand and fresh air.

"That's nice," Hally said at Pam's drawing, as she took a place beside her.

"Sure," Pam muttered as a reply. "Blake's putting up a wall or something. He just needed Piet and Tom, so I thought about using some of the paper and pencils I found."

Hally took some sand in her hand. "I saw them working outside. What's that wall for?"

Pam shrugged.

"No idea."

"Hey girls," Lukai greeted.

"Oh great," Pam moaned, "now it's a party. Yay," she rolled her eyes.

"C'mon," Hally replied. "Play nice."

Pam sighed and gave a forced smile.

"Yay, now it's a party," she repeated in a higher pitched voice.

Lukai laughed.

"That's alright, I'll take it." He sat beside them as Pam kept drawing the waves with her black pencil.

"Where did you learn to draw like that?" Hally asked.

"Art class, it was the only one that was open after hours," she explained.

"Hey! Beach party!" Ayala shouted as she ran towards them.

"You have to be kidding me!"

Pam sighed.

"Really? More people?"

"Well dear, we're about seven," Isla replied back. "You'll have to get used to us."

"I suppose so," Pam growled and again grabbed the pencil between her fingers.

Hally looked over at the nice waves. There, on the very edge where the white foam formed, everything seemed to be so perfect. She took a deep breath of that salty air, this was heaven. With no Gang, no Elowen, no Superiors, no problems.

"Do you think we'll be here a long time?" Ayala wondered.

"I wouldn't mind," Pam said before Hally could.

"You didn't like your home?" Isla asked.

Pam put down her pencil one more time and sighed.

"My father's a drunk and my mother loves to play mute. On the best days they were asleep when I came from school and I didn't need to talk to them. In the worst cases, he was waiting for me with a bottle in one hand and a belt in the other."

The kids remained quiet. Pam resumed her drawing.

"Sorry for being the black sheep in your dream-like lives," she muttered.

"I wouldn't go back home if I was given the chance either," Isla said. "My mom probably didn't even look for me and when Blake called her to tell her I was with him, I'm sure she begged him to keep me. I was never a part of her plan. Like she always said, 'I'm the result of three bottles of booze and a big party'."

"Sorry," Pam muttered under her breath. "I didn't mean to assume-"

"It's alright." Isla fixed her hair and smiled. "The trick is not letting them know how much it hurts."

Pam looked at her.

"I'll toast to that," she chuckled. "What about you?" She turned to Hally. "You don't go around life being the way you are without having some scars."

Hally had to resist the urge to hide her right arm.

She chuckled.

"There's really not much to say. We all moved from Costa Rica to Tirabia when I was younger for my mom's research. My dad used to be around more , but after we moved he mostly disappeared into his work. My mom was there, some-times. I guess after two kids they thought the third would be capable of taking care of itself."

"Try being the middle one of five," Lukai blurted.

"YOU HAVE FIVE SIBLINGS?" Isla exclaimed, her jaw dropping.

"Four, I'm the fifth. Actually the third one, but... you get it," Lukai mumbled

Hally gave him a pat on the back.

"I take back what I said. Being three is amazing," Hally proclaimed.

Lukai laughed.

"Well, I had a good life. My parents are both great, and I only have one sister," Ayala said.

The kids cheered for her.

"How's your home? Kiribati?"

"Tuvalu," Ayala corrected Lukai. "And it's sooo boring!"

The kids laughed.

"I'm serious. Nothing ever happens. Nothing! It's so small and everybody knows everybody. There was one time that an ambassador called the mayor by the wrong name and that was the most interesting thing in months. You hear me? MONTHS!"

The kids laughed even harder.

"Hey," a voice called from a far. "What's this party without me?" Piet exclaimed.

Piet ran down the sand panting.

"I've looked everywhere for you."

"You've found us," Lukai said.

"Did you finish up the wall?" Pam asked.

"Yep, all set and ready for tomorrow."

"What's it for?" Hally asked.

"I have no idea whatsoever."

"How can you work on something and still not know what it is?" Hally exclaimed.

"Just like this, not caring," Piet joked. "You could maybe ask Tom, he was actually paying attention to what Blake was saying."

"Where's Tom anyway?" Hally asked.

"He went to Center," Piet said.

"Is he okay?"

"I don't know. We were walking by the river when he got all pale and excused himself. Surely lunch didn't sit right with him."

Pam grabbed a bunch of sand and threw it at the young boy's face.

"Are you stupid? It wasn't lunch. Tom's scared of the water and with reason. What the Generation did... You didn't see it, it was inhumane."

Hally looked at her, unlike Tom, Pam's face was still covered with the bruises and scratches.

"That makes sense!" Piet exclaimed, getting another bunch of sand thrown at his face.

18

YOU REMEMBER TOM, RIGHT?

To be fair Tom tried, he really did. I know he tried, he knows he tried, now everyone can know that he tried.

He did his best to repeat Hally's words in his head over and over again, as if it was a prayer or a mantra. He repeated it each time the side of his eye caught the flowing water, each time the smell of wet dirt hit his nose and each time his already cured wounds came back like ghosts. Yet, it was never enough. He still wanted to throw up off the fear, he was still shaking, and his eyes still watered. He didn't want to cry, not because it wasn't manly, but because if he did then he would accept he couldn't control it, and he couldn't do that.

"I think that would be it, boys," Blake said.

"Finally," Piet panted as he cleaned the sweat off his forehead.

"What do we do now?" Tom asked.

Blake looked at the newly installed wall in the middle of Three's open space and grunted.

"I suppose... um," he thought about it. "What would you normally do at your house?"

"Dinner, we would have dinner," Tom answered kindly.

Blake smacked his forehead with the palm of his hand.

"You're absolutely right, I have to feed you. How did I forget?" He turned to the kids; eyes as wide as saucers. "Get the rest and don't tell Beira I almost forgot about dinner, she would kill me," he said before rushing towards Center.

Tom and Piet shared a chuckle.

The sun was already setting, making Platz look even better than before. The golden hour shone against the grass, shining as if millions of diamonds had been encrusted inside the small green leaves. All the birds that were on Four twittered their last songs of the day, all the butterflies flew around searching for a better place to sleep, and the light bounced against the river.

Tom had to hold back the tears one more time. He had once gone snorkeling, he loved swimming, he loved the beach and he had even gone surfing once. He loved the water! Or at least he used to. How had a bunch of people been able to rip the beauty of something Tom loved so much?

Piet started mumbling about something, Tom paid no attention to his words. His mind echoed with one and one thing only: Ulyssa's voice saying the word 'drink'.

"I'm sorry," Tom excused himself. "I'll be in Center," he couldn't be close to that river, he just couldn't do it.

The walk to Center was lonely and quiet: the way Tom liked it.

When Tom made it to his room, he determined Piet had already found the rest and called them for dinner. He calculated thirty minutes before everyone came back, thirty minutes to get his head straight , thirty minutes to wipe his worries away. The whole world could be falling apart, metaphorically, but whenever Tom grabbed some detergent, he was able to ignore it.

Tom started by cleaning Piet's mess, the boy certainly had never heard of drawer organizers or hangers. And let's not discuss his bed, whoever taught him how to make a bed should get their money back because Piet hadn't paid any attention to that class. If Tom hadn't known better, he would have said that part of the room belonged to a five-year-old but that would be mean to some five-year-olds considering that when Tom was that age, he already organized his clothes based on the color theory.

After organizing Piet's belongings Tom moved to the opposite side of the room, towards Lukai's not-as-bad-as-Piet's-disorder. Lukai at least folded his clothes and made a decent bed, what Tom could absolutely never agree with was the mess he had created with the cook books Blake had given him earlier. Once the books were organized based on color and alphabetical order, Tom's heart filled with some pride. It had only taken him half the time, now he could calmly ask Beira for some detergent and a mop to finally clean the floor.

He took a step backwards and admired his good work with a smile.

"This is how it's done."

Plop!

The smile dropped.

Plop!

A shiver came down his back.

Plop!

Tom looked at his hands, they were shaking uncontrollably.

He turned, just in time to see the small drop fall from the faucet.

Plop!

He marched, stomping his feet, and twisted the wrench. Another drop appeared. Tom turned it over and over. The stupid drops kept appearing.

"SHUT UP!"

As the next drop was about to fall Tom grabbed it before it could make a sound. His heart stopped. He opened his hand, there it was, an innocently evil water drop.

"Drink," Ulyssas' voice echoed.

"Ahhh!" Tom threw the drop and fell against the wall into the floor.

How had he become so weak that a drop could make him fall?

"Drink."

"SHUT UP!" Tom yelled.

"Drink Bellator."

"SHUT UP! SHUT UP! SHUT UP!"

His arms shook, but this time it wasn't out of fear.

A spark of energy surging from his stomach, rising up through his throat, arms and into his fingertips.

The light started to flicker.

Tom smiled; he wasn't scared anymore.

The energy disappeared.

"Tom, are you there?"

Tom rushed to wipe his tears and stood up. Hally couldn't know, he couldn't let her know.

"Yes," he answered.

"Okay." There was a pause. "Are you okay?" Why did she keep asking?

Tom smiled. "Never better." He looked at his hands, he wasn't sure if it was true.

"Alright, I'll be downstairs with the rest."

"I'll be there in a second."

Tom was making his way downstairs when something caught his attention.

"I don't trust him. I know Blake is wise, but Mr. Treacher is a man I would never trust with anything. He's bad and evil, and you know all those rumors…"

Pepper spoke quietly and rapidly, trying unsuccessfully to ensure that the words didn't reach any of the kids.

"I've heard the rumors," Beira interrupted Pepper. "And I'll not lie saying that Treacher is the person I had in mind for the Magister. But these Íroes are powerful, more powerful than what we expected, more powerful than what we could've ever imagined. I felt it the second they walked in. You must have felt it too!" Beira said.

"I did…," Pepper replied.

"The Bellator river has never shone this bright and there are only two Bellators in here. The Naturae section has never been so alive and there are also only two Naturaes. Even the Veteris is as strong as the others, and he *is* a Veteris. And the Woldier… Lukai… He's so strong, well trained and with a little help he could grow up to be a match for Hally. Blake may be the expert, he may know every single page of the history books and he may have the patience to teach the Bellators, Naturaes and the Veteris. But he never believed the Magisters to be real, and he may not be capable of getting a hold of such a powerful Woldier. They deserve to get to know their limits, not Blake's."

"I get it, but Treacher? Out of all the myth scholars of the world, why would he be picked? He has an *obsession* with the Magister!" Pepper exclaimed.

"And that's exactly why he is the perfect teacher. He knows everything there is to know about Magisters, myth or no myth. He basically prepared his whole life for an Íroe that could achieve an Imperium Orb bigger than a soccer ball, which is what *they* need," Beira responded calmly.

Pepper took a deep breath; it sounded as if she was getting ready to debate every single word Beria had just said.

"As for the rumors," Beira continued, making it clear that Pepper stood no chance with her debate, "those must not be ignored. You'll be responsible to make sure he doesn't do anything suspicious. But listen to me, *without* messing with him or the Íroes training. Am I making myself clear, Pepper?"

Pepper let out a tired sigh.

"Yes ma'am," she muttered. "But you have to promise me that you'll talk to Blake about this. We don't want the kids exposed more than what they have to be," Pepper demanded.

"I will," Beira promised. "Although it is going to be difficult to catch his attention tonight, his mind is only on the kids, he loves them as much as a..."

"As an uncle," Pepper finished Beira's sentence.

"As a father," Beira corrected Pepper.

"Hally is getting a real teacher? I want a real teacher," Tom mumbled to himself, a part of his heart roared with anger. He had felt it in the bathroom, he was supposed to be powerful. Why wasn't he getting a real teacher? There was nothing wrong with Blake, he knew a lot and he was a good man, but he was sort of a... amateur, Tom would say, and he wanted the best. Not only did he want it, he needed it. He couldn't help being afraid, he couldn't keep hiding behind doors, letting others get beaten because he was too much of a coward to do something about it.

"I will be her equal. I will do so. And then they'll see my real power and I'll be the best," he whispered to himself reaching the first floor.

"I will be the-" the worried looks on the other kids' faces stopped his whisper.

"Don't move her," Blake ordered.

Tom rushed to his unconscious sister.

"What happened?" suddenly the whole power thought disappeared.

"She mumbled something about feeling off on the way here," Pam said to him.

"The next thing she is hugging the floor," Piet added.

"What should I do?" Lukai asked, he was holding Hally's head the best he could.

"Just lay her down, softly," Blake ordered as he ran towards the kitchen.

Tom rushed and helped him.

As Hally touched the ground a wave came off her body. All the tables and benches levitated centimeters off the ground. The dishes that Blake had just placed on the counter flew across the room and the spoons of the kitchen joined them.

"Whoa," Piet said as he gently pushed a spoon out of his face.

"Nobody move," Blake said.

"Should we try to wake her?" Isla asked.

"No... I know what this is about. Hally's a powerful Íroe. Power needs energy, a lot of it. She's getting acclimated to her new self. She will be alright once she sleeps it off," Blake responded.

"Is this going to happen to all of us?" Ayala asked.

"I don't think so. She released all her powers yesterday, without any warning whatsoever, that may have helped this situation. And-" Blake stopped.

"We're not as powerful as her," Tom finished the sentence for him.

"In a way. Yes," Blake responded.

"We should take her upstairs," Lukai proposed.

"Here, I got her," Tom said and picked her off the ground.

"Don't you need any help?" Lukai asked.

"No, thank you," Tom said as he walked towards the stairs.

Gently, he made his way to the girls' room and placed Hally, in what was noticeably her bed.

"You'll be fine, Hally," he whispered and walked towards the door. There, he stopped just beside where all the shoes had been lined. He looked at her for a second.

There was this feeling that he couldn't really get a hold of. He stared at her for a minute and the feeling became strong enough to be recognizable. It was a mixture of jealousy and pain.

Jealousy because Hally was the Magister. What she held in her veins, that was power. Moving things around while being unconscious. Even having trouble getting adjusted, that was power. It was clear now what he had to do. If he wanted to be someone, if he wanted to not be scared, to not be a coward anymore, he had to be like her, he had to be better than her.

And pain, because how could he feel that way? He knew better than everyone that Hally was not a braggart type. She didn't consider herself better than anyone, even if she was.

Especially when she was. Tom couldn't be holding those harsh feelings against his best friend. Against the person that made sure to be there for him, always. Against the person that always made sure to help him and motivate him before anyone else. He couldn't be harboring these feelings against his sister, it was wrong. Wasn't it?

19

NO-SLEEP CLUB

Hally woke up to the ear-piercing sound of Ayala's snoring. Don't get me wrong, Ayala slept like an angel. She looked as adorable and cute as a puppy. Even her snoring was like that of a newborn puppy. It was the echo of those snores that piercedHally's ears.

"I would say good morning, but I don't consider it to be morning or good, yet," Pam muttered from her own bed.

Hally sat and looked around, the room's only light came from the lamps at the corners.

"What time is it?" Hally asked with a yawn.

"Almost midnight," Pam answered. "You passed out, Tom brought you here. Then Blake gave us a really nice and inspiring speech," Pam said sarcastically.

"What did he say?"

"Not much, just a few rules, like we can go anywhere as long as we stay within the boundaries of Platz. No fighting, he reminded us of that one. And always to seek help if anything happens. He also told us how our schedule will work. In the morning from eight to noon we'll have group training. After lunch we'll individually be assigned an hour for solo training time, meanwhile the rest should be focusing on our Ommon learning, that way we don't lose our whole touch with the normal world," Pam stopped to think for a second. "Ayala mentioned she wants to be a veterinarian in the middle of a conversation. I have no idea why, but how ironic it is considering her powers? Anyway... that's about the best explanation you'll get from me."

"So I didn't miss much..." Hally sassed. "Why does he say all the important stuff when I'm not there?"

"Why are you falling unconscious out of the blue?"

Hally chuckled.

"No idea, I was feeling alright, and then I felt as if I had just run a marathon and turned off."

"It's got something to do with your powers drawing too much energy according to Blake. He said you have to get used to the energy they are demanding and the energy you're giving them. He actually added later that you have to be careful. Íroes can't really lose their powers, but they do have limits. And if you use them to the very limit, energy wise, they tend to disappear for a while."

"Good to know," Hally mumbled.

Pam nodded. "I'm going downstairs, Lukai was cooking something. Isla is taking a shower and Tom went to sleep about fifteen minutes ago, do you want anything?" Pam asked.

Hally looked at Ayala, that weird sound was truly making her head hurt.

"I'll go with you," Hally said and started to slowly and carefully get out of the bed.

"Are you feeling good enough to do that?" Pam asked worriedly.

Hally smiled.

"Wow, the old angry bitter Pam cares about others," she said. Pam immediately rolled her eyes and recovered her usual annoyed expression.

"Do what you want, I don't care," she said and started to head out the girls' room followed slowly by Hally.

When Hally got out of the room and closed the door, the weird noise disappeared. She let out a sigh of relief and looked at Pam's confused face.

"Didn't you hear that?"

"What?" Pam asked.

"The weird-window-breaking sound."

"No," Pam responded oddly and headed downstairs.

Before following Pam, Hally poked her head into the boys' room silently, she felt she had to speak with Tom about something. However, the room was pitch black.

Maybe I should let him have one night's sleep, he has gone through much.

The dining room was filled with an exquisite smell: bread.

"Look who woke up!" Piet exclaimed as he saw Hally enter the dining room.

Piet was sitting in one of the stools at the counter of the kitchen and Lukai was inside the kitchen with an apron on. The girls sat beside Piet.

"How are you feeling?" Lukai asked Hally from the kitchen.

"I'm alright, it's just as if I had gone to sleep and woke up. Nothing hurts, or aches. No scars, no scratches." Hally said. That was a first.

"You have to keep that in mind, the energy thing I mean. Blake said-"

"Yeah yeah, Pam already told me about powers and stuff. I suppose I'll have to make some changes to my diet to keep up with my powers," she mumbled, the last words left a weird taste in her mouth. "What are you cooking?" she asked Lukai.

"Bread," Lukai said with a smile, "but don't worry, I left half of it without raisins."

"Okay, okay, okay," Hally said, trying to calm herself while looking around, offended. "We really need to settle this. Only people that want to feel like they're eating fancy or healthy while eating bread, put raisins inside the bread."

"Also chefs who want to make better bread," Lukai argued.

"That's insane!" Hally exclaimed and turned to Pam. "What do you think?"

Pam looked at Hally plainly.

"Frankly I couldn't care less."

"Aggghhh," Hally let out a sigh. "What about you, Piet? What do *you* think?"

Piet looked shocked to have been asked and thought the answer carefully.

"I guess any option is alright," Piet said confusedly.

"No!" Hally slammed the counter, Lukai laughed.

"See, raisins are good," he said laughing and putting the freshly baked loaf in front of Hally, the raisin side pointing at her.

"They're a crime to the real cuisine," Hally said, turning the plate so that the non-raisin side pointed at her.

"Can you stop whatever this is," Pam said tiredly. "Raisin or no raisin, it doesn't matter. Let's talk about something that won't give me a headache," Pam complained.

"Well, that will be difficult considering anything gives you a headache," Piet said and Hally and Lukai laughed with him.

"I'm not that bitter," Pam snorted.

"If someone made a video of you right now, muted you and edited a knife into your hands it would look like a scene from a horror movie," Hally said.

"That's not true! I am not that scary or mad looking!"

"So you admit you are a teddy bear?" Hally asked.

"Ugh!" Pam exclaimed, letting her head fall into her hands. "Lukai, would you give Hally a piece of bread so that she can shove it into her mouth, and I don't have to hear her anymore."

"I would, but I'm afraid the bread is still too hot, she would just spit it out," Lukai replied. Pam let out a frustrated growl.

They ended up eating a little bit of bread, the best bread Hally had ever tasted. The taste in her mouth brought back memories of a Costa Rican afternoon with her grandparents, the time where everything was how it was supposed to be. Even the raisin side tasted good, not that she would ever let Lukai know that. The raisin war had started and Hally was not about to surrender.

"I'm glad you joined our club," Piet said after taking a fifth piece of bread with his mouth still full of the last. "We do need food."

"Club?" Pam exclaimed; her mouth also full.

"Yeah...," Piet answered. "This," he said pointing at all of them, "is like a club. It is the... No-sleep club," he said with a proud smile.

Hally chuckled, one hand over her mouth.

"I like it, I have never really been in any kind of club."

Pam, on the other hand, rolled her eyes, as usual.

"I guess I'll have to live with that," she sighed.

Lukai was the only one not to add a comment, he just smiled. He too was happy to be included in the 'No-sleep club'.

Hally stared for a while at the empty plate where the bread had been.

"Have any of you tried using their powers on your own?" she asked, she was trying to move the plate, but she wasn't able to find that same feeling she had had with the Unicorn Powder or the night before or even when she was about to faint.

Lukai looked at her. His charming brown eyes smiled at her.

He shook his head, and his eyes told her everything she needed to know. He was scared of burning something and leaving nothing but dust.

"I have," Piet said disappointed. "But it doesn't work, not even with the special bracelet," he said looking at the bracelet Pepper had given him, one that he never took off.

"I try almost every second that I find some free time. But

unlike you, Hally, I haven't felt them ever since the day we met," Pam said.

"Well, I hope that changes tomorrow, it's been three days. I want my powers," Piet said with enthusiasm as Lukai turned back to the kitchen, he wasn't done cooking.

"What are you going to cook now?" Hally asked.

"What would you like?" Lukai asked back with a smirk.

"Anything but raisins."

Lukai clicked his tongue.

"I'll see if I can make that work."

The next morning started with good weather. The sun shined bright in the clear sky, yet there was enough of a breeze for the day not to be too hot.

After the delicious breakfast, made by Pepper, (she could use some lessons from Lukai), the kids were given ten minutes to gather in Three. Hally had washed her teeth and ran downstairs hoping to catch Tom and walk together to Three, only to find he was long gone. It felt like he was trying to avoid her, but there was also nothing weird about Tom being punctual and to follow a strict routine, one that Hally didn't usually fit into.

Eventually Hally ended up waiting for Lukai and Pam along with Piet, she now knew what Tom felt every morning when he waited for her back at home. When they finally did arrive on Three the clock marked five minutes later than when they were due, fortunately Blake was nowhere to be seen, therefore no one there to scold them.

"Frankly I'm shocked," Hally mumbled between her short breaths.

"Why?" Piet asked the same way.

"It's been four days and I'm not surprised to find a built-in wall in the middle of nowhere," Hally said calmly. "Who would have said you can get used to weird in so little time." She chuckled.

When Blake finally appeared, he came from inside the building. He was dressed formally, like a university professor.

"Are we all here?" Blake asked, he counted the kids. "Yes. Fantastic! We may start today's lesson," he took a look at the paper in his hands and the many sentences he had been practicing since last night, before starting. "Today... today we are going to push this wall!" Blake pointed at the brick wall.

The kids gawked at it confused.

Hally's hand went straight up.

Blake frowned.

"Is that a question?"

"Yes."

"Go ahead."

"Where do you get a single wall from? And why do we need a single wall?" she asked.

"Oh," Blake chuckled, massaging the back of his neck. "There are many rooms in these buildings, you have no idea of how many interesting things you can find once you start looking," he said and cleared his throat. "As for the why, well, this wall is a wall, as you can see, obviously. It doesn't really have any special name now that I think about it... But it *is* indeed a special wall. As a matter of fact, now that I think about it I'm not sure if this is how it is supposed to be used. Though it does respond to powers and-" Blake realized that he was losing his way and the kids had gotten lost a while back. He cleared his throat again. "I'm going to need a volunteer," he finally admitted.

The kids remained quiet, some of them still too confused about the introduction and others a bit scared of the insecurity. One of them stepped up front.

"I'll do it," Tom said.

Hally looked at her brother, his set of brown eyes that mirrored her own had never been darker, emptier and colder. And in the very center, deep down, invisible to anyone who hadn't trained for years, there was a pinch of anger and jealousy: greed.

What's he doing? What's he trying to prove?

"Perfect, I didn't want to have to handpick one of you. Tom, the brave, you may step near the wall," Blake said with a smile, ignorant of what Hally knew that was going on inside that thick head of his. "The wall will measure the strength of your powers. The stronger they are, the more it will move."

He paused momentarily for the kids to digest the information.

"You may go ahead and start pushing the wall."

"Just that?" Tom asked, eyebrows raised. "I just push, and it tells me how strong I am?"

"Exactly."

Tom stepped closer to the brick wall. He looked one more time at Blake searching for assurance. A single nod gave it to him.

"Just push the wall as hard as you can."

He placed both of his hands against the wall and with what looked like all his strength he pushed it. The wall, however, didn't seem to have received the memo, and stayed rigid in its place, as a wall tends to do.

Tom grunted and stepped back to regain his breath.

"Is this a joke?" he asked, angrier than before. "This is a wall, walls don't move."

"That's because you're looking for your physical strength," Blake turned to the kids, happy that the moment for the lesson had finally appeared. "The first thing you must learn is that your new powers are like a muscle you've never used. You have to work on it to build it, take care of it and maintain it. They're not magical and won't disappear if you don't use them, just like your calves don't disappear even if you don't walk anywhere. But you have to train and strengthen it, just like you would with your body. Yet, your powers aren't exercised with weights and running, they're built with the mind."

Tom smiled cockily, if there was something he didn't have to doubt was his mind, the one he bragged so much about, the same one he knew was one of a kind.

Oh no.

He placed his palms once again where they were supposed to be, and he pushed again and again and again. The wall remained in the same place it had been built.

"It's still not moving," Tom grinned between his teeth.

Blake scratched his chin.

"You're still thinking too materialistically. Go deep, find the strength of your person. Each one of you has an idea, an ideology and trait that makes you so unique. Find that thing you're willing to fight for."

Tom rested his forehead against the wall taking one more deep breath.

"Maybe you should take a break?" Hally suggested.

Immediately she realized it had been a foolish idea. She saw as the thunder of anger rose from Tom's feet up to his head. He looked at her, his eyes speaking a language only the twins understood. 'You would like that huh? For me to be nothing. I'll show you.'

He closed his eyes and pushed.

"AHH!" he exclaimed, all his muscles, physically and mentally, pushed harder than he ever did.

"Yes!" Blake was the first to react, the wall had been moved half a meter back.

Tom recovered his posture and the rest of the kids applauded, even Hally gave a small gentle clap.

What the heck is going on with you, Tom?

Give him time. Give him patience.

"That's what I call strength," Blake celebrated. "High five! Do you still do that? I mean I'm not sure. I did it when I was young."

Tom chuckled, a nice normal Tom chuckle.

"I'll take it," he said.

The sound of hands hitting each other filled the air.

"Now what about us?" Piet asked. "What do we do now?"

"Now's your turn."

Hally found out a few interesting things that first morning. Isla appeared to be afraid of failure, and therefore refused to do the exercise at the beginning alleging that it was not lady like to do it. It was until she was the last, then she did it and moved the wall fifteen centimeters making her face fill out with a smile. Also, Ayala was stronger than what she looked, and ended up pushing the wall twenty centimeters, a real example that being kind and nice is not a weakness.

At the end, the ones that moved it more were Lukai, Hally and Tom. Tom being the best and Hally and Lukai tied with twenty-five centimeters.

Just as Blake had explained, the strength hadn't come from her body, rather from her mind. At first it seemed hard, difficult, but then... then Hally'd let her mind alone. It came naturally, in some kind of way, as water comes from a river. She just took a breath, cleared her mind and let all that power she'd been trying to hide for so many years come to light. She didn't have to make anything levitate or fly, just the thought was enough to be liberating. Even though there was still something inside, something that was fighting to stay there.

The kids continued to do this exercise for half the morning, each of them taking turns. There was only one problem that Blake had not taken into consideration, unlike our silver girl, the rest of the kids hadn't used their powers on command before (considering that the river accident and Elowen's session had been controlled) and they had no control whatsoever on them. Isla made a patch of grass grow up to her knees. Ayala became a bear for a while without changing back to human form and roaring all the time (Blake had to help her turn back). Piet and Pam had an unintentional fight for a moment, Piet would turn Pam's shoes to rock and she would separate the matter of leaving *him* without shoes every time he moved. And Lukai accidentally burnt the same grass that Isla had grown and later threw a shot of light directly into Pam's face, earning a really angry glare.

Around ten o'clock Blake gave the kids a break when Beira came over to hand them some pineapple juice and repositioned the wall the way they had placed it the afternoon before.

When the 'break' ended Blake had the kids arrange themselves into a circle, Hally ended up standing face to face with Tom, who was still acting way too weird to be normal. Hally had tried talking to him while the others did the wall exercise, yet he'd found a way to avoid her at all cost either talking with Blake or suddenly disappearing. Then, during the 'break' he'd excused himself to the bathroom and hadn't returned until Blake made the announcement that the training would restart. And now that they stood in front of each other, Tom made the impossible not to make eye contact with her.

"What are we moving now, Blake? A building? A car? A city?" Piet asked.

"Oh please don't, no more pushing, it gets me all sweaty," Isla cried.

"How do you plan on moving a city? You barely moved the wall!" Pam exclaimed.

"Hey!"

"Maybe he'll imagine he's being chased by a bear and the city is on his way," Hally joked.

Ayala smiled and turned to the young boy.

"Roar," she mimicked a bear.

"Ugh," Piet shrieked at the sound and took a step away from her and closer to Lukai. "C'mon Canada boy, back me up. Bears are evil and frightening right?"

Lukai grimaced.

"I don't know, kid, in my motherland we would hunt bears wearing nothing but underwear and covered our heads with their skins after we invited them for coffee."

Piet eyes opened widely at the idea.

"Really?"

"OF COURSE NOT!" Lukai replied.

The kids laughed.

"I assure you Piet, there are no bears in these woods," Blake said, then he gave it a second thought. "Well... um... I assure you they won't come here. They're scared of the lights... I can absolutely assure you're here, though."

Piet looked at the teacher even more scared and confused than before.

"Anyway," Blake regained their attention. "As I surmised you already understood, the wall helps you find your strength, and it can be used to measure it too. However, there is an even better way to search for strength and measure your powers."

"Then why did we move the wall?" Isla whined.

"The wall is a starter, the first of all, the unplugger. This next exercise requires the powers to have already been unplugged. You'll like this one Isla, I'm sure. This one won't make you sweat. Well... I mean-"

"Just stop assuring things, you're just digging even deeper," Hally advised.

"As I was saying, in the past they used another method, a method that will prove to be effective whenever you don't find yourself in Platz. Although now that I think about it I don't know why you would need to prove your power outside of Platz..." He refocused. "They are called Imprerium Orbs. In ancient times, these were used when two Íroes got into a duel, they would call on their Imperium Orbs to prove who was stronger. Unlike with the wall, Imperium Orbs won't be altered by your emotions. If you face the wall and you have a rush of adrenaline or manipulate your strength with your emotions whether they are love, fear or anger, it will have an effect. The Imperium Orbs will demonstrate the strength of your powers and your powers alone, they will never change unless your power grows stronger or they weaken."

He paused momentarily and reached for a book he had gotten from the building.

"Now, I'll read the instructions from one of the books of an original teacher of Platz," he moved the yellow pages between his fingers and started reading. "Before reading the steps to make an Imperium Orb I'll give a list of what I have studied in the last few years. According to my latest research, there's a usual order from the weakest type of Íroes to the strongest. (It is valuable to mention that there are exceptions, my closest friends destroy this whole investigation just by breathing. Yet there are far too many coincidences out there not to put them in here.) The weakest Íroes usually are the Veteris. They are commonly followed by Naturae and then Bellators. Finally, the strongest, commonly, are the Woldiers," Blake made a pause for a clarification. "Magisters are not included on the list, probably because either the researcher wasn't in their capacity to reach Queen Sila or because they didn't consider that the representation of one was enough to prove a point. With that clear I'll continue the reading."

"The first step for making an Imperium Orb is putting your arms horizontally across your chest forming square angels with your elbows and placing one hand on top of the other," Blake said and raised his eyes to the kids. "Go ahead and do that."

The kids asked for the instruction again and Blake showed them a hand drawn picture from the book.

He continued.

"The next steps must be done by each person's focus on their powers, they may focus on the feelings their powers give them or on the power themselves, just make your only thought to be about your abilities. Link it to your breathing. Let your powers exit your body as you let air exit your lungs when exhaling. Did you all get that?" Blake asked.

The kids all nodded.

"Second step. Rotate your hands in opposite directions so that the hand that was underneath now lies on top. Meaning if the left hand was underneath the right hand it shall be on top, same goes for the other way around. While rotating the hands stay focused on the foregoing discussion. The student may choose to do it with their eyes open or closed, whichever is easier for them to focus on their breathing."

Hally breathed slowly and deeply. Her heartbeat slowed down and that powerful feeling took over her veins again. It was such a feeling that Hally wondered if she was making something levitate unintentionally. No one was complaining so she considered it unlikely.

"Finally," Blake now spoke quietly in a hushed tone not to disrupt the relaxed kids. "Separate your hands vertically while you exhale and as the air leaves your body, release your power. It is important to note that not all students will be able to do it on their first try and that whether the Imperium Orb is very shiny and big or dim and small it does not affect the quality of their holder," Blake read the last sentence and closed the book gently, there was no need for further explanation, each of the seven was focused.

Hally escaped from the world, leaving only her and her orb. Whether Ayala was breathing loudly, or Piet had been able to achieve his focus, wasn't her concern at the moment. For a second it was only her and the air around her. The blood rushed through her veins moving the oxygen around, keeping her alive. Her feet kept her straight without much effort. Her mind was at peace. When she felt ready, she separated her hands and created her Imperium Orb.

She opened her eyes and let herself see what all the fuss was about. Let me tell you, the fuss was completely and utterly worth it.

Between her hands, causing a slight tingle on her fingers, floated a 'gigantic' (not exactly gigantic), silver glowing ball. The ball was smaller than a gym ball but a little bit bigger than a medicine ball. It obviously glowed silver, silver being the color of Magister. It in fact glowed so brightly that Hally thought she wouldn't ever have to worry again about not having any light, she could now shine her way through darkness.

Several minutes had to pass before Hally took her eyes off the hypnotic Imperium Orb. The ball was fire-like, dancing with the wind, dangerously ready to attack, persisting under any circumstance without much effort. It was fighting, fighting to be something more, to be even bigger.

The kids enjoyed the moment, moving the orbs around teasing each other... Even Blake enjoyed it with them.

"Now kids, creating an Imperium Orb isn't energy demanding. On the other hand, when you dissolve the orb you might experience a big decay of energy. Right next to you I'll put one of these." Blake showed a small cup with what looked like a gummy. All gummies were different colors. "When you cease to create the orb, if you feel dizzy, and only if you feel dizzy, you may take the pill by your side. Every pill is made specially for you and for your powers. Beira made them. They'll give you a boost of energy. They're not to be taken without actually needing them or you might end up hurting yourself and creating an addiction. You hear me? Only if you need them," Blake said quite seriously and didn't put a cup beside each kid until he made sure they all understood what he had said perfectly.

As Hally's orb dissolved and the power was set free, the peacefulness was replaced by a blur. For a second the world spun around, the floor dissolved, and her heart seemed to want to stop beating.

Gently Hally let herself fall to the ground and grabbed the pill, her orange flavored pill. In no more than a couple of seconds Hally's veins filled again with that common adrenaline rush, and everything went back to normal, her normal and not Íroes normal. And it raised a thought, taken in normal conditions, that pill could give any of them enough energy to beat an army on their own. Hally chuckled at the thought unknowingly that there, on the exact opposite side of the circle, as Tom finished chewing his pill, his mind filled with the same thought.

20

TOM'S TRAINING

Tommy boy was going crazy. The last thing he really wanted to do was not to talk to Hally, but he just couldn't bear to look directly in her eyes, not with what he had been thinking the night before. He'd had to eat the fastest he could that morning, shoving food like crazy into his mouth to avoid sharing a table with her. And then, at training, he'd had to run around like a dog chasing his tail, pulling the worst excuses to prevent the dreadful conversation. After lunch however, as Blake gave each a schedule, Hally got too occupied chatting with Pam and Lukai and mocking Piet to pay much attention to him.

Tom arrived at the Veteris quadrant, where he had been cited, leaving the rest on the beach, enjoying the water and laughing until their ribs hurt. When he reached the quadrant, he thought that maybe that day could really turn around, just maybe. He came with hopes that drowned the fear and trembling sensation from his heart. He was mistaken

He tried, he worked his back off and tried. But then the voice would always come back to his brain, his legs would start to shake and every drop of sweat that fell from his forehead was easily confused with water. He didn't quite understand what was happening. He had been able to do it, he had been able to do it before when he was forced by Elowen and Gunner. Before, when he was a warrior and a Bellator.

Tom opened his eyes and gasped, leaning against his knees.

"Focus," Blake advised, the best advice Tom had ever heard (more like sarcasm).

Tom looked at the golden pin in his shirt, he was still a warrior, he was still a Bellator. Nothing had changed.

He closed his eyes, and he felt the power growing from beneath his feet, all the electricity that had been held inside the ground and rock for years waiting for someone to call it.

A drop of sweat fell to his nose.

"Drink!"

He was once again forced into the water, his lungs burning for a breath and his brain begging for it to stop. He wasn't a warrior, much less a Bellator. He was the same kid that had seen Carlos arrive at his classroom and did nothing more than wait for the banging to stop.

His eyes opened and gasped again, leaning one more time against his knees.

"It's not working," Tom managed to say while hoping that the shaking wasn't obvious in his voice. He doubted Blake would understand what was happening, he hadn't been there. Not even Pam who *had* been there would understand either. They weren't the ones that had felt the blazing powder moving through their veins, crushing and burning anything that stood in their way, even if that was the same flesh that controlled it.

Blake gave him a pat on his back.

"You're doing great, kid."

"Am I? Seriously? Is this what it is supposed to be?"

"Not really, no."

Tom snorted.

"Are you aware of what the word Íroe means or where it comes from?"

"It means hero. Greek, I believe."

Blake smiled impressed.

"Yes, I had to look that up myself. You're quite smart."

Tom shrugged. "I just read."

"That's more than what half the world does."

"Hally reads too," Tom added.

Blake sighed.

"You have to stop that, Tom. What Hally or Piet or even Pam are doing will always be different from what you're doing. It doesn't matter if you're genetically similar or even if you both are Bellators. You're you and they are them. That's literally why we are having solo training!"

"I don't understand this," he opened his hands pointing at his surroundings. "I want answers, Blake. I *need* answers."

"I know kid, they'll come, with time. Look at me, I've been studying this all my life, that's twice your age. And I still have many questions. You got into all this three? four days ago? It'll take a few more."

He didn't have time. He knew fairly well that his own sister was sitting at the beach at that exact second wondering every day if she was a curse. He had to prove her the contrary, he had to show her that they were a miracle, not a problem. But how could he if he couldn't even make himself work right?

"Have you ever seen X-men Tom?"

Tom laughed.

"No... movies are Hally's thing."

"That sounds about right... anyway. Your abilities, what we call powers, can be affected by emotions, just like the wall in the morning. Things as strong and rash as fear, shame and especially anger can manipulate them like nothing else. You must be careful with that, anger-based powers poison the mind."

Tom studied the grass underneath his feet.

"Base your powers in you... yourself. Who are you Tom? There's a reason, a value, something you stand for and will fight within your soul that separates you from all the rest of the Toms in the world."

Blake gave him a pat over his shoulder.

"Why don't we finish here? Restartt tomorrow?"

Tom walked directly to Center avoiding the beach and the rest of the kids entirely, his mind clouded with thought and his body covered with sweat.

Silently and calmly, Tom marched into the empty building and directly to the boy's room.

"Hey!" Hally yelled from beside the door.

"Hally! Gosh! How many times have I told you not to do that?" he exclaimed, he hated being scared, it clouded his mind.

"Oh no. You!" One finger pointing to his face. "You have been avoiding me!" she exclaimed frustrated.

Tom stared back; his eyes opened widely.

"Ummm..."

"When I try to talk to you... you act as if I'm the harbinger of death and run away. How the heck are you even avoiding me? This isn't that big a place!" Hally made a small pause, calming her tone and lowering the finger. "I just want to know if you are okay. We're far from home, really far. We have to stick together, for our sanity."

Tom took a deep breath and looked at his sister's eyes.

He gave her a small smile.

"Life is different here, Hally, but I'm fine... I'm just trying to... find how all this works... My powers, the place, the people," Tom pointed at the room that in spite of his efforts the night before it had gone back to disaster.

"So... are you really fine?"

"Yes," he lied.

Hally figured it out.

"How are you feeling?" Tom asked before Hally could keep asking.

"I'm fine," she answered dryly. "I'm happy here," she added sincerely. "Are you?"

Tom smiled.

"I'm on my way to getting answers. Can you believe it? We are finally figuring out what all this is! You'll never have to worry about your eyes glowing again or the curse thing."

"I'm a curse Tom," Hally replied, she had accepted it, why couldn't he? "There is no way to change it."

Tom rolled his eyes.

"C'mon Hally, I begged Mom to give you away the first five years of our lives, then I realized you're not that bad."

Hally laughed.

"Yeah... I grew on you. Like fungus!"

"Exactly." They both laughed.

"It will all sort itself out, right?" Tom asked.

"I have no idea, I have as many years of life experience as you," Hally babbled back.

"Shouldn't you be at training?" Tom asked.

"Probably. And you should take a shower, you smell terrible."

Tom smiled

"Just when I feel like hugging my little sister." He opened his arms.

Hally stepped back.

"You stay away from me Mr. Sweat. I have things to do!" she argued as she ran down the corridor.

Tom laughed, one of those honest and heartfelt laughs only Hally got out of him. If life was that simple...

He turned around. "You should take a shower," Hally had said. Just the thought of water gave him shivers.

"C'mon Tom pull it together, it's just a shower," he mumbled.

"Drink!"

He closed his eyes; he couldn't do it. He was just another coward.

Something stumbled down the stairs. Tom walked out of his room already picturing the messy haired Hally getting up from the floor and getting his laugh ready. In its place, there was a teary-eyed Bobby struggling to pick up some fruits.

He looked up.

"I'm sorry," he mumbled. "I'm so so sorry," he continued, babbling.

Tom's heart felt a warmth. He bent down and carefully helped all the fruits find their way back to Bobby.

"I'm so sorry," he kept repeating.

"Don't apologize, it's alright," Tom assured him.

"I-I-I am bothering you," he sniffled.

"No... not at all." Tom helped him onto the couch and handed him a tissue.

He looked worriedly at the stairs; would it be wise to call for Beira? He didn't know how to calm the big guy but calling her so desperately might hurt his feelings even more.

He decided to sit by his side and wait a few minutes before reaching for the lady.

Bobby kept crying, using tissue after tissue to wipe his tears. As he did so, Tom noticed a scar on his neck, it was deep and big, right where the main vein was. Either he had had a terrible accident, or he'd almost been murdered.

"Bobby, are you in here?" Beira called from the stairs.

Bobby rushed to wipe off his tears. Was he aware that Beira wasn't going to notice them?

"What's wrong Bobby?" Beira asked.

"I-I-I-" Bobby struggled.

"He dropped the fruits coming up the stairs," Tom explained.

"Tom, you're here," she greeted him with surprise. "Was there any mess?" she asked Bobby, keeping her sweet and soothing tone.

"No ma'am."

"Then there was no problem, Bobby, you did nothing wrong."

Bobby sniffled and covered his neck as if anyone would come at any time and reopen the scarred wound.

"Really?" he asked.

"Sworn."

The promise was enough to cheer him up and send him back on his way, wherever he was taking the fruits.

Beira chuckled and smiled at Tom. How was she aware of where he was?

"He likes helping us collect food for a poor town nearby, he gets sad when he doesn't think he did a good job."

Tom smiled.

"He has a tender soul…"

"He wasn't always like that though," Beira continued, her tone shifted to melancholy. "Elowen has a big, weird obsession with clean genetics, even before she'd realized Íroes had been born. When Blake found Megalo Dentro she went even…" she thought of the perfect word, "crazier."

Tom had to suppress his laugh, that was certainly not the word he would have thought of using.

"Blake found Megalo Dentro? I thought it had always been there."

Beira laughed, showing her pearly white teeth.

"Megalo Dentro is not any tree Tom, it can only be found if it wants to be found. It's not magic though, it's something to do with electro waves and baffling the brain… You'll have to ask Blake about that one, about everything actually." She chuckled.

"Were you from the Western Guarders?" Tom asked although he knew the answer, he wanted to hear it from her.

Beira's smile faded.

"I was, at one time. The Guarders were where I lived, never my home. Humans love to judge who we think deserves something or not. It has been like that for all of history and it will be like that for many years to come. The Guarders weren't like that and stood by differences for many centuries, until they eventually succumbed to the tendency for stereotypes. I wasn't the stereotype Elowen wanted. I never was."

Tom's arms filled with goosebumps.

"I thought I was her type, didn't really help me at all."

Beira moved her hand softly around until it found Tom's cheek.

"I wasn't born blind Tom," she confessed. "'Til this day I don't know if it was a bad joke or a planned disaster."

Tom shuffled awkwardly in his seat.

"The fear will go away. With time you will stop caring about it, and then one day you'll wake up and that awful sensation will have disappeared completely."

"Are you sure?"

"Yes. Blake helped me, I helped Bobby, we'll help you. Even through your training."

Tom's muscles tensed. Beira felt it.

"I'm sorry," she apologized. "Pepper saw it partially and she isn't much for keeping secrets," she chuckled delicately.

Tom licked his lips.

"You don't get it, my problems go far before the Generation even appeared," he struggled. "I have always been a coward, always waiting for someone else to fight and fix the world. There's nothing changing it now."

"You're not a coward."

"Yes I am," he insisted.

"No, Tom. You *don't* understand. A real coward would never accept they're a coward. Real cowards are too afraid of their own fear to even accept it. There's nothing wrong with being a little afraid. Bobby's afraid. Blake's afraid. I'm afraid. Fear doesn't make you a coward. Fear makes you human."

She paused before she continued.

"Not all heroes wear capes, Tom. I know it's a saying..." She strived for the right words. "It's true. All heroes fight differently. Some fight for peace, others for family, others for love. Find what you fight for, sometimes we don't even realize it, but we all fight for something. Especially Íroes."

What if she was right? What did he actually fight for?

Tom's mind filled with images, all the time he had spent teaching, all the times he had explained math problems time after time. Why had he done that? Why had he spent so much time? The images changed into a memory. He was too young when he saw a teacher yell at a boy, insisting he would do everything in life except get anywhere, all because he couldn't add. He'd seen the joy leave that kid, the hope and more importantly the life. He'd seen that kid come every single day afterwards, watch the wall and ask himself over and over again why he'd been born if he was stupid. It was then he'd decided that he didn't want to let others lose everything as that kid had done, their joy, their smile, their life. That day he'd decided he wanted to fight for hope, even if it was a little of it.

His face filled with such pride he wished Hally was there to see it. He had figured it out, with help, but he had done it.

"You got it?" Beira asked.

"I think so."

Beira smiled. "You have no idea how lucky you are, most of us never become brave enough to even think about fighting for something." Then as a thought entered her brain her smile broke.

"You still have to be careful, Tom, with your training. Knowing what you fight for, is a big step. Getting the fear back down is another. And fear has a tendency toward anger. Anger poisons the mind."

"Blake said something similar."

She grinned

"Promise me you'll take the training gently until you manage the fear. Íroes have lost their minds before, cities have been destroyed and blood has been drawn because of it."

"I promise."

"Beira, could you help me?" Bobby's voice echoed through the stairs.

Beira stood up.

"I loved talking with you Tom."

"The pleasure was all mine," Tom replied.

21

SOCCER MESS. SHADOW GAME

Treacher, (Screecher how Lukai and Hally had nicknamed him) was a tall, pale, blue eyed, serious looking guy who liked screaming, a lot. And even though Blake had reassured the kids there was no one better to train them, ten minutes after having started, Hally was questioning if he was trying to teach them or kill them.

"Hally Black!" He spoke with force and a thick accent. "Focus girl!"

Hally grunted, her legs ached from the five miles he had forced them to run, and her forehead was filled with the sweat of the afternoon sun. The problem wasn't the powers, after the morning Imperium Orb, she'd made peace with her abilities and they came when she called, just like breathing. But not always exactly how she called them, just like sneezing.

"Again," Treacher commanded with his notoriously unique hand movement, Lukai mimicked him at his back.

Hally choked back laughter at her throat.

She placed both her hands at her sides, movement helped focus. She bent her knees like Treacher had asked and straightened her back. The three overfilled water glasses rose gently from the ground.

She inhaled.

Keep them straight. Keep them straight.

"Not one drop on the ground," Treacher ordered, Lukai mimicked him again.

"Sure," Hally mumbled.

The glasses reached mid-air and stopped rising. Hally froze as a statue. *Not one drop.*

"Keep them steady. You might be powerful, but without control you're just chaotic."

Hally swallowed hard, she needed the control, she knew it. The Imperium Orb and all the exercises Treacher had pulled had only left it clearer, her powers were far from the limit. Which made her question, *how much damage am I capable of doing?*

Hally's hands started shaking slightly, the feeling of a thousand cold needles filled them. The sweat fell and her back atrophied.

"How long am I supposed to keep them here?"

"Until I get bored of seeing you do it," Treacher replied.

Hally sniffed, then her sigh changed into a smile at Lukai's mimicry.

Treacher turned around to face the Canadian boy, the same one who had left his own exercises forgotten a while before.

"What are you doing?"

Lukai's face paled at the Russians' angry look.

"No! That's not right!" Pam's screams from the Bellator quadrant echoed.

"Well, it is how it is done in the upper class! I get that it's hard for you!" Isla replied.

Treacher's eyes didn't move from Lukai, his mouth curled down.

"Boy controls light. Light confuses brain. You make a clown out of light, I laugh with you."

Lukai looked at his hands. From them a slight warm light came out. He focused on it, trying to tell it how to act, where to go. The light grew.

"More," Treacher dared him.

More light appeared. Then more and more, until it went out of control and flooded the air like a second sun.

"Off," Treacher grunted, hiding his eyes behind his hands.

The light disappeared.

"I'm sorry," Lukai apologized. "I can call it, but I can't make illusions."

"Mmmm," Teacher replied disappointedly. "Boy give me fifty pushups."

Lukai's face filled with such an expression Hally chuckled.

Treacher turned around as fast as the lighting ready to scold his student.

"Not one-" His words were cut off by the one water drop frozen in mid-air with such precision. "Mmm," he grunted for a moment. His expression changed into a different person entirely, admiring the drop.

His eyes rose to Hally and his expression returned to normal.

"What?" Treacher asked. "What's that face?"

"I have to sneeze," she admitted in a high-pitched voice.

This time it was Lukai the one that let out a chuckle.

"This is not how training's supposed-"

"Achooo!" Hally interrupted Treacher. The glasses flew in all directions bursting against the ground, water splashing the three of them.

Hally covered her face with her hands, an invisible shield appeared protecting her head from the water.

"Hey!" Lukai complained. "The water is supposed to stay in the glass."

"And the light is supposed to look like a clown," Hally replied.

Lukai put up his hand calling a gentle and warm light strong enough to blind Hally but also to dry her clothes.

They laughed.

"This is it!" Treacher snapped. "No more training! Tomorrow, I bring chess game. You learn discipline with chess, or you run until I get bored."

Lukai's smile faded.

Hally bit her cheek to keep the smile from appearing.

Mr. Invincible doesn't know how to play chess.

Nope, he has absolutely no idea.

"Dismissed."

Hally sighed, she was ready for a shower and an eternity of just laying in bed.

"Heads up, Hally," Pam threw an old dirty ball at her. "We're playing soccer."

She could say no, say she was tired.

A malicious smile appeared, there was no way she was missing that game.

These were the teams: Hally, Piet and Isla vs Tom, Lukai, Pam and Ayala.

Good teams considering none of them really knew how to play the game. Ayala tried to take the ball without hurting anyone. Pam didn't really mind about kicking whether it was the ball or the other player's legs. Tom did a quick math calculation before every shot. And Isla didn't run but walked rapidly and elegantly, hands at her sides. Nonetheless, it was a lot of fun.

From time to time an enormous root appeared out of the ground, tripping the players with the ball. Isla argued that it was accidental, although sinceit only kept happening when the other team had the ball her word lost its veracity real soon. There was a moment when Ayala turned into a bird, and she decided to bother the other team by sitting on their heads until she was able to turn back. Lukai blinded Hally once to get the ball, just for Hally to call over the ball with her mind later making her own team cheer and the other team complain endlessly. Even Pam would make the ball go through the feet of the other players. And we can't leave out the part when Piet turned the ball into rock, and everyone yelled at him until he turned it back.

With a lot of sweat, even more cheating, but especially laughter, soon enough the halftime arrived. They were two against three, Tom's team winning in spite of all problems.

Hally sat up, the sun was already hiding on the horizon. Her legs ached, and she had never felt more alive. She couldn't even remember when she had so much fun, nor when she had laughed so much. And then her senses... she could feel everything around her sharpened, as if she had gained a sixth sense. She could feel the steps of the kids around her, the birds flying around, the ball bouncing through the grass, Treacher's smile forming in his face as he watched the game and a new figure walking towards him.

Hally turned around; Blake had finally made it.

Cheers came from her side, Piet had just scored another goal.

"Hey!" Tom complained. "When did the game even restart?"

The cheers turned into yelling.

Hally focused on Blake. Her abilities were incredible. She had known her powers were more than capable, but she had never imagined this. Even if she closed her eyes, she could still tell that he was tall, wearing a winter coat, his hair was a mess, and his shoes were covered in mud. She could feel the mud in his shoes! She focused on his lips; she could tell what he was saying without hearing a thing.

"Treacher," Blake said, by the look on his face he wasn't very amused.

"Blake," Treacher greeted back

There was a visibly awkward silence.

"How did they do?" Blake asked.

"Great, they're great specimens," Treacher responded.

"They are kids, not projects," Blake growled silently back at him

Treacher scoffed.

"Did they manage to do the exercises you gave them?" Blake asked.

"Some. The boy needs confidence, the girl discipline. But she's powerful if I could..."

Suddenly Hally's leg met the ball.

"Hally, stop wandering and play!" Piet screamed at her.

Hally rose up, this wasn't her conversation. She kicked the ball and ran down the field scoring another goal.

They continued to play, Blake and Treacher watching, they weren't talking anymore. Treacher had moved to the far side, bordering the other quadrant.

When Blake announced that there were five more minutes before dinner, the kids decided to run a final play. Piet came running for the ball, Pam behind him. The ball went through his foot directly into Pam's. Pam ran with it, but Piet recovered rapidly and kicked it right into the Woldier quadrant.

Hally sighed. "Seriously?" She ran after it into the short green grass section. She was about to reach it when a root wrapped around her foot, and she fell face down into the grass.

"Isla," she mumbled under her breath.

"Hally!" Blake screamed.

Hally pushed herself up, looked back at Blake and smiled. Blake's eyes weren't staring at her, they were looking at the grass. Beneath her hands the green had been replaced with black, the darkest shade of black you can imagine, like a shadow. The shadow grew until it covered the entire quadrant and then rose into a full humanoid form.

Hally stood up rapidly, backed away a few steps, heart pounding in her chest. In front of her stood a three-meter-tall shadow who's only features that could be seen were its long and pointy limbs, its yellow eyes and its dark mouth filled with yellow teeth sharp as knives.

"Hally don't move," Blake ordered, she felt as he took a few steps closer. "Everybody take slow and quiet steps back"

The game had stopped, there were no more cheers or complaints. The only thing the other kids did was breathe as they watched the creature from all of their childhood nightmares become real. Blake repeated the order.

The shadow creature looked around and sniffed as a dog does when you pull some bacon out of the microwave.

"That's a Shadower," Blake explained as he got closer. "Hally, you're its creator, therefore the Shadower will obey your commands. But only if you prove to be a stronger being. If the Shadower believes that you're weak it will go out of control."

The Shadower studied Hally's fear-filled face. It didn't appear to be convinced that Hally was a fit master.

"Show that you're stronger than him, that he should fear you, not the other way around. Show him that he *has* to do what you say because they are not suggestions, they are orders. Show him your power. And whatever you do, don't turn around," Blake croaked and took a few steps closer.

Hally took a deep breath and stared back at the dark empty Shadower's eyes. They were horrible and evil.

The Shadower growled, it was a deep ugly growl that could make its debut in a horror's story.

Hally's face hardened and the growling was silenced.

I won't be afraid. I won't be afraid. I won't be afraid.

Hally took a step closer to the shadow without taking her eyes off of his.

He should be scared of me.

The Shadower looked back and smiled, showing off all those ugly and deadly teeth.

Hally's face remained emotionless, her whole body was shaking, but her face wasn't going to show it.

The dark creature, disappointed that Hally was not screaming her lungs out, took his eyesight off and looked at the rest of the kids behind her.

"Don't," Hally ordered. "Don't do that," she repeated the command.

The Shadower's eyes lay once again on the girl. She was smaller than him, way smaller and he was starting to notice.

"Sit," Hally demanded.

The Shadower didn't move.

Show him my power.

The now natural fire rose from inside her chest. She formed a shield around the creature and pressed it firmly. Her eyes glowed silver showing she could do it, she could do it if she wanted to.

"Sit down, now," Hally repeated.

The Shadower sat and growled.

Hally raised her hand, the growl disappeared.

A hand reached Hally's shoulder. It was Blake, his touch made her feel safe, like a parent does to a small kid.

"It is your servant now," Blake said. "Tell it to go away, to where it was, and not to come back."

Hally took a deep breath.

"Leave. Go to your home, where you came from. And don't come back," Hally ordered.

The Shadower slightly nodded, his eyes fixed on the ground, too scared to look at Hally's. Slowly it dissolved into ash, disappearing into the wind. The grass turned back to green.

"You can stop shaking now. It's gone" Blake said kindly to Hally.

"What just happened?" Hally faltered; she wasn't fighting the tears anymore.

"Let's discuss that inside, I think we had enough of outside for a day," Blake replied, behind him Treacher stared at her, studying her.

"Centuries ago, there was war," Blake started to say.

Hally looked at her half-eaten dinner. She would have thought that after a hot shower and having eaten a few bites she would calm herself a little... her body was still trembling.

Treacher was gone and Beira, Pepper and Bobby had done their best to calm them.

"When Platz was founded, Princess Dawn, the Princess of Woldiers, was tired of war. She believed that there were better solutions than spilling blood, so she forbade war in her kingdom and in the Woldier quadrant, as it was still considered her property. The other armies didn't take her seriously and to mock her decided that any fight was going to be taken in the Woldier quadrant harming pacifist soldiers just for the sake of it. As revenge, with the help of other Íroes, the princess arranged that no drop of blood could be spilled in her quadrant without consequences. If blood touches the ground of Two a shadow figure, called a Shadower, will come under the command of whose blood was spilled. If their master doesn't prove worthy, they'll be free to cause chaos all around."

The dining hall remained quiet.

"That's why we don't train in Two or near it. I must say I'm impressed at how you handled that Shadower Hally, a born commander. But please make this the last time we have to face one," Blake begged the kids. They didn't reply.

Beira cleared her throat.

"Changing the topic. Why don't you tell me what your favorite part of the day was?"

"I liked my solo training, I got to be as strong as an elephant," Ayala mumbled.

"And I liked mine too. I can turn on my powers on command now," Pam added.

"The problem is turning off," Lukai said as he prevented her third glass from falling through the table.

"I liked the wall, it proved how strong I am," Piet said with a wink, a soft laughter spread around the table.

"I believe that the wisest thing to do is not to let you play football until you get them under control," Isla said to Piet as she held an ice pack on her foot, she had kicked the ball when it had been turned into rock.

"What about you, Tom?" Blake asked.

Tom smiled at Blake, a soft half sad smile.

"Today might not have been my day, but I have high hopes for tomorrow," he answered.

"That's how you talk," Beira encouraged him. "Cheers, for tomorrow."

The kids picked up their glasses filled with strawberry juice.

"Cheers," they all repeated.

Hally listened closely, talking from time to time. Smiling when the others smiled and laughing when the others laughed. Nothing ever took away that awful sensation that something was behind her, watching her, waiting for the right moment.

That night there was no official No-sleep club meeting, in fact, after dinner, both Pam and Hally had gone to sleep. She had laid down ready to rest. One hour later she'd grabbed the lightest flashlight and headed downstairs to see if anyone was still up.

She was tired, no question, yet the fear kept her up.

Hally reached the stairs and smiled. The first floor reeked of cinnamon; Lukai was up.

She walked to the dining room and then to the kitchen, the Canadian freckled boy was moving inside, his apron on.

"Hi...," Hally said, slipping onto a stool.

"Couldn't sleep?" Lukai asked kindly.

"No... their powers are going crazy. Isla left the window open so there's a tree that's invading our room, growing with every breath she takes. Pam already made my bed sink twice and Ayala somehow snores and makes an awful ringing in my ears that no one else hears."

Lukai stared at her.

"And I thought I had it bad when your brother suddenly filled the air with static," he replied sarcastically. Hally laughed, laughing was way better than trembling.

"Hey. Do you know how to play chess?" she asked.

Lukai looked up from the oven.

"Not really," he said, a little bit ashamed.

"Do you want me to teach you?" A board game was all she needed to calm her mind. "I don't know about you but I'm sure Treacher will get creative if we don't play chess."

Lukai smiled.

"Would you do that? Would you teach me?"

"Sure."

His smile grew bigger.

"Do you have a board?"

Hally shook her head.

"There's one in the storage room, I remember seeing it yesterday," she said. "I can get it."

Lukai smiled.

"That would be awesome."

Hally got off the stool and walked a few steps before stopping at the sight of the tree's shadows.

Lukai came out of the kitchen.

"C'mon," he said with a smile. "We'll get it together." Without waiting for Hally's answer, he walked out.

The two of them moved through the trails, the moon shining up high. Hally couldn't stop from looking around. She knew the shadow thingies weren't going to come back unless she went spilling blond in Two, yet fear is not always logical. If you are angry or sad you can talk to someone, but if you are scared, you can be in the safest place in the world and still feel insecure and nothing will change that.

"What were you baking?" Hally asked, a conversation was way better than that overly creepy silence.

"Cinnamon rolls," Lukai said. "And an apple pie. In my house there are three people that are allergic to cinnamon, so I don't get the chance to bake those things back there.'

"Three?" Hally asked. "That's a lot of people."

"It is," Lukai assured her.

There was once again silence. As they came closer the shadows of the building grew.

"Well, I was impressed that this place, being as old as it is, didn't have any dark secrets. Now at least we know it. And considering this one only threatens you if you spill blood, I suppose it could be worse," Lukai jested.

"I suppose," Hally said quietly. "Although if you think about it, every place has their dark secrets, but we are so used to certain dark secrets that we don't see them as dark or secrets at all."

Lukai stared back at her.

"Sorry sometimes I talk like a boring grandma."

"Oh no, no at all," he replied. "I think you actually have a good point."

Hally answered with a small smile.

"You know what's weird? I didn't scratch my hand."

Lukai continued to stare at her confused.

Hally looked at her palm.

"When I fell, I hit my hand and it was red, but I didn't scratch it. There was no blood."

"Maybe it was a very small cut, or maybe it healed instantly, don't you do that?"

"I do..., but I didn't scratch it."

Lukai remained silent.

"I didn't scratch it, I know it. Whatever blood rose from the Shadower, it wasn't mine."

"It did follow you," Lukai argued.

"Because he felt what I was capable of doing."

Lukai turned his face to the glowing river beside them.

"You don't believe me."

"Yes, I do. I mean no… I mean- Who's blood could it have been?"

Hally's mind flooded with the image of Treacher standing at the very edge of the quadrants.

"I don't know."

They reached the storage room.

"I think it was over here," Hally said and looked into the boxes near the entrance. Lukai didn't stay by her side, instead went to the back of the room.

Hally ignored him and kept searching until she found it, a fancy and old wooden box.

"Found it," she announced proudly, and Lukai appeared from behind some boxes.

"So did I," he said, carrying a small plastic box with some headphones attached to it.

"What's that?" Hally asked.

"A walkman," Lukai answered as if it was obvious. "I saw it when we were over here yesterday. Pam mentioned you were complaining about some weird noises and today you said the same thing about Ayala's snoring. So, it got me thinking. Ayala is a Naturae, which means she has that singing dangerous voice thing. Maybe, Ayala is unintentionally doing that when she's sleeping and somehow, you're more sensitive to it. Just like Magisters are more sensitive to Unicorn Powder, maybe they are also more sensitive to Naturae's singing," he said almostlike a question. "You can use the headphones to drown the noise if you don't mind going to sleep with music..." He handed the walkman to Hally.

She looked at the old music cassette player.

"That's a good theory, I'll try it," she said with a smile. "I also found something." She handed Lukai the wooden box. "It's a little old but it should work for you to at least learn what every piece does."

"I have to warn you though, I'm terrible at chess," Hally admitted later

"You can't be worse than me," Lukai declared.

"Believe me, I'm an expert doing things that people tell me I can't," she said, and they shared a laugh.

Lukai took the wooden box and they started to walk back to Center. On the way he turned to her.

"I do believe you, Hally, the blood thing. I really do."

22

A HISTORY LESSON AND
A CHESS MATCH

Blake clapped.

"Ah!" Piet woke up with a scream.

Laughter went around.

"At least try to stay up," Blake asked.

Piet grumbled and threw himself against the sand.

"Can't we just lay down here and learn about clouds or something?" Ayala sobbed.

Blake stared at her; she already knew the answer.

"Ah," she sighed quietly, smashing the pile of sand she had been playing with before.

"What's with you today? We've barely had a day of training!"

"I vote for one day of training, two of rest," Hally proposed, knowing far too well that soon enough Treacher would arrive and despite her running aches, she would have to train. But hey! A girl can dream.

"Can't you see us?" Pam asked, her lower half was buried in the sand. "We need the vacations!"

Blake laughed.

"You know, when the first Íroes appeared, they were forced into slave labor or burnt at the bonfire."

Isla rolled her eyes along with an exasperated sigh.

"Why are we always hearing about the past and the first Íroes?"

"Learn from the mistakes of the past and you'll know the choices for the future."

"Dang it! A history lesson," Lukai exclaimed.

"Do you want another training session?" Blake asked.

"No sir, I will take history gladly," Lukai replied.

"Everybody just shut up, let him talk. I can't take another training session," Tom begged.

Blake smiled.

"No one really knows when the first Íroe appeared, just that there were few known by the Middle Ages. People used them as the most valuable coin, as an asset. The most noble of families held an Íroe and if they ever wished for power or money, that Íroe changed hands. But then, the king came, Queen Sila's father. Having been raised by an Íroe himself he showed a lot of interest in them and set out to find more. In one of his southern quests he found the Revelateur, a rock that glowed at the presence of Woldiers. He brought the rock back and planned to find all the Woldiers in his kingdom and protect them. Eventually his work blossomed, more Woldiers than ever were discovered. Then Naturaes, Bellators and Veteris, all through different methods. For years historians have tried to explain why or how suddenly there were many Íroes. Did they appear just by luck?" He paused. "You know what I believe?"

"We're like worms that come out with the rain?" Piet guessed.

"No…"

"What do you believe?" Hally asked.

"There weren't many Íroes to start with. There was one, one that was strong enough to shine on his own. Then another followed their example, and then another one, and another one. The courage they had spread like wildfire. All it takes is one, or in this case seven."

"What happened to them later? To those Íroes." Tom asked.

Blake's previous smile faded.

"They became greedy in their quest for power and riches. A dark war fell upon that kingdom, many lives were lost, and many more homes were destroyed. Many of the Íroes were poisoned by fear and ran away, and others were poisoned by the anger of revenge and lost their way. Some even forgot what they had been fighting for at the start. Most importantly, however, they didn't stick together. A big fire is spread by the wind, but a little one is extinguished by it."

Hally looked at the water moving around the small circle of dry sand she had covered with a shield.

"Blake," she called to him. "You said the past helps with the future. What's our future? I learn to move things with my mind and then... Then what?"

Blake nodded at the question as if it was a challenge he was willing to accept.

"There's a place where you might find the answer for that, an old castle I could take you to," he mumbled.

"I thought we shouldn't go out of Platz," Pam questioned.

"Mmm, this place shouldn't be in too much trouble. Is far, touristic, pretty..."

"Blake," Pepper calmed him from the top of the hill. "Mr. Treacher is here."

Hally looked at her face, Pepper didn't like Treacher, her despicable tone and narrow stares left it clear.

Do you think she feels the same thing as we do?

That bad feeling in our gut?

Yes.

Don't know, but she certainly feels something.

Hally looked at her palm, the red caused by the fall had been long gone. The shivering and the fear had decided to stay a little longer, uninvited.

It wasn't my blood.

"Hally, Lukai, seems after all you won't save yourselves from training."

Both of them moaned. The rest laughed at their expressions. They shared a look; the time had come.

Lukai was terrible at chess. Hally was actually impressed that someone could be so bad at it. Even after the whole night she spent explaining the basics he still confused the knight with the rook.

"Lukai, your move," Treacher reminded the boy, he had gone five minutes in silence staring at the board, occasionally looking at Hally for help.

"Mmmm," Lukai replied thoughtfully.

Treacher switched his weight from one leg to another.

Hally bit her tongue.

Common Lukai, do a stupid move already, I can't run.

"Done," the boy finally said.

"Your turn," Treacher hissed at her.

A shiver went down her spine, the memories of the Shadower fresher than ever.

You're making no sense, it wasn't him.

Why would it be him? What would he get from the Shadower?

"Move," Treacher ordered.

Hally gulped and looked at the board. She frowned.

"Discipline girl!" Treacher snapped. "He moved his knight to the left!"

As soon as the words escaped his mouth, he realized what he was saying. His eyes rose to Lukai.

"Lukai, it is not chess that you're playing," he replied.

Lukai's face paled even more than before.

"Who taught you how to play?"

Hally looked at him.

Better start stretching, it seems we'll be running the rest of the day.

"Well... umm... I didn't really have the most experienced teacher," he lied.

"Maybe you weren't the right student," Hally argued. "Who knows?"

Treacher massaged his temples.

"Discipline, it is what you're supposed to learn! Not faking and cheating!" he moved his hand to snap the knight Lukai had just placed, the figure went right through him.

Treacher froze. Hally and Lukai locked eyes.

"You made an illusion!"

"I made an illusion."

"YOU MADE AN ILLUSION!" Hally exclaimed; the kids shared a cheer until Treacher managed to quiet them down again.

"Does this mean no running?" Hally asked.

Treacher moved his head from one side to another.

"Boy managed to learn from chess, Hally must learn as well."

"But I'm all taught, see," she moved one of her pawns, "discipline."

Treacher grabbed the pawn she had just moved and threw it at her face.

She covered her face with her arms and the heavy chess piece bounced from an invisible wall into the ground without touching her.

"Hey!" Lukai complained.

"Moving things require patience, attention, dedication, serenity and steadiness. Shields require firmness, strength, aim and discipline. Do you still think you have what it takes?" he asked as he picked up another chess piece.

The question almost sounded like a challenge: 'Prove little girl that you're worth powers'.

Hally remembered Blake's warning before the first training.

"Treacher is an expert with Magisters, he has studied all the writings of Queen Sila and all the myths that came after. He might be what we call-"

"Obsessed?" Hally had asked.

"A fanatic," Blake had corrected her. "Just make sure he still remembers you're a kid, not an experiment."

At the time it had seemed a senseless warning, how obsessed could he be? But now that he stood there, daring to hit her just to see what her limit was, the warning seemed barely enough.

She looked at the pair of blue eyes, waiting for an answer.

"Go ahead," she accepted the challenge.

Lukai jumped out of his chair between Treacher and her.

"You're not about to throw those things at her! They're metal, heavy metal."

Treacher looked over Lukai's shoulder, waiting for Hally to speak.

Hally stood up.

"It's okay Lukai, they're not reaching me."

Lukai turned to her, real worry moving through his caring eyes.

"It's okay," Hally reassured him.

He nodded and stepped away.

Treacher stared at Hally, Hally stared back at him. She wasn't the weak little girl he thought he was playing.

A wicked smile curled up at the sides of his mouth.

"Eyes closed," he asked as he picked more pieces off the board.

You can't be serious.

Hally closed her eyes.

"Hally!" Lukai exclaimed.

The first hit came before she expected it. She opened her eyes, the piece froze less than a finger from her face.

"Eyes closed," Treacher reminded her, Hally could almost swear his accent was disappearing.

She looked at Lukai to her left, he had one foot in front of the other, ready to intervene whenever she asked.

She closed her eyes again.

The second piece came, directly at her stomach. This time she didn't even bother keeping it in the air. The knight bounced from the shield and fell on the the grass. Then came another one, and another one. Each of them bounced back. Then came two at the same time.

Hally let out a small chuckle as she heard them hit the ground, her senses were stronger and faster than whatever Treacher had imagined.

Treacher must haven't liked the chuckle, because then came one more, stronger than before, bigger, faster.

Hally gasped and opened her eyes. Far from herself, a millimeter away from Lukai's nose, was the piece. Lukai's fearful eyes looked at her, the piece had taken him as much of a surprise as Hally. Still, she had won. The white king fell to the ground joining the rest of the pieces.

Treacher smiled at her, whether he was amused or entertained was impossible to know.

"No more running?" Hally asked.

Treacher pulled out his index finger.

"Just one more exercise, indulge me," the accent was back on.

Hally had to keep herself from rolling her eyes.

What does this señor want to prove?

"Fine."

Treacher nodded and left them for a minute.

"This is getting out of control. Do you want me to call Blake?" Lukai asked.

"It got out of control since the Shadower, Lu..." Hally corrected him. "Face them, show them, beat them."

"Mom advice?"

"Life lesson."

When Treacher came back Hally was surprised. She hadn't really expected anything, but she certainly didn't expect a watermelon.

He placed the watermelon where the board had been.

"Watermelon has seeds. Find them."

Hally looked at the fruit and pointed at it.

"They're there, inside."

Treacher grumbled.

"With powers."

Hally looked again at the fruit.

'Indulge me', next time I'm going to punch you.

"What's next?" Hally asked.

"Pull them out."

Sure, let's destroy the watermelon.

Hally focused on the small weight of the seeds inside the watermelon, they were easy to find, to feel, and even easier to move. The watermelon made a ripping sound as hundreds of seeds burst from inside.

Treacher looked at the seeds in his hands, there were too many for him to hold. He then stared at the leftover pieces of watermelon at the table, the juice was streaming down to the grass, pieces of the green peel covered the chess table, and the watermelon was so destroyed that it was no longer recognizable.

The same evil smile curled up from the Russian's mouth.

A dreadful feeling filled Hally. Why did she feel like she had just walked into a trap, a horrible trap?

"You're dismissed, there will be no running today."

As Lukai and Hally were a few steps away Treacher called them.

"Has Blake already given his past and future seminar?" he asked almost in a mocking way.

"He did today," Lukai answered. "He said he's taking us to an old castle to finish up the lesson."

"Tell him not to bother," Treacher replied. "I already know your future." He looked at Lukai. "You're a tool. And you," he turned to Hally, "you're a weapon."

Blake caught up with Hally just after he took Treacher home, there was only one way in and out of Platz, and only Blake knewit. He had taken a whole five minutes to explain about the rare existence of a traveling powder called Wisatawan powder, capable of taking anyone anywhere as long as they knew the place.

"Hally!" he called.

Hally stopped walking, she had managed to wash the watermelon out of her hair, and she was on the way to the beach, where, by the screams, she knew already that Pam and Isla awaited her. Ayala on the other hand, had excused herself with Lukai as the boys were planning revenge against a cricket that hadn't let them sleep.

Blake stopped in front of her and leaned on his knees to take a breath, he was a mess. His clothes needed to be straightened out, his hair could use a brush and his hands glowed with a mysterious substance.

"Sorry," he apologized. "Watermelon mess in the dining hall."

A sudden blush covered her cheeks.

"That might have been us in training. Well, me."

"Ahhh I see," he nodded. "A masterpiece by yin and yang."

Hally frowned.

"What?"

"Oh it's nothing, just what Pepper calls you two. You know, because of the balance... and the power... Never mind," he gave up. "Tomorrow, we're going on a field trip."

Hally couldn't help a shiver down her back and glancing at the scar on her right arm.

Pull yourself together, they aren't here.

Blake followed her glance.

"It'll be alright," he calmed her. "It's been quite a few days. Most people have already lost trace of you, or they are looking for you on the other side of the world. We'll be careful."

She swallowed her fear, and the shiver went away. She straightened her back and raised her chin.

"Fine," she managed to say with a smile.

"Is it Treacher?" Blake asked back.

"What?"

"You both, Lukai and you, have this look. I see it in you, and I saw it before, when Lukai passed by with Piet and Tom running from Ayala."

Hally chuckled at the idea of the three boys running.

"Did you manage to know what happened with the cricket?"

Blake laughed.

"Well, it's them three against one cricket and Ayala."

Hally nodded.

"I'll tell Pam, they might need a fourth."

"Or a fifth."

They laughed, Hally appreciated it, laughter was always the best medicine.

She grabbed her rips and wiped off the one tear falling down her cheek.

Blake gave her a second to get herself together.

"Is it Treacher?" he insisted.

Hally smacked her lips together.

"It's not him. I mean it is him but he's … I don't know if the right word would be bedevil." She shook her head and sighed. "He's a bad vibe, that's it."

Blake looked baffled.

"I didn't take you as a 'vibes' person."

Hally let out a sigh and let her hands fall down her sides.

"I'm really not, but the situation calls for it. He's…," she thought of a better expression, "a bad vibe." There wasn't one.

"Did he say something?"

She nodded.

"What did he say?"

Hally played with her new silver ring she had been given at the ceremony, now a permanent part of her.

"Yesterday he said I was powerful, but without discipline I was just chaotic. And today he said we didn't have to bother about searching for our future because he already knew it."

"What did old Treacher say?" Blake asked, almost challenging the answer to be a bad one.

"He told Lu that he was a tool."

She paused.

"And you?"

"That I was a weapon," she finally said, a little weight off her shoulders disappeared with the word.

Blake stood in silence as his eyes revealed his brain studying the words.

"Am I a weapon? Elowen tried making me one. Clearing up my mind into an empty one to be played with. And now Treacher says this, and he seems so sure of himself that I can't help but think if it's real. Is this what I have become? Or what I will become? Nothing more than something to be moved and controlled?"

She fought the tears back; she didn't want to be a weapon. A weapon had no mind but brought only violence. The weapon was as filled with blood as the hands that willed it. And a weapon didn't rest, didn't bring peace, only more pain.

"Yes," Blake finally answered. "You're a weapon and you're dangerous."

That's not helping.

"You speak your mind, you stand your ground, and you fight for your values. If that makes you swim against the current, you do it. If that's what it takes to stand against a crowd and scream your lungs out, you do it. Because you're that type of person, the type that is capable of things. However magical or mythical all this looks like, this is still the twenty-first century Hally. Out there, and in here, the world is still moved by people with power and money. Money they all made by stealing, cheating or bringing temporary solutions to the same problems they create. The real world is an infinite web of people covering each other's back to acquire more by doing wrong. And that's a problem, a problem capable people like you can and will fight to fix. So, yes, you're dangerous and you're a weapon, to everyone out there that stands against you, against your values. And there's nothing wrong with that."

A small proud smile showed up on Hally's face, what if Blake was right?

"Blake," Beira called him from Center, it sounded urgent.

Blake looked back and then to Hally.

"It's alright, go on," Hally replied.

"Not until you tell me you understand what I said."

"I understand, and thanks." He would never have an idea of the impact those wise words had.

Blake smiled and gave her a hug, a gentle, warming, fatherly hug.

"And I'll talk to Treacher, try to keep him at least to hide his bad vibe. He might be the best expert out there, but that doesn't give him the benefit of acting like a jerk."

He turned one more time.

"You have been doing great Hally, keep going."

The beach was the perfect place for that afternoon. The wave's white foam reached the sand leaving sights of colorful seashells. The sun, placed near the horizon, painted the sky a golden color.

Hally breathed in the fresh sea air, if there was ever a smell that she could call home, this one was it. She played with the soft warm sand beneath her palms and between her bare feet. With her eyes closed she could almost sense it as she fell asleep.

"What do you think?" Pam asked.

Hally opened her eyes and sat up. She looked at the white canvas Pam was showing her and then at the great model behind it, Bobby. His shiny eyes glowed with the sun and his bright smile shone along with the yellow shirt he had insisted on wearing for Pam's portrait.

"I don't know Pam, you're still not capturing his adorableness," Hally joked.

Bobby's eyes filled with pride.

"Beira says I'm too adorable, maybe that's it."

Pam glared at them and turned the canvas around.

The shiny pair of dark eyes opened, so big that they were suddenly double their normal size.

In a single movement Bobby was on his feet jumping up and down.

"I love it! I love it!" he cheered over and over again.

"Shhhhh, you're getting sand everywhere," Isla calmed him down, and moved a little to her left, just in the perfect position for her green choker to shine with the sun.

"I love your choker," Hally said, even after how things had ended the way they had with the Guarders, in an unspoken agreement all the kids had decided to keep their objects. Hally wore her silver ring, Tom's pin always shone on his chest, Piet lived with his two permanent bracelets and even Pam, who wasn't someone that struck Hally as a jewelry person, wore her golden earring every day.

Isla played with her choker.

"I love it too, it's so minimalistic and at the same time elegant. I can wear it with everything! It reminds me of a story that my mom used to tell."

"I love stories!" Bobby exhilarated.

Isla laughed.

"It was actually more of a song," she cleared her throat and sang.

Before the first note finished, the wretched sound reached their ears, searing its way into their brains. Pam and Hally covered their ears.

"Please, no singing," Pam asked. Isla stopped.

"Pardon me... I know it. With my talent, I always kill it."

There was an awkward silence before Hally let out a laugh.

"Are you alright?" she asked Isla. "You just made a joke."

Pam bursted out laughing at Isla's reaction, and Bobby joined her.

Isla frowned at them and let out another high-pitched note.

"Okay okay, no more bullying," Hally apologized with her hands on her ears.

Isla stopped.

"Thanks, I already have enough with Ayala's snoring."

"Ayala's snoring?" Pam exclaimed. "What about your eighties rock and roll playlist? How can you sleep listening to that?"

"Like a beautiful, chubby baby," Hally replied.

The boys arrived, the three of them looked tired, messy, sweaty and absolutely beaten.

Tom and Lukai let their bodies fall into the sand. Piet on the other hand, gently touched the sand and turned it into a little rock for him to sit on.

"Royalty much," Pam exclaimed.

"What?" Piet asked back. "I have to keep the sand off my hair, the ladies don't like sandy hair."

"They don't?" Bobby asked.

"They don't."

"What girls are you talking about? We're the only ones here!" Pam exclaimed.

Piet smiled.

"You never know," he turned to Isla and winked.

Isla rolled her eyes.

"I don't date babies."

"I'M NOT A BABY!"

"How did the cricket situation end?" Hally asked minutes later.

The boys groaned.

"Damn cricket," Tom muttered. "That six-legged creature is costing me more brain cells than calculus."

"We wanted to kill it but Ayala insisted on taking it elsewhere, away from us," Lukai explained.

"I promise you, if that thing shows up again, or anyone related to him. I'm going to smash it, slowly," Tom threatened. "And then, I'm going to sleep."

"Like this," Lukai looked at the sand where a cricket appeared and he smashed it.

"Hey, those illusions are getting better!" Hally applauded.

Lukai lifted up his hand, a small real looking brown insect was looking up.

"I know!" he cheered back.

"Maybe you can make me look taller," Piet proposed.

Lukai looked at him.

"I don't know…"

"You should ask for parental permission before you do it," Hally suggested.

"I'M OLD ENOUGH!" the blond boy cried.

Hally and Lukai shared a high five.

Bobby joined them.

"Yin and yang," he mumbled between laughs.

"Oh no, not you too!" Hally exclaimed.

"Who are yin and yang?" Tom asked.

"Apparently that's what Pepper's calling us, Lukai and I. Something to do with balancing our powers or something."

Lukai chuckled.

"Are you serious?"

"That's what Blake said. Can you imagine? Hi, I'm yin."

"And I'm yang," Lukai concluded.

"Oh please don't, it sounds like a fricking kids show," Pam growled.

"Language!" Isla barked back.

"I didn't say anything wrong! I used FRICKING!"

"Fricking," Bobby copied. "I like that word."

23

THE FIELD TRIP

Wherever Ayala took the cricket it wasn't far enough.

Tom turned to his side, wrapping the pillow against his ear, drowning out the sound.

"Cri."

He tightened the pillow, sticking his recently washed hair against his forehead. Tomorrow would be a very bad hair day.

"Cri."

"That's it, I'm done," Piet exclaimed. He jumped out of bed directly to the corner where the sound had come from.

Tom sat up at the sound of books hitting the ground.

"Where are you!" Piet exclaimed.

"Cri," at least the cricket had the decency to answer.

"Damn you thing, I'm going to-" a book flew through the air into Lukai's head with a dull thud as it hit.

"Hey!" Lukai complained as he too jumped out of his bed, one hand pressed against the back of his head.

"Cri."

Another book flew by, this time Lukai was fast enough to duck for it, not fast enough to stop him from bringing all the other books off the desk to the floor.

"Hey!" he complained again.

"I'm trying to find the thing," Piet explained.

"You can't even see it," Tom replied. He stood up and placed his palm against the wall, instantly the light turned on.

Piet squinted at the light and returned to his search, making more of a mess.

Tom took a few steps closer, staying far enough to avoid the flying books and shoes.

"What exactly is your plan when you find it? Ask it to leave?"

"Or are you going to crush it?"

Piet froze and turned to Lukai, his eyes opened as big as plates.

"Shut up," he shouted, and he looked at the door as if

expecting someone to barge in because of the comment. "You can't say that. What if Ayala hears you?"

Tom chuckled.

"You're scared of Ayala?"

Piet took a second look at the door before turning at Tom.

"She growled at me! A deep real lion growl!"

"Cri."

"She's not going to do anything, she's the sweetest girl," Lukai said. "Just growl back."

Piet shook his head. "It's not the same."

Tom looked at him.

"I guess you're right. Maybe in a few years when you get your man's voice."

"I HAVE A MAN'S VOICE!" Piet was suddenly aware of his squeaky sound. "Well, maybe not a man's man's voice, but a man's voice," he explained.

"Cri."

"Shut up!"

"You can even talk with the cricket," Lukai replied.

Before the kid snapped back, Tom placed a hand on his shoulder.

"Don't worry, in a few years it will come."

"A few years? What the heck are you talking about? I'M NOT THAT YOUNG!"

"Cri," the cricket added to the conversations.

The boys turned to the sound; this time stronger. The brown, dark-eyed creature was looking at them, mocking their futility to catch it.

"Cri."

"Nobody move," Piet whispered. He slowly stood up.

"Cri," the cricket replied as a farewell and jumped out of the window into the darkness of the night.

"No!" Piet ran to the window and poked his head. "I will find you!" he screamed.

He turned to see his blankets on the floor, the clothes Beira had gotten and neatly organized spread throughout the room, shoes and socks hanging from the lamps and books laying on the beds. "Did I make this mess?"

"Yes!" Lukai and Tom replied at the same time.

Minutes later, when Piet was 'taking a break' from cleaning, Lukai had finally picked up all the books, and Tom had finished with the clothes, he grabbed the chair from his desk and sat, the sleep was long gone.

Tom moved his hand across the desk, he could feel the electricity gently playing in his fingers, asking where he wanted it to go. He touched the lamp, and it turned on, brighter than ever. Tom smiled, he was getting better at this.

On the other side of the room Piet was staring at him.

"I wonder-"

"Oh no," Lukai replied from his bed. "I have four siblings. It never ends well when one of them starts a sentence like that."

"You're going to like this one," Piet promised. "Tom calls the electricity. You control the light. What would happen if Tom brought electricity to a light bulb, and you stopped the light from appearing?"

Lukai looked up at Piet, a spark of curiosity shining in his eye. He turned at Tom, Tom smiled.

"I got the bulb."

Tom took a bulb from one of the lamps and placed it in the center of the room, where Piet had already moved all the clothes.

The three of them sat around it, admiring it closely.

"Isn't this dangerous?" Piet asked.

"It was your idea!" Tom protested.

"Dangerous, interesting. Potatoe, potato," Lukai smirked.

"Fine."

Tom looked at the light bulb, he could feel the electricity moving through the floor, as if it was trying to speak to him in a language only he could understand. He placed his hand on the floor, the light bulb lit up.

Lukai lifted up his hand on the other side, the light dimmed.

Tom pushed more electricity. Lukai tensed his hands. The light flickered. Just a little bit more electricity.

Blap!

Piet jumped in his place. There was no more light.

Tom looked at the bulb, where light had once shone, there was nothing more than broken pieces and black stains. A small tail of smoke coming from it.

"That was awesome!" Piet gasped. "I can only do this." He touched a book near by his foot, nothing happened. He lifted the hand and touched it again, this time the book turned into a shiny silver rock.

Tom and Lukai laughed when he struggled to turn it back.

"It doesn't matter," Piet continued. "Because I still have my charming ways."

"Charming ways?" Tom asked. "What charming ways?"

Piet pointed at himself.

"This, of course."

Tom and Lukai laughed again.

"Hey I can charm anyone," Piet continued.

"Who would you even charm?" Lukai asked.

"Anyone. I could charm Isla or Hally."

Tom's smile disappeared.

"No one's charming Hally," he threatened.

Piet's color dropped; his eyes opened wide.

"I-I totally forgot she's your sister," he babbled. "Sorry, definitely not happening."

Tom glared at him.

"Good.

"Are you sure you don't want me to go?" Beira asked Blake the next morning.

Tom fixed the bag on his back. He had insisted on taking one for a water bottle and a sweater, soon it had become a communal bag.

"Stop moving!" Hally snapped.

Tom rearranged the bag.

This time a slap hit the back of his head.

"I said stop moving."

"What are you smuggling?"

"Band Aids, sunblock, socks, bandages, insect repellent. The important stuff."

Tom mumbled something under his breath.

"Blake already has that in his own bag."

"But two is better than one."

"Ehh-"

Another slap came.

"Sun block?"

Tom sighed.

"Yes."

Blake called for attention.

"I don't think I have to explain to you why you must not use your powers outside of Platz, in any case," he muttered, he was having a hard time getting the first aid kit inside his backpack. "That's the first rule. Second, always stay with the group, never wander off. I would have a heart attack if I lost one of you. It hasn't even been a week!" Finally the backpack closed. "And third. This is still the real world guys, and even though you're being looked for in America and not the European side, if you see any weird activity, any one gets close to talk to you or anything, you say something. Understood?"

"Yes," the kids agreed, three rules, not that hard.

Tom couldn't keep the emotion from rising. He had never been to Europe. And a field trip? His powers were working, his fear of water was declining and now they had a field trip? It was the best he could have asked. Maybe after all, life wasn't that hard, you just have to survive enough storms to see the rainbow.

Hally squeezed his hand gently.

"Europe," her eyes shone with the word. "We're going to Europe."

Tom chuckled. "I wonder what May would say?"

A deep realization sunk in. How long had it been since he had spoken to his older sister? A week? No it had to be longer. A month? What was she doing? Did she have any idea that they were no longer with their parents? Was she safe?

As if his thoughts had escaped his mind Hally turned to him.

"She's fine, we'll see if we can call her when we get back," she whispered.

Tom nodded, Hally had always been the one to carry the family weight and he was the one with the knowledge weight. It has always been like that, in balance. Hally made sure the family didn't shift away too badly and he made sure to find enough knowledge to keep them safe. But then again, he had never been able to find any knowledge and Hally had always worked, remembering every one of their birthdays, doing the jobs they didn't want to keep the peace, calling May every day, congratulating their mom, and even enduring conversations with their dad that she wasn't remotely interested in, just to make him feel better. Even then, with the sunblock, she might have been extremely irritating, but she still took care of him, she was still his little sis. And he hadn't been bothered with it ever, but now he couldn't stop. How different would it have been without her?

He gave her a one arm tight squeeze around her shoulders

Hally looked at him strangely.

"You stuck something in my back, didn't you?"

She looked over her shoulder and tapped her shirt to trying to find the note.

"I didn't do it. I'm just happy we're here together," he smiled.

"Oh stop your hallmark monologue, it came in the package instructions, there wasn't any choice," she muttered, but he could see a smile forming as she turned her head.

The kids surrounded Blake with a potato shaped circle and watched him closely as he took a jar with a white powder, similar to Unicorn Powder, from his backpack. They had all heard the explanation a couple of nights before, when Piet had asked how their kidnappers had been able to get them all in a few hours.

"This is called Wisatawan powder," Blake had explained. "It is extremely rare nowadays, they probably just had a jar and used it all. It comes from the flowers of Micro Dentro, which is the tree brother of Megalo Dentro, it has never been seen in centuries."

Tom watched as Blake poured some in his hand and threw the powder into the ground. As it touched the grass, the ground seemed to melt like ice cream. The kids and Blake were sucked into it and disappeared.

For a moment Tom didn't know where the heck he was. Everything was so crowded and dark. Then a light came. He was standing in the middle of the living room of an old camping cabin. A cold wintery smell reached his nose, a chill came over his arms.

He looked around, there were old paintings hanging on the walls, a couch covered with a white bag and lots of dust. The cabin didn't appear to be used, yet it didn't look like it was completely abandoned either.

Tom's attention was brought back to the real world by the sound of Piet throwing up.

"Take a seat if you feel like you need it," Blake said, holding the trash can for the blond boy. "First time travel with the Wisatawan powder can be really messy for your stomach."

Tom sat even though he was alright. He looked at Hally, her hands were shaking, her forehead sweating, and her skin was pale. She took a sip of water.

"Whoever invented this is evil," she murmured before taking another sip of water and noticeably fighting to keep her breakfast where it belonged.

After Piet had thrown up more food than he could have eaten in a whole day and Isla recovered a little bit of balance, they were ready to start the adventure.

"I thought we were going to a castle. There's nothing but forest out there!" Pam exclaimed as if she had been scammed, face pressed against the dirty window.

"We're not staying here. This is merely one of Platz's safe-houses. We are going to the nearby town, a very touristy town. We're going through the forest over there to the ruins of a castle," Blake explained.

"Wait, we are walking?" Isla asked.

"Yes."

Her jaw dropped to the ground.

"I didn't bring my walking shoes," Isla let out.

They indeed walked, and walked, and kept walking along the street, cars passing by, leaving nothing more than a rush of wind in their faces. But they weren't the only ones walking.

"Where are all these people going?" Tom asked Blake. At the other side of the street, he could see the third family that walked, their children by their hands, nothing more than a bag on their backs.

"They're moving to the military city that just opened nearby, they offer protection from the Superiors," Blake replied.

"Are they really going to be safe there?" Tom questioned.

"As long as they don't question what the soldiers say."

The town of Bled, Slovenia, was a beautiful town and that's saying little. The reason why it was a well-known place for tourism didn't have to be clarified. The blue clear water of the river nearby was enough to impress the most bitter critic. The superb color filled architecture of the houses and build-ings were breathtaking. And the refreshing green mountains that lay behind formed the perfect picture for a painter.

Blake took the kids directly into the middle plaza to freshen up, by the souvenir shop. And, after looking at their amazed faces, he allowed them to get anything they wished, he would pay for everything they wanted.

Acting as mature as decent kids they didn't go crazy with shopping. Most of them, like Piet, Pam, and Isla, simply got a snack and some water. Ayala got Bobby some candy. Lukai got some traditional snacks from Slovenia to try later and some traditional recipes magazines. Hally got herself a deck of poker cards with pictures of Bled and the mountains on them. And Tom got himself a bottle of water and a bag of cookies.

When Tom was done, he stepped out of the shop and sat beside Blake and Hally.

"Hey," Blake said after a while, "I'll go make sure these kids don't get in trouble, would you keep an eye out so that none of them leave the plaza?"

"Sure," Hally said, and Blake walked to a nearby store where Pam and Piet were having a discussion about whether the Slovenian soccer team was going to win the match on tv.

Blake hadn't entered the shop when a man got close to them.

"Help," he asked in broken English, putting a can with a charity foundation name and picture in front of them.

"Sorry," Tom replied. "We don't have anything," he said, tapping his pockets.

The figure glared at him, he wasn't looking at Tom, he was looking at the corner of his golden pin. Tom zipped up his sweater and stood up to keep the man from looking at Hally's silver ring.

"Sorry mate, we don't have anything," he repeated.

The man looked at him, his eyes as clear as the sky, as if considering a million possibilities. Then he turned around, leaving them.

"What was that about?" Hally asked.

"I don't know," Tom took his seat back. "He kept looking at my pin."

Hally shrugged.

"It looks like real gold, maybe he was wondering how you can wear that and not have a spare coin."

Shopping done and the soccer game finished (with a tie) they all finally met in the fountain and set course for the mountain despite Isla's complaints.

"Sorry, the mountain is closed," were the words that silenced the whole group and drew their attention to the guy at the entrance.

Tom's heart sank.

"Excuse me?" Blake asked, confused.

"You heard me well, sir. The mountain is closed, you have to leave," the guy spoke in a despicable way, as if Blake had wronged him, and kept looking back at the kids.

"The schedule says that the mountain is open for tourists until seven o'clock."

"Look sir," the guy said wearily and rolled up his sleeves as if he was ready to fight. "It. Is. Not. Open. Now leave."

A figure behind the entrance caught Tom's attention, it was the same man of the plaza, the one with the charity can. He was pointing at them while talking with uniformed officers. The officers kept looking at them, up and down. No. They weren't looking at the kids, they were looking at Piet's bracelets, Ayala's necklace, Hally's ring... Sure, the jewelry looked expensive, but it didn't really stand out unless someone was looking for it. Did the tin-can man think they had stolen it?

"Kids let's go," Blake said and got out of the line, turning back to the town.

"But-"

"Let's go, now," Blake squashed Pam's comment.

Keeping most of their complaints to themselves, they matched Blake's fast pace.

"Did he not let us in because we are foreigners?" Hally asked quietly, when they were far enough away.

Blake looked at her, there was some caution in his eyes.

"I'm not sure, but it can't be good," Blake said in the same way. "Look at his wrist."

Tom turned discreetly and looked at the guy he was talking to, with a smile on his face, to the people that had been behind them in the line. There, on his right wrist, there was a white bracelet with golden straps, a bracelet he had never seen.

"The Superiors," Hally let out under her breath. "But that's the bracelet of the northern Superiors, of America. What are they doing here?"

"I don't know," Blake replied as if the words singed his tongue, he stopped walking. "Everybody come close."

The kids made a really tight circle and looked at Blake.

"I need you to be honest with me, has anyone used their powers?"

There was silence.

"What if he's only one of those extremist Superiors that hate everybody, especially foreigners?" Hally asked when the silence had answered Blake's question,

"I don't think so, look at the line," Lukai argued.

In the line there was every kind of person and the same guy that had made them go away was treating them nicely and decently.

"I don't know what to say. Whether it's because of your ethnicities or because they suspect you are the Íroes we must leave here, now. Better safe than sorry Beira would say," Blake said, his preoccupied tone kept the kids from complaining and made them walk behind him, faster, and without looking round. The field trip had turned into a dangerous situation.

They hadn't crossed two streets before the first cloaked figure started to follow them, white bracelet showing on their wrist. Then another came, and another and even more.

"Left," Blake whispered, he was trying to lose the figures.

The kids followed him rapidly, the figures were obviously trying to keep their distance not to get caught.

In the corner they gave a quick turn and started to walk faster.

Blake had called an old friend, there was a car waiting for them just outside the town, there they would be absolutely safe.

"Over here," he said and made a right turn, they were now between walking and running. "Oh no," Blake let out, in front there were other four figures. "Back where we came from," he changed his mind and the eight of them walked back, now they were being followed by seven and they were nowhere near leaving the town.

"Why don't you call the car over?" Tom asked Blake as they walked.

"There is a group of Superiors that's not letting any cars inside."

"And why don't you use the Wisatawan powder?" Hally asked.

"Because right now you're only suspects, if they see us using the Wisatawan powders your faces will be known in every corner of the world and even if you wanted to go back to your normal lives the Superiors would never allow it," Blake said

They went down a new street and started to run, really run now.

Tom looked back; the figures had lost all interest in disguising their intentions.

A right turn, a left turn, two streets, another right turn, another left and another right turn. The figures continued to appear wherever they went, each time more and more.

Maybe they stood a chance, maybe they had a real slim chance to get out of that town without facing the Superiors.

As I said, maybe they stood a chance, a chance that was gone the second they walked into an alley. They were surrounded, trapped.

Blake looked at them, for the first-time fear covered his face.

"Kids get behind Hally, Hally get behind me. If anything goes wrong you create a shield and protect them," Blake said to Hally, she didn't even question the fact that she had never, ever created a shield that big.

Tom stood one step in front of everyone, almost by Hally's side, he wasn't leaving her alone.

The figures, now more than ten of them, stopped at the entry to the alley and stared at them in the shadows of their cloaks, their creepy purple cloaks, not moving. Then one more figure appeared, a smaller figure with their cloak hanging around their shoulders.

The figure walked into the light revealing her face. She must have been near her fifties, with crooked teeth and evil eyes. She looked at Blake.

"I heard rumors. Never thought the filthy creatures were going to show up in my backyard," she spoke with a northern accent, Hally was right, they were from America. Lukai clenched his fists, straightened his back beside him. Tom knew this look from Hally's face, this wasn't the first time he was facing them. "They do things differently here, but not us. My people will be happy seeing all the Íroes in cages, defeated, waiting for their deaths," the lady spoke, she had a snake-like voice and as she pronounced Íroes she made sure to spit as much as possible.

"What?" Blake asked, he didn't know anything, at least he had to act that way.

"Skip the act, we know everything about Íroes."

"The... the what? I have no idea what you're talking about?"

The woman scoffed.

"Then why did you run?"

"Because I have heard my own fair share of rumors, I know

what your group does to people, and I know that even some police stations are involved."

The woman laughed and turned to a guy behind her who handed her a jar with white powder, this one Tom recognized, Unicorn Powder.

"Then you'll have no problem with this," she said and threw the powder into the air.

For a moment Tom wanted to laugh, that wasn't how the powder was used.

And then he remembered Blake's words: Magisters have a connection with Unicorn Powder, it is very sensitive to them. As he realized his heart sank and he looked at Hally's arms. The powder that had reached her was floating around her, dancing like dandelions in the air.

"No..."

The woman laughed as she looked at Hally.

"Get them!" she ordered.

Blake took out a small marble from his pocket and smashed it to the ground, a cloud of smoke surrounded them.

He turned to the kids. They couldn't leave the alley the same way they had entered.

"Quickly, climb," Blake said, pulling ladders at either side of the alley. The kids started to climb, some on the right building and others on the left building. They didn't have much time. When Tom made sure Hally was climbing, he went to the other side and climbed the ladder.

Once on the roof the smoke disappeared, and the purple cloaks started to look for them. Eventually they started to climb.

"What do we do now?" Hally asked. Tom looked at her. She, Pam, Piet and Lukai were on one roof. Blake, Ayala, Isla and he were on another. Tom walked to the edge, the jump was too far, there was no way to cross over.

"We can't leave them!" Tom exclaimed.

Blake placed his hand on his shoulder.

"Nobody is being left behind," he said.

Blake looked over at the stairs, they were getting closer.

"Look at me, Hally!" Blake exclaimed from the other building "Take this," he said and threw his backpack over.

The backpack barely made it, with Pam's help Hally grabbed it.

"Take the Wisatawan powder and go back to Platz, I'll take this group to the cabin and from there we'll travel back. We'll meet you there. If anything goes wrong, don't trust anyone, once the news gets out to the Superiors' media they'll know your faces."

"Are you sure you will be alright?" Hally asked Blake, looking at Tom.

Tom nodded, reassuring her.

"Yes," Blake said. "And Hally... trust your instincts and protect them."

Hally turned to the backpack Blake had thrown and grabbed the white jar. She poured some in her hand and looked over. A few more steps and one of the figures was going to get to the roof.

Tom took another look at the alley, he wanted to jump so badly, he couldn't leave her alone. He couldn't do it.

Hally gave a quick look at Tom on the other roof. She smiled at him. He smiled back, their way of saying see you later.

"See you in a couple of hours Tommy," that's what her eyes read.

The first purple cloak stepped on the roof. Hally threw the powder to the floor, and they disappeared. They were no longer on a field trip.

24

WHEREVER IT IS,
IT'S DEFINITELY NOT PLATZ

This isn't Platz.

That's the only thing Hally managed to think before her stomach claimed all her attention. She lost all her balance, the food tried to make its way to her throat, her legs gave in, her head spun. Blake made it look so easy; she would've never guessed a portal would take so much energy.

"Where are we?" Lukai asked quietly.

Hally forced herself to stand back and wiped the few drops of blood that fell from her nose.

"I have no idea," she replied the same way.

The whole place was pitch black except for the 'emergency' lights that glowed on the floor. It reminded Hally of the corridor of an airplane at night.

"What do you mean you don't know where we are? You brought us here!" Pam exclaimed.

A sound came from afar.

"Shhh," the others turned to Pam.

Pam growled quietly, Hally didn't have to see her to know that she had rolled her eyes.

At that moment Hally felt something, a tingle at the nape of her neck.

"Someone is coming," Hally whispered. They all looked around.

"I can't see shi-"

"Shih tzu. We have to keep it PG for the baby over there," Hally interrupted Pam and remembered the backpack Blake had given her. "Wait, I think I saw Blake pack a torch," she said.

"A flashlight," Lukai corrected.

"Whatever," Hally replied. She put the backpack on the ground and started looking for it, there were indeed a million things in there.

"Why do you need a flashlight? Can't Lukai call light?" Piet asked.

Hally sighed.

I'm so stupid.

She stood up just as Lukai let off a gentle warm light from his hand.

"We're in some kind of maze," the Canadian said, looking at the wall. "It looks like the laser tag back at home."

Whatever was getting close came closer, Hally felt it. It was heavy weighted, a figure. A man.

She grabbed Lukai's hand and pointed the light at the figure.

"Ahhh!" Piet exclaimed when the light showed the face of a really angry guy with a gun. He punched his face. The guy fell to the ground, he was turned to stone.

Hally bit her tongue to keep herself from screaming.

"What did you do?" Lukai hissed.

"I got scared, it was an accident," Piet cried.

"Turn him back," Hally said, this was a complete mess. "Now."

Piet walked slowly to the fallen guy and touched his forehead, the rock turned back to flesh.

"Is he alive?" Pam asked.

"Yes... he's just unconscious," Piet said, relieved.

Hally let out a sigh.

What's going on!

Piet is turning people into stone.

This can't be happening!

What are we going to do?

Hally took several deep breaths, this was no time to have a panic attack. They had to get out of there and find a way to get to Platz.

"Guys," Piet stuttered. "I think I know where we are." He showed an ID badge the unconscious guy had been wearing.

"You gotta be kidding me," Pam said, the badge was no joke. "I have to give it to you Hally, you can't get us into Platz but you get into the fricking FBI!" Pam exclaimed quietly holding the very real ID.

"Hey, it's not Hally's fault. It's no one's fault," Lukai replied. "Let's get out of here before another agent finds us. I have a feeling that Blake wasn't lying when he said that some Superiors are police officers."

"Yeah," Hally said, she was still a little stunned. "Help me look for the Wisatawan powder." She handed the bag to Pam.

Both girls kneeled and desperately looked for the jar with the white powder.

"Here," Pam said after a while and handed Hally a jar.

Lukai pointed the light at the jar, it was sugar-like, not flour like.

"This is Unicorn Powder, not Wisatawan powder."

Pam looked at Hally and Hally saw something dour in her eyes.

"That's the only jar there is in here."

"No it can't be it, I used it before," Hally said.

"I think this is the one you used before," Piet said, inside the jar there were a few silver spots.

"How does that even make sense?" Pam asked.

Hally stared at the jar blankly.

"So now I create portals?"

"Guys, we must go now, someone is going to be here soon," Lukai exclaimed. He pulled Pam and Hally unto their feet.

Hally's senses sharpened, she didn't need light to see where the walls were, where the maze opened and where it closed. She could feel several people around her, far, but still too close for comfort.

At least Hally could add something new to her adventure list, running through an FBI training center trying not to get caught.

"Even if we make it out of this maze, how are we going to get out of the fricking FBI?"

"I don't know, I have never been in the fricking FBI," Lukai replied to Pam.

"Can you please stop saying the 'fricking FBI' we're in Quantico, right?" Piet asked.

"Don't look at me, the closest I have ever been to the FBI was in my living room when I watched Criminal Minds," Hally blurted out.

They continued to run, Hally and Lukai in front. Hally kept them away from people, towards the exit, Lukai keeping a dim light, barely enough for them to see.

After running for what felt like the same distance of a hundred blocks, still far from getting out, Hally abruptly stopped.

"What happened?" Pam asked.

"I... I don't know," Lukai managed to say between breaths, he was staring at Hally.

Hally felt the two corridors that extended at their sides, from the two of them a set of figures were approaching. She focused on where they had come from, when a figure was behind them.

"We are surrounded," Hally said, she felt as they grew closer.

Lukai turned off the light, and the four of them pushed into a corner together, each of them shaking against the other. There was nothing more to do.

They waited there like statues until the flashlight shone in their faces.

"What the he-?" said one of the officers, they appeared to be playing some kind of laser tag, some wore a red band on their head, others a blue band.

"Hands in the air!" yelled another. The kids slowly put their hands up. "We got trespassers, turn the lights on," the same guy said on their radio.

For a moment Hally was blinded by the white light.

"Who are you and how did you get in here?" one of the officers asked, still pointing the flashlight into Hally's face for no reason.

"You do know this is the FBI?" asked another, more kindly.

"I'm sorry sir," Lukai said, he was the first to find the words to express himself. "I told my friends that I had found a hole in the fence and wanted to take a look inside."

"Seriously?" asked the guy with the flashlight, turning the light to Lukai's face.

"Stop that. You're going to blind the kid," said the other officer, the nice one. The rest of the officers stayed behind quietly. "Sadly boy, this is cause for an arrest, you barged into the FBI. You'll have to come with me and call your parents to come pick you up," he said as he took out a pair of handcuffs and made a signal to the other two officers to help handcuff the rest of the kids.

The kids looked at each other, for the first time Hally didn't know what to say. It wouldn't be long before the Superiors realized they'd been arrested, and then their lives would end.

Hally stood frozen as the officer pulled her hands into the ice-cold metal rings. She had no idea what to do. Usually, she was the one with the quick thought. Now, she just wanted to call her mom and cry for help.

This can't be happening. This can't be happening. This really can't be happening.

"Wait!" Lukai exclaimed to the officers before they closed the second metal ring around Hally's wrist.

"What is it?" the flashlight officer asked.

"Please don't drag them into this. At least not the girls, they are exchange students. They just arrived in the country. They don't even know how to speak English. They didn't know what we were getting into," Lukai begged.

The officer looked directly at Lukai, he wasn't convinced at all. He gave a second look at Pam and Hally, they did look their part.

"I'm sorry to say that they'll have to come with us, but I guess I can take the handcuffs off," the nice officer said.

The officer with the flashlight turned to him.

"WHAT?" he proclaimed.

"Please, where can they run to? And besides, they're girls, they're defenseless."

That was it, that was the spark Hally needed to start that fire in her soul again.

The other two officers followed the orders and took off Hally's and Pam's handcuffs.

As soon as that horrific metal went off Hally's hands, she hit the officer's nose with her elbow. She pulled Piet and Lukai closer, and she focused, she could do it. Before the other officers could react to their partner's mistake, the four kids were surrounded by one of those silver-ish transparent igloos she had grown to love: one of her shields.

"What are you doing? You just assaulted an officer!" Lukai exclaimed, although his voice couldn't hide it, he was impressed.

"Oh, shut up," Pam said and she grabbed the keys one of the officers had dropped and freed the boys.

"So what's the plan?" Piet asked.

"It's actually a Kung-fu Panda moment, I didn't think I would make it this far," Hally said.

"We should start thinking about one," Lukai said, the officers outside were yelling and hitting the shield, they were so confused and pissed. Hally didn't have to be an expert to know that they had already called for back-up.

"Are you sure you can't create another portal?" Lukai asked.

Hally nodded faintly, she was starting to tire from the shield, just like when she had dropped her Imperium Orb.

"I don't even think I can hold on much longer," she said as she kneeled down for support, her back was sweating, the trembling of her legs had returned. If she continued, she would throw up and faint.

"What about an illusion?" she asked Lukai.

Lukai shook his head.

"I would never manage to create one big enough to be helpful."

"Easy, Piet can turn them into rocks," Pam proposed.

"We aren't hurting anyone," Hally mumbled between her teeth.

"I'm pretty sure it's painless," Pam said.

Hally looked up, she still had enough strength to glare at Pam.

"Well not *that* sure," she said.

Outside, more officers than Hally could count had appeared and they were all hitting the shield. Oddly, she could feel every hit, it was not as if they were hitting her, more as if she was hiding behind a mattress and they were hitting the mattress.

"Blake's backpack!" Piet exclaimed, that was his breakthrough.

He walked to the backpack, still in Hally's back, and started to look inside.

"There must be another marble like the one Blake used with the Superiors," he mumbled.

"That's not a bad idea," Pam said and joined him.

"Hurry up."

Hally closed her eyes, that shield would be gone in the next five minutes.

"Have you found it yet?" she asked, her voice trembled.

"Does it look like we have found it," Pam answered back.

Hally couldn't read their faces.

"Here it is!" Piet exclaimed victoriously, a small blue marble in his hand.

"Hally, at the count of three you pull the shield down. Piet, you throw the marble. Then we run away from here," Lukai commanded.

Hally looked at the crowd of officers outside.

"That's a failing plan."

"It's a trying plan," Lukai corrected her. "If we fail, we fail trying." He helped her stand up and placed her hand around his shoulder to keep her from falling. "One. Two. Three!"

The shield went down and a fresh breeze hit Hally's face. The silence was replaced by the yelling of the officers. Those that had been hitting the shield found themselves hitting air, some even falling forward.

"Now Piet," Lukai ordered, there was no millisecond to lose.

Piet moved his hand; the marble was about to be thrown when a sting came to Hally's neck.

She fell to the ground with her friends, completely paralyzed. Her breathing turned raspy, her eyes closed. She was faiting.

"This will be taken care of by the special department, they're just what we have been waiting for," a new voice said as Hally lost consciousness.

25

A NEW HOME? OR A JAIL?

Tom was not fond of running, that much was clear. He wasn't really good at it either, much less when it was on six story high buildings. The others didn't seem to mind it that much, at least Blake and Ayala. Isla did make it clear several times that she wished to be on the ground drinking some fancy coffee instead.

Gladly the Superiors cut short Isla's complaining.

"Come kids!" Blake exclaimed.

They were at the edge of the roof.

"What do you want us to do?" Isla exclaimed.

"Jump!" Blake answered.

"Jump?" Ayala asked, scared.

Blake looked at Ayala.

"Ayala, have you tried to turn into a bird or something?"

Ayala shook her head.

"My powers aren't working," she cried.

`Blake sighed.

"Then you'll have to jump."

Ayala looked over at the other roof, it was barely one meter away.

"I'll do it," she said, and took a few steps, bent her knees and jumped.

She made it to the other roof safe and sound.

"Keep going! Don't stop!" Blake exclaimed at her. "It's your turn kids."

Tom glanced behind him; the purple cloaks were close.

He studied the other roof; it wasn't a hard jump.

He took a step backwards and jumped. For a second he was in the air, for a second gravity was gone, he was flying.

His feet bumped against the cement. The strike traveled from his feet to his waist. He didn't stop, he just kept running.

He ran across the roof, another jump, this time longer.

Still, he didn't stop.

Behind came Isla and Blake, not much farther were the purple cloaks.

He found himself the third jump, the biggest of all.

He watched as Ayala did it, she barely made it.

"It's just math," Tom said to himself. "Do a little math or find yourself with the Superiors."

He looked down, the floor was too far down for him to survive a fall.

"Tom, just jump!" Ayla exclaimed from the other side.

"It's just math," he said once again.

Tom took a few steps back and ran with all of his strength. When he was a centimeter from the edge he jumped.

"I'm not going to make it," he whispered in the air.

He reached the other roof, barely in the edge.

Tom smiled, he'd done it.

His foot slipped.

"Tom!" Ayala exclaimed, grabbing his hand.

Tom peered up; he was hanging. If it wasn't for Ayala he would be dead.

He moved his feet frantically trying to find some support.

His hand slipped.

"Don't let me go!" Tom screamed, his heart racing fifteen meters from the ground.

"Just hold on," Ayala hissed. She closed her eyes and growled as she pulled him up.

Tom's body was thrown against the roof.

"Thank you," he said with a smile, he was still alive!

Tom stood up. The smile faded, they were surrounded by purple cloaks.

"Stay away!" Blake commanded from behind Tom and threatened the group with one of his marbles.

More purple cloaks appeared.

"I really mean–" he was interrupted when one of the cloaks threw themselves on top of him.

"Blake!" Isla sobbed.

"No!" Blake cried.

The rest of the purple cloaks were doing the same with the kids.

Tom could feel it later sometimes, the weight of five grown ups on top of him, pushing to the ground, his face smashed against the concrete, his hands tied with rope, and later a cold and hard hit behind his head.

Tom woke up all sweaty, it was the third time he tried to sleep. Like the time before, his dreams turned into memories that woke him.

His head had stopped hurting a while back enough for him to be aware. Ayala, Isla and he were in some kind of dungeon no bigger than two small cars put together. It was very dark, with a single small window high on the wall. The walls were made of a black rock and the only entrance was blocked by thick iron bars.

Inside the cage, there were some old chains and a wood table used as a bed. Tom had no idea where they were exactly, nor the girls. Five minutes after all of them had awoken, a couple of guards with purple cloaks covering their faces had arrived and taken Blake by force. They had later brought some blankets, pillows and food. If they were going to kill them it wasn't going to be through starvation, not that that brought some peace.

Something that *was* going to kill Tom was being trapped in such a small place with Ayala and Isla. They were great people, and he liked them. He just didn't like being trapped with them.

Isla was alright as long as she wasn't complaining. She had spent the first couple hours trying to find a plant near the window, complaining and working. Later, she had gone on only complaining after not finding anything.

Ayala was nice, just too nice for Tom. She kept encouraging Isla and giving positive comments like, 'Blake's going to be alright', 'we are going to be alright', and worst of all, 'we just have to stay positive, you'll see everything will work out'.

"No! We won't!" Tom had responded. "Don't you see! We are going to be dead by nightfall and no positive thinking will change that! Shut your stupid words and your stupid voice!"

Ayala had looked at Tom. She opened her mouth, ready to respond. Instead she shut her mouth and kept her mean words to herself.

"Hey! Show some manners. That's not how you treat a lady," Isla had replied.

"What did I do?" Tom had hissed. He had remembered once he had ripped apart one of Hally's favorite toys and he had asked that same question to his angry mother. Just like back then, he knew perfectly well what he had done, but he was too mad to apologize for it.

"You insulted her," Isla responded, pointing at Ayala. She sat quietly, her eyes lost, staring at the wall.

Tom's heart filled with remorse; he wasn't a little kid anymore.

"I'm sorry," Tom apologized and gave Ayala a comforting pat on her back. "I don't do well with positivism. I'm more of a numbers person, but it seems like math isn't going to get us out of this one."

"It's alright," Ayala replied, she looked at him and smiled. "I'm used to it."

Eight hours later they were still there, just as they had been left. It was already night; Tom could tell by the small window. Isla and Ayala were fully asleep. All there was to hear was

Ayala's quiet snoring and the sound of some water dripping. There was no other sound from the outside world.

Silence, if Tom couldn't sleep at least he could enjoy it. Suddenly he ached for Hally's sloppy paces around the house and her whispers when she finally decided to wake him up. Where was she? Hopefully Platz. Yes, she had to be safe, in Platz. Soon she would realize he was in trouble, and she would start scheming.

"Please don't do anything stupid," he begged quietly.

"Beautiful night, isn't it?" a voice asked from the dark.

Tom jumped in his place. The voice was coming from the other side of the bars where it was way too dark for him to recognize anything.

"Answer!"

"I can't really say," Tom stuttered.

"Then come, I'll show it to you."

Tom looked around the place, he wished that Blake was there.

"I think I'll stay here," Tom replied and held his breath. He didn't know if what he had just happened had been something wise or something extremely dumb.

The figure remained silent and left, only to return a minute later with the key to the cage and a flashlight.

He came by and opened the door but did not step in.

"It wasn't really a question," the voice added.

Tom crawled slowly a few centimeters back against the wall and stared at the door.

The guy let out a tired sigh.

"Either you come out or I'll make my people kill Blake," he said and pointed the flashlight at his face. "I got the power to do so."

The figure wasn't any person, it was one that Tom had met earlier. It was James, the Superiors guy.

Tom didn't move. James took out a phone from his pocket and dialed a phone number.

"Get him," he said into the phone and immediately the air filled with a scream, Blake's scream. "Do you still want to stay there?"

Tom stood up, shaking.

"That's good," James said as Tom walked to the door.

Before he stepped outside James stopped him.

"Give me your wrists," he ordered.

Tom moved them slowly. James took two bracelets made of plastic tubes and filled with a white powder, Unicorn Powder. He wrapped those around his wrist, the powder instantly turned golden. Tom felt as if energy was being drained from him, his powers were going to be useless as long as he wore those bracelets.

James grabbed Tom's arm and pulled him. After closing the door behind him, he pushed him through the dark corridor and then outside.

Where were they? At first he assumed it was a camp, like a summer camp. Later, he realized it was more likely the headquarters of the Superiors.

There were beautiful wooden cabins surrounding him, all with signs on the doors. Although it was late, there were purple cloaked people walking through the place. All kinds of people, from some that seemed like gang members, to people that Tom was sure to have seen in some kind of political campaign. And there were all kinds of staring and hatred.

Tom looked at the empty spot on his shirt where his golden pin had been before, one that just like Isla's and Ayala's necklace, had been taken before he had woken up. How different would they see him if he was wearing that pin? He pushed the thought out, these weren't the Guarders, they were the Superiors. He was just a prisoner, not a hero.

"You really are as smart as Blake claims," James said.

Tom raised his eyebrows; he wasn't expecting that comment.

"May I ask what took you to that conclusion? You barely know me."

James laughed.

"You didn't come with me the first time I ordered you to."

Tom remained quiet, he was still a little confused.

"Why does that make me smart?"

"It means that you think things through. You don't let emotions like fear cloud your judgment."

They walked past what looked and smelled like a cafeteria. Tom's stomach growled, he was very hungry.

"If I'm being honest I'm surprised that you haven't escaped the prison already. I have heard that your powers need some work but I doubted that your brain wasn't going to be enough to get you out," James continued.

This time Tom felt both ashamed and flattered.

"A man can do as much as the resources he's given," Tom answered, which he thought to be an answer clever enough to continue the conversation to appeal to James.

James, as Tom expected, smiled.

"Exactly."

"Do you know what the Superiors goal is?" James asked after a few minutes.

Tom shook his head.

"Most people believe it's hate. I won't deny that there are smaller groups that do hate and create chaos around the world. But there is an even bigger dream we wish to accomplish. Our mission is not against people, but against the Villagers. You see Tom, just like you, I had my bad experience with them. When I was young, my brother and I were orphans in London. A girl that was studying in London took us in and later took us to her childhood home, the Western Guarders. The Villagers hated us as outsiders and made our life growing up miserable. While I lived there I couldn't help notice that the Guarders have resources, a lot of them. They could give homes to a lot of people if necessary, they know science that Ommons dream about, they even know ways to cure diseases and yet they never tried to share it. When my brother and I grew up we chose to change this. My brother, your dear Blake, helped by bringing kids in need to the Guarders who only accepted them because they believed they would secretly get the Íroes. I chose another angle. See, you, more than other people, should know that the Guarders don't deserve anything."

Tom remained quiet. James and Blake were brothers! They did look a little alike.

"My goal is to take away all those resources and share them with the world. I can't do it alone though."

Tom still kept his mouth shut, he wasn't sure if James wanted him to say something.

"For my people to attack, the Guarders will have to lose their security, one that Helden Platz is responsible for. To get to Helden Platz one needs Wisatawan powder and even if I had some, I would need someone who knows exactly where it is. Usually, I would torture Blake until he revealed it, but I know that he would die long before he helped me. So I'm forced to hunt a myth. It's said that Queen Sila's people had a portal made out of ancient objects. In the past, people have tried finding them. No one has been able to. They didn't count on Íroes, however."

"I'll send you and your two *classmates* to gather these objects in several missions for me. While you do good in them, I'll personally train you and make you a powerful Íroe. Once you are trained you will be given the choice to stay with the Superiors or to go back to whatever you were doing before you came here. If you don't succeed, I will give you back to the American groups and they'll gladly have you and your friends killed along with Blake. Do you understand?"

Tom nodded, as the conversation continued James' tone had turned more and more threatening.

"Do we have a deal?" James asked and extended his hand to Tom.

Tom looked at the nearly skeletal hand and swallowed hard. He wanted to have some time to think and give a thoughtful answer, a good one.

James noted Tom's indecision and laughed.

"Ohh sorry," he said, placing his hand back on the top of his cane. "A deal would mean that you have a choice. You'll do as I command or whatever the Generation did to you will be the last memory you and your friends will have. Am I making myself clear?"

Nope, he wasn't going to have time to think about it.

He gulped. He wished Hally was there, to give him hope or to help him punch James' horrific look out of his face. He wished to be back in Platz, where he was safe talking with Beira. He even wished to be a few hours in the past, when his worst problem was his heavy backpack. But life wasn't a fairy tale, and he couldn't just jump the pages all the way to the nice ending, if there was one at all.

Isla and Ayala deserved that ending, Blake too. And if working with James was what it was going to take, he would have to swallow his fear.

"Yes, sir," Tom muttered.

"Great," he cheered. "Now I can give you a tour, I would have given it before, but there's no point in showing the place if you weren't going to live long enough to see it. Tell me, can you create your own lighting?"

Tom got enough courage to look at his eyes.

"No?"

"We'll work on that."

26

THE FSC

And there was Hally, in a moving truck. Her hands tied to her back, and her head covered with a sack. The situation was almost laughable. First, she could move things with her mind, tying her hands wouldn't change that. And second, the sack was as thin as paper, she could see everything through it.

But she didn't laugh. Why? Because whatever they had used to sedate her left her powerless. And all she could see was a masked police officer holding a gun ready to shoot Piet's head off if he moved.

Hally moved her eyes across the truck, she couldn't let them know she was awake without risking another dose.

The truck looked like those she had seen on TV, the same ones they used to move criminals. Was she now a criminal?

There was a metal bench on either side. Above each bench there was a long metallic bar, one of those they used to tie the criminals' hands. However, Hally's hands weren't tied there, none of the kid's hands were, they were so small compared for whom the truck had been designed for that tying them would leave them in a really uncomfortable and dangerous position.

There were a total of four weirdly uniformed officers and a driver Hally couldn't see. The officers wore face masks, like superheroes. Their uniforms were mostly black, with red detailing here and there. They wore big black pants with a thousand red pockets, tall and fierce looking black boots and a bulletproof vest on top of a long sleeve red shirt. On each side of their waist bands each held one small gun and a knife.

Three of the officers looked too young. The fourth one, Hally could even dare to say, looked too old. Sitting by Lukai's side, her gray hairs had managed to escape from her mask and her vivid blue eyes looked like those that have seen too much of life already.

Hally gave her another look. Yes, that lady could really be in her sixties, and she was the boss.

She studied the rest, they were ten years older than her, surely. The young man sitting beside Pam, across from Hally, had short, black hair and deep-sea green eyes: Tony. In front of him, sitting beside Hally, there was a girl: Rumi. She had long, pink hair and light blue eyeliner. Lastly, besides Piet, there was a shoulder length red headed boy: Henry.

Hally looked at the doors, even if she managed to walk all the way through the back of the truck without being noticed, it was locked. She turned to the boss, the one the others kept referring to as Madame Rosemary, she had to have the key. The others, as uniformed as they were, were too young, too chatty, too untrained to have been doing this for a long time. She wouldn't have trusted them with a key, not with...

Not with us here, we're valuable merch now.

The truck stopped and the officers ceased their chattiness. The boss grabbed a key from her pocket and opened the door. Hally stiffened.

I am asleep, act like it.

She relaxed her muscles.

Rumi, the pink haired girl, grabbed her waist and picked her up easily onto her shoulders. She stepped down from the truck.

"Rumi, be careful with that one. The officer back at the FBI said she knocked out one of them," Madame Rosemary said.

"They were trainees, anyone can knock out a trainee," Rumi scoffed.

"It was with her elbow and a single blow," Madame Rosemary added.

Rumi remained still.

"I swear it's like the smaller ones are the maddest," replied Henry through his teeth.

They walked into a building, up one floor. Wherever they were it was a new place, clean and without much use. No one had bothered to take all the plastic off the furniture. Wet paint was still in the air. Most doors didn't have a handle yet.

Before Hally realized it, she was alone. Her heart stopped when she couldn't see Lukai, or Pam, or Piet. They were still asleep, what would happen to them?

Rumi walked into one of the few rooms that held a handle and a lock. She sat her down and placed her head gently against the table before leaving the room.

Hally stayed frozen.

Let them come to me, not me to them.

She sighed, the silence burning her ears. Her winter jacket was too warm for this place, her hands started to sweat, her throat to close. Just the thought of Tom being in a similar situation.

No, Blake was with them.

But did they make it out? Were they grabbed by the Superiors?

The air tightened around her face, and she couldn't deal with it any more. She took the sac off and breathed the fresh air.

She looked around, the dark walls could have used a little decoration, and the paint smell could have been replaced by a vanilla scent spray. But this room wasn't meant to be comfortable, it was an interrogation room. Hally knew it just by looking at the wall-sized mirror in front of her.

Her hair was a mess, her clothes had been all wrinkled. She looked terribly, then again it made sense she'd been arrested. Or was it kidnapped? She wasn't sure.

Suddenly she had that warm feeling that someone was looking at her.

Hally looked at the mirror, she could almost make up the set of blue eyes staring from the other side. What did they see? A small Latin girl? A threat? A myth? A criminal?

The door opened and in came Madame Rosemary, accompanied by Rumi, her pink hair flowing around her shoulders. They had dropped their masks along the way, somehow it only made them look less serious.

Hally followed both with her eyes, and for the first time in her life her mouth stayed shut.

Madame Rosemary sat in front of her, Rumi stood behind her boss. The lady pulled out a yellow file and placed it on the table. Hally had seen too many movies to know that the file was empty, they didn't have anything on her, much less a file. Yet, she could be mistaken, and they could have already figured out her name and address.

"I'm agent Rosemary," the lady introduced herself.

Rum forced a cough by her side.

"They call me Madame Rosemary so I suppose you can too..."

She opened the file.

"Full name?" Madame Rosemary asked.

Hally looked at her, with the corner of her eye she noticed a camera, red light on, they were filming.

"Full name," Madame Rosemary repeated.

Hally bit her tongue.

I don't speak English. I don't speak English. I don't speak English.

"Tell me your full name," Madame Rosemary asked.

"Ah?" Hally asked.

"Maybe she doesn't speak English," Rumi proposed.

Her comment was met with a glare, a warning for her to stay quiet.

Madame Rosemary returned to her file.

"Hally Razo Arinoa, pretty name."

Not mine.

"Seems that you're the troublemaker. Out of the four only you have a file."

Sure.

"Either that or-" her voice trailed off. "Or someone was very fond of you and your 'abilities'."

An image came to her mind, she was young, perhaps too young. She and Tom were lying in twin beds, facing each other. A single flickering light shining over their faces. A person came in, face unseen. And she pulled out a needle.

The image faded.

"Sealed, of course," Madame Rosemary continued. "Wanna take a look?"

She flipped the file for Hally to look at.

There *was* a file, and it was *her* file. At least her baby self. In it there was a young picture of her, back to when she hadn't even started school. Underneath, her name did read: 'Hally Razo Arinoa.'

Who was that girl? Maybe a cousin's name. Or grandparents... she stopped, she didn't know her grandparents last name, she'd been too young the last time she'd seen them.

Madame Rosemary studied her, her movements, her response, anything that would provide any information.

Hally relaxed herself, her muscles untensed, her breathing deep and slow. She wasn't going to let the old lady read her body.

That lovely spark appeared in her stomach once again. Her powers were there, she was just too stressed before.

Blake's voice echoed in her brain, she repeated the breathing exercise and she let her powers move through her veins. On the other side of the mirror there was another person. At her right in another room there were two more, an officer and a kid. Whether it was Piet, Pam or Lukai she couldn't tell. She could feel their hearts though, heartbeats increasing, they were waking up.

"Where are the others? My friends," Hally finally asked.

"She talks, and in English," Madame Rosemary said and looked at Rumi, the 'I told you', stayed unsaid.

"Where are my friends?" Hally repeated.

"Why don't you start by telling us how you got here?"

Hally slammed the table.

"WHERE ARE MY FRIENDS?"

The mirror on the wall cracked.

Madame Rosemary looked at Hally. No, she wasn't looking at Hally, she was looking at the silver ring on her hand.

Hally hid her hands underneath the table, it was too late.

"Rumi," Madame Rosemary stood up, "put her to sleep."

Rumi nodded.

"No," Hally tried to fight her. "Where are my friends? My friends! Where are–"

Rumi managed to place the cloth over her mouth. Her eyes closed.

When she awoke, her head rested against the table. She was no longer alone. By her side there were three other chairs, Pam, Lukai and Piet. A small smile curled up the side of her mouth. Piet looked up at her, he too was pretending to be asleep.

"Ok ready," Henry said from the front. "What do we do now?" he asked.

"Bring four chairs and wait," Madame Rosemary replied.

"I'm scared," Piet mouthed to Hally.

"It will be alright buddy," Hally whispered back.

A slap came on the table and the two of them straightened up.

"We have two awake," Madame Rosemary chuckled.

"Three," Rumi corrected as she pulled the sack off Lukai's half-asleep face.

"Four." Pam was waking up as well.

Madame Rosemary took a seat and looked at the kids' faces curiously, studying them, just like she had done before. Something had changed in her.

Then Madame Rosemary started with the questions.

"Who are you?"

"What were you doing in the FBI training center?"

"How did you get in?"

"Who are you working for?"

Question after question the kids remained as quiet as Rumi, Tony and Henry in the back.

Madame Rosemary sighed after the tenth unanswered question. She massaged her temples.

"Look, we're the Force for Special Cases. My name is Madame Rosemary, this is my squad, Tony, Rumi and Henry. We want to help you. But if you don't give me anything, when the General comes tomorrow, he'll take you to Kidutta and from that prison there's no coming back," the gray-haired lady explained.

Hally saw Lukai tense up from the other side of the table.

There was something funny in the way she was speaking, as if she was begging. As if the last thing she actually wanted was for them to end up in that so-called Kidutta.

"Without a trial?" Pam scoffed. "I know my rights."

"Yes," Madame Rosemary said, almost ashamed. "Without a trail."

Pam's cockiness disappeared.

"And you'll spend the rest of your lives there," Madame Rosemary added.

"I was the one that got them in, and I was the one from the silver igloos, not them. Let them go," Hally admitted.

"Good, we are making progress now, keep talking," Madame Rosemary said, but only silence filled the air again.

"Justice isn't going to be fair with you. We're trying to keep you alive whether you like it or not," Rumi said from the back.

The kids stared at them.

"Look, we know you're the Íroes," Madame Rosemary finally blurted out.

"Allegedly," Henry murmured in the back.

"*I* know you're the Íroes. *We,* the FSC, are the special unit to deal with this," she pointed at them, "if it ever happened. Now it has happened, and out there, the senior heads are already making plans. They saw a taste of what you're capable of doing, they'll want to know more. They *will* do experiments, turn you into soldiers to fight in *their* wars. So please," she begged, really begged, "if you don't know what we are talking about say so. But if you do, which I believe is because of the ring you hold, then let us help you get as far away as you can before the General arrives."

Hally looked at the camera in the corner, the light was off. She looked into the cracked mirror; her hair was still a mess.

It could all be a facade.

"Trust your gut," that's what Blake had said.

The file in the middle of the table levitated a few centimeters, the papers came out as if they were dancing with the wind, a little to the left, a little to the right. They all fell back on the table.

The FSC agents looked at each other, jaws dropped, and eyes opened. Henry pulled out a bill from his pocket and placed it in Rumi's hand.

"Told ya."

"Who did that? Please tell us who it was," Madame Rosemary begged.

There was silence, Hally could feel the stress pouring from the others.

"I did it. It was me," she admitted.

The lady looked up.

"Tell us the story, please."

Hally looked at the others. They trusted her.

"Well-" the story took long, longer than what they all expected. Eventually Piet and Lukai started adding details here and there. By the end it was being told solely by Pam. They told them everything, from the kidnapping of the Gang, the ceremony in the Western Guarders, the training in Platz and finally the mess with the purple cloaks on their field trip.

"We have no freaking place to go to now. We don't know where Platz is so we can't walk there, we have no Wisatawan powder, the portal maker has no idea how to create portals and we are running from Superiors. And now the FBI!" Pam exclaimed.

"Maybe we could search for some of the other Guarders and find refuge between the Villagers meanwhile," Piet suggested.

"That could work," Lukai supported.

"No," Henry stepped in, firmly. "The last place you wanna be is with Villagers." His voice seemed like he spoke from experience.

"Henry's right," Madame Rosemary added. "If there are really four Íroes right in front of me now, if there's a real Magister here, then you don't want to get anywhere near the Guarders. Believe us, we're from the Northern Guarders and we were often told the tales about how Elowen was the most merciful of all the four leaders. The Superiors, if they find you, they'll kill you. But if the Villagers find you, they'll torture you until you're nothing but an empty vessel they can use as puppets. They are like that, the Superiors seek power, and the Guarders seek only to remain above everyone else."

Hally remembered her last day there, all that Elowen had done to her, all that she would've done if Hally hadn't run away.

"We aren't safe with the government either... We're screwed," Lukai blurted out.

"They already knew you were there, existing somewhere. I supposed they always knew, if not the FSC wouldn't exist. Either way, the stunt you pulled on the FBI made it a reality. They now know your faces, soon it will be your name and addresses. They will look for you, until a better deal comes in and I doubt that will be soon enough," Rumi confessed.

"What do we do then?" Tony asked. "Should I create fake passports to send them home?"

"No," Madame Rosemary said firmly. "They can't go to an airport, too crowded. And if anyone sees their pictures, they will be toast. Once the Villagers find out that they are no longer in Blake's care and therefore the Western Guarders' protection, you'll be hunted like turkeys in November. And the Superiors are probably already hunting you. You'll need to take trains; they're the safest transport. I'll pull some strings, write to my closest friends in the Guarders and get in contact with Blake."

"Why don't we take them by helicopter?" Henry asked.

"Sure, because taking four kids that broke into the FBI and made some magic voodoo will not make the General suspicious," Rumi replied. "The General will insist on taking a real look at them before they leave and she *will* find out. This way they have a chance."

"Henry's right, the General can never know there are actually Íroes out there," Tony quavered.

"We'll have to make it look like you escaped from here, from us," Madame Rosemary explained.

"The safest way they can make it will be through the forest. Once they reach the city and then into the university campus, they won't be noticed among the students. There they can find some shelter for a few days and get back into the forest to cross the river and reach the safe house," Henry proposed.

The rest of the agents agreed.

The kids looked at them and then at each other, they had gotten lost quite a few sentences earlier.

Madame Rosemary stood up, her chair scraping the cold floor.

"You'll have to rest, tomorrow you'll be criminals."

27

THE "GREAT" ESCAPE

Hally lay on her bed unable to sleep when Pam stood up and locked the door.

"Too much?" she asked.

"Maybe just enough," Hally replied.

The FSC members had given them a small room they used for breaks to rest and a change of clothes, similar to the uniform they wore.

Hally had tried to sleep, her powers prevented her from doing so. When she had been able to explain to the others that their powers weren't working because of the stress Madame Rosemary had stepped in.

"Sometimes fear is what makes you hide away," she had said.

"Have you noticed that this morning we were on a field trip

and now we are being hunted by people that want to either kill us or turn us into puppets." Hally let out.

"And experiments, don't forget the experiments."

"And the experiments," Hally chortled.

Pam murmured.

"If my parents knew it, they would laugh. They would ask why someone would want me, I'm not worth the kill. Or they would say they were right by telling me not to leave home so that I would be safe. The funny part is that I feel safer than I felt at home," Pam said.

Hally studied her.

"You know what I think is also funny"

"What?"

"I wish to be home safe, I won't lie. But this is in a way the best and scariest adventure I have ever had," Hally laughed.

Pam joined her.

"You're right."

"I'm always right."

"What are we doing with our lives?" Pam asked minutes later.

"We're creating our way through them," Hally answered. "Even if that makes us a little crazy."

It was a couple of hours after midnight when Hally and

Pam's door was knocked. Rumi had asked them to get ready and meet everybody else in the interrogation room.

Hally picked up her old clothes and placed them into the bag Blake had given her, one that Tony had been kind enough to return. Then, along with Pam, she walked to the interrogation room.

There Madame Rosemary awaited each of them with a backpack.

"Tell me, was Blake really taking you to the castle in Slovenia?"

The kids nodded.

Madame Rosemary let out her breath.

"Why is it important?" Hally asked.

"It means it's time... If Blake thinks so, then it is," she told Henry, the young man smiled.

"Time for what? Redecorate?" Pam frowned.

"When I was a child in the Northern Guarders, they used to tell us the story of a group of soldiers known as the Guardians of Kinds, who ensured peace and balance. They protected the Íroes from the Ommons, and the Ommons from the Íroes. They protected the world from the animals and the animals from the world. They protected everyone. Today, when I see you, I see a new generation of those soldiers. Heroes."

Piet scoffed.

"Lady, we're not heroes or soldiers, we're kids."

"Who says a kid can't be a hero?" There wasn't any answer. "Besides, if you weren't heroes, you wouldn't be Íroes. This is who you're meant to be, that's what Blake wanted to show you there."

She handed Hally a red backpack.

"Here's a letter, it'll explain better."

"Wait a sec, lady. What do these soldiers have to do with the castle?" Piet asked.

Henry stepped in.

"That castle used to be Princess Dawn's castle, she founded the Guardian of Kinds."

"I thought Princess Dawn was a peaceful princess," Hally bleated.

"She wasn't peaceful," Madame Rosemary corrected her. "She fought for peace, and that takes as much strength and work as fighting for violence."

"What if we don't want to play you heroes?" Pam blurted out, glaring at the red bag.

"You may try to run from it. But just as a dog chases its tail, it would be pointless. Eventually, you'll end up doing it, because it's who you are."

The kids remained silent, not one of them convinced of their new title.

"Your lives will never be the same now, you know that, right?" Henry said.

"We've known it since the first day," Pam replied. "And we're okay with it, I guess," she smiled, sharing a look with Hally.

The four agents looked at them, sorrow and mourning filling their expressions.

"We'll be fine," Hally assured them. "We were born for this. Diamonds are forged."

Madame Rosemary nodded. "You're right."

She let them through the stairs into the backyard, where two bikes awaited them.

"Take the motorcycles, I assume you must already know how to ride," Madame Rosemary said, there was some sorrow in her voice. "Ride as fast as you can until you reach the fence, then take the motorcycles out and camp in the frontier. If you leave now there's a big probability that you'll meet the General on your way out. Don't leave that camp until mid morning and then ride even faster than before until you reach the train station in the neighboring town. There are five backpacks, all we could give you to help," she took a deep breath. "I wished we had more time... When you get out of all of this come visit me, I have a beautiful summer home away from all civilization," she said and couldn't resist giving them all a hug.

"You really are going to change the world," she added. The kids gave their thanks and goodbyes.

"Inside one of the backpacks there is a map with your route highlighted. There is also a place where you can meet one of us in the city. We want to make sure you get there safely," Rumi added.

"And I'll advise you to stay away from technology, it's a really easy way to find people that don't want to be found."

"Thank you, for everything," Lukai told them.

"It was our pleasure," the agents replied.

The kids turned around, not sure if they wanted to take the next step. They took it anyway.

"I have always wanted to drive a motorcycle," Piet exclaimed as he took the keys.

"No, you're a baby, I'll drive," Pam snickered and took the keys out of Piet's hands.

"But... but that's not fair!" he argued.

"Piet stop whining like a five-year-old," Hally said.

"But aren't you the ones that always say that I am like a five-year-old," he replied.

Pam looked shocked at Piet.

"Was that back talk I just heard?"

"I believe it was," Hally added.

"That's it! You're grounded!" Lukai exclaimed.

Piet's eyes opened widely out of confusion; the rest laughed at his expression.

Each of them grabbed a backpack and Piet and Hally grabbed the extra two backpacks, as they were the ones in the back.

"I think I can make us invisible," Hally said as she sat on the motorcycles. "Keep us away from cameras."

"You have invisibility?" Piet asked.

She shrugged, remembering a couple of the many accidents she'd had before everything started. When she'd explain them to Tom, he'd call them an optic illusion. What would he say now?

"I think so," Hally replied. She looked at the motorcycle. She took a deep breath trusting her powers to do what they did, when she opened them, the motorcycle was nowhere to be seen.

"I'll take that as a yes," Lukai said and sat in front of her.

Before the engines started, they gave a last wave to the FSC and then they set their way, invisible and invincible.

After driving for an hour Hally wasn't sure which one was wasting more fuel, her or the motorcycle. The invisible cover she gave both motorcycles was tiring, not really at first but after the first thirty minutes a break wouldn't have been a bad idea. Still, like the others Hally held on, they had to until they reached the fence.

When they reached the fence, a brick wall, Pam helped them cross one by one, each more doubtful of her abilities than the last. Good to say no one was trapped inside the wall, although she felt tempted to do it just for fun.

As Madame Rosemary advised, the kids camped there and took out a few blankets and coats. Eventually they also took their premade food packets they had been given and started to eat, well three of them. Lukai mostly complained about how the food could have been better if it didn't have that much salt.

Once the 'food' (not nearly as good as Beira's or Lukai's) was gone and they were all comfortable, at least the most they could be, Hally's curiosity finally took over.

"Who wants to see what Madame Rosemary gifted us?"

Pam sat up, she had been trying to sleep unsuccessfully. Lukai looked up from the list of ingredients he was reading on the food packet. Piet moved closer.

Hally opened the backpack and on top there was a green envelope. Carefully, Hally pulled the envelope. Inside there was a letter.

"What does it say?" Piet asked.

"I would know if I've read it. Have some patience," Hally snickered as she opened it up.

It read like this.

Today is my honor to receive the Guardians of Kinds. I know this title might not be what you expected or wanted, but it is yours. This responsibility can't and won't be held by another. From this day on, consider yourselves informed and remove ignorance from your list of excuses. With honor and heavy duty, I give up the weapons I had been entrusted to keep safe for their rightful owners: Updated versions, of course, from Princess' Dawn secret vault that have been waiting for you for centuries.

As you know, or should know, Princess Dawn was a pacifist but that never stopped her from being a great warrior. Her weapons were special, they were forged in a way they didn't hurt, yet they gave real temporal pain as if the wound actually existed. The ones with a red stripe give pain for a couple of hours and the ones with yellow stripes give pain for a few minutes. These aren't toys, they are sacred, old, and they carry a heavier burden, don't pick them unless you're ready to use them. Once you pick them up, they'll be yours forever and whenever you call upon them, your weapon will appear by your side.

The first weapon is Piet's.

Piet, I see you clearer than water, you're what we call a field agent at heart. You have the bravery to attack upfront and the loyalty to never leave the side of your friends, even on the worst of days. We've decided to give you the nickname of Pebble as you turn things into rock, but you are also the youngest of the group.

"They have to be kidding me!" Piet exclaimed.

"Shhhhh!"

Your weapons are nunchucks; they require strength, coordination, attention, discipline and training. All a set of skills that you have.

The next one is Pam's. Pam, we have given you the nickname of Trusty in honor of your friend's jokes of your trust issues. You too are a field agent at heart, you lack no strength to fight as a warrior and beat some people. You and Piet both are warriors of the front line. Your weapon is a katana.

Pam looked at the long and thin sword she had taken from the backpack. It was beautiful; it had a golden handle with a red stripe in the middle. Its metal was shiny like a mirror, strong as iron, and as light as a feather.

Pam gave it a few hits on a nearby tree.

"Awesome!" she exclaimed with a smile. "I can hurt people now."

"We are not hurting people," Hally reminded her. Pam let out a disgusted snarl.

"If you say so."

"Continue reading," Lukai told Hally, he was waiting enthusiastically for his own suit.

Lukai unlike the two previous ones, you aren't a field agent, your abilities lie in another way. You are a planner at heart. As when you cook, a good chef must know his ingredients well, a good planner must know his team well. You always take time to think thoroughly and have the ability to make fast decisions for your friends. Your weapon will be a sword. Your nickname is Sunny and I believe that I won't need to explain why.

Lastly, there's Hally's. Hally you're the spy. You are clever and agile. Your powers give you the ability to lay undetected and your senses are heightened in a way that no other humans are. You alone can get into places that are unbreakable and can get things that are unstealable. For our invisible agent I send you weapons that are easy to hide, a set of knives that I hope will be of use. Finally, to you too, I give you my own medical kit for you to call on. We have given you the nickname of Silver.

Again, I hope you don't find any use for all of these items. Take care of each other and I hope with all my heart that you reach the safehouse as planned. It was indeed a pleasure meeting you.

-Madame Rosemary and Henry

Hally took out the knives, all different sizes. They were small, shiny and sharp. She placed her finger on the tip of one and pressed, where the cut should've been there was nothing, just a little pain.

She looked up. Piet trying the nunchucks and Lukai and Pam taking turns to kill a tree. They were laughing like kids on Christmas. Like this was what they had been expecting all their lives.

She took out a last letter and a golden bag that were at the bottom of the backpack. Outside it read: *For Hally and only Hally.* Her heart dropped, forced back to reality. She was supposed to be a warrior now and whatever that was, it couldn't be good.

28

LIGHTNING

"Again!" James snapped as a whip does on your back.

Tom lifted his eyes from the ground and cleaned the blood coming from his nose. The mission relied on him being able to create lighting on his own. James hadn't been kind enough to explain how.

He'd been trying that for three hours fifty-five minutes and thirty-seven seconds, unsuccessfully. The first hours he'd been encouraged, happy that he was learning. The learning soon turned into humiliation. They were allocated an open space near the center of the camp, perfect for everyone to see his powers, or his failing.

By his right side, Isla and Ayala were still being forced to watch him, a guard standing on each side. On their wrists the Unicorn Powder bracelets shone bright green, keeping them both from their powers. The two girls were tired, the sun had already managed to start burning their faces and the dark circles underneath their eyes were just a reminder of how Tom felt. An hour of sleep and a single piece of toast in his stomach.

"AGAIN!" James snapped one more time, his voice showed what Tom had learned, he didn't like to repeat himself.

"Einstein once said that for different results try different methods," Tom muttered between his teeth, too quiet for anyone to hear, or that's what he thought.

James walked up to him until he was close enough to choke him.

"And. I. Say. AGAIN!" he screamed, spitting into Tom's face.

Tom sighed and stood back up. He nodded giving the signal he was ready. The two purple cloaks, James's training assistants, Beatrice and Roberts, grabbed another jar of sand and threw it into the air. Tom waited for it to be at the tallest point and then extended his hand.

The jar fell into the ground, adding more glass and sand into the pile.

"Ahhh!" James screamed. "You imbecile…"

Tom looked down, he had a bruise on his right cheek as a lesson not to look at James when he was mad.

Tom sniffed, there was nothing for him to do. He had never done anything similar. He had once been close to using lightning, but even then, there had been a storm, he had just redirected the lightning, not created it. This time the sky was clear as water. It didn't matter how many times he lifted his hand, there was always something inside of him that was pulling the power in, instead of out.

"What am I going to do with this... useless boy?" James asked himself, hitting the ground with his cane.

Perhaps set him and his friends free.

"May I give you some advice, sir?" asked Roberts, his dark hair and eyes contrasting against his white skin and soulless mind, he was one of the 'best soldiers' that James had introduced to Tom. Compared to the other men who'd spit in their faces and yelled the worst insults even the Jilsons were saints.

Tom looked at him, he couldn't be much older than him, perhaps five years.

Roberts smiled, the evil smile that had accompanied him all the morning as he made the worst, most evil, suggestions to James. One suggestion was to use Ayala as the target for practice.

"The first lightning I create is going directly at you," Tom whispered between his teeth.

"Tell me," James allowed with a tap of his cane. Roberts walked to him and muttered some words into his ear.

James didn't answer, he moved his hand as if he was getting

rid of a mosquito and Roberts returned to his assigned position beside Isla.

Isla looked at Tom, she moved her hands signaling him to breathe.

"Roberts does seem to have a good point," James said and turned to Tom. "I still need you to be capable of moving though." He made a pause as if he was preparing for the worst. "Seems we'll need to go with my brother's approach. Textbook. You're an Íroe because of who you are. Who are you?"

Tom looked up. He still had a hard time relating to Blake and James. One was warm, the other cold. One was good, the other bad. If they were brothers what had happened to them to end up so differently? James was nothing like Blake. However, if he squinted, and listened to these words, they did seem related.

"Answer me!" he yelled.

Tom swallowed hard as he did every time he had to eat broccoli.

"I'm Tom Black Sols from Costa Rica, a Bellator," Tom let out the last part out of necessity, that was why he was there after all.

James clicked his tongue.

"No, you aren't that anymore," he said with a different tone, a soothing one. His blue eyes staring back, moving his cane from side to side. Tick. Tack. Tick. Tack. It was almost hypnotic. "Now you're Tom Black Sols, part of the Superiors family. You are *my* champion. You are *the* Bellator, *my* Bellator," he said. "Focus on that. Again!"

Tom resisted the need to puke at the words he'd just heard. This guy had a serious need for an anti-narcissism class. Scratch that, an anti-narcissism intensive camp.

Still there wasn't much choice and he decided to do it, just to prove to himself that what James was saying was not who he was.

He nodded to Roberts and Beatrice. There they went, again. It couldn't get any worse, could it?

The jar was thrown up. As it moved through the air, Tom waited. He filled his mind with pictures of the Superiors, of him fighting for them and of him living in the camp. Something was set free in his stomach. He extended his hand; a strong force rose from his chest. He set it free. The electricity came from the ground, made its way up his whole body. He didn't command it, he just asked it to move, and it listened.

"Ah!" he screamed, the currents moving through him.

Lightning shot from his hand, into the jar. This time when the jar fell there was no new sand added, only crystals.

James laughed. What was happening?

"Again!" he roared, this time as a cheer rather than an order.

Two more jars were thrown into the air, time after time, they turned into crystals. Tom leaned, gasping for air. He wasn't going to be able to shoot many more.

"Leave him alone!" Isla barked.

Tom looked up, the sweat pouring down his forehead and back. The residue electricity, still moving through.

The crowd stifled a groan, how was she speaking like that!

He wanted to scream for her to shut up. He could take it. The more James was busy with him the less time he'd spend with them or looking for Hally. He didn't have any strength for the scream.

James touched her chin with the tip of his cane. Isla stiffened.

"You want him to be okay? Then sing little bird."

She glared at him, studying all the ways she could refuse. She gave a second look to Tom.

Her concern triumphed.

Isla opened her mouth. A melody came, suffocating and beautiful.

Tom's heart turned; the electricity danced in his veins. It burned and it danced.

She shut down; the crowd amazed.

"I could sell you; your voice would make me rich."

Roberts coughed.

"But there are things to do first."

"Amazing! Isn't it?" James exclaimed to the crowd that had built in the last minute, more amazed than disgusted. Power was their natural language, one they all understood.

"Our job here is done. Roberts, Beatrice take them to their chambers," he ordered and left the training arena, Isla and Ayala already being pushed to their newly acquired cells.

Tom didn't take his eyes from that jar while Roberts and Beatrice put back the white powder filled bracelets and pulled him away. That couldn't be possible. Was he supposed to be part of the Superiors? His powers shouldn't have worked.

"Move along, Pawnsie," Beatrice said, and they entered one of the cabins. Tom gave the last look to the smashed jar and crystals on the floor.

"And into your cell," she added a long last push into the dark room. The door closed.

"Maybe you can sing to me someday," Roberts said.

"You wish," Ayala replied.

"I will."

Tom fell to his knees, head between his hands, steps faded further, until they were silenced. He was so tired. The powder on his wrists sucking all the energy he had had before. The electricity had left him.

"Tom, what did they do to you?" Isla asked from her cell. "The lightning... It must have been a trick," she argued.

The kids were no longer together or in the dungeon. James had claimed they should never be in a horrible place like that, and he'd decided to place them into other cells inside the 'prison' cabin: a big wood building that held nothing but cells, just three of them being used.

Tom pushed himself off the ground and sat on the thin mattress in the corner they called a bed.

"Right now I'm too exhausted for this. If you don't mind, I'll sleep for a few minutes before having to recall the events from this morning." Isla didn't reply, she knew she too could use a good nap. He laid back staring at the ceiling.

"We'll wait for you to wake up," Ayala replied from her own cell in the back.

Tom's heart filled with remorse, it wasn't their fault, any of this.

The new cells were a big change from the dungeons, for their luck. They did have the same bars for an entrance and similar rock in the wall, yet they were more *comfortable* if that word could be used. In a corner there was a thin mattress, with several blankets and one pillow. On the opposite side of the 'bed' there was a small wall hiding a toilet and a really small shower that didn't work. When it did, it brought nothing more than brown colored water. Against the small wall there was a sink that only gave a small freezing waterjet.

Tom closed his eyes and clenched his fists. He hated that place. There was no silence. There was no hygiene. He couldn't keep up with his routine. He missed his shower, his chess board, Beira's food, and Blake's training. He missed Hally. He hated the Superiors. He hated those stupid, purple cloaks. He hated those stupid bracelets on his hands that took away his powers. He hated James. He hated everything.

But he couldn't hate, he wasn't allowed to hate. Hate was an unpredictable feeling and right now the numbers said they stood more of a chance to survive if he helped James. He had to stop hating him and play along. For the next few days, he had to be a 'member' of the Superiors and get James those stupid parts of a portal. He was the only one capable.

Tom wondered what Hally would do in that situation. She would have already given three escape plans, each crazier than the one before. She was the one that knew about sneaking in and out of places, she was the one who knew about saving people. She was the hero, not him.

He was once again running through rooftops, the wind against his face and the dried sound of his feet hitting the concrete. He knew perfectly well that it was all a dream, still he tried his best not to get caught. He ran, harder and faster than before. He felt his muscles being torn apart, he felt that agonizing pain starting on his side, he kept running.

A splash of water woke him.

"Move along, Pawnsie. James wants you to attend dinner,"

Roberts said, he had a now empty bucket in his hand and a towel in the other.

Tom rubbed his eyes; he didn't remember falling asleep.

"You have five minutes to get ready, call me when you are ready and don't try anything stupid," he said, leaving the towel behind.

Tom looked to the front, Isla was glaring at Roberts with hatred and giving Tom a worried look afterwards. So was Ayala.

"Is everything OK?" Ayala mouthed to Tom.

He nodded faintly and picked up the towel. He couldn't tell if having dinner outside his cell was good news or bad news. He couldn't tell potato from papaya in that place.

"Hurry up!" Roberts yelled from the entrance.

Tom picked up the pace. He dried his face, combed his hair and put on his shoes. Without a shower there was nothing he could do about his smell except hope that no one noticed.

"I'm ready," he called Roberts. The purple cloaked soldier came up to him and opened the door.

There was a wicked smile on his face.

"Why does James want me for dinner?"

Roberts laughed.

"Either he really likes you or he is considering killing you, Pawnsie," he said. "Anyway, it will be interesting."

Tom gave a scared look to Isla and Ayala.

"Mind your manners," Isla whispered as he walked by her cell.

"I tried getting one of the girls to join us. James said they'll be for later," Roberts laughed.

Outside, it was dark. Wherever they were, they didn't get many daylight hours. Perhaps the weather just copied their hearts. People were still moving, from one side to another, running here and there. The Superiors never stopped working: destroying, killing, torturing.

The far northern side of the camp was filled with cabins where people stayed. The size of the cabin was determined by the rank each person served. The wooden cabins were separated into two groups. The more extremist, the ones that believed in true blood purity, were on the left side. The least extremist, the ones that believed that there was more than one pure blood, were on the right side. The closer the cabins were to the outer side, the bigger they were.

On each side there was a park for the smaller kids. There were about twenty kids younger than twelve in the whole camp and there were no more than five teenagers or that's what Tom had seen.

In the center of the camp, where everyone seemed to be the same, there was the biggest cabin of all. It was made of shiny wood with lots of windows and a front porch. That one Tom had assumed to be James' house. It almost reminded him of Elowen's cottage back at the Guarders.

Just beside James' supposed house there was another big cabin: The cafeteria.

Pushed by Roberts and Beatrice, Tom stumbled inside. Most tables were filled with people talking and laughing. Exactly like the cabins, the extremists were on the left side and the rest on the right side. At the very end, in a table taller than the others, there was James, wearing a suit, drinking wine, and talking to another woman Tom swore to have seen on TV talking about politics.

Roberts and Beatrice walked the Bellator past the tables causing some conversations to stop and catching some hate filled looks. Most people were already oblivious to his training that morning.

"Oh here it is!" exclaimed the woman by James' side when they reached their table. She was ugly, no sugar coating it. Her nose was permanently swollen, her cheeks redder than normal, her fried hair raised into a bun.

"Ms. Duckstein," Roberts and Beatrice saluted.

"What a fine specimen," Ms. Duckstein said. She walked past her chair and looked at Tom closely. "Doesn't look like much up close," she said. Tom thought the same thing of her.

James laughed.

"Not at the moment, no. With a few training sessions he will become my champion," he said.

Ms. Duckstein turned to James, her badly painted eyebrows raised up her forehead.

"Your champion?" she scoffed. "Don't take it wrong, I know he's an Íroe but he's half-blood. Surely his abilities don't compare to the ones of my commander Atonal, the Superiors best soldier, *your* champion," she spoke as a reminder of who she was, she knew better than to order James around.

Roberts and Beatrice scoffed at the comment.

"Ex-champion," James corrected.

Beatrice smiled; this was the entertainment they'd been waiting for.

Tom studied them, angry looks were shared. Which one was going to blow up first? Even the farthest table had ceased their conversation to hear what was going on.

A young man stepped up to Ms. Duckstein's side, he was probably the champion she was talking about: Atonal.

The young man kneeled in front of James and stood up, salute in hand.

"I'm sorry sir, I wasn't aware of your change of champion," he stated respectfully, facing the front, looking at nothing in particular.

James looked down to 'Atonal', perfectly done considering the soldier was a head taller.

"The moment you couldn't get the first piece of the portal you lost your rank boy."

Atonal stayed frozen, only his eyes changing from respectful to perplexed and offended.

"I admit that my commander did make an awfully bad mistake, surely that won't make him lose his rank to a useless fifteen-year-old boy," Ms. Duckstein whispered.

"Believe me, no one can be more useless than your commander," James replied. "Besides, it is *my* champion. I choose."

Ms. Duckstein took a deep breath, searching from the last ounce of strength to control herself.

"I beg your pardon, Sergeant, I believe there is only one way to prove who is strongest. I demand a duel, between my commander and this scum you call your new champion," she said pointing at Tom when she mentioned scum.

A duel? Tom wondered if the Superiors were aware of how very much alike they were to the Guarders.

Tom turned at James, he wasn't going to let that happen. Was he? Ms. Duckstein's commander was a decade or more older, he was in complete military uniform with several stars on his chest. He was also armed with two guns by his side and several grenades. Tom could only imagine the training that guy had, he stood no chance. He ran the numbers in his head, even though he miraculously grew a few centimeters, gained some muscle and learned how to use a gun in the next seconds, his probability to win was almost imaginary.

James smiled, his teeth showing more like a threat than manners. If he was thinking about it then probably the duel was not the kind Tom was thinking about. James had seen him train, he was barely able to create a single lightning, much less fight a commander.

"Sure, amuse me," he grabbed his cane and walked down his chair to Tom.

James took the keys to Tom's bracelets and opened them up. Instantly Tom's hair spiked and the lights above him flickered. All the desire to keep his fear quiet, gone.

"You hear me well," James whispered to Tom. "You show them what I saw this morning, a power they can't even dream of. Let it be clear to everyone that you are *my* champion, that you are the strongest of every soldier in here, and they should fear you, not defy you."

Before Tom got to argue his point, he was gone, back in the chair, the quiet place echoing with the dry click of the cane meeting the ceramic tile.

The closest members rushed to move their tables clearing the center of the cafeteria. None one was mildly bothered that their dinner had been interrupted. This was what they lived for.

Tom gulped. It was the kind of duel he was thinking of.

Ms. Duckstein took the seat beside James and Atonal and Tom were left alone in the center.

Tom's whole body was shaking, he was about to get killed and no one would care as long as he put on a good show.

Atonal smiled and put his guns and grenades on the ground. It appeared that the duel was old fashioned, with punches and kicks.

Looking at Atonal's fist, Tom swallowed hard. He remembered Gunner's punches, somehow, he understood those were going to be nothing compared to Atonal's. James was right about something though; he had a power none of them possessed. He only had to throw one lightning bolt at Atonal and the fight would be over.

"Begin," James announced, Atonal's smile grew bigger.

Atonal started to run towards Tom. Tom did what he knew, he closed his eyes and extended his arm forwards. He felt the energy in his chest. He filled his head with images. He was the champion. He was the best. He was the strongest. He had to be feared. He was going to prove all of this.

He called and the electricity answered.

Tom screamed as the strongest current he had ever experienced left his arm and hit Atonal in the chest. The commander was thrown through the air against a wall, where he fell to the ground unconscious.

"Bravo!" James exclaimed, applauding as the lighting dissipated and the crowd joined him. "The duel is over, my champion wins."

Ms. Duckstein was paralyzed, she kept looking at the motionless body of her commander, muttering under her breath, 'useless, useless'. No one helped him up.

Roberts walked to Tom holding the bracelets, his powers had done the job, now they had to go away.

"Stop that," James ordered Roberts. "He did a great job; he deserves to have some fun. Let him free, it's time for dinner. Today, we celebrate my new champion," he exclaimed, and the cafeteria filled with cheers. Even the extremists joined, once again Tom spoke their language: power.

Tom looked at Atonal's body, he was starting to wake, he wasn't dead. He was injured and burnt though.

He wanted to feel bad. If Hally was there, she would be giving him a speech about how they don't hurt people. But Tom didn't feel bad. He enjoyed the feeling of power. He enjoyed the cheers. He enjoyed the respect. He enjoyed the salutes everybody was giving him. He enjoyed sitting down beside James. There, in that place, he was the best. There, he didn't have to be his sister.

29

THE TRAIN STATION

Hally's dreams were usually weird, not usually this weird, but weird. She was sitting down in the middle of a forest, the same forest her parents used to take her to picnics when she was younger. She was there, alone, with a basket. She opened the basket; everything had been eaten by purple worms.

She looked up, there was her mom, a smile across her face. Hally smiled back and felt something on her arm. She looked at it and there were over ten tubes coming out of her. Hally tried to take them out, her mom stopped her.

"Lie down, we are almost over. Just a little bit more," she whispered.

Hally nodded and laid on the ground. She looked up at the clouds, they had weapon-like shapes, knives, arrows, nunchucks, katanas...

A yellow bird flew by and sat on a tree.

"Do you think I should wake her up?" asked the yellow bird in Pam's voice.

"No. It's her turn to sleep, let her sleep," replied the tree in Lukai's voice.

Hally smiled, even in her dream she knew that she wanted to keep sleeping.

"Piet's annoying me," said the yellow bird.

"I don't know. I'm starting to really like it up here. As long as Hally doesn't make me levitate into space, I'll be fine," replied one of the worms in Piet's voice.

Wake up.

The first thing she saw was Piet floating three meters into the air. Beside him, a few blankets, branches, leaves, food packages, Pam's sweater and Lukai's sword joined in the air.

"Sorry about that," Hally apologized with a yawn as she rubbed her eyes.

She put everything back onto the ground and Piet let out a sad sigh, he was actually enjoying the levitation.

Hally was getting stronger, she knew it. She had found that the clearer her mind the easier it was for her to use her powers.

"Good morning sleepy head," Pam mocked even though Hally had literally slept less than everyone else.

"Good morning," Hally replied with the same tone. "What time is it?"

"About nine o'clock, we should be leaving here in an hour," Lukai said. "Eat something," he added and gave Hally one of the apples that came with the food packets.

Hally took the apple happily and took a bite, it was better than the food from the night before, anything was better than that. Even Tom's failed attempts at pancakes he always made on their birthday.

"I still think that half morning is six o'clock," Pam muttered.

Lukai rolled his eyes.

"Pam, we've been through this. Half morning is ten o'clock," he said.

"I thought it was eight o'clock," Piet replied innocently from behind a tree. "Hally, do you think you could levitate me again? I left my sweater up there," he said pointing at the wool sweater hanging from a branch.

"Sure," Hally answered. She carefully moved Piet up the air.

"Why would it be eight o'clock or six o'clock?" Lukai exclaimed, ignoring the flying blond boy over his head.

"I have always thought that it was ten o'clock," Hally added, another bite into her apple. She was so hungry!

"Ugh," Pam complained. "We are wasting time! I asked Mr. Light here if he could create an illusion with those powers of his and make them look for us in another place. He didn't want to! We could be on our way already," she said at Hally, pointing at Lukai.

"I already told you, it doesn't work that way," Lukai replied. "I can barely create small illusions in front of me, much less one on the other side of the world," he added, and he leaned against a tree looking at Hally. "Are you hearing this?".

Pam hit the floor beside the tree where Lukai was leaning, making him go past the wood and fall to the ground.

"Hey!" he cried. Hally laughed.

"Hally?" Piet called; he had gotten the sweater.

"Sorry," she apologized and put him back on the floor.

As Piet reached the floor he accidentally turned his sweater into rock.

"Dang it!" he exclaimed and tried for several minutes to turn the sweater back to its normal form.

Hally turned to Lukai who had gotten up on his feet again.

"Talking about your powers, last night it was far too quiet so I started thinking-"

"Oh no."

"Shut up Pam. *I* have a question. Do you think perhaps that you could illustrate a whole movie? Like a portable cinema?" Hally asked.

"Not really or not yet," Lukai replied as he cleaned the dirt off his clothes, he wasn't sure either. "I can barely create static illusions, much less a movie."

"Ah," Hally sighed disappointed. "It would have been nice to watch a movie."

"What would be nice would be to know if Pam can turn charcoal into diamonds applying pressure," Piet said, still trying to turn his sweater back to normal. "Now *that* would be a real money maker."

An hour later, when Pam's complaints about their incredible stupidity regarding the half morning topic were one step from making Hally's ears bleed, they started to pack everything. Madame Rosemary should have code named her Complaints rather than Trusty.

"What's that?" Lukai asked, pointing at a small golden ball on the top of Hally's backpack

Hally hurried to close the bag, all possible lies rising in her brain. An apple? An illusion? A family relic? A gift? She finally went with the best one.

"Oh nothing," she answered.

Lukai didn't ask any further, the subject disappeared.

The special letter of the night before had explained what Hally feared the worst. She was the Magister and so Madame Rosemary trusted that she would make the best decision regarding that golden orb with the carving of a sunflower. She had done her best to explain the situation, what it was, and what it was capable of. Now it was up to her to make a decision.

Fifteen minutes after ten, the four of them, the newly Guardians of Kinds, were back on the motorcycles. Hally once again riding with Lukai and Piet with Pam.

As the night before, during the whole ride through the forest roads Hally made sure to make both motorcycles invisible, just as a precaution.

By the time they reached a highway she took down the invisibility cover, she didn't want to end up being rammed by a truck. They had survived so much, something like that would just be a bitter end.

Fortunately, after a trip of about an hour, the kids reached the small colorful town, and they reached the train station.

Between the small houses and the many cafes, the train station was big, bigger than any other building there. The walls were made of bricks and the columns that filled the place were covered in paintings. The roof had been designed to let the light in creating beautiful patterns, birds, flowers, butterflies. And just like the FSC had explained, there was no security and lots of people, the perfect place to disappear.

They left the motorcycles outside. They would have to find another transportation mode later to cross the forest after reaching the university city.

"There's something poetic about this kind of place, don't you think?" Hally said.

"Here we go-" Pam replied.

"I mean it. It is almost like a... a cocoon of stories. Look at all these people, how many are planning to visit family? How many are running from their family? How many will meet the love of their life? How many are starting their dream? How many their nightmares? And for how many this is just like any other day? There's a thousand stories all in the same place. Parallel stories, touching but not affecting each other, perhaps colliding for the first and only time in history, and only a few will remember it." Hally inhaled deeply. There she was, just another story.

"You done?" Pam asked.

"The only poetic thing is that smell," Piet declared.

Hally laughed. It had a really good smell.

"Can we have a real breakfast?" Piet asked.

Lukai had to visibly bring up the strength to say the next sentence.

"First let's buy our tickets and then we'll see if there's any time remaining," he said.

Hally nodded

She walked to the front desk.

"Hi," she said to the young girl at the desk. "Could you give me four tickets for the next train to... Opinnot City, please."

"Sure, that would be twelve dollars, lovely," the girl said nicely.

Hally handed out the money, Madame Rosemary had packed money in all types of coins just in case. The girl handed her back four tickets.

"Your train will be leaving in twenty minutes. It's on the other side of the station." She leaned closer. "I advise you to hurry up," she said and Hally's hope to eat in a restaurant died.

"Thank you," she replied and walked back to her friends.

She handed each a ticket.

"Our train leaves in twenty minutes and we have to cross the whole station," she muttered.

"Does that mean no food?" Piet asked, his lips curling down.

"I mean if we make it to the platform on time maybe we can buy something to eat on the ride," Lukai proposed.

The others took it as badly as her but didn't fight it, they knew that to enjoy food they had to stay free.

The four of them walked through crowds and great-smelling restaurants until they reached their platform, 6A.

"We have thirteen minutes before the train arrives..." Pam insinuated.

"Twelve minutes," Lukai corrected her, she rolled her eyes. Pam was the easiest person to annoy.

"Twelve minutes, the same. I'm going to the bathroom. I've been holding it in since last night."

"That's because you didn't want to use the bushes," Piet said.

"Yes, because I'm not an animal."

"Neither am I."

"You're closer."

"Hey!" Piet groaned.

"One of you, pick up some food," Pam continued.

"I'm also going to the bathroom," Hally said and started to walk with Pam.

"Wait," Lukai came after them, he took two really small earphones from his pocket. "Found these in my bag yesterday. If any happens, press them, we'll hear you," he said, giving one to each girl.

Hally looked at the black earphone.

"You do realize that we're going to the bathroom, not to another city," she said.

Lukai shrugged.

"Just in case."

"Okay," Hally said, she put the earphone in her ear, Pam copied her.

They walked a few meters down to the bathroom. Pam turned to her.

"Take the earphone off for a second"

"Why?"

"I'm going to pay him back," Pam answered. "Just take it off."

Hally did as told. Pam took hers off as well, brought it up to her mouth and yelled the loudest she could.

Piet and Lukai jumped in their places.

Piet glared at them; they were definitely annoyed.

"You!" he mouthed at Pam. Their expression was enough to make the girls laugh all the way to the bathroom.

In the bathroom Pam got into one of the stalls and Hally walked towards the sinks. She would have done anything for a real bath, but she settled. The cold water took away the dirt and some of the stress.

As she moved her arm to grab a paper towel, she hit a lady beside her, and the sound of things falling to the ground was unavoidable.

"I'm so sorry," Hally replied and holding the paper towel with her mouth she kneeled to help the lady pick up her things.

"That's all right," the lady said nicely.

She could be in her forties. She seemed to be rich, all she was wearing was of expensive brands.

Hally picked up the lipstick, sunglasses and the ticket the lady had dropped. When she picked up the ticket, she looked at it.

Same train as us.

"Here you go." Hally gave the things to the lady.

"Oh thank you dear," the lady responded.

Oh SHOOT!

Hally swallowed hard; her eyes glued to the white bracelet with golden stripes on the lady's wrist. She lifted her head. They locked eyes and the lady recognized her.

Fast as lighting the lady grabbed her by the neck and pushed her against the wall.

Hally moved her legs trying to hit her. She brought her hands to her neck, she had to make the lady loosen her grip, the air wasn't reaching her lungs.

Relax.

Think thoroughly, you can't achieve anything if you just move like a fish out of the water.

Hally relaxed, there was a way of getting out of this. She kicked the lady's her to the ground. She then grabbed the hand the lady had been using to choke her and brought it to her own back. The lady, who had definitely had some kind of fighting training, pulled her hand back and kicked Hally right in her stomach.

"What the fu–" Pam, who had just gotten out of her stall, was interrupted by a punch in her face.

Hally brought herself up ignoring the pain, that lady knew how to kick.

"Hally, Pam, the train is going to leave in five minutes," Lukai said through the earphones.

Hally pressed her earphone.

"There's a Superior lady attacking us, she's supposed to be on the same train as us. Pam and I'll take care of her, you guys have to make that train, wait for us," she said without taking a breath.

"How?" Piet asked.

"I don't know! Turn the rails into stone or something!" she screamed.

"Hally, a little help," Pam cried, it was now her, the one pinned against the wall.

On the lady's hand something reflected the light. She was holding an injection, most likely a sedative.

Hally focused on the object. The injection flew off her hand to the other side of the room.

"Ah," the lady groaned.

Hally pushed her against the sinks.

Pam, now free, tried to kick her. The lady grabbed her foot. Pam fell against the floor.

Hally punched her jaw, a crippling pain moving from her fingers all the way to her arm.

The lady let go of Pam only to turn her attention to Hally.

She stood up and tried to kick Hally's stomach again. Hally made a shield. The lady bounced back to the sinks.

Pam touched the cold ceramic, letting her sink halfway into the furnishings and then hardened them back, leaving her head and hands trapped inside.

"Ahhh!" the lady grumbled. "Let me go." The ceramic made a sound like 'bleh blee blo'.

Hally leaned on her knees and took a few deep breaths. Her stomach hurt so bad that she was sure she was going to have a bruise. Her knuckles were filled with her own blood and her forehead was all sweaty. Between the punches and the kicks, making shields and levitating things wasn't as easy as she expected.

Pam stood up, she had a cut on the side of her mouth.

"We can't leave her like this," Hally managed to say.

The lady was struggling against the ceramic.

"Tell me a reason why not, she punched me in the face and was trying to kidnap us," Pam said. It did sound like a good argument.

"If she stays long enough there the ceramic might crush her ribs and then her lungs."

Pam wiped the blood from her mouth.

"So? She would probably do the same to us," she replied.

"You can't fight fire with fire, it will just get bigger," Hally said. "You use water or sand. If we want to stop this violence the Superiors have, we can't solve it with the same violence. We have to be better."

Pam looked at the lady, she was having some trouble breathing.

"Ugh, I hate my good values," she replied and turned to the sinks, giving them a buttery form.

Hally pulled the lady out and Pam returned the sinks back to normal.

"Grr," the lady managed to say as Hally grabbed her, still recovering from the ceramic pressure.

"So now what do we do? Do we just let her follow us?" Pam asked.

"I said we didn't use violence, not that we didn't use our brains," Hally exclaimed, making the injection the lady had fly across the room into her hand.

Pam smiled.

"I like the way that you think."

Piet's and Lukai's expressions were priceless when they saw the girls return from their bathroom break. Pam with a bruise forming on her eye and Hally with a bleeding hand.

"What happened?" Lukai asked.

"Dealt with a problem," Pam responded.

"What does 'dealt' mean?" Piet whispered.

"Gosh Piet! We didn't kill her!" Hally shrieked. "It means we sedated her and locked her in a storage room. She should wake in a couple of hours when we are long gone," Hally said. "How did you guys do?"

"We also dealt with a problem," Piet added.

Hally raised her eyebrows.

"Meaning?"

"Meaning that I turned the rails into stone so the train couldn't leave," Piet answered proudly.

"When they finish up their investigation and realize there's nothing wrong we should get going," Lukai added.

"Everyone on board, train 974 will leave in three minutes," said a voice through the speakers.

"See," Lukai said, turning to Hally and Pam, they were a little too proud of delaying the train and still being able to get pastries.

Inside, the kids got themselves their own small compartment with big windows and a beautiful view.

When the train started moving, Lukai closed the door and Hally called her medical kid. Just like that, the big duffle bag filled with medicines appeared on her legs. She cleaned Pam's small cut and put on some bandages on her knuckles. Then she took two ice packs, (magically frozen) one for Pam's face and another for Hally's stomach. In the meantime, Piet called his nunchucks until the rest scolded him enough to put them away.

When the doctor was done, and the duffle bag disappeared, Piet offered the girls some food. He had bought four sandwiches for them for lunch and a bunch of pastries like donuts, brownies and some bread.

And just like that, they had dealt with their first stop. They were only missing two more and then they would be back in contact with Blake and into the safety of Platz. Hally thought about it, for them to end up with few wounds, delicious food, a comfortable seat, and all of them alive, they weren't doing that bad on their own. She just wondered how Tom was. She hoped with all her heart that they had truly reached the safe house back in Slovenia, not only because this whole plan relied on Blake picking them up in the safehouse, but because she couldn't handle the feeling of Tom being in trouble.

If anything happens to him it will be my fault.

Hally started shaking her foot and scratching her wrists. Suddenly she was way too hot and her heart beat faster than when the lady had attacked her.

Everything will be good.

But if the Superiors caught him...

Everything will be good. Everything will be good. Everything will be good.

Hally took a deep breath. And another deep breath. The air didn't seem to find its way to her lungs.

"Hey," Lukai called her. "Look what they gave us at the bakery," he showed Hally a long thread with beautiful colorful silver beads. It was a key chain.

"That's nice," Hally responded, almost indifferent.

"It's yours, take it."

She turned, giving it a second look.

"Really?"

"Yeah," Lukai shrugged his shoulders as if it wasn't a big deal. "The beads are silver, that's kind of your color so..."

Hally took the keychain between her hands and played with the beads, her breathing slowly returning back to normal.

"Thanks," she managed to say.

Lukai nodded, a small smile forming.

*Everything is alright. Everything **will** be alright.*

Hally wouldn't or couldn't lie to herself. Even with the Superiors and the Villagers after them, she felt like she was just where she was supposed to be. It just felt right, the way it had to be, despite all the problems. Almost as if that same adventure had been waiting for her to come all along.

She turned her face to the window and accepted a piece of bread Lukai handed to her. Without looking at it she took a bite. She felt that awful taste in her mouth.

"What is this?" she said forcing herself to swallow the bread, so she didn't need to taste it anymore

"It's bread with raisins," Lukai said. "See everybody does it this way."

"Everybody who is out of their mind!" Hally exclaimed and gave the bitten piece of bread to Lukai. "Take it, you eat it. I'll take a brownie thank you very much," she said and took a brownie out of the brown bag Piet was holding.

"I don't understand your thing with the raisins," Pam replied.

"Shhhh, no one invited you into the conversation teddy bear" Hally replied, making Pam raise her eyebrows offended and the rest laugh.

She turned again to the windows and looked at the beautiful mountains moving from afar. She smiled. Yes, she was just where she had to be, with who she was supposed to be, doing what she was supposed to do.

30

LOVING IT OR HATING IT?

om woke up with a terrible feeling, both physical and mental.

He sat up on his thin mattress, holding his head with both of his hands. His eyes burned with the faint light of the entrance; his head ached as if a drill was trying to go through his skull.

He looked up, trying to find a drop of water to calm the longing thirst of his throat.

He could only remember a few glimpses from the night after the duel. It had appeared to be the greatest time of his life at the moment. Now the party and all the drinking just seemed like the worst mistake.

He rushed to the toilet and threw up more food that he never remembered eating.

When he was done, he washed his mouth, face and hands in the sink. Above the sink there was a thin piece of metal encrusted in the wall, it was shiny and clean enough to give back an almost recognizable reflection.

Tom looked back at his own face. His hair was a mess, he had puffy eyes and he looked tired. He was tired. This wasn't the same Tom he was used to seeing.

He looked at the door of his cell, beside it there was a bottle of water, a change of clothes and a letter.

Tom took the faint yellow paper, it read like this:

For you, my champion. Rest a little and rejuvenate yourself, you had a great party. Today you and your friends shall take on the first mission for me, and I will not tolerate any failure. Although I believe that I don't have to worry about that, after all you are _my_ champion.

The words made Tom let himself fall against the wall and take a sip of water. He liked the sound of champion, he felt special, he felt better. But he couldn't keep his guilt from drowning that pride. How could he feel that way when the words came from a person like James? He knew him, and his Superiors, brought only chaos. He had experienced that chaos. He had seen blood drawn; violence cheered on.

Tom drank the water bottle in seconds, for a moment he wanted the water to become something else for him to forget everything that was on his mind. When the water was gone, he rushed to the sink and filled the bottle again and again.

When his stomach was filled with water, he threw himself on the mattress he was calling a bed. He wanted nothing more than to lay there and cease to exist, to close his eyes and to open them to find out it was only a bad dream. An illusion. It was all just too overwhelming. He missed Hally, he missed her curiously wise advice for her age. He knew that she would actually have the words to bring him to his senses.

But Hally wasn't there, so Tom would have to give himself a pep talk.

"Who am I?" he whispered to himself. "I'm not from the Superiors. I'm Tom Black Sols, an intelligent guy. That's it! I am intelligent. In fact I'm a genius and that's what I'm doing, a genius choice. I'm not starting to feel part of the Superiors. I'm getting James' trust to get out of here. I'm not starting to feel part of the Superiors. I'm getting James' trust to get out of here. I'm not starting to feel part of the Superiors. I'm getting James' trust to get out of here," he continued whispering the same lie over and over until it didn't feel like a lie. He stood up and changed his clothes.

It was not until that moment that he realized the silence of his cell. He took a look at the cell in front of him and the one across, they were empty.

He ran to the bars; they were nowhere to be seen.

"Ayala! Isla!" he called, silence was his answer.

A drop of sweat fell from his forehead. Were they okay? Where were they? Had James decided they were useless after the presentation of the night before? Or worse, had he called them to turn them into champions just like him?

The cold feeling crawled through his skin: jealousy.

"How can I think like that? I'm a monster," he mumbled. He walked to the sink and splashed his face with water. "Wake up you stupid bag of bones, wake up. You're not thinking straight."

The door opened.

"Good morning champion," Roberts declared from the entrance with a smile, there was no sass or intention to mock in the comment.

Tom looked at Robert's teeth, it almost felt unnatural to see him smile that way, as if it was one of those things that he wasn't meant to be looking at.

"Where are Isla and Ayala?"

"Good morning," Roberts repeated.

"Morning, where are Isla and Ayala?"

Roberts laughed.

"Your *friends* are fine, James doesn't let us hear them sing. Beatrice took them for a walk before taking them to the central cabin, where James is waiting for you right now," Roberts said as he opened the door. "Come champion, he's waiting with a warm lunch," Roberts said. Tom doubted for a second. Warm lunch? Was there a possibility that they had confused James with someone else? Or was James just playing a prank?

A thought arose for a slight second before Tom pushed it away, what if he just had the wrong idea of who James was?

They walked out of the cabin.

Tom looked at his companion as they moved through the camp. Roberts was walking beside him, not pushing him and calling him names like the day before. If Tom didn't know better he could say that he was even starting to act friendly. That was stupid. Right? Had a single lighting changed so much of his life? Or had he done something else throughout the night to make them like him?

He begged that wasn't the case. He had seen what made them laugh and cheer, if he had done something they liked, maybe it was better for him just to drop dead in that exact moment. That only thought was enough to promise not to drink again.

The food was good, too good. Delicious. Perfectly seasoned. Gracefully done. It was all Tom needed to feel better. If he dared to close his eyes and just savor the butter melt on his mouth he could almost pretend to be in paradise. Nonetheless he wasn't in paradise, he was as far from it as one could be.

"Take those silly things off," had been the first words James spoke to Roberts when they entered. Inside the big cabin by the cafeteria, in the center of the room there was a round table. James sat at the farther end; his evil cane placed in front of him. Did he really need it, or did he only take it to be able to hit from a distance?

Tom took a seat, receiving more pads and congrats. Meanwhile, he noticed Ayala and Isla in the corner, both still forced to stay standing up, bracelets on their wrists, mocked and bullied time after time.

"Today's mission is to retrieve the first of the four pieces of Queen Sila's portal to Helden Platz," James announced after. "Rengas, as we know it. After months of searching the team finally found it's one of the tires of the first chariot of Queen Sila, currently being held in the Próta museum in Greece."

Tom choked on his food.

"Is there anything you want to say?" James snapped dangerously, Tom couldn't tell whether he was mad or actually cared for any comment he could say.

"Nothing," Tom muttered in the most respectful way he could.

"Oh no, please. If there's anything you want to add to this conversation feel free to do it," James replied, the same game continued. Was he mad? Was he not mad? Was he mad but pretending not to be mad? It was impossible to know.

Tom swallowed hard.

"I've read of this place... The chances of any person getting inside the Próta museum and stealing something, I assume that's where this is going, are incredibly low."

James smiled back, there was anger in his eyes. He gave a pat to Tom's back.

"That's why I created a plan for this mission," he explained. "Besides, my champion is unstoppable, and some silly security won't stop him," he added, looking around like trying to find someone to defy him. Tom noticed there was an empty chair, Ms. Duckstein's chair. Suddenly he was uncomfortable. Was he sitting in Atonal's?

James gave a final look at Tom, no smile on his face. It simply read: 'Never, ever doubt me again.' Tom took another bite, his food didn't taste as good as before, and for a reason he could only think of that for the rest of the meeting.

The first time he had heard it, Tom had thought that it was a good plan. Maybe not really good, but a half-decent one at the very least. It was not until he was there, five in the afternoon, sun still burning bright in the sky, waiting for the museum to close, to fry the security system from outside when he started to think otherwise.

Tom looked at Roberts, laying on the grass beside him, eyes fixed on the door. Each of them had been assigned someone to keep them from escaping. Isla had a guy called Jaden. Ayala, for her bad luck, was with Beatrice. And Tom was with Roberts.

The three companions had only one role in the plan: make sure that the Íroes did their jobs and keep them straight if they got creative. Hanging on their waist was their instrument. Although the colorful and bloody threat James had given the kids and the fact that he still held Blake in custody somewhere and wouldn't hesitate to torture him to death would help to encourage them not to screw up.

Roberts took off Tom's bracelets, he'd ignored James' orders and put them back on the jet on their way there.

Tom rubbed his wrist and closed his eyes, the natural electricity of the ground rising through his feet, charging his heart. He had to relax himself to make sure this mission went well.

Roberts laughed.

"You look like your teacher when we let him go," he mocked.

Tom's heart stopped.

"You let Blake go?" he exclaimed.

Roberts laughed.

"Of course, he's an Ommon. The Superiors legally don't attack Ommons unless they are Guarders. Doesn't matter how much James hates that guy, your teacher is technically not part of the Guarders, and he can't find a legal way to hurt him without creating a window for his own people to turn against him," Roberts said.

"I wasn't aware you actually had laws," Tom mumbled, eyebrows raised.

Roberts laughed again.

"They are very general rules, nothing too specific, they are there though," he explained. "Most of them are because of The Company Committee. They like how James solves their problems; it's quick and efficient. But they can't have too much blood cover their accounts. Now that would be a real-Look, that's your cue," he interrupted, pointing at the other side of the mountain where Jaden moved his arms like those who guided the airplane's landings.

James had been clear that the Íroes were not to be together until the mission officially started to prevent them from escaping.

Beatrice, Roberts, and Jaden took the Íroes to the back side of the museum, they had one hour before the night shift started, during that whole hour there was no security but the electric one, the best moment for a heist. In a way it only made it worse, the Greeks trusted people enough to leave it one hour without security. Now because of Tom that would change.

"Here you are, do your job," Beatrice said, giving Ayala a final push against the wall and walking away with Roberts. They would guard the other entrances.

"Do we seriously have to do this?" Ayala asked, rubbing her cheek.

Isla looked at Jaden, far behind her. He had a gun between his hands ready to use.

"Unfortunately, it looks like it," Isla sighed.

Ayala and Isla turned to Tom, the three of them too embarrassed of what they were going to do to say anything to each other.

Tom saw the electronic panel beside the door. He touched it with the tip of his fingers. A few volts of electricity came out of his hand, and it was deactivated.

Ayala looked at the locked door. A green mist appeared at her feet and covered her up to her head. When the mist dissipated Ayala was no longer standing there, in her place there was a small green spider. The spider, Ayala, made its way through a crack in the door and in a few seconds the door opened, human Ayala standing on the other side.

The three kids walked inside, and the door was shut, creating an echo through the empty room. They were officially criminals now, and there was no going back.

Tom looked at the room, it was the new exhibit the posters on the front wall spoke about. Shelves were filled with statues, pedestals showed relics, paintings decorated the walls. It was enlightening.

Ayala stopped at one of the first paintings: green trees, blue sky and happy animals.

"That's beautiful," she sniffed.

"I don't know if this is mean... does it feel like home?" Tom asked.

Ayala chuckled at the question. His eyes opened as plates.

"I might have fauna powers Tom, I'm still a human," she reminded him. "But yes, it does bring a special feeling. Nature, it's alive Tom, in a way we'll never understand. It is free and balanced... We should learn from it more often. And we must respect it, respect every small life in it. People think I'm just stupidly nice, the truth is I learned to respect life. We are all here for a reason and whether someone is a good or bad addition I can't judge. I just know what I'll be."

Tom smiled.

"That's why I don't like taking the animal shape."

"You don't?" Tom asked bewildered. "I thought we all enjoyed our powers." He remembered the electricity in his veins, it was the best feeling he'd ever had.

Ayala continued to stare at the painting.

"I like my powers, not turning into animals. It is unnatural, it doesn't feel normal. It's like taking their shape just to use their advantages and then dumping it as it gets hard. It's a cheap cheat. I much rather use their abilities without using their shape. It's more respectful."

She turned to him.

"What if we find a window and just run?"

"A window?" he scoffed.

"They can't guard every window at the same time."

"We don't have any transport. How long do you think it will take them to find us if we run?" Isla asked.

Ayala shrugged.

"An hour, or two. Any time would be worth it."

"Don't be silly," Isla snorted. "We would put Blake in danger."

A lump crossed Tom's throat.

"You're right," Ayala confided.

"Let's get the dumb piece already, if they want it to decorate their houses it's their problem. At least we won't spill any blood."

They continued walking, following the plan James had created. Tom followed them, mouth shut. He didn't know why; he just couldn't tell them that Blake was free.

Isla opened the doors to the next exhibit, according to the grid the kids had been given, Tom's damage to the security measure ended just there. "You activate the alarm, I'll kill you," James had said.

"Wait," Ayala said and pulled Isla back from entering the next room. "There are cameras up there," she said, pointing at the very next corner of the room, invisible to any normal eye.

"I shall take care of that," Isla said sorrowfully. She threw some seeds from her pocket into the ground.

From the seeds a set of big green vines came out and moved through the walls until they reached the cameras covering every single one of them.

"I hate this," Ayla muttered when they walked into the now safe next room. "It's so dishonest and wrong."

"This isn't what a well-educated human being should be doing," Isla agreed.

They walked, a now heavier burden on their shoulders. At the end, two heavy metallic doors awaited. Isla pulled them open.

The air filled with the emergency alarm; they had tripped one of the security measures.

Tom covered his ears and looked up. The room was filled with lasers, shooting from wall to wall in many angles. The door on the other side of this exhibit, the one that led to the storage room, started to be covered by another security door, one that was impossible to open. They had thirty seconds before the police were called.

Fortunately, they knew what to do. James didn't leave anything to chance.

The green mist appeared, and Ayala turned into a small bird. She flew past the lasers and covering herself with mist, she went back to her old self. With inhuman force she pushed the door and kept it from closing.

"Isla!" Tom yelled; it was her turn now.

Isla brought the vines from the previous room, covered the cameras from that new room and helped Ayala with the door, the thick vines pushing upwards beside her.

Tom placed both of his hands against the wall, he called the electricity away, trying to draw it from the alarm and the lasers. It was too much for him to handle alone.

"Seven seconds," Isla alerted him.

Tom pulled even harder; he couldn't take all of it. Not draining it anyway.

He took a step back; he would have to try something new. He raised his hand, anger soaring through his veins, why couldn't he just do it? Was it really going to be his fault?

"Two seconds."

A lighting bolt escaped from the tip of his fingers to the wall.

The lasers turned off. The metallic door stopped and retrieved back into the wall. Smoke filled the place.

The three kids took a second and gasped for air. They were once again living on borrowed time.

"That was too close," Isla mumbled, before fixing her hair and crossing the door, Ayala not far behind her.

Tom wiped the blood off his nose and the sweat off his forehead. He took a deep breath and looked at the wall, a black circle marked where the lighting had entered.

"Tom?" Ayala called.

"On my way," he replied.

He was about to follow when a small door opened on the left wall. A hidden door, an old one for sure. It had probably been created centuries ago for Queen Sila's workers. The lightning must have activated it. Tom stared at it. Through the small crack he could see the trees, the mountains and the sun still shining up high.

Tom looked at it and then to where Ayala and Isla had disappeared.

The three of them were being held hostages and forced by James' to do the dirty work. They were miserable, mistreated, underfed. If that was a secret door there was a good chance that it wasn't being observed. They could use it to escape. This was their chance to get away and save themselves. Now that Tom knew that Blake was no longer in jeopardy, they could try it without putting any life in danger besides theirs. All he had to do was to tell Ayala and Isla about that door. All he had to do was open his mouth.

31

OPINNOT CITY

"You're still up," Piet yawned from the other side of their compartment.

Hally looked up. Pam's head rested against the window, her breaths clouding the glass against her cheek. Lukai lay asleep beside her, turning to either side every once in a while.

"You guys were all completely zoned out, someone had to stay awake in case anything happened," Hally whispered back. She kept her weird dreams off the topic.

Piet rubbed his eyes.

"How long till we get there?"

Hally looked at the dark scenery outside, the sun had set no more than half an hour before.

"I asked a while ago, I suppose one more hour, maybe two," she answered.

Piet yawned again.

"Why don't you sleep? I'll stay awake," Piet proposed.

Hally gave him a small smile.

"It's not a problem really. I'm not that tired," she lied. Truth be said, she didn't want to have another of her weird dreams.

Piet glared at her, he might have been naive but even he wasn't stupid enough to be fooled by that.

"Alright," Hally reluctantly accepted. "Don't talk to anyone, don't leave the cart and if anything, I mean anything, looks suspicious, wake us up," she said as she arranged her jacket into a pillow shape to rest her head.

Piet laughed.

"I mean it Piet," she grunted.

"I know, I know…"

"Night, Piety."

She closed her eyes. Despite her wounds curing, her muscles still ached. Yet she was warm, her belly filled, and the constant movement of the train comforted better than a lullaby.

Hally was about to fall asleep.

Time went by, dozing on and off. The world silent as it slept.

Someone sniffled. Then again. And again.

She opened her eyes slightly, in the corner of the cart Piet wiped his tears with the edge of his shirt, eyes red and cheeks pink.

"What's wrong?" she asked, sitting up.

Piet straightened at the sound of her voice forcing a smile in the middle of his sad face as he wiped the last tears off his cheeks.

"I thought you were asleep," he replied, embarrassment clear in his tone.

"I'm not," Hally replied softly.

"Yeah," he rushed to rearrange his shirt and smiled again, the same fake smile that Hally had mastered.

"Crying's alright Piet. It really is."

Piet lifted his eyes from the ground.

"Even if the reason is dumb?" he dared to ask.

"There is no stupid reason for crying. There are only stupid people that don't do it."

Piet chuckled and then broke down, tears pouring down his face.

Hally switched seats and hugged him as he continued to cry silently, letting the tears of his eyes wet his face and his sweater. Hally stayed there, comforting him like she had done to many refugees back in Tirabia. She'd knew, eventually if he wanted to talk, he would.

Between tears and sniffles he started to whisper.

"I have a sister. Her name is," he paused, "was Joy... After I was born, Mom abandoned us and Dad had to raise us alone. When she was seven, she was diagnosed with leukemia. I never knew, she insisted my dad not tell me, so I wouldn't change the way I looked at her. For months I was angry because I thought she had abandoned me like my mother. She was fighting for her life at the hospital. There was a time when she came back home, and everything was alright, two wonderful years. Then she left again. This time I was sure that she had left me. I was so angry that I threw all our pictures in the trash crying myself to sleep wishing that she came back. My dad isn't bad at all, he does his best, but he isn't Joy. Joy... she never came back and I never got to see her again, not even to say goodbye."

He sniffled.

"She called me Piety."

A heavy weight struck Hally's heart.

"I'm so sorry Piet, I had no idea."

Piet wiped his tears once again; he was calmer now.

"You don't have to apologize; you did nothing wrong. It's just that...," the words were having a hard time coming out of his mouth without bringing tears as well. "I lost a sister and every opportunity to ever say goodbye properly, but now God gave me another chance with not only one but with two more sisters and a brother," he said and smiled, a real smile.

Hally hugged Piet once again and his face filled with comfort.

"Just don't tell them I said that," Piet muttered pointing at the deeply asleep Pam and Lukai with his chin.

"Why? Because you'll lose your cool guy vibe?"

"Yes and no... Mostly because they'll make a goal of their lives to annoy me and treat me like a baby."

"Believe me. It already is," Hally replied, and Piet let out a laugh. "But I promise, a sibling's promise, those are never broken.

They reached Opinnot city by night, along with other college students. As if it had been planned, the university was having an open house for international students providing thousands of different faces to disappear within, and too tired seniors that let them in without checking their stolen names, ID badge and dorm key included. Boys on one side, girls on the other.

The dorm was pretty, or at least not horrible.

"Thank you Giselle Henderson," Hally mumbled as she threw herself onto her bed thinking about the whole mess there was going to be when the real Giselle appeared. She would probably get another room; the seniors would think they hadn't added her to the list. Either way she was now too tired to even care for her dreams.

It was not until four in the morning that Hally forced herself to wake up. She had been back at that metal table, tubes coming out of her arm in her dream. There was a point where weirdness beat tiredness.

She stared at the ceiling, her eyes adjusting. Pam was sitting at a small table in front of their even smaller kitchen. She was eating something, her hair wet against her face.

Hally stood up, she was still wearing the same clothes as the day before, all filled with dust, blood and sweat.

Against her will, one that told her to go back to sleep, she put both feet onto the frozen cold floor and walked down to the kitchen. In the afternoon they were going to meet Tony in the mall, until then they were as free as birds.

"You're eating a hamburger? At this time?" Hally asked, sliding into a chair beside her. "Where do you even get a hamburger at this time?"

Pam swallowed the piece she was chewing.

"The college students know how to party. Whatever they were celebrating didn't end until a few minutes ago," she said with certain astonishment. "Piet was walking around a while back. He said he found a guy in a food truck that was giving away the last hamburgers and he got one for each of us. Yours is in the microwave," she said before taking another bite of the juicy hamburger.

Hally let out a tired sigh and got herself up to the old-almost-falling-apart microwave.

"Where are they now? The boys I mean," she asked.

"Mmmm," Pam said, still chewing her food. "Why should I know? I'm not their mom!" she complained.

"Sure, yet you were the one awake, therefore the one that could know that information," Hally said returning to the table with her burger, it smelled delicious.

Pam let out a quiet growl, put her burger down, and closed her eyes trying to remember.

"I think, let's better say guess so it can't be upheld in court, that Piet is walking around the place and Lukai... well I have no idea," she offered and added an eye roll.

Hally took a bite of her burger. She was so hungry that she finished hers before Pam.

With the burgers gone, Hally sat in the kitchen admiring the dreadful attempts at art hanging on the walls, the corners of moss forming on the paint and the dust accumulated in the cracks of the floor. Eventually her eyes fell on Pam, combing her hair. The white light revealed the new bruises forming over her old ones.

"How are you feeling?"

Pam didn't pay much attention to the question.

"Better, whatever that lady did certainly pulled a number on my knuckles," she said.

Hally looked at the bruises and cuts. She recognized them perfectly. Some were clearly new ones; others could perfectly have been from weeks ago.

"I was thinking-"

"Here we go again," Pam groaned.

"Let me finish!" Hally muttered. "Do you know what the university must have?"

Pam remained quiet for some seconds and then let the word come out of her mouth.

"No."

"An incredible and amazing art studio," Hally said.

"And how am I supposed to go, it's for students only," Pam grunted.

Hally threw the ID badge.

"Monica Stefson is a student."

The moment Hally's words entered Pam's head her dark eyes shone, her mouth almost formed a smile.

"You're right," she said, putting the comb down. "I'm going to find it," she said excitedly and grabbed a coat from her bed.

"It's four in the mor-." She was already gone.

Hally looked around, again. Her eyes fell in the small bathroom, she could use a shower and a change of clothes. Without discussing it too much with herself that was exactly what she did.

Her stomach full, her hair brushed, and the dirt and blood cleaned off her skin, she made sure to have her backpack ready to go just in case. She looked at the window.

The sun had still not risen, the perfect opportunity to go and see it.

Door closed, the key in her pocket, she walked to the elevator and pressed the button to the rooftop, one she had her eye on since the night before.

The metallic door opened, the cold air hit her face; it was the perfect morning.

The rooftop was not much. There were a few chairs and a fireplace, all looked like they hadn't been used in a while. The place was quiet except for a few birds singing their praises on the tree and a few students going to the gym or finishing an all-nighter down at the plaza.

Hally walked to the edge and leaned over the brick fence.

"Jue...," escaped from her mouth when she saw the bottom from that far. She had never been scared of heights, but she had to accept that she had probably never been in a building so tall either.

"Long trip down, right?" a voice asked behind Hally, she turned around just to find herself in front of Lukai's friendly freckled face.

She smiled.

"Are you here to see the sunrise?" she asked.

"Not really," Lukai said leaning on the brick edge beside Hally. "I was here for the lake," he pointed at the far left, where shiny waters met the first sun rays of the day. "The sunrise is just a nice addition. You're too." He quickly rephrased. "Not that I was looking at you." His eyes opened even bigger. "Not that I was not looking at you. I mean- I better shut up," he hid his red face between his hands.

Hally laughed.

"Worth the view certainly," she added, eyes on the horizon. She crossed her arms, the wind hitting, she should have gotten a jacket.

"Here, take this," Lukai said, taking off his coat and placing it around her shoulders. "I'm used to Canada's cold, this is home," he said. "And after coming ten floors up the stairs I don't need it."

"Stairs?" Hally laughed.

Lukai's face turned red one more time.

"I couldn't find the elevator."

Hally laughed, one of those heartfelt laughs

"Now you're laughing at me."

Hally bit her inner lip, trying to keep the laugh from coming.

"Sorry."

"Don't be, I repeat I have four siblings, you're just making this place more like home, each time."

Hally laughed again.

"If this were my home, we would be speaking Spanish under the heat of the morning sun." She tightened the coat around her.

"This is a weird question but, do you miss speaking Spanish?"

Hally remembered the first day she'd been forced to speak English alone. She'd cried and cried. Stumbling with a language she didn't understand.

"*A veces como que me hace falta. El inglés es precioso, pero no es mi lengua natal. Por más que lo hable siempre.*"

"I'll take that as a yes."

"It's a yes."

Hally chuckled.

"Now that we're not on a comfortable beach, what do you think about home? I mean before, we had a chance back there. Now we can't go back to our lives even if we want to."

Lukai looked at her.

"Who said I wanted to?"

"I mean it," Hally replied, turning her face to look at him.

The thin line of light in the horizon had gotten bigger by now, his freckles and brown eyes shining. His hair, just like hers, fighting against the wind.

He took a few seconds to answer.

"I'll tell you if you tell me," he finally said.

"You first," Hally replied.

"I guess... I guess that I am missing home a little bit," he finally admitted. "Even the shoveling."

"It's not like I want to go back," he continued, "this, whatever it is we are doing right now, it feels like... like..."

"Like you are just where you are supposed to be," Hally finished his sentence, turning to the horizon one more time.

Lukai smiled.

"Exactly," he said. "Your turn. Do you miss your home now that you can't go back?" he asked, turning to face her.

Hally could feel the faint sunlight hitting her face.

"Ummm," she was trying to formulate the answer in her mind. "I don't know..." she finally said, she had spent so much time in Tirabia missing Costa Rica, that the home-sickness had become a natural feeling. "I miss not being hunted, just another name in the public records. I'm sure of that."

She continued.

"I suppose that this is just a new experience, a new chapter. Just because you turn the page it doesn't mean you forget the last one or that you suddenly don't miss it. Yet you can't help but enjoy how the story is turning out," Hally answered.

She took a deep breath, the fresh air as the best medicine for all stress.

"That's deep," Lukai chortled. "Are you sure you aren't a little bit emo?"

"Do I look emo to you?" Hally complained.

Lukai grinned.

"You look like a troublemaker."

"I'M NOT A TROUBLE MAK-" Her mind flooded with the many classes with Ms. Knox. "Forget it. I'll take it as a compliment." She gave in. "But that's a good thing, because we need balance. Pam can be the-"

"Cheerleader," Lukai proposed.

"In another dimension maybe." Lukai laughed. "No, she's from the dark artist clique. And Piet... He's too young to be in a clique. And you..."

Hally turned at the Canadian boy.

"Which clique were you in?"

His cheeks flooded red.

"I wasn't in one," he lied.

"Oh my gosh!" she covered her mouth with her hands. "You were a jock!"

Lukai's eyes doubled their size.

"HOW DID YOU KNOW?"

Hally threw her head back and roared in laughter.

"What's so funny about it?" Lukai asked.

Hally's laughter grew louder as an answer.

"Sorry, sorry…" she mumbled, forcing herself to stop laughing, wiping the tears away. "You were saying?"

Lukai stared at her before opening his mouth.

"There's nothing to add, I just played…"

Hally looked at him eagerly waiting for the end of the sentence.

He crossed his arms over his chest.

"I'm not saying, you're gonna laugh."

"You started it, you must finish it. It's the rule."

"Whose rule?"

"My rule. Finish it."

Lukai sighed.

"I played baseball," Lukai said, turning red.

The roof filled once again with laughter.

"Why are you laughing? And why am I embarrassed? It's baseball!"

Hally leaned on the border, her stomach aching. She laughed harder.

"So..." she said when she calmed down. "Baseball?" she didn't manage to say the word without smiling.

"Are you gonna laugh again?"

Hally pressed her lips and shook her head.

"Yes, I played baseball. I even took my dog to the games."

"Awww, you have a dog?"

Lukai nodded.

Hally looked down at the plaza, at the few students that remained there, waiting for the last of the sun to rise.

"I wanted a dog, but my mom isn't a fan of them. Maybe when we get back, I can ask Blake if he lets me have one," Hally said. "It would be nice to bring a dog to the team. We can argue a service dog would help tighten the group dynamics."

Lukai clicked his tongue.

"I don't think he'll let you."

"Why?" she exclaimed.

"I don't know, he looks more like a cat person to me."

Hally pictured Blake's face.

"What are you even talking about? He's a hundred percent a dog person, I'm sure."

Lukai tilted his head from side to side.

"I don't know."

"Treacher on the other hand, he's definitely a cat person. You can tell by his George face," Hally continued.

"George face?"

"Yeah you know, he looks like someone who should be called George."

Lukai thought about it.

"You're right," he finally admitted. "He does look like a George. And like a cat person."

"Told ya."

The kids shared a laugh. Together, up there, with the world at their feet, life felt easy enough for them to beat it. It all just seemed to fade away, worries, fears, anxiety. And in its place came a type of peace Hally couldn't remember feeling in all of her life. She just wanted to stay there forever.

By midmorning, still a controversial topic between the four Guardians, the kids reunited and got some breakfast, a real breakfast. It felt like a lot of time had passed by since the last day at the refuge, the bus, the Guarders, everything. Hally had a new life and she liked it.

Once the sun had completely risen Lukai and Hally had had some self-inflicted training. They had played with the light on the rooftop for Lukai; he had made a few small illusions. Then they had gone to a tennis court to practice Hally's reflexes and telekinesis, as well as her shield making ability (all of them better each time) and even tried and successfully made three small portals that transported a pencil across a room.

Finally, they had visited the library where they had found Piet who had been enjoying guided tours of the university (yes, there was a crazy guy giving tours since three in the morning). He joined Hally and Lukai's training for the last hour, his own powers proving to have improved a lot, being able to turn small objects at will. Hally wondered if his improvement had come with the training or with the talk they had had the night before. She couldn't help but think the things were connected.

Eventually they bumped into Pam, her face and hair filled with glitter, and her clothes splashed with paint, confetti and traces of wet clay.

After eating their traditional American breakfast they returned to their rooms, got their things and walked to the mall, getting lost twice on the way.

The mall was packed. Apparently, the college students never rested, they went from party to party and when they weren't at a party they were shopping for one. Although Hally had always disliked such places, too many people for her taste, this time it brought her the relaxing feeling that she could sit in a cafe and shop for new clothes like a normal teenager. And for better or for worse she wasn't the only one that felt like that.

After looking through a couple cafes in search of Tony, he hadn't specified on the map which one he usually visited, the kids started to lose a little focus, entering store after store, looking at pretty things and saying things like 'I've always wanted one of those' or 'When I have the money, I'll surely get one'. They even started to get turns to choose the next store they visited.

Eventually, and I mean a real bunch of stores later, they reached the third floor, the surprises-filled-floor. In one of the cafes at the end they could see Tony, sitting at a table, sipping his cappuccino. And on the other side there was a shop Hally had never seen but made Piet go nuts, better said desperate.

"Please, please, please, let me go," Piet begged the rest.

"You can go to the store later, we're actually here to see Tony," Pam replied.

"Easy for you to say, you took us to five different art stores. I didn't know there were so many kinds of paint," Piet moaned. "Technically it's still my turn to choose the store."

"Can't you go after we speak to Tony, we don't know how much time he has been waiting," Lukai said, now the time they had spent fooling around was making him feel guilty.

"No!" Piet cried. "Please," he begged once again, for some reason that store had some importance to him.

"Fine, I'll do it," Hally finally accepted. "Lu, hand me two of those earphone thingies. I'll take Piet to his store and you guys can talk to Tony."

"Don't take too long. We'll call you if anything happens," Lukai said, handing an earphone to Hally and one to Piet.

Piet thanked them and pulled Hally inside the store before she even had the chance to put the thing in her ear.

It's literally like having a five-year-old kid

The store was a furniture store. There isn't much to say in that respect. I mean, Hally liked some of the furniture, at least what she was capable of seeing. Piet kept pulling her through aisle after aisle rapidly. At first she thought that he was looking for a lamp or something but then she saw a pretty girl at the other side of the store and she understood what was happening.

"Please tell me you didn't bring me all the way here just to see a girl," Hally let out.

"I was thinking of talking to her, actually," Piet replied with a stupid, flirtatious smile.

"That makes it so much better," Hally blurted sarcastically.

Piet let out a sigh and looked over at the long-black-haired girl.

"I guess you're right, we should leave."

"Nah," Hally said, stopping him. "We're already here, now do something Romeo."

Piet looked at the girl once again.

"I'll talk to her," he gloated.

Hally nodded in agreement and looked around. A kid with a white bracelet and golden stripes entered the store. She had seen him before, on the first floor. He seemed harmless, more focused on talking with his friends than hunting anybody, but now that they were close, she couldn't risk it.

"Fine. I'll go with you."

"No! That'll look so creepy."

"Ohh, chill. I'll go invisible."

"That's even CREEPIER," Piet cried.

Hally looked straight into his eyes.

"It's that or nothing."

Piet moaned.

"Don't make a sound," he warned.

Hally followed Piet, now invisible, holding on to his shoulder.

Piet walked to the aisle where the girl was, the candle aisle, and acted as if he was looking for candles as well. He grabbed a long white candle that allegedly had a coconut smell, sniffed it a little too hard. He sneezed, dropping the candle and bringing a bunch to the ground.

Hally had to keep her hand on top of her mouth to keep her giggling quiet.

Piet picked the candles sloppily from the ground and continued as if nothing had happened. He then took another candle and looked over at the girl, he was getting up his courage to speak.

"So, are you looking for a candle?" Piet asked.

The girl looked at him and then to the candle she was holding.

"Yes," she frowned.

Piet's cheeks flooded with embarrassment, that was a dumb question.

This time Hally had to pinch herself to stop from laughing and even then, a few giggles could be heard. Piet smashed where he thought Hally's foot was. He missed by a centimeter.

Hally serious up.

"He-," sounded through her earphone before the line cut. "Ca-." It was Lukai's voice, it sounded urgent.

Hally's heart started racing, something felt wrong.

She tapped Piet's shoulder a few times letting him know she was walking away a few meters. She walked to the next aisle far enough to whisper and not be heard.

"Lukai? Pam? Everything alright?" she asked through her earphone.

There was no answer.

"Hello? Can you hear me?" she tried again, the same silence remained.

Something is wrong.

Relax, just breathe.

Something is very wrong.

Maybe they lost signal.

That doesn't make any sense. Something is wrong, I know it.

Hally looked around anxiously. Her palms had started to sweat, and she had this need to move around in circles. She took out the keychain Lukai had given her from her pocket and played with the beads. They had to go to the cafe.

She walked back to Piet, who was having a better conversation by then.

She whispered into his ear.

"We have to go, now."

Piet jumped; he wasn't expecting the whisper. He played it cool enough and continued the conversation.

"So, yes Mabel. If you want a candle for the whole house you should go for the cinnamon one, but if it's for the bathroom you should go with the mint, it's more refreshing," he winked at her, and Hally had to keep the retching sound silent.

The girl, Mabel, laughed and grabbed the candles.

"How do you even know this much about candles?"

"School project a few years ago, never thought it would be useful until now," Piet answered, Hally could see through his face that he was having a great time.

She pinched his arm again to hurry him up.

"I think I have to leave now, can I get your number?" Piet asked.

Mabel smiled.

"Just if you promise to call sometime," she said and Piet promised. Hally rolled her eyes.

Mable wrote her number on a sticky note and handed it to Piet.

"Thank you," he returned the smile and before he could continue talking leading to a never ending conversation, Hally pulled his arm into the next aisle.

"Bye," he mumbled as he was pulled by an invisible force, leaving Mabel with a very confused face.

Once in the next aisle Hally dropped her cover.

"What's wrong with you? I was killing it!" Piet said to Hally.

"Sure. You were talking about candles!"

"Hey! I got her number!"

"Still. Candles?"

"There wasn't much to say-"

"It doesn't matter now," Hally interrupted him, she remembered why she had pulled him away. "Something is wrong with Lukai, Pam and Tony."

Piet rolled his eyes.

"Let's go to the cafe and when we make sure everything is OK we come back," Piet said walking to the exit.

"Why? Missing your girlfriend already?" Hally asked.

"SHE'S NOT MY GIRLFRIEND!" Piet muttered under his breath, cheeks red.

The two of them walked to the end of the floor, to a beautiful small cafe. From afar Hally read the name on the sign, Scienza Cafe, it had a weird seal beside it with a chemical compound. From the same distance Hally could see Tony through the window, his face buried in a newspaper. Lukai and Pam sitting across from him, rather serious.

Piet opened the door; a welcoming bell rang.

Inside, the cafe was very pretty, it reminded Hally of Four back at Platz. The walls were stone and filled with plants and flowers of all kinds. All the chairs and tables differed from each other. And the whole place smelled like coffee and rain. It seemed the perfect place to read a book or listen to music.

"See, everything is perfectly good," Piet moaned to Hally.

Hally looked at Pam and Lukai, they both were quiet, fear filled their eyes.

"No it isn't-" Hally mumbled.

Behind her a guy locked the door. Hally turned; they were the only ones in the cafe apart from five shady looking guys.

"What is going on?" Piet asked Pam and Lukai, but they kept quiet just looking at them trying to warn them of something.

"Tony?" Hally asked.

Tony looked up from the newspaper straight into Hally's eyes.

"I'm sorry dear, I believe I will disappoint you in that aspect," the guy said standing up. He wasn't Tony, he was just a very similar guy. "*You* on the other hand will make my boss very happy."

32

THE GUILT CAUSER

"Tom, are you coming? Or must we leave you behind?" Isla asked, from the other side of the room.

"Sorry," Tom muttered and walked through the room and into the other, the hidden door he had just found was a secret he had decided to keep.

Tom's legs started to shake, what had he just done? There was still time, the door was still open, it hadn't disappeared. All he had to do was open his mouth and say the words.

He kept moving, staring blankly at the map James had given him, he didn't dare raise his eyes and look at the girls.

They crossed the last doors; the storage room waiting exactly where it was supposed to be.

Tom raised his eyes, finally, and looked at the one entrance. The door that now stood between success and failure was guarded by two passcodes and two heavy metal doors.

They could still make a run for it. He dismissed the thought.

Ayala took out of her pocket the yellow note with the passcodes, at least the Superiors had done something to help the kids.

Tom watched quietly as Ayala pressed the numbers, mumbling them under her breath as the tiles lit up.

He just had to talk up.

He kept quiet.

The red light turned green, and the metal doors opened wide. Tom felt the cold AC hit his face and stared into the dark room as the lights turned on one by one, revealing hundreds of years of history.

"In we go," Ayala muttered.

The three of them walked inside, closing the door behind them. The storage room was by far more interesting than the actual exhibit. It was bigger, way bigger, and it was divided into three parts. The first was a small room dedicated to restoration and research. The second part was occupied by carefully organized boxes. Tom could only assume that inside those boxes were equally organized objects, perhaps small paintings or old tools. The third one was exactly the same as the one before, but it wasn't for the small things, this one dealt with the bigger gear. Through this room there were gigantic vases, statues, parts of monuments, important art pieces and a chariot: Queen Sila's chariot.

The chariot was simple and that made it beautiful. No. It wasn't beautiful. It was gorgeous. Lovesome. Venust... Such a beauty that a thousand words wouldn't be enough to describe it. It was made of pure burnished agarwood. At the front there were gold carvings formed into trees, flowers and birds. It was made to be pulled by four horses, even the reins were golden. Although there were tons of other details, Tom didn't pay much attention to them, his mind was focused on one single problem.

"Where's the fourth wheel?" he asked.

"You gotta be kidding me!" Isla groaned. "The freaking wheel isn't even here!" she shouted. Her eyes opened as she realized that the sentence was crude. "Pardon my frustration," she said, cheeks as red as a tomato.

"We don't mind it," Ayla said, giving her a comforting pat on her shoulder. "How do we know Rengas isn't one of these wheels?"

"James said that Rengas was made of gold and it contained Queen's Sila's seal, a crescent moon, a sunflower and rainwater," Tom sighed, he circled the chariot in search of a hint of where Rengas could be.

"I don't get it. Is this a trap? Or are others looking for the same pieces as us?" Isla protested.

"It's hidden," Ayala blurted out, catching Isla's and Tom's attention.

"Ayala, what do you mean?" Tom asked.

Ayala turned to him, her kind brown eyes smiling at him kindly. A shiver crossed his neck. He just had to tell them of the door.

"The chariot has a particular smell," Ayala sniffed the air. She walked towards the wall focused on a thin crack. "Right here, there's a slight breeze coming from the other side of this crack and it has the same smell as the chariot."

Tom and Isla walked to the wall. The three of them studied the crack, it covered the wall, forming what looked like a secret door.

"You're a genius!" Isla exclaimed.

"You really are," Tom gasped. "We have to open it."

He looked around the room trying to find a way to open the door. "Physics. If I find something to lever it-"

"Oh! I just want this over," Isla complained. "Make way," she said and signaled for Tom to get out of the way. She took a deep breath "For Blake."

For a split second, Tom's heart stopped. The Superiors didn't have Blake, he knew that. He knew it. All he had to do was say it and the whole situation would turn a complete hundred and eighty.

He opened his mouth, no sound came. He couldn't. If he did, he would lose all of it. He would lose his power, his influence, his title. He would be no one again.

He looked at Isla, mouth sewn shut once again, that secret was not going to leave him.

Isla threw a few small seeds through the crack and put her hands on the wall. She closed her eyes.

The green leaves grew out coming out the crack pushing the hidden door open. She took a step back. She had revealed a long and creepy dark corridor.

None of the kids wanted to step inside, it looked old and smelled bad. However, they always ended up with the same conclusion, either they faced the darkness, or they faced James. They all chose the darkness.

Holding a single small flashlight, step after step they got deeper and deeper into the darkness, with only hope to live for. None of them spoke, Ayala guiding them. Eventually they made it to the end of the corridor, into a giant chamber.

The chamber was a little bit less terrifying than the rest of the place. It was made of rock all of it covered with bright green moss. In the corners several water drops fell killing the dreadful silence that Tom actually enjoyed. And the air had a much more tolerable smell than elsewhere.

There was only one problem with the enormous chamber: nine different tunnels opened up in different directions, only one of them leading to Rengas.

"I lost the smell," Ayala wept. "What are we going to do?"

"If we pick either of them, we have an eleven percent chance of making the right choice," Tom said. "89% of making the wrong one."

"Or none at all," Isla replied harshly.

Tom frowned.

"That's not how probability works."

"I'm just saying. To get into a place properly you usually have to be invited in, it's bad manners if you just enter and bad luck if you don't even care."

"Isla, this isn't one of your fancy parties, *we* have no invitation," Tom snapped back. They were taking longer than expected, he just wished that James wouldn't get disappointed if they came back with Rengas a little bit later than the plan dictated.

"Actually, I think Isla has a point. Maybe the tunnels aren't the right answer," Ayala proposed nicely.

Tom took a deep breath and prepared his brain for stupidity. Ayala was an angel, a good person that meant no harm to anyone, but he considered her deeply beneath his intellectual level.

He opened his eyes, snapping out of it, what was he thinking? How could he say something like that?

"Could I have the flashlight please?" Ayala requested. Tom handed it to her. He felt the need to apologize for what he had just said, but how would it go? 'Sorry, I called you stupid in my mind, I'll try to not think about it anymore'?

Ayala took the flashlight from his cold hand and walked to the center. Instead of looking at the tunnels she looked at the floor. There was writing on the stone: "Si domum meam voles pervenire, audebis vincere".

"Latin...," Tom gulped, he didn't know latin.

"If my home you want to reach, then my dare you must complete," Ayala read. "What dare?"

"There must be another writing around here that explains it," Isla said.

They started looking.

Tom walked; flashlight high. He felt weird, as if he had to remember something but he couldn't figure out why. As if his mind was foggy and unmanageable.

He focused on the light trying to get his thoughts in order. His eyes fell on what looked like a stone button covered with moss.

"Found something," Tom called.

Both girls walked to him and looked at what the bright white flashlight was pointing at. It read: "Paratus es".

"Are you ready?" Ayala translated.

"Absolutely." Isla pressed the button all the way to the bottom.

The whole chamber shook.

"Maybe that wasn't the best idea," Ayala whined. From the rock a light came, each second brighter, creating a human form. When the light figure was complete it shone brighter. Two times brighter. Three times. Four times.

Then, it stopped.

Tom opened his eyes. In front of him, standing, there was a rock statue of a human (fully armored) with the button as its heart in his chest. The rock glowed a dim light, enough to kill the darkness.

"Perhaps we must speak to it. Convince it with respect and manners that we deserve Rengas," Isla suggested. "James said he needed Íroes, maybe we just have to show him."

The statue answered before Tom could.

"Certa me et cor meum!" the statue shouted; it raised its fists. Its voice was deep, cold and dry, like rock.

"It's... it's telling us to fight. And get his heart," Ayala stuttered, scared.

None of the kids moved. *That's why I needed the lightning, to kill the statue.*

"Pugnare!" the statue shouted again.

"What did it say now?" Tom asked, his hand raised ready for the lighting.

"He's insisting that we fight."

Again, none of the kids moved, there was something about a talking statue that made it difficult to process.

"Tum vitam tuam capiam," the statue exclaimed and there was no need for Ayala to translate, it was them or the statue, not both.

The statue turned to the wall and ripped a piece of rock, giving himself a self-made sword.

"Pugnare," the statue repeated and charged.

Tom raised his hand. He called, no one answered.

For a second he froze, the statue still charging.

"Tom!" Isla yelled.

He threw himself out of the way into the cold and wet rock.

He looked up at the sound of struggle. Isla had taken the instructions clearly. She had thrown seeds into the floor and was already charging back at the statue with vines and roots, wrapping around its body and sword. Each time the statue broke free. Ayala was back in a corner, fists raised ready to fight but not quite convinced that it was the best decision. All her beliefs kept her away from the struggle.

Tom pushed himself off the ground. There wasn't much he could do. The lightning wasn't coming, not from him. And electrical powers didn't really come handy when the enemy was made of rock, a non-conductor. Unless of course the rock was wet.

Tom turned to the corners, there was a small pool of water, maybe just enough.

He ran to the corner, Isla still dealing with the statue single handed.

"Ayala! Help me!" she growled while evading a sword strike. The rock against rock sent an echo through the chamber.

"But- It's a living creature," Ayala cried back. "I can't hurt it!"

"I know," Isla replied, "but I need help," the words burned Isla's mouth as they left it.

Tom took off his sweater and dipped it in the puddled water until it was soaking wet.

"Tom!"

"Coming!"

He ran towards the statue leaving a water trace beside him.

"Ahhhh!" he screamed as he reached the rock. He threw the wet sweater on top of it, covering it with water.

The statue stumbled back.

Tom raised his hand, ready to throw a lightning bolt into his heart. He felt the tickling sensation in his fingers. He drew all the anger and frustration that roared inside him. He was the champion!

The statue growled. It grabbed his wrist before any lighnting came out and threw him against the wall without any trouble. He was no champion.

Tom lifted his eyes, his vision blurry, ears ringing, several parts bleeding.

Isla was shouting again. To Ayala, possibly. Her voice sounded more desperate. The statue was cornering her.

"Ayala! Please!"

Ayala didn't answer. She looked at Isla, her red hair a mess behind her ears. She stood frozen. Isla's vines missed as the statue grabbed them, reaping them from the ground. She saw how the statute grabbed Isla and pushed her against the wall. She saw how it brought the sword to her throat. And then, she couldn't bear to watch.

Before Tom knew it, a bang rang against the walls. A full-grown elephant ran through the room and pinned the statue against the wall, one of its big teeth going through its heart.

The rock stopped moving and the elephant was covered in a green mist. Ayala was back to her normal form, her eyes were stripped of life, filled with shame

"I'm sorry. I'm sorry. I'm sorry," she repeated to herself and to the statue, each time more and more miserable.

Tom stood up, along with Isla. There was a little bleeding in the back of his head, one of his elbows had an awful cut and his ears still rang, but he would live another day.

"It's alright. You had to do it," Isla reassured. Ayala kept looking at the rock.

"I didn't have to, I chose to." She gave the fallen rock a head bow.

Tom walked to the statue and looked at its heart. It was once again shining and the writing had changed: "Dignus es, accipe".

Tom pulled it out of the stone corpse.

"Tom!" Isla exclaimed disgustedly. Ayala turned her face, unable to see such atrocity.

Tom ignored them and studied the statue's heart; he would have time for apologies later. When it got closer to the wall it shined brighter, like a hot and cold game.

He walked around the chamber until the button glowed its brightest. He found another hole in a wall, one where the heart fit perfectly, Isla still scolding him. He put the heart in it and another secret door opened just above it.

That was the first time he laid eyes on it. It was gorgeous. Brighter than the stars. Perfect in every sense of the word. It wasn't just a wheel. No. That would be wrong. At its side, it had carved the crescent moon and rainwater, Queen Sila's crest. Tom smiled, his heart finally stilled. He had gotten Rengas. He had accomplished the mission.

He took the golden wheel out with both hands; it was unexpectedly light.

Behind him the secret door closed and the statue's heart returned to its owner like a magnet. The chamber shook one last time. The statue stood up, gave a respectful bow to Ayala and returned to its original position in the rock, leaving the kids once again in the dark.

"The statue's OK," Isla assured Ayala one more time pointing at the wall with the flashlight.

Ayala gave a slight nod, still ashamed, but she made peace with what she had just done or at least Tom assumed, he didn't care in the least. He had Rengas! And that's what mattered the most. In fact, that was the only thing that would matter when he gave it to James.

What is wrong with me?

He shook his head. That feeling taking over one more time. The fogginess and the confusion.

The kids left the museum the same way as they had entered, by then the full moon shone brightly in the sky.

The first look Roberts, Beatrice and Jaden gave them, had the usual kind of hatred. Then their eyes fell on the wheel in Tom's hands, and it all changed, just as darkness changes into light. They gained respect for the Íroes, the ones that had done what no one else could. Even to Isla and Ayala, but especially to Tom.

See, I'm a champion here. Why drop it?

Tom smiled as he walked. As he received the pats on the back. He'd felt wrong before, now he couldn't remember why.

All he could focus on was the wheel clutched against his chest. He wanted to be the one to give it to James.

"We've arrived Champions," Roberts announced.

Tom took a deep breath and looked at the wheel. He walked proudly off the jet, like a proud general who had just won the war, directly to the cafeteria. It was dinner time, James would be there.

He walked into the cabin; every conversation stopped. For a second he stood paralyzed at the front door, all eyes on him.

I'm the champion! He straightened his back, head high. He walked towards James and kneeled before him.

"I bring you the first piece of the portal to Platz, Rengas," he announced.

James laughed, pride written all over his face.

"Stand up, my champion," he said, descending from his tall chair and giving Tom a pat on the back. "Today we party," he cheered to everyone, "those filthy Guarders are going down!"

The whole room roared.

"And it's all thanks to my champion and his helpers!" James continued; the cheer got louder.

Tom glanced at Isla and Ayala, they had been forced to come by Beatrice and Jaden. Their faces were terrified of what he was doing.

"Such party poopers," Tom whispered to himself and turned to James.

"What have you done?" Hally asked behind James.

Tom jumped, his blood froze. He looked again, there was no Hally.

He must have been tired.

He turned to the rest of the people.

And there it was, centimeters away from his face. Hally, a very angry and disappointed Hally.

"You could have saved them. You didn't. All for what? Fame? What are they going to do when they realize you aren't the champion you say you are?"

Tom shook his head. Hally disappeared.

He was very tired. He had to eat and go to sleep, then he would wake up sane.

He sat at the very first table he saw and turned to his side.

"Failure. Liar. Swindler," the illusion of his sister exclaimed.

Tom jumped out of his seat. His heart almost jumped out his chest and his hair spiked up like a cats'.

"You alright mate?" asked one of the guys serving food.

"Of course," he lied, taking back his seat.

The server wasn't convinced.

"Take one of these, it'll help you," the young man insisted, giving him a glass with a watery liquid.

Tom thanked him. The liquid had a strong smell, surely it wasn't something his parents would be happy to see him drink. But he did, each drop making the glaring Hally from the other side of the room fade a little bit more.

He drank until there was nothing left in the glass. And then he stood up.

"Server! Another!"

33

THIS IS STARTING TO BECOME
A USUAL THING

Hally didn't like being kidnapped. At all. The first time hadn't been all terrifying and nerve racking. More like ninety-five percent creepy, five percent laughable. This time, however, was so bad it made Hally wish she was still helping Piet get girls' numbers.

For starters, they weren't in a truck this time, they were in an airplane. Which was pretty much worse. And second, this wasn't the same as last time, where Hally was so small the chains were loose and where she had been drugged and woke up early without anyone noticing. This time she had no advantage. Her wrists were chained in an 'x' position, way too tight to move at all. Her ankles as well. All the chains shone with Unicorn Powder. This time her kidnappers were not taking any risks.

The plane they were on brought Hally memories of those military airplanes from the movies. It was large and had a kind of green tone. Where she and the rest were sitting, (chained), was a big hangar with nothing but seats at the sides, a few metal boxes, also secured, and a big opening that had been used to threaten Hally of being thrown off the airplane every time she opened her mouth.

The captors were some private force, almost paramilitary, or that's what she had managed to understand. Yet they weren't the Guarders, nor the Superiors, that was for sure.

The only thing Hally understood was that whoever was the boss kept talking about wanted them, badly. So badly, that the captors did their best not to hurt a single hair of the kids. In fact they had tried to make the kids cooperate and it hadn't been till Piet turned a guy into stone, Pam trapped four guys inside a wall, Lukai blinded five guys and Hally threw two guys against another wall that they had finally sedated.

Once inside the plane Hally had gotten back all her senses, only to really realize there wasn't a way out of this one.

For the fifth time Hally focused her curious mind on the looking normal chains.

The powder wasn't enough to make her sick and weak, but enough to neutralize her powers, well most of them anyway. Hally had felt it the very second she had woken up, that tingle in her stomach, like the first training sessions, barely enough to count.

Hally clicked her dry tongue; she could use some food and water. She studied her surroundings; her hands were cramping, her stomach growled, and she could use a walk. There were five guards, their guns ready in case she tried to use her telekinesis, again. She smiled at them, a mock smile, they stayed frozen.

I hate this. I hate this. I hate this. I. Hate. This. I hate…

I know! I know. This isn't exactly a trip to the beach. But we can do it. We have been kidnapped before.

Before we had sheer luck that our kidnappers ended up being actual, good guys that helped us out. It was rare to happen once, much less twice.

They could be taking us to the General. Does that mean that the FSC betrayed us?

No. Someone that takes that much trouble as they did to bring us into freedom is too much to be fake.

Really?

Yes! Right?

I don't know.

I don't know either! I'm you!

Okay, I have to relax. We've been here, what? Three hours?

Four, the soldier's watch has ringed four times.

And we have been flying directly to our destination.

Although they could be trying to just mess with us.

No... The guy from the right checks his clock and goes to the pilot cabin every thirty-ish minutes, they must be late.

And they aren't just carrying us, they are carrying those weird boxes that they check every so often.

Yes! So they probably aren't from a specific organization but recruited. They wouldn't waste fuel messing with us, they just want to deliver us and get paid. To whom?

That's the mystery.

Let's see. There are the Superiors, the Guarders and the FSC. The FSC isn't really a threat but the General, whoever it is, Madame Rosemary surely made it sound creepy.

So... The Superiors, the Guarders and the General. The Superiors wouldn't hire someone, they have more than enough resources to get us themselves.

That leaves the Guarders and the General.

But the Guarders at least respect us? Don't they? And besides they believe themselves to be better than the rest of the world. Their pride wouldn't allow them to hire someone to do their job.

The General is then. Should I risk it?

No I shouldn't.

But I could.

But I should not.

Something caught her attention. Hally lifted her head, her eyes falling on Pam and Lukai up front. They kept signaling her.

She frowned, how was she supposed to understand what they were saying?

Pam waited for a soldier to turn around and pointed. Then she shifted her eyes. Hally followed hers. There, just at arm's reach, between Pam and Piet, the soldier with the keys tempted every fiber of their being.

Hally glanced at Piet, the young boy nodded, sure that he was ready to try it. He could get the keys, but he needed all eyes looking the other way.

The four Guardians exchange looks, they were really doing this.

Hally took a deep breath, her job came implicitly, she was the distraction.

"I guess the General won't be happy to see you late." The soldier who kept looking at his watch raised his cold eyes to where the words had come from.

For a second everything stopped, as if a bomb had been dropped. Perfect, she needed all the attention on her.

"What did you say?" another soldier asked angrier than any would have liked.

"I guess the General won't be happy to see you late," she

dared to speak, she'd already started, now she'd see it through.

There was a pause, the same soldier, the one that looked like Tony, stood up, hand on his gun.

"How did you know that?"

Hally chuckled at him and pointed with her head to the soldier that kept checking his watch.

"The time won't change any quicker even if you check it every five minutes," she replied.

Fake Tony, the boss, took a step closer to the Latin girl without taking his eyes off her. Hally copied him, her shiny brown eyes defiant against his cold green dead ones.

"I mean how did you know that we worked for the General?" he asked, getting closer, hand still on his gun.

Hally had the audacity to laugh.

"Oh please, the answers are all written on your faces, you wouldn't survive an interrogation even if they tortured you," she mocked.

His features hardened.

"We have."

Oh shoot.

"You on the other hand don't seem very strong to start with," the man continued, switching the gun in his hand for a small knife from his pocket.

"You wouldn't do it," Hally dared directly in his face.

He brought the knife to her throat.

"Hally–" Lukai babbled from her side.

"Really?" Tony asked.

Hally stared at his eyes, emotionless, she'd played this game before.

"Yes. This plane is far too big for you to afford without your pay. And I believe the General, who does not like tardiness, won't like that the merchandise also comes in rough shape," she replied.

Fake Tony didn't move the knife.

"I could lie and say that you came with several old cuts."

Hally let out a weary sigh.

"Quit saying things we both know you won't actually accomplish. We both know that for the General to know that we are coming you had to send some kind of proof and if it was the case that I already arrived hurt you would have provided that information too. Which means that you would risk losing a client. Not any client, a very powerful one that can put you behind bars or better, out of service."

Hally made a small pause and licked her lips; she *really* could use some water. Her palms were sweating and her whole body shaking, but her face remained the same.

"So go ahead, make the cut, ruin your life," Hally dared with a cocky smile.

Fake Tony looked into her eyes, he wasn't happy, not one bit. Not that Hally considered him capable of happiness.

"That cleverness will get you killed one day," he said, putting the knife back to his waist.

"Only if they get me," she said and gave him the most innocent smile ever, a smile that said 'after all, I am just a little, harmless girl'.

Fake Tony took back his seat and turned to the other soldiers.

"Tape her mouth," he ordered.

Hally looked up, Pam shook her head, they needed more time.

She twisted her wrist. A guy flew against the wall, boxes knocked out of place. The soldiers rushed to their guns, too far to suffer from her powers with the chains on.

"Was that panic I just saw?" fake Tony scoffed.

"No," Hally answered coldly despite the sweat and dizziness her powers had caused. "I just prefer a handkerchief. It damages the skin less."

The soldiers turned to the boss; they were enjoying the show of a trained military guy sparring with a fifteen-year-old girl.

Fake Tony grunted.

"Just grab a damn handkerchief and shut her up!" he ordered furiously.

The soldiers did as ordered, and Hally was once again at her thinking place.

When everyone had gone back to what they were doing, and the Chief relaxed enough to leave her alone, Hally dared to look at her side.

Piet smiled, between his fingers, almost invisible, were the keys to their freedom.

She smiled underneath her handkerchief.

At the end, the flight to who knows where, ended up taking around twelve hours.

During the hours after Hally's and fake Tony's, who was always addressed as the Chief and never by a real name, skirmish, nothing interesting happened.

Around hour five the kids were given a small sandwich each and a glass of water but were told not to drink much as they weren't going to be able to pee until they landed. By hour seven they were unchained ten minutes each, one at a time, and escorted by seven soldiers through the hangar so they could stretch their legs. While one of them was walking, the other three were blindfolded and forbidden to talk to prevent them from causing any trouble, especially Hally.

By hour nine, when most soldiers had finally dozed off and the ones that were awake were doing anything but paying attention to the hostages, Piet finally gained the courage to use the keys.

He pulled the smaller key and shoved it into the handcuffs. They didn't give. He tried the second key. Still, it didn't work.

Hally looked at the cabin's door, the one that would open any minute.

Hurry

Sweat dripping on the pale boy's face he tried the third key. It slipped from his fingers.

Pam had to stifle a scream.

Piet grabbed the key and tried again. This time it fit in the hole. He turned it. His handcuffs opened with a melodic 'click'.

The other three kids cheered silently in their own seats.

Rapidly, he moved on to the rest of his chains and got rid of every lock. Then he placed them over, just as they were. As long as any one didn't pay him attention, they wouldn't be able to tell he was free.

Piet looked up, the proudest smile crossing his face. He looked at Hally, ready to throw the keys.

Hally shook her head, whenever the Chief came out, she was going to be the very first thing he saw. And after the skirmish before he *would* notice if she was free.

Pam coughed. A couple soldiers looked up for a second, then returned to their card games.

The Asian girl opened her hands, ready to catch the keys.

Piet grabbed the keys tightly. His eyes fell on the soldiers. He took a deep breath and prepared. He moved to the edge of his seat, more sweat coming down his forehead. He nodded; he was ready to...

The cabin's door opened. The Chief came into the hangar.

The kids returned to their positions. Pam's angry face, Lukai's lost eyes, and Hally's mischievous look.

Piet slipped back in his seat, a chain moved a little too much. The boy hurried to place it where it was.

The Chief cold's eyes fell on him, he walked towards his seat.

"Ummmm... hi?" Piet mumbled once the man was in front of him.

"What are you doing?" the Chief asked, having removed his dark jacket a long time before, exposing his scar filled arms for the kids to see and fear.

Piet looked at him without any words.

"Aa- ummmm-"

"What are you doing?" he repeated.

"I have to go to the bathroom," Piet stuttered, that would explain all the movement.

The Chief stared at the kid, perhaps he actually had a gram of sympathy in his heart or maybe he just didn't want his merchandise to arrive all wet and smelly.

"You get five minutes," he agreed.

Five soldiers were called to escort him.

Piet gulped as the men moved towards him. He wrapped his fingers around the chains to keep them in place when he stood up.

He was pulled to his feet.

Hally dared to breathe; they weren't going to notice.

Piet moved, step after step, eyes widened more than what can be considere normal. His fingertips white from holding on to the chain and the keys.

He was a few meters from the bathroom when a soldier bumped into him. The keys fell from his hands, the handcuffs followed.

Piet's scared blue eyes locked with the Chief's.

"Wha-?" escaped from the Chief's mouth with the realization. His face was tomato red. "Handcuff him. And search them! Search them all!"

With a word every single soldier was on their feet. Between the bunch of them they all took one of the kids to each corner of the hangar, as far aways from each other as possible, and asked them to empty their pockets.

"How did this happen?" the Chief exclaimed to his people. "Explain it to me!"

"We don't know sir," a soldier answered. "We tied them before."

"But they got free! They got keys!"

Hally tried to remain as still as possible, disappearing between the soldiers that held her against the wall.

"They have been tied all this time sir," another soldier responded.

"How would they get a key without being able to move?" another asked.

Hally felt the Chief's eyes fall on her.

"Bring the girl!" he commanded.

"Which one?" a soldier asked.

"The Latin one!"

Hally was forced to stand in front of the Chief, chains still keeping her at bay.

"You did this?" he asked, showing her the keys.

Hally raised her eyebrows at him, she still had a handkerchief tied around her mouth.

"It can't be- Take the handkerchief off morons!"

The soldiers moved clumsily.

"Hurry!"

"Sorry sir," one of the soldiers apologized. "It's a pretty tight knot," he mumbled, the cloth slipping through his fingers.

Chief took a deep breath, massaging his temples.

"You're trained assassins, take the damn thing off," he ordered.

The soldiers kept trying, unsuccessfully.

"I can help them," Pam proposed.

"They don't need your help, they are capable of doing this." He turned to the soldiers. The handkerchief was still there.

"All right!" he finally accepted. "Bring the Asian one, don't dare say a word."

Pam nodded and gave small steps towards Hally, the fastest she could move with all the chains.

She came and unwrapped the handkerchief. As soon as the handkerchief was off, she was escorted once again to her corner, forced to look at the wall.

Hally licked her lips.

"I'm sorry, it's been so long I forgot the question. What was it?"

"Did. You. Do. This?" he asked.

Hally looked at the keys.

"No. I don't work with metal, but I do know a very crafty locksmith that can help you if you like."

The Chief glared at Hally, anger building up from behind his eyes.

He slapped her. Hand against her cheek. Just like they do in movies. Or in this case, books.

Hally felt the burning feeling on the right side of her face. She tasted blood.

"Hally!" Lukai exclaimed, the soldiers held him in place, facing the wall.

Hally licked the blood off her teeth, her eyes looked up at the Chief.

"Did you do this?" he asked again.

Hally didn't answer.

Another slap came.

"Hally!" Lukai cried.

"Stop it!" Pam exclaimed.

"Hold them there," the Chief ordered.

The soldiers pushed the kids against the wall inhumanely.

"Either you answer me or I'll kill one of them," the Chief said.

"You wouldn't," Hally replied, but she wasn't so sure anymore.

"Wanna try?" He aimed a gun towards Piet's head, the young blond boy looked the other way.

I tried his ego.

And it is way bigger than his need for money.

Hally lifted her wrists.

"Take this off me and I'll show you what I'm capable of."

The Chief chuckled. He leaned in.

"But you're in them, what are you going to do then?"

He stepped back, a proud smile shining through his face.

Hally looked down.

"Thought so," the chief replied.

The airplane shook.

Hally raised her head, her eyes glowing the brightest shade of silver. She reached inside, searching for that peace she longed for, all she stood for, all her strength, all her fight, all herself. And, for the first time she didn't keep it at bay. She let it all go.

The airplane shook again, stronger. Some soldiers fell to their feet. The metal outside made a horrible sound as it was being ripped apart.

"Sir," the soldiers cried.

The Chief's eyes looked up at her. There was a single emotion: fear.

A cold blow came to the back of her head and Hally fell to her knees, eyes returning to normal, the plane steadying.

The Chief rushed and poured one more jar of Unicorn Powder, his last one, on her wrists. Hally looked at the powder disappear in the metal; she felt the sudden lack of energy. Her muscles atrophied, her head spun, her eyesight blurred.

"Fine," Hally mumbled. "I did it. I moved the keys around when you were too distracted talking to me."

She raised her eyes. The Chief was pointing the gun at her, not as a threat, but more as defense. She smiled. She'd done it, she'd gotten in his head.

"Put the handkerchief back. And blindfold them, blindfold them all," he commanded, the quiver in the back of his throat trying to be silenced.

The soldiers didn't move.

"NOW!"

The four were forced back to their seats and Piet didn't get to go to the bathroom.

Hally let her head fall, the room was circling.

And now what?

She looked up, the others' minds were as blank as hers.

What else can we do? Looks like we're going to have to face the General with no cards left to play.

34

THE FAILURE AT BEING A FAILURE

"Such a disgrace!"

Tom's eyes burst open. Even in his dreams he couldn't get rid of the yelling.

The light of the room burned into Tom's eyes; his head hurt as if it was being impaled.

"Mmmmm."

Tom covered his eyes with the cold pillow, that was nice.

The world was moving too fast for him to catch up. He pressed his stomach; he wasn't feeling that well. He was too hot, too sweaty, too confused. He threw himself over the side of the bed, all the food he had had the night before making its way back from his stomach onto the floor.

"Such a piece of trash, couldn't even make it to the toilet."

Tom lifted his head, mouth dirty, eyes red, cheeks pink. There, clearer than crystal itself, it was Hally, better said the illusion of Hally.

"It's not even real," Tom muttered to himself, he knew it, yet somehow the ghost refused to leave, and its words hit him as hard as if they came from Hally's real mouth.

"You remember when you were ten, you had that math competition in Heredia. You thought you were going to win, you didn't. Remember why?" the ghost asked.

"Because you have never been someone, you're just a nobody. No one will remember you when you're dead."

Tom covered his ears; it was of no use.

"Do you also remember when you tried for that scholarship? They didn't give it to you, they gave it to Hally. Now that's a winner. A champion."

"Stop," Tom begged.

"Stop what? You're the one who continues to be a loser. What will James say when he realizes he got the wrong twin? You're no champion, Hally is. You can't even talk to someone without trying to sound more intelligent, Hally doesn't try. You give your all to be the best, Hally is always second without effort, what do you think will happen when she puts in some work...? Bye bye Tom."

Tom felt the acid of his stomach rising a second time. He managed to keep it inside.

"She would have saved Ayala and Isla," the illusion continued.

His heart stopped. He could picture perfectly the mountains, the trees, the freedom. The girls would have had it if it wasn't for him. But if he had taken that choice, he wouldn't have been able to bring back Rengas to James.

Tom closed his eyes.

"No, no, no. I'm smart. If I had said anything about the door then we would have been caught and harmed. I made the best decision. I made a good choice," Tom muttered to himself shaking his head, he was trying to convince someone. The illusion or himself.?

The door was opened.

Tom threw himself off the bed right in front of the vomit, whoever it was, he didn't want them to see him in that position. Weak, disgusting, dirty.

"Morning, Tom," Ayala said, her natural high-pitched sweet voice echoing inhumanly against the walls.

The sound pierced Tom's ears.

"Hi Ayala, may I help you?" Tom asked, all his muscles tensed up as he hid the food that had just been inside him.

"I heard a weird noise. Came by to see that nothing bad had happened." The red-haired girl smiled. She looked like she just had a shower, her hair was combed, and for the first time in the last few days her clothes fit her.

Tom sighed.

"Oh. Don't worry. I merely dropped something under the bed. As you can see, I'm currently looking for it." He added a smile at the end to make it look more believable.

Ayala returned the smile at him, unconvinced.

"Tom." She paused. "Are you okay?" she asked softly and low key.

Tom frowned, the vomit smell reaching his nose. He hoped Ayala didn't notice it.

"Yes, of course. I'm perfect."

"No. I mean, are you fine? Last night Isla and I saw you a little bit...," she stopped trying to look for the least hurtful word, "lost..."

"Oh," Tom said, abandoning his smile and the kindness in the past, he didn't like where this conversation was going. "I was only tired," he lied.

"I mean with the drinks," Ayala continued. "First you took the credit for everything, I believe it was for our best, Isla doesn't. I understand it though, James knows what you are capable of and therefore he keeps an eye on you, if he knew what Isla and I can do, he would also keep an eye on us. Then it would be harder to escape."

"They could have escaped last night, if you weren't such a traitor," Hally's voice rang behind Tom, bringing back the dreadful cold feeling. Isla and Ayala could never find that out.

"And then, you started to act all scared and paranoid. And kept having drink after drink," Ayala continued, as she kept talking she found it harder to see the good side of Tom's actions.

"I know what I'm doing!" Tom blurted, he was the champion, he didn't have to be questioned. "And I have no need for your worries, so *don't* worry about me," he replied harshly.

Ayala looked at him with a mixture of pity and the look that puppies give when they are scolded. Tom had no heart for such feelings.

"Is there any other reason why you're still in my room?" he asked, she was starting to give him 'Hally' vibes, he wanted anything but that.

Ayala recovered from her puppy gaze.

"Isla is waiting downstairs for us to have breakfast. She really dislikes us to not have good manners."

"Well, is there anything Isla doesn't dislike?" Tom replied with a chuckle.

Ayala joined with a small chuckle, awkwardly.

"James sent you this," she said and stepped into the room to hand Tom a letter, then stepped back outside as if being inside was a line she wasn't ready to cross.

Tom gloated at the card; butterflies flew in his stomach followed by fear. Had James realized that he wasn't the champion that he had made him think? Or was he even prouder?

"I'll be downstairs, don't take too long to not upset Isla," Ayala said. "Please." She closed the door.

Tom moved the letter in his hands, the paper felt warm and thin. He smelled it, it smelled like old books and markers. What it contained meant the world to Tom.

"A letter," the illusion scoffed.

Tom looked at the vomit behind him, it would be more respectful to clean it up before opening the letter.

He stood up. His legs were weak, his head stuffed.

Slowly he went into the fancy, big bathroom and got some toilet paper.

Out of the few things he could remember from the night before he remembered James telling him he wasn't going to be sleeping in the dungeons anymore. As a reward for the successful mission he and his team were going to stay at a proper house.

Tom stepped back into the beautiful bamboo-walled room. He had the softest bed ever and ten servants at his disposal. James wouldn't give any of those things to someone who wasn't worth it. He just wouldn't. It made no sense.

Neither these words nor all the drinks made Hally's "ghost", Aina, leave.

"You should be there," Aina said, pointing at the trash can where Tom had just thrown the toilet paper. "After all you are simply a piece of trash."

Tom didn't respond, he knew the second he responded to his imagination it would be the second he would accept that he definitely lost all sanity. Still, Aina followed him, disappearing from time to time, sometimes from afar and sometimes from centimeters away, never truly gone.

He understood Aina wasn't a ghost or a hallucination of the result of a drug. He understood, whether he let himself acknowledge it or not, that Aina came from his guilt and fear. He felt it was his fault that the girls were still imprisoned by the Superiors, partially because it was a hundred percent his fault. Yet he couldn't avoid it. He had to be there. He couldn't leave.

In previous days he'd been beaten, trained, forced to use his powers, to lie... to survive. But he had never, ever, in his life, experienced the kind of honor he had received daily under James' wing. This kind of attention he didn't want to risk losing. He just had to put all the things in balance, the love and attention or Isla and Ayala's freedom?

Tom sat down on his bed and looked at the freshly cleaned room with pride. He took the letter.

"Bye, bye, liar," Aina whispered as he opened it.

My dear champion, after yesterday's amazing job I gladly inform you that today you and your team will have a second mission to retrieve another part of the portal, Pláka, in the afternoon. Take the morning off and make sure your team is well rested to meet after lunch. I'm proud of you, but remember my pride is a benefit, don't squander it.

Tom read the letter several times, each time his smile growing larger. James still trusted him!

The balance tilted. He made a choice. He was still the champion!

Suddenly the sun alone was enough to make Tom smile. He danced around the room. He'd not lost his worth.

"Not yet, anyhow," Aina hissed, it meant nothing to Tom.

He went down the stairs jumping two by two, like Hally used to back at their home. Each time he was passed by a servant he greeted them and wished them the best day possible. He surely was having one, himself.

He walked inside the dining room, a *real* dining room. The room was connected by two doors, one that went to the kitchen and another that went to the hallway. The walls were covered with fancy wallpaper and expensive museum paintings. The dark wood table was covered with hundreds of dishes, big and small, all of them filled with food.

Tom couldn't resist the smell.

"Good morning," Tom greeted. He took a seat at the head of the table, where he belonged.

A servant came and helped him get his napkin.

"What would you like to eat?" the servant asked, he was a young man, barely in his twenties.

Tom inspected all the dishes.

"A french toast would be fine."

"It'll be right here, sir."

The servant hurried into the kitchen and brought a dish perfectly decorated with two pieces of toast.

"Oh no, I'll only eat one," he said.

The servant's eyes opened with fear.

"I'm so sorry, please forgive me," he cried with a bow. "I will fix it right away."

The servant hurried once again, and rapidly brought another plate, this time with only one piece of toast.

"I apologize again, please forgive me."

"It's alright," Tom replied with a smile. This was true respect, and he deserved every inch of it.

The servant stood paralyzed by his side.

"You're dismissed," Tom added.

The servant gave another bow and walked to the corner, where he stood frozen with eyes front.

Tom took a bite from the toast, it was warm, soft and delicious. He had barely swallowed the first piece when Isla's gaze glared at him.

"What?" he asked, his mouth filled with food.

"You shouldn't be talking with your mouth full. Neither answering that way to a lady," Isla scolded him.

Tom returned his attention to the toast; he was having a very good day to let Isla ruin it.

"Will you please excuse us?" Isla asked the servants.

The servants nodded; they didn't seem to understand the question.

"Please leave the room," Isla ordered.

The servants looked at each other perplexed. They didn't have the same respect for Isla as they had for Tom.

"Is it a command coming from all of you?" a servant asked Isla, but looking at Tom.

Isla's green eyes landed on the poor servant. Tom had to admit she looked beautiful.

"Yes," she answered, offended.

The servants nodded once again and left the room, closing the door behind them.

"What's wrong?" Ayala asked.

"Wait," Isla said. She lifted her hands. All the flowers and leaves that had been used to decorate the dishes grew, vines intertwining each other, flowers growing into abnormal sizes. All surrounding them, growing more and more until they created a sphere around the three kids.

"What is going on?" Tom asked, his gaze lost in the nearest flower.

"This is such a pretty power," Ayala said from the other side looking at the flowers.

Isla snapped her fingers. Ayala and Tom turned.

She placed one finger in front of her mouth, telling them to be quiet. She started to move her hands and with it the vines started to dance.

Tom looked at the vines, moving up and down, from side to side, it was hypnotizing. It wasn't until they stopped that he realized they weren't dancing, the vines were forming letters.

"We don't know if we're being looked at or listened to, answer yes or no with your head," she spelled and waited for Ayala and Tom to nod, showing they understood.

"Blake's free," she spelled. Tom froze, how had she realized that? Even worse, what was she going to do knowing about it?

"You sure?" Ayala asked.

Isla nodded and continued spelling.

"The next mission is this afternoon, it'll be in a much less guarded place than the last one. This may be our chance to escape," she spelled out. "We have to make a plan for..."

"You have to be kidding. This is ridiculous!" Tom stood up, his chair scraping the ground.

"Shush!" Isla exclaimed.

The vines started to move again. Tom didn't wait for them.

"This is stupid! I'll take no part in it," he exclaimed. "Now let me leave or I'll electrocute you," he threatened.

"Thomas," Isla snapped, she wanted to be heard, or read. "Please we have—"

"Now!"

"You should let him go," Ayala declared, for the first time she saw him with anger building behind her eyes. "He isn't on our side."

Isla stared at him head to toe, analyzing him as a math problem. She gave in.

The flowers moved around until there was a hole big enough for him to leave.

His good day was now ruined. How could Isla even propose something like that? James had put him in charge of the whole team, if anything happened that he didn't like, Tom would lose his title. He would cease being the champion. He would not be loved.

Tom stormed out of the house; he needed a walk.

He walked through the camp. He saw a few people he recognized and returned greetings when they said hi. Then he had to pretend to know a lot of others that knew him, but he didn't remember. Aina walked beside him, staring when he greeted anyone, and staring when he was alone. Always quiet, even his own guilt recognized that he really needed time to think.

Tom kept walking, no destination in mind. For a moment he stopped seeing houses and tents, admiring the purple cloaks working, laughing, living. He kept walking, each second running the numbers. What was the possibility for an actual escape? What was the possibility of staying there? He had always known that sooner or later he would have to leave the Superiors camp. Either Blake would come for them, or worse, Hally, and he would have no actual reason to let them know he wanted to stay. But he didn't want to leave, not yet anyway.

He made it to the fence, to the actual fence of the camp. It was a tall, electrified metal fence keeping the wildlife from the camp. On the other side Tom couldn't see anything, just dirt extending further than his eyes could see. In a way the fence seemed unreasonable, there was nothing out there that would attack him. Although he knew the truth, it was to keep things inside rather than things outside.

Tom monitored the fence closely. It meant nothing to him. The charge was barely a fraction of a lightning bolt, he could easily cross it, and leave everything behind. Adventure himself into nothing, leave all of this behind. His title, his life, his sister, his name.

"I hope you don't make me regret taking off your handcuffs," a voice said from behind.

Tom turned, this wasn't Aina talking.

"James," he babbled, "I'm sorry, I wanted to clear my mind. Hadn't realized I'd walked so far from the camp."

"It's alright my champion" James laughed, he was wearing workout clothes all filled with sweat, his cane nowhere to be seen. "I'm just joking. I understand wanting a relaxed mind before an important mission, I personally like to run to free my mind. I know you wouldn't abandon this place," he said, giving Tom a pat on his back. "If you excuse me, I'll continue my running." He jogged a few meters away.

"Wait!" Tom called before thinking. "How are you so sure I won't leave this place?"

James turned around and smiled.

"Because I have already tamed you," he answered and kept running, leaving Tom standing there watching him, each second further away.

"You're nothing but a dog in here," Aina said.

For the first time Tom agreed with Aina. Tamed? He wasn't an animal. James made it sound like he was. Nothing more than an object, an asset.

He looked at the fence, he was being held like a penguin in a zoo. And not even the loudest cheers in the world were going to change that fact.

He returned to the house, he had made up his mind, sort of. He didn't give it much thought, if he did, he knew it would be hours before he finally came to a decision.

He made it back to the center, walked inside the house, directly to the dining room. Isla and Ayala were still there.

"Out!" He ordered the servants. They were left alone in seconds.

The girls looked at him both scared and worried.

"This might be the right moment to add that yelling isn't the correct etiquette," Isla said.

Tom shook his head.

"I'm not here to yell, I'm here to let you know I've made up my mind."

"Made up your mind of what?" Ayala asked.

Tom took a deep breath.

"Let's make a plan to get out of here."

35

THE PLAN. THE FAILURE?

Tom looked at the camp at his feet, the view was much better from up there.

After a few lies he had been able to convince Roberts to hand him the plan of the mission beforehand *'to prepare his team properly'*. Meanwhile Isla had spoken with some of the servants from around the big fancy house and had found out that the only place in the whole camp that had no microphone or cameras was the roof. A time before there had been cameras there, but after a few accidents with birds James had realized it was easier to restrict anyone from the roof.

Ayala tightened her grip around the chimney, for being the only one who could fly she was too worried about the height. Isla babbled things under her breath as she looked through the papers. The plan for the second mission wasn't much easier than the first. Pláka was an old vase. It had been lost for a long time until recently recovered from an antique store by an old man.

"This time we have to steal from an old guy?" Ayala asked. "It isn't better than stealing from a museum. It's worse!"

"Technically we wouldn't be stealing the man's legal property, we'll be stealing from the bank's safe vaults," Tom clarified.

"Still, stealing," Ayala sobbed. "My mom's right, all my hair is going to fall out."

"I know it goes against all etiquette. But we need to survive," Isla consoled Ayala. "Let's hear the escape plan one more time, the first step–"

"This plan won't work," Tom interrupted.

"Excuse me, I was tal–"

"Why won't it work? If I'm going to be bald at least make it worth it," Ayala exclaimed, interrupting Isla again.

"Seriously?"

Tom paid no attention to Isla; he focused on Ayala's question.

"I have run the numbers over nine times already, there's a big chance of being caught by the police."

"How big of a chance?" Ayala asked.

"97%, give or take."

Isla let out a growl, an annoyed growl.

"Isn't that what we want?" she asked.

"If we get caught James won't be happy. We might lose every chance to escape," he replied.

"Are you saying these things seriously or are you just scared to lose your master's pride?"

Tom took his eyes off the other houses and glared at Isla.

"Don't underestimate James' power. If I'm right he might control around one fifth of the population of the world, if we get caught by the police we'll be back at this camp in our old cells. So yes, I'm talking seriously. The Superiors may not hold power in the surrounding neighborhoods, but they own the whole system" he snapped. "And I don't care about James' pride," he lied, well, half lied.

James was a bad guy, *the* bad guy. Obviously, Tom understood he never cared for him. And if the time came when he became useless, he would throw him away like garbage. Yet, he couldn't stop himself from liking to be praised, to be needed, to be loved. And that's why there was always that guilt, that conscience, that Aina that followed him every-where, hunting him, confusing him on his decisions. He knew it far well without Isla adding wood to that fire.

"But, if the plan won't work, what do we do?" Ayala asked.

"We shall build our own plan. We'll need a computer," he muttered the last part to himself.

"I know where you can get a computer," Ayala said, happy that she could finally contribute something. "I'll be right back."

She went inside the house through the same window they had climbed out.

A few minutes later she returned with a bright white fancy laptop in her arms.

"Where did you get it?" Tom asked, opening it, knowing better than to assume she had stolen it.

"I asked Joseline, one of the servants, if she had a laptop. She asked Martino, the chef and he lended us his. They are such nice people once you start speaking with them. Most of them aren't even Superiors, just underpaid workers," Ayala added.

Tom moved his fingers across the keyboard. He had learned a few hacking skills here and there. He could only hope they were enou-

His face paled as the screen poured thousands of numbers he didn't understand.

"Do you need any help?" Isla asked,

"Ummm," Tom mumbled.

He licked his lips and swallowed his pride.

"Seems we're going to need someone that knows a fair amount of code and is willing to hack a bank."

Isla laughed at his failure to ask for help. She took the computer from his arms and sat elegantly on the roof.

"What are you doing?"

"I know it's completely contrary to the etiquette I usually follow, but I was the best programmer in my school district, I can deal with this," Isla said.

Tom looked at her, he was impressed.

The numbers quickly changed into more numbers and then into an elegant website.

"I'm in," she blurted. "What do we do now?"

"You do know code! Why didn't you say something before?"

Isla smiled at him, her green eyes shining through her long lashes. "You never asked."

The next few hours were filled with discussion. Tons of ideas went back and forth between the three of them to create the best plan possible. They considered every single thing that could go wrong as well as a solution. It was set, they were leaving the Superiors behind, or not coming back at all.

By three o'clock, fueled on breakfast and several cups of coffee alone, they made it to the meeting room. Yellow folder underneath Tom's arm, hee couldn't rid the sweat off his hands. One single misstep, and nothing would be able to be turned around. Was this really what he wanted?

Tom lifted his eyes, Aina looking back at him. The answer came naturally, yes.

"*My champion*, perfect," James cheered. "'We were waiting for you and your team to start explaining."

Tom stepped close to him.

"As a matter of fact, James, we have created a new and more effective plan," Tom whispered.

James stared at Tom and the girls, who were standing behind him.

When you try to fix or improve someone's job it can go two different ways, the person can be grateful and happily receive the criticism, or the person can believe that they are considered stupid. James was the second kind.

"Let me take a look at that." He snapped the folder from Tom's hands, cane already in hand. Tom took a step backwards, in case he striked.

He stared at James as he read the plan Tom had drafted, maybe he should have done it simpler, more direct. Or maybe James was going to realize that the plan had a thousand holes and Tom would lose it all.

The whole room stood motionless; fear prevailed not only in the three kids but in every single person. They all had that terrified look, the Champions had screwed up, big time, and if James didn't like the paperwork inside that folder his anger wasn't going to be reserved for them.

"Explain this plan in five simple steps," James said, throwing the folder on the table "Take away all those fancy, useless words and explain the plan that a bunch of teenagers propose and is supposed to be superior to my professional staff's plan."

Tom licked his lips, he didn't have the talent Hally had with words, he could barely speak with people about something important when he had something rehearsed, much less if he had nothing planned.

"Firstly-" Tom struggled

"Excuse me, I'll take over," Isla gently pushed him out of the way and moved in front of James. "We hacked inside the bank's system and created a fake position for Ayala. When we arrive she will take a security pass and open the door for us from the inside, giving me the opportunity to deactivate the bank's security long enough for us to get in. Then Ayala will use the security pass and her powers to open all the doors and gates we need, meanwhile I will make sure to erase our trail behind us. We've searched the guards' schedules and are prepared for them. When we reach the final vault Tom can use his electrical immunity to get inside through the electrified tunnel and grab the vase. With the vase in our possession the second security system will be denoted, which with some hacking I can delay for a few minutes giving us enough time to get away and successfully end our mission."

James stared at Isla, his eyes couldn't lie, the plan did sound legit.

He turned to the rest of the room.

"Be careful with these kids, they'll be coming for your jobs in a few years," he said with a smile and invited Isla to sit beside him.

For a second Tom felt this burn in his stomach. He was the champion, not Isla. Why should she sit beside James? That was what Isla wanted, to take his place! No. Of course not, Isla wanted to get out of there more than anyone. Besides, she would never be able to become James' champion. How would *she* compare to *him*?

He swallowed his pride and sat in the chair furthest from James. If the plan worked, he wasn't going to see him ever again so what would it matter? He looked behind him for a second, Aina seemed to be smiling, he couldn't tell if she was mocking him or if she was proud.

The actual job was very similar to the half-true plan Isla gave to James. The start was the same. Ayala got the security pass from one of the employees turning herself into a cat in an alley. Roberts had been kind enough to escort them down the jet and into the black vans just to leave them there, by the garbage bags.

Though he didn't leave before giving a last wink to Ayala.

"You and me, karaoke." Ayala had replied , sticking her tongue out.

"Found it?" Isla asked, they were waiting by the back door of the bank.

"Here it is," Ayala replied, a white card in her hand.

She came to the door and swiped the card. The door opened with a nice ring.

Inside Tom had to stop for a second and admire the bank's architecture. It was modern, all white with touches of black and gray. The roof was tall. The desks were decorated. The hallways were long and elegant. Even the floor was made of marvelous, patterned ceramic.

The only part he disliked, due to the circumstances he was there, was the heavy security. There was a guard in every corner and every hallway, standing watch like statues, cameras in every corner. And five guards walking around, leaving no centimeter unwatched.

Of course, Ayala's, Isla's and Tom's powers were more than enough to overcome or destroy any of those measures, but it took time, more time that they could afford losing if they really wanted to escape.

The first hallway filled with green mist for a second.

Tom looked at Ayala, she was now a small cat.

The white cat went ahead silently into the bank. Isla and Tom walked behind.

"Meow," echoed.

"Hey, there's a cat. Get it out of here!" a voice yelled.

Isla prepared the seeds from her pockets.

The white cat came running, behind her three guards followed.

Before the guards could finish processing the presence of the kids, huge flower vines wrapped around them covering them from their toes to their mouth.

Tom rushed to move the bodies and hide them behind a desk.

They continued inside, their soft steps echoing more than what they would have liked.

"Open the door," Isla ordered Ayala.

"Meow."

The cat walked again deeper down the hallway, Isla and Tom followed quietly behind her.

They walked through three more hallways before they came upon another guard.

"Hey." The poor woman stood no chance before her body was covered by vines,

Tom moved her body.

He wiped the sweat off his forehead, he felt as useful as a match in the ocean. Ayala walked in front and opened all the doors; Isla took care of all the guards. Meanwhile he just stood behind them, watching, and moving guards. This was the price he was paying to escape, back to being a nobody.

Five more guards, seven doors, ten hallways later they made it into the vault.

"It's not opening," Isla cried.

"Let me give it a try." Isla made way for Ayala.

Tom's watch vibrated against his skin, not much time was left. He looked up, there was an empty space. Aina hadn't followed him inside the bank. He wanted to believe that it meant that his guilt was diminishing, but he could still feel that cold stare on his back, a constant reminder that it hadn't yet died.

"We're running out of time."

"Actually, we aren't running out of it. If we were running, we would still have time, we're more like slow walking out of it," Isla replied, her hands raised ready for anything. Soon somebody would find a vine wrapped guard and the alarm would be raised.

"Did you- Did you just make a joke?" Tom asked, with a smile. "Are you feeling alright?"

Ayala chortled; her head turned as she tried to get rid of the lock.

Isla's jaw dropped, she looked at Ayala and then Tom.

"I'm quite funny for your information, just not in English."

Ayala and Tom laughed.

"What about you Tom? Are you as equally excruciating in Spanish as you're in English?"

Tom fixed his jacket.

"I'm pleased to tell you that I've been told that my abilities do extend to both languages."

Isla looked at him, holding her belly as she laughed, hand in her mouth to keep it quiet.

"Tom, your turn," Ayala muttered, holding the heavy metal door over her head.

The sound of the metal moving caught the kid's attention back at the mission. Isla stopped laughing.

Tom had to be quick. Ayala wouldn't be able to hold the door forever. And the Superiors team was going to be there in five minutes. They had to be out of there in two.

Tom slid through the small hole, it was a tunnel. He crawled through the small and warm metal cylinder, easier said than done. He could feel that familiar tingling sensation around his whole body, the electricity running through the air. He could feel it moving around the walls, deeper than what could be considered normal. It was meant to keep intruders away. But he wasn't an intruder. It didn't hurt him, it welcomed him.

His spiked hair first, worn out shoes later, the boy made it out of the tunnel and into the big empty vault that held one thing: a white pedestal in the middle of the room.

"That's it?"

He walked to the pedestal, there was an old wooden box on top of it.

He opened up the box. He gasped. Pláka was nothing like Rengas, except both were made of gold and both had Queen

Sila's seal on it. Pláka was much smaller, more elegant and obviously, it was a vase.

Tom picked it up gently, afraid that the remaining electricity in his body would damage it. The three of them had reached the same conclusion. They couldn't let James get into Platz. They had to destroy the vase.

Tom made his way back out the tunnel to once again, the swank and glamorous bank. He suddenly felt empty as the electricity left him.

"It's precious," Isla babbled, grabbing the vase from Tom's hands, "such a shame we have to destroy it. It would look lovely beside my bed in Platz."

"It is a shame," Tom agreed.

Ayala let the metal door close, sweat rolling down her face and neck, pressing her red hair against her tanned skin.

"But it has to be done. For Platz," Tom continued.

"For the rest," Ayala said.

"And for us."

Tom nodded. Isla placed the vase on the floor, right in front of them.

"At the count of three, we throw everything we have."

The girls nodded.

"One. Two. Thre–"

A metallic bang interrupted them. Tom felt a horrible cold strike his leg. He fell to the ground, blood flooding his clothes. This wasn't part of the plan. He looked at his leg, he'd been shot.

More bullets came.

Isla raised vines to cover herself and Ayala. Superiors' guards came out of nowhere and pinned them against the ground, handcuffing them with Unicorn Powder before they moved too far. The vines fell dead to the ground.

The girls struggled, it was pointless.

"I'll be honest, I'm amazed by your courage but even more by your stupidity. I used to think you were nothing more than a pawn looking for a master," James appeared from the shadows, gun in hand, he was the shooter.

Tom crawled away, against the wall, leaving a trail of blood behind. He was scared, terrified, and hurt, really hurt. He stood no chance against a furious James.

James walked slowly towards Tom, his cane hitting the ground. He pressed Tom's bullet hole with the tip of the cane.

"Ah!" Tom yelled.

James retrieved the cane.

"Stand up."

Tom tried, he couldn't.

James growled. He leaned in and pulled him to his feet, choking him against the wall.

Tom grabbed his arms, gasping for air. Eyes failing. The electricity is too far to be of any help.

"Please–" he begged.

"Let me be clear, for your own good you have to leave that independence here. You're mine and you'll do what I say. Don't ever try me again! If it wasn't that you're one of the few lucky people that have powers you would be dead by now." He looked away. Was that it, just a threat? "I'll make sure you remember that, forever."

Tom fell to the ground. He took a deep breath.

A guard came to his place and forced him to his feet, bracelets back on his wrists.

Tom screamed as his weight fell on his injured leg, blood dripping all the way down.

The guards held him in place, their grips ripping the skin of his arms.

Ayala and Isla were forced to stand beside him.

"Put your arms in front of you!" James ordered.

The kids didn't move, they were too scared to. They had been so close, they had practically been free. Isla had even made jokes. Isla! Now it was all gone.

"Now!"

The soldiers grabbed the kids' arms and forced them in front of them.

Isla and Ayala fought. They were no match for the strong guards, not without their powers.

James placed his cane against the wall and looked at the kids, his cold dead eyes cursing them.

"You don't need your hands to use your powers," he pulled a knife out from his pocket.

He walked to Ayala.

"No!" Ayala cried.

"Shut up!" James ordered.

The guards covered their mouths leaving only a muffled sound. Tom cried in the hallway. Where was the police? The rest of the guards? Where was the help?

Reality came like a storm. James had more power than what they had seen.

James looked at Ayala's scared eyes and smiled viciously. He took the knife and slowly moved it across her arm, from the elbow to the wrist, leaving a bright red trail behind it. Ayala's screams were muzzled by the guards. The tears that covered her whole face were her only show of pain.

James didn't flinch, he was used to doing things like this, dispensing pain with the least amount of harm. When the cut was done, he did a similar one in her palm and moved to her other arm, he repeated the process. When he finished there was blood dripping to the ground and Ayala crying harder.

He then turned to Isla. He repeated the process. Knife to arm, blood followed.

Finally, he turned to Tom.

He was too defeated to try anything when he saw the monster get near him. He bit his tongue as the knife touched his skin, he wasn't going to scream. Then James started moving it. His vision blurred, the sudden need to faint followed.

James slapped his face. Tom closed his eyes.

"You're feeling it, whether you like it or not."

He moved to the other arm. Tom watched his blood staining the purple cloaks of the soldiers at his side, face firm. He felt the battle ending. Thick, warm, texture falling down to the floor, drops echoing like the screams he didn't dare let out.

"This is only a small demonstration of what I can do," James said when it was done. "Listen well, you're not champions, you're a bunch of working dogs that are useful as long as you cooperate. The second you stop working you'll be thrown into the trash like used toilet paper. And if you ever try or even think about pulling another scam like this I'll take every tooth out of your mouth, rip your nails from your fingers, put your eyes in jars and burn you alive. Am I clear?"

The kids remained quiet, there wasn't anything to say.

"Answer me!" James screamed.

"Yes sir," the three of them muttered.

"Take Pláka, we're leaving," he ordered the guards.

"Should we bandage them?" one of the guards asked, the pools of blood were even making *them* anxious.

James glared at the kids.

"No, let them bleed until we reach the jet. As for the *boy,* he will wait for one of our special doctors," he said and laughed.

Tom's heart sank. Why had he ever tried to escape?

36

THE LAB

"Wakey, wakey," Chief said, the plane had finally landed.

Hally opened her eyes, behind her blindfold, there was nothing for her to see besides plain black. She hadn't been able to sleep at all, not that she felt comfortable sleeping in mid kidnapping, even though it would have been a good use of the time.

The cut inside her cheek was still bleeding. Her legs were weak, her head was buzzing, her whole body covered in cold sweat. The extra powder was surely pulling a number in her.

"Let's go everybody, move it. We're already late."

Hally shook as her chains were finally separated from the big iron cage.

With the blindfold still on and a soldier on each side, she was forced to her feet. For a second she believed she was going to faint.

The soldiers pulled her a few steps, she felt blind and empty, as if there was something missing. Her powers had become a part of her, a part they had dared to take away.

"Open the hangar," Chief yelled.

The loud noise of metal moving and mechanics working echoed in the cold air.

A cold breeze hit Hally's body. The sound stopped.

"General! Your packages. Just like you asked," Chief exclaimed proudly. That's what the kids meant for him, another achievement, one less thing to do. A few dollars. Hally wondered if he was ever going to lose sleep because of them, if in the years to come he would ever stop and consider what had become of them.

"Let me see them," a thick raspy female voice asked.

Hally's blindfold was taken away.

It took a few seconds for her eyes to adjust.

The four of them were in a line, separated by five guards between each other. In front there was a big group of people, most of them in white coats. A chill covered Hally's back. She didn't need to watch more movies to understand that powers and a bunch of scientists were never a good combination. She remembered her dream, lying beside Tom, a big needle in her arm. Was this the day that horrid nightmare turned true?

"Tell me, what did you bring?" asked the same female voice as before, now Hally could finally see its source.

Between the scientists the short, black haired beautiful woman, near her fifties, fully dressed in military uniform, managed to stay unnoticed. On the right side of her chest hung seven different medals, and above them there was a small golden name tag, it read two simple words: "The General".

The General walked slowly looking at each of the kids carefully, cold eyes reading them like a book. The Chief talked to her, sharing all details, the authority Hally had heard during the plane ride was gone. At least it meant that he knew his place, but it also meant that Hally wasn't going to play the General the same way she had done the Chief.

"We brought you what you asked for. We followed the trace to the FSC. We have no idea what they are. Or who they are. Just know that the last girl is more powerful than the rest. We used our last powder on her chains."

The General came by Hally and touched her hair carefully and creepily. Hally stood still, before doing anything stupid she had to understand what kind of person The General was.

She moved Hally's chin up, her gray eyes admiring her features.

Hally studied her back. The General's face was filled with scars and wrinkles, all from lessons she'd learned, and the ones she'd taught.

She took a step back.

"Morons!" she snapped at the Chief. "The only thing that you're doing here is killing her slowly. And for her luck we need her alive. Take the chains off," she ordered.

The Chief and his soldiers looked at each other.

"But ma'am-"

"Yes?"

No one dared to speak.

"Take the chains off," she ordered.

Chief looked at his workers and nodded. One of the hired soldiers came with a set of keys and one by one took the seven chains off, leaving nothing except a black anklet and a simple set of handcuffs on her wrists.

Hally took a deep breath, her powers moving weakly through her veins. She closed her eyes, there it was, the part that she'd been missing.

From the anklet came a horrid sound. Hally had never been electrocuted, except for one time when she was small, and she had accidentally touched an outlet while putting up Christmas lights. She remembered she had cried, swearing it was the worst feeling in the world. She had had no idea.

She leaned on her knees, the pain reaching her heart.

"You have no idea how much I wanted to do that," Chief chuckled. He gave a small remote to the General. "As promised. Now they are your problem, not mine. Where's my money?"

The General looked at the remote, analyzing it, a small smile curling at the corners of her mouth. Then she looked at the Chief.

"Before you get your money, I have to make sure they are what we need. Doctor Tanner! Would you do me the favor to check out that your new toys are actually what we are going to pay for?" The General asked.

From the group of scientists, a young guy, mid-thirties, came forward. He was tall, really tall, with short, curly, black hair and serious heart-piercing blue eyes. The stethoscope around his neck brought no peace to Hally. Somehow, she knew it was mostly used to listen for dead heart beats more than live ones.

Doctor Tanner, walked to the kids followed by an assistant.

"Remove the handkerchiefs from the suspects," he ordered the Chief.

Chief shook his head at him.

"You really don't want me to do that."

Doctor Tanner looked him dead in the eye, whatever his

actual title or power was, he knew that The General was on his side.

"Fine," Chief finally accepted. "You want to listen to them? There you go, listen to them."

The soldiers took the handkerchiefs off.

The Hally licked her lips, she could taste a little blood, the handkerchief had caused slight burns on the side of her mouth.

Peace filled her heart, all her power was back. She knew fairly well her biggest weapon was her words. Now she only had to wait for the right time and the right person. And maybe, they would survive.

Tanner, that's what Hally started to call the doctor since that day (she wasn't going to call him doctor until he gained her respect), examined each kid. He made them open their mouths, counted their teeth, checked their vision, hearing and lastly, he leered at each of the kids handcuffs and the color of the Unicorn Powder inside it.

He started with Piet. Tanner did his exams slowly, thoroughly and seriously until he glanced at the brown powder. Then he laughed, an ugly, bully laugh.

"This one is going first. A Veteris! He's the basis for everything we have to know. We study him and we'll understand everything else," he said to The General, she didn't share his enthusiasm. "What are the others?" he asked the hired soldiers.

The soldiers remained quiet and shrugged.

"What colors are in the other handcuffs?" Tanner asked this time as if he was talking to a three-year-old.

The soldiers checked the handcuffs on the kids.

"Blue, gold and silver, sir."

Tanner smiled at the kids with a 'I'm going to have a lot of fun with you' smile.

The scientist continued with the exams. After he was done with Piet he went on to Hally. Hally took her exam quickly and obediently, she wanted to convince everyone she was nothing more than an innocent quiet girl.

Pam didn't share the feeling. When Tanner went to check her she spit in his face and muttered what Hally was sure was an insult in Mandarin. The General pressed her remote and a shock rose from her ankle. Pam grunted but didn't move. If they wanted to actually hurt her, they would have to do more than that.

"Doctor, are they really worth the money?" the General asked once Tanner was done checking Lukai.

Tanner looked at The General, a smile crossing his face unnaturally.

"Indeed they are. We have a Veteris who is the basis for everything. Then we have a Bellator and a Woldier who will be able to teach us about the two opposite sides of Íroes. And finally, by luck or destiny, a Magister. She'll help us understand more complex matters such as Megalo Dentro and how their powers are created."

The General massaged her temples.

"I have other things to do. In one sentence?" she asked tiredly.

"We have them. We replicate their powers. You get your weapons and I get to study their organs in jars."

Hally's stomach gave a turn.

"Actually, I would prefer for my organs to stay just where they are," Hally said before the words went through her brain.

Tanner laughed.

"Don't we all?"

"Take them inside," The General commanded. That was it, the deal was done.

As Hally walked past Chief she overheard him and The General talking.

"Forty thousand, correct?"

"Yes."

A stack of cash exchanged hands.

The kids were forced inside what they would continue to call The Lab. (I love these kids, if they were to name everything in the universe, stars would be called The Little One, The Dark

One, Luisa... Instead we have names such as Polaris, Rigil Kentaurus and AS0039, try to say the last one seven times in a row quickly, I dare you).

The Lab was a lab, I know that was hard to figure out. Sadly there wasn't a brochure or welcome slide show the kids got to see to know what that place was. No one was interested in them having a good stay.

At first Hally tried to keep count of how many turns and corridors they went through, but within minutes she realized it was useless, the way the scientist and guards moved was planned to confuse them. They wanted to make sure that even if they escaped, they never found the exit between the long and dark hopeless corridors.

The deeper they went the more rooms and signs the kids were able to notice. There was lots of top-secret research going on in that single building. In a way it felt illegal to see all of it, though no one cared to make sure the kids didn't see everything. They all knew the same thing: the Guardians of Kinds were never going to set foot on the outside world again.

I'm going to be okay.

We're all going to be alright.

We're getting out. We're getting out. We're getting out.

Not even she herself believed it. All she wanted to do was to cry, she was scared, more scared than ever in her life. She was never going to see her mom again or her dad, or May and Tom. None of them were going to be able to see their family again. Lukai's siblings. Piet's dad and date. And Pam. She hadn't had the opportunity to experience a real family. They were already dead and the best they could do was accept it.

"When was the last time you guys ate?" Tanner asked Hally as they walked.

For a second, half-a-second, Hally felt an emotion similar to happiness. Between the fear and her shock, she hadn't noticed that she was hungrier than she had ever been all her life. Maybe she would be fed before dying. Then it wouldn't be such a bad death after all.

"In the plane, several hours ago," she answered quietly.

Please, at least a sandwich.

Tanner smiled.

"Let's take the four of them for samples, they are in perfect conditions. Deprive them any liquid or food for the next twenty-four hours. I want to see the survival mode of their systems." Murmurs moved among the excited scientists.

Hally's stomach sank. No food. She was going to die hungry.

The scientists moved, some took needles, others gloves and others notepads and pens. And the kids were forced in different directions, with no final looks to each other.

Hally was taken to a room that looked like a medical comfort suite , except all the walls were made of glass, rows of chairs outside prepared to hold an audience. One of the guards grabbed her and forced her into the bed, hands and ankles tied before she managed to move. Nobody gave her a second look, no one questioned why there was a teenage girl tied there. The scientist and the nurses just kept moving, like robots programmed to do their jobs without hesitation.

She looked to the side, on her left was Lukai and on her right Pam. Next to Lukai there was Piet, too far to talk to him.

A young nurse entered the room, needle and tube in hand.

"Stay still, this will be over quickly," was the only thing she said before she pushed the needle in and the blood started to come out.

Hally glanced at the blood filling tube after tube. She counted twenty in total before the nurse grabbed her stuff and left without saying anything else.

Hally watched her leave. Outside, the chairs had already been taken by young students eagerly waiting for something to happen. Her handcuffs were still around her wrists, powerless to challenge the two gigantic guards in the entrance. Pam had tried it, she had refused to give blood. Tanner had shocked her so many times she had been left unconscious, her nose bleeding and staining her clothes.

Whenever no one was looking Hally turned to Lukai, maybe he had a plan, a way for them all to get out of this. Lukai never looked back at her. He was the biggest of the four. He was tall and strong, so he had more guards, too many to try anything.

"Do you know where we are?" Hally asked a guard, then a nurse, and one of the students lucky enough to step into the room. They never answered. They knew better than that.

Then the second part started. The students in the chairs got their notes ready.

After the blood was taken and apparently analyzed, Tanner had decided the experiments had to start.

Ignoring every single thing he had said about dealing first with Piet, Tanner did his rounds looking at every kid, making sure there wasn't anything he hadn't noticed.

"How's this one?" he asked a nurse in Hally's room.

"Weak sir," the lady replied, the first words she'd said in hours.

She *felt* weak, and hungry.

"Take away the handcuffs," Tanner ordered.

"Are you sure doctor, she could be a threat," the nurse advised.

Tanner laughed.

"Let her get stronger for a few minutes before we start. I will personally take care of her. Meanwhile make sure the other teams are ready, we'll start with their bacteria reactions. Immune systems. Then viruses. And then..." He laughed. "Then we'll see."

Bacteria?

"If you say so doctor," the nurse replied, and he came by.

Hally felt how she was freed, unable to even sit up, she felt how the cold metal was removed from her wrists and for a second she was the most powerful being in the world. Her senses strengthened; the power moved through her veins. Then everything went back to normal. She had no food in her stomach, no energy to feed her powers. Her consciousness started to fade.

Tanner walked to her; Hally's muscles tensed.

"Relax, I'm peaceful," Tanner said with a smile.

"Are you peaceful or just harmless?" Hally mumbled, head spinning. Her thoughts were as scrambled as eggs for breakfast.

"What did you say?"

"Are you peaceful or harmless? You can only consider yourself peaceful if you choose peace over violence, but if you are just defenseless then calling yourself peaceful is just a mistake," she mumbled back.

Tanner laughed.

"I am peaceful," Hally added, vision going back to normal.

The laughs were gone.

"Oh really?" Tanner scoffed.

Hally turned to him and stared at his eyes.

"Yes."

Tanner smiled; he enjoyed Hally's defiance.

"I wonder if you'd say the same thing in a dark shadow filled room?" He leaned closer. "I've been told the mighty Magister is afraid of the dark, just like a little girl," he whispered.

Hally's mind filled with the vivid images of the Shadower. The cold feeling of being watched took over. How did Tanner know about that? Was it just a coincidence? Either way this wasn't the moment for that.

"I would say it any time, any place."

"She says it while being tied to the bed," Tanner taunted.

"Yet I'm not the powerless one."

The smile faded.

"You see," Hally continued, "the worst idea you could have ever had was to let me loose without my handcuffs and truly believe I wouldn't bring a knife to your throat."

Tanner looked around mockingly. He put his hands up in the air as a joke.

"The problem is that I see no knife against my throat."

Hally smiled.

"You know what a metaphor is, right? I never said it was actually a knife or that it was your throat."

Tanner's smile faded, this wasn't a joke, he'd just realized that.

Hally looked down at her leg.

"No!" Tanner screamed standing up immediately.

Hally smiled even harder, she was telling the truth, she was weak, not powerless. With her very little energy she had taken a shot into her leg.

"Penicillin, in case you forgot. Works against bacteria."

A nurse rushed inside.

"Doctor," she gasped. "I'm afraid the experiment has been compromised."

"Let me guess, the other specimens have had a shot of penicillin?" Tanner angrily asked the nurse.

"Yeah..."

"Ahhhh!" Tanner smashed every visible piece of glass into the ground shattering in all directions.

Hally closed her eyes, avoiding glass in her eyes.

"Get them inside cells and as soon their systems are clear, get them out of here!" Tanner yelled.

"Ok-kk-ay," the nurse stuttered.

Soon the room was filled with people and Hally fell asleep, wherever they were moving her they didn't want her to know how to get out.

"Halls."

"Halls."

"HALLS!"

Hally woke up as she was being shaken.

She immediately got up on her feet ready to fight anything and anyone.

"It's all right, you're okay," Lukai calmed her. "We're fine."

He hugged her. She hugged him back, a short calming hug.

She looked around. They were in a box, a literal metal box, handcuffs back on her wrists. They were doomed, that was a fact.

She looked at Lukai, she wanted to cry so bad, she had wanted to cry since she had woken up in the plane.

"I'm sorry, I did the first thing that came to mind. I didn't really think about it. And now we're trapped, who knows where," she mumbled, her words mixing with each other, her voice breaking, her eyes filling with tears.

Lukai grabbed both her shoulders gently, his own kind brown eyes looking back at her.

"Hey, it's okay. You did what you could, and you saved us. If it wasn't for you, we wouldn't be able to talk right now. You bought time."

Hally sniffled. She felt stupid crying like a little baby.

She wiped her tears with her hands.

"I kept looking at you, waiting for you to have a plan," she sobbed.

"I know," he answered. "I didn't want to call attention by looking back," he said regrettably.

"Instead, you left me with my stupid ideas," Hally replied.

Lukai looked at her.

"You have to start giving yourself the credit you deserve, Hally. You're more than what you think."

"Sure, everybody thinks so now that I can move things with my mi-"

"I didn't mean your powers, I meant you. Your person. Your powers weren't the ones that got us out of the Gang, or the ones that stood to Elowen, or to the Shadower. That was you. You were the one that when there was no way out, you looked up with that twinkle in your eyes and did something stupid that gave us hope."

Hally shook her head.

"Hope is a bunch of empty lies."

"No. Hope is courage, it's strength. And it's in your veins. There's something about having a shot of penicillin brought into our hands in the middle of the most secure military lab that makes one think that anything is possible. *You* make us believe that everything is possible, because that's what you do. And I know you know it; you just don't know yet that you know it. But when you see a fight in front of you, you roll up your sleeves with that look that screams 'if I'm going down, I'm going down with a mess'."

Hally remembered her science classes. She frowned. There was something bothering her, as if she knew something but couldn't figure out what.

She remembered Madame Rosemary's letter, she said something similar. 'I know it'll be safe with you; you won't give it up.'

"So, stop your sobbing. Take a deep breath and let that awesome mind of yours start-"

"Rosemary!" Hally's eyes lit up, fire burning in her heart. "How could I have been that stupid?" she asked herself.

"What? What is it?"

"The bags," Hally answered as if it was obvious. "The weapons. Everything. I had utterly forgotten about them."

"Madame Rosemary's weapons," Lukai said putting his hand on top of his head, he had also forgotten about them.

Hally closed her eyes and focused, she called her medical bag and the weapons. In a second they were there, like magic. Perhaps reality did hold a little bit of magic.

Hally looked at herself, a set of belts had appeared on her. One on her waist, one on her lower leg, another on her arm, all holding a different shiny knife ready for her to reach it.

She grabbed one of the biggest ones with such a silvery shine that she could use it as a mirror.

She focused on that one, the rest, just as they had appeared, vanished.

"Wow," slipped from Lukai's mouth.

Hally smiled; she thought the same.

"You have to try it, call yours."

Lukai closed his eyes, a long golden sword appeared in his hand.

"Dang it, now I look like an actor from Mission impossible," he said. "But with a sword."

"You look fine," Hally assured him while she looked for something in her medical bag before disappearing again. She was still weak, but she remembered the pills Blake had given the kids, they were for energy and even though she was sure they weren't made for her just to eat, she needed the energy right now if she wanted to stand a chance.

"Have you seen the pills? Blake's pills?" she asked

"Yeah, I think I have them." Lukai looked in his bag and pulled them out. He handed one to her.

Hally shoved the red pill into her mouth, Lukai shoved one into his as well.

"Help me find the door so we can force it open."

They pushed themselves against the walls, looking for anything that showed the location of their salvation.

"Here," Lukai finally said, a thin small crack revealed the entrance and exit.

Hally took out her biggest knife and he took his sword.

"At the count of three, are you ready, Halls?" Lukai asked.

Hally was ready to push the door, pressing her back against the wall and her legs against the knife.

"Halls? Where did Halls come from?"

"I don't know. I guess I was looking but couldn't find the why."

Hally glared at him, rethinking every decision in her life.

"C'mon, it was funny."

Hally shook her head, she was disappointed.

"I'm just happy you're a chef and not a comedian."

Lukai laughed.

"One. Two. Three."

Together they pushed. Hally heard a crack coming from the force of the knife and her wrist and she kept pushing. The door started to open, centimeter by centimeter until it was wide enough for them to come out into a long empty hallway.

The white walls and floors sent chills over Hally. She looked up at the walls. No cameras, not visible anyway. She focused her hearing, waiting for a guard to come any time and send out the alarm. They never came.

"Come," Lukai called Hally.

Covered in sweat the kids ran down the mysteriously empty and quiet hall and found another cell, they knocked on it.

"Pam?"

"Hally? Hally! Get me out of here," Pam begged.

"Give us a second," Lukai said.

They repeated the process. The door opened. From inside a very angry and crazy looking Pam emerged. But Hally's attention was in another place. Another crack had come from her wrist.

She looked down at her wrist, she didn't feel the pain, she felt power. One of the handcuffs had cracked, Unicorn Powder pouring slowly down her hand onto the floor.

She focused on the left handcuff around her wrist and ripped it apart, like she had done with the watermelon in Treacher's training. Her full power rushed back; her eyes glowing. She was unstoppable.

She turned to Lukai.

"Don't move," she ordered, and his own handcuffs broke in half and fell to the ground, then Pam's.

She turned. Where the fourth had to be it was empty.

"Where's Piet?" she asked.

"They took him, like ten minutes ago," Pam said, she had also taken a pill from Lukai.

Hally's heart sank.

"Then let's go get him," Lukai replied. "We're all getting out of here. Or none at all."

The three of them looked at each other, they were stronger than ever. They were getting Piet, getting out of the Lab and returning to Platz. There was hope once again.

Then it all changed.

Hally's smile faded.

"I can't see."

"What?" Lukai asked.

"I can't see," Hally repeated, she had been fine just one second before.

"What do you mean you can't see?" Pam asked as she waved her hand in front of Hally. Hally didn't move.

"I mean I can't see!" Hally exclaimed as she moved her head around terrified.

In one second her eyes had ceased to work. She was completely and utterly blind.

37

DRUNK

There was blood everywhere, I think I already made that clear.

They were on their way back to the Superiors' camp, at least that's what the kids hoped.

The three of them had been thrown in the airplane hold. Their mouths, hands and feet were taped. James had been nice enough to cover their cuts for them not to bleed to death, after all they were worthless dead. But that didn't stop the blood from going down Tom's arms, to his clothes, and onto the cold floor.

Isla had passed out. By his side the cuts from her arms were bleeding worse than Ayala's and Tom's together. Tom lay quiet. He wasn't going to pretend that the cuts from his arms, the bullet in his leg, and the pain from his heart weren't killing him. But he had reached the point where all his tears had already dried out.

There wasn't a single drop of anger inside him. Somehow, crazy somehow, Tom was sad. Not because of the cuts, but because he'd let down James. He'd been a champion; he had been someone for a few days, and he had thrown all of that through the window just to try to escape and fail.

Now he was back to his normal self, his worthless self.

The flight didn't take long, or it didn't seem long for the half-conscious kids. Either way they reached the camp sooner or later. When they arrived, he watched the patient and malicious soldiers force them out, step after step. Tom walked, nothing in him as a will to live.

A few steps into the camp Isla fainted. Tom watched the soldiers beat her so badly that she would have bruises over her face and arms for weeks. He watched as Ayala was forced out with a leash on her neck, everybody who looked at her barked mockingly. And he suffered as he was paraded as a war hero by James, except the people spit at him and laughed.

The next day Tom was woken by a dish of spoiled, fried eggs thrown at his face.

"Wake up! James wants you out in five minutes!" Roberts screamed and left before he answered.

Tom moaned; he had barely slept. He cleaned the eggs off his face carefully; even though his wounds had already healed he felt the ghostly ache.

After the parade the kids had been thrown into their old cells and made to wait until James decided to call for a doctor. He couldn't remember much after that. He knew they had been taken one by one, first Isla, then Ayala, and finally him. Ayala and Isla had been given the cheapest medicine and few bandages for their arms. After that he could only remember his screams

"Coming?" Isla whispered as she walked past his cell, she was way too hurt to try to talk fancy. Her face was almost unrecognizable. All her beauty hidden behind her bruises. Her confidence shattered to pieces. Her bandages had blood spots. He remembered the first time he'd seen her, in that bus so many days before. She couldn't have looked more differently now.

"I'll join you in a minute," Tom moaned. Isla continued walking.

Tom sat up; the cold floor bringing the only relief he had for the pain.

With the help of a tall, thin old stick the doctor had given him he stood up, a piercing pain going through his leg. He was cured, why was he still aching?

He noticed a bottle by his bed. He should've left it there the last night he had spent in that cell, even though he didn't remember doing so.

He picked up the bottle; it was full of the transparent liquid.

What would he say if he'd known a month before that he'd be there? Would he have enjoyed his mom's cooking more? Would he have laughed every night when Hally woke him up? Would he still worry about the homework he hadn't done? Would he still be looking for answers?

Tom opened the cap and smelled the liquid. It was rancid, and old, not all that delightful, but he knew perfectly what the liquid was going to do if he drank it.

"No...," Tom whispered and put the bottle back, that wasn't him.

"One minute!" Roberts screamed furiously from outside. Tom heard Ayala being slapped. This was hell, he couldn't afford being himself.

He retrieved the bottle and drank it until there wasn't a drop left.

"Your breath smells," Isla whispered to him.

"Your nose is swollen," Tom whispered back.

Isla closed her mouth and turned her head, deciding not to direct her words to him again.

Tom couldn't care less.

The three of them were in a line facing the cabins, the cold rain falling against their bodies washing down the blood on their bandages. James was talking to them. No, he wasn't talking. He was furious, screaming and yelling. Yet the words didn't seem to find their way into Tom's brain.

He tilted his head, admiring the rain falling down. He found it funny. The pain was gone, momentarily, but gone. That was good.

He stared at James, it felt like that was what he was supposed to do. From time to time he wiped a few drops of blood coming from his nose. He looked at James' mouth moving up and down, side to side, big and small. Until a guard that looked quite like a penguin interrupted him respectfully and whispered some words in his ear.

"You didn't find Sfaíra?" James snapped.

Tom smiled at himself; he liked that word. Sfaíra. Sfaíra. Sfaíra. If he wasn't wrong it was another of those dumb things James was looking for, the portal pieces, right?

He chuckled. Sfaíra.

"What do you mean that you didn't find Sfaíra," James asked again.

The guards started to explain to him something about someone else having it. Tom didn't pay attention. He just stood there, enjoying the emptiness in his mind with a hiccup here and there. Several times Isla tried to get him to stand up straighter, show a little respect to avoid the guards' anger, Tom refused.

Hours later, when the alcohol had gone through his system, his mind got clearer, and the pain returned.

A guard pushed him.

Tom fell face into the mud.

"Drink," he remembered Ulyssa's voice.

He tried to push himself from the ground, he couldn't.

The guard pulled him to his feet and dragged him to the center, the same place where days before he had shot his first lightning bolt.

James looked at him and frowned. He nodded to the guards. Tom's handcuffs were taken off.

Tom looked at his wrists, what days before would have made him powerful, only increased the pain. He felt the sudden electric currents going through his arms, his recent wounds, blood tinting his muddy bandages. It wasn't nice, not at all.

As punishment, sobriety quickened. He felt that cold whisper on the back of his neck.

Tom didn't even bother to turn his head, only his eyes. There she was, Aina.

She wasn't mad or angry. She wasn't talking either, just whispering.

"You have to get out of here."

"You have to get out of here," she repeated.

"You all have to get out of here."

The words started to echo in Tom's head, over and over again. Nothing stopped them, even though he didn't understand why she was repeating them.

"Thomas!"

The words stopped.

Tom turned his head where he thought the sound had come from.

"Thomas!" He turned his head to the other side, the right one this time.

Behind James, in a line, fifteen well-dressed ladies and gentlemen stood watching and analyzing. The Company; James bosses.

Tom looked at them, he recognized some, from billboards, ads, television shows. They were important rich people that controlled the world and now desired to control him. And James was doing the favor of showing them off. Isla had sung. Ayala had turned into an elephant. Now it was his turn.

Tom looked at James, his mind still not clear enough.

James' face was stone.

"Fire it up," he ordered looking at a diana that stood in the empty field, fifty meters away.

Tom looked at the diana as a third grader looks at calculus.

He gulped.

He couldn't do it. He knew he couldn't do it. He knew deep down in his soul, whether he accepted it or not, the second he had decided to betray James, his powers had minimized. And now he was hurt, really hurt, and he was drunk, his mind flooding like a tsunami. He was as lost as a kid in a forest.

"Fire it up," James repeated, the words 'or we'll fire *you* up' implicitly.

Tom raised his arm.

He closed his eyes and tried. Again. And again.

He lowered his arm, the diana standing untouched.

Before his arm was completely down the strike came.

Tom felt it terribly. He would never know if it had been the alcohol or just his mind playing games, but that strike, that wooden log breaking against his back was more painful than being shot.

Tom went down to the floor, his head hitting the mud.

James kneeled beside him and grabbed the collar of his shirt.

"You were supposed to prove that you were still the champion," he said so close to his face that drops from his saliva fell onto his cheeks, "but you're no champion. The second this mission is over, when I have what I want in my hands and your powers prove worthless, I'll pretty much enjoy killing you myself."

The evil man pushed Tom's head into the mud before standing up. The Company was still there, nobody argued about what they were watching.

The guards forced Tom onto his feet and the scene repeated. Tom was told to "fire up" the diana and he raised his arms for a minute or so, but it never worked. The electricity never came. And then, a wood log smacked his back.

Hours later, or what seemed hours later, when the diana still stood at the other side of the field, one last log was broken against his back, and he was dragged to his cell.

Tom looked at himself in the little broken mirror on the wall. He was unrecognizable, pale, eyes red, hair bloodied, purple bruises hiding his face.

"When will it be enough?" he asked. "When will I have had enough crap? When will I be free?"

No one answered.

He reached down by his bed. Desperate, he moved his hands, until his fingers wrapped around the cold glass. He smiled, at least something was going well.

He pulled the bottle up to his face and he looked at it disappointed, it was the same bottle he had drunk that morning.

He stood up. There it was, Aina.

"You have to get out of here," Aina whispered.

"How?" Tom asked furiously, it was the first time he answered the illusion. "I'm not a champion. I'm no one in the

Superiors world. I'm no one in the Íroes world. I'm no one in Platz. I'm no one in my school. I'm no one in my house. *How* am I going to achieve something if I'm a nobody?" he yelled at Aina.

Aina stood there, but didn't answer. How could she? She wasn't real.

"Why would you know? You're just a mirror of my conscience," Tom muttered, and he threw the glass bottle against the wall, smashing it to pieces.

"May I come in?" a voice asked from outside the bars.

Tom turned, it was James holding a tray with food and drink, his cane in his other hand.

He looked at him. Although it sounded like a question, he knew that it wasn't one.

"Yes," he whispered, eyes fixed on the ground.

James smiled, the side of him that had shot him and screamed all day, long gone. He entered the cell and carefully laid the tray on the floor.

He placed one hand on his shoulders. Tom tensed under his touch.

"I know I said you're no champion. And you aren't, *yet*. But I believe that you can achieve it, actually achieve it. One day, I think you can actually put to good use those powers of yours. That day you *will* be a champion," he said to Tom.

Tom continued staring at the ground.

"Today, we can drink for that day is to come," James cheered and grabbed the bottle with the funny looking liquid. He poured a whole glass for Tom, none for himself. "Here," he said.

Tom took the glass; he again knew that there wasn't a question in the sentence.

He drank the liquid. Almost instantly he felt a burn in his heart and then he smiled. For no reason he smiled. He was happy, really happy. His mind wasn't clouded with torment anymore, or pain, or with anything at all. Only with happiness and one question. Why had he ever wanted to leave that place?

38

BLINDED

"What do you mean?" Pam asked hysterically.

"I mean I can't see," Hally responded, her eyes meeting nothing but darkness. "Me. No. See! Put your hands over your eyes tightly and look around, that's what I'm looking at!"

She was panicking, hand wrapped around Pam's wrist in search of balance.

"But... but... Why?" Lukai asked himself. "Did they give you something? Maybe a pill? Or an injection?"

"No..." Hally responded, shaking her head. "I only took Blake's pill."

"Yeah, I gave it to you, the red one," Lukai said.

"Wait, wait, wait," Pam interrupted. "Didn't each person have their specific color?"

"Yes," Lukai and Hally answered at the same time.

"Then why were you taking the red one, that was Tom's."

For a second Hally's ears clouded. She revisited the memory of that morning. The wall, the Imperium Orb, and the pill. Her pill was green! Not red. Green!

Oh no...

"I'm so sorry Hally," Lukai apologized. "I swore it was yours."

"I mean they are twins, it was a fifty-fifty chance," Pam said.

"Yeah, at least I got that one right-"

"Hey!" Hally exclaimed. "Still blind over here."

"Sorry. What now? You took the wrong pill, and you stay blind forever?" Lukai asked.

"I guess it could fade away once the pill gets out of my system. We just have to hope that there aren't any more side effects."

There was silence between the three for a second.

"How are we going to get Piet?" Lukai asked.

"Well... let me think. Maybe... Maybe, we could start by looking for him!" Hally exclaimed as if it was obvious.

"Hally you're not looking for anything, literally!" Lukai exclaimed.

"Don't worry about me, I'm not completely blind. My powers

let me feel things around me a little bit. We only need to find Piet and then get out of here," Hally added.

Pam and Lukai gave it some thought.

"Where could they have taken him? To another experiment?" Pam asked.

Hally shook her head.

"Another experiment could mean another building, we can't afford to think like that, not yet," she replied.

The silence continued. Hally could feel their eyes on her.

"Why are you looking at me?" she exclaimed.

"How could you even know we are looking at you?" Pam asked.

"I can feel your eyes piercing my soul. And I don't understand why?"

"You're the one that usually knows how the rest of people think, why did they take Piet?" Lukai asked.

Hally licked her lips.

"I mean..." she closed her eyes, even though she couldn't see anything but darkness. The answer came. "Because I injected all of you with penicillin. The second I did that it became a declaration that we, or at least me, are a threat. Now Tanner has to be more cautious and that's why he took Piet. If we are actually a team, we would never leave without him and even if we did, he would still have one of us." It wasn't an answer, just a guess.

"So we find a map or something and try to figure out where they could have taken him," Pam proposed.

"I know where the security room is, I saw as they took us here," Lukai said. "Come," he said, and Hally heard as he walked away.

Using her powers and guided by her hearing she followed him, a few steps to her right. She hit a wall. She was used to her powers being an added sense, not her eyes.

"Ughh, seriously?" Pam exclaimed.

"Just take my hand." Lukai grabbed Hally's hand, guiding her through the aisles carefully.

A little late, but still soon enough to be an inconvenience an alarm filled the air.

"Careful," Pam called out.

Before the kids realized it, they were being pursued by guards. At first, they kept their distance waiting for the right orders. When they came through, they brought out the batons and tasers cornering the kids.

The first guard dealt with Lukai. The second with Pam. The rest just made their way into the fight.

"Duck!" Hally yelled at Lukai when she threw a guard's taser away before punching him. Lukai was right about something, she didn't give up, even if she was blind.

Another guard walked towards her, she followed her instinct, her powers knew what to do. She grabbed her hand tightly around her knife. The guard swung his baton. Hally ducked before disappearing, if she couldn't see, it was only fair that they couldn't see her either. She made a clean slice on his leg. The guard stepped back. Hally raised her hands. The young woman flew all the way to the back of the corridor. Then another came, she dealt with him the same way. Then another. And another.

Yet, it wasn't enough. It never was.

"We have to separate!" Lukai exclaimed to the girls.

"I'll distract the guards, you guys get to the security system," Hally blurted out as she fought another guard.

"Are you crazy?" Pam asked. "You're blind, Hally!"

"I am pretty sure that's called discrimination," she argued before dodging another baton. "I can still distract them," she assured her. She threw a knife and heard a guard exclaim as it made a clean cut at his side, his pain would disappear with time, hopefully after they'd had the opportunity to run away.

"No! Lukai take her with you to the security system. I'll distract them," Pam announced and made her way through the guards taking them to the other side of the building.

Lukai didn't wait a second, he took Hally's hand and together they made it to the security system temporarily free of any followers.

They entered the room; Lukai closed the door behind them.

"Stay here," Lukai sat Hally in a chair hidden from the door.

The Canadian boy walked away.

The door creaked open, somebody slipped in.

Hally stood up, quiet, and ready to face someone. Before she used her invisibility a hand came from behind and carefully pulled her against the wall. It was Lukai.

"Did you get the plans?" Hally whispered.

"Yes, I know where Piet is. No eyesight yet?"

"No. But my head is clearing and it's easier to sense what's happening around."

Lukai clicked his tongue.

"It *is* something."

The two of them waited for the door to be free. Then quietly they walked to the door and Lukai opened it slowly to stop it from creaking. They stepped into the creepily quiet hallways. Hally was about to turn them invisible when she felt a tingle in her neck. She made a shield.

A tenth of a second later the shield was hit, exactly where her heart had been. Another hit came. They were being shot at, not bullets, sleeping darts.

A warm feeling came from her right: light.

The guards grunted, blinded.

Now they know how it feels.

"It won't last," Lukai said with a short breath. "Let's go."

He pulled Hally to the other side.

They turned around the corner and Lukai stopped, frozen.

There was someone in front of them, staring.

"Lukai?" she whispered. "What's happening?" The person was a grown adult, probably a man, either a doctor or a guard, neither of them being good news.

The figure didn't move, Hally felt as it tensed.

"It's alright?" he tried to affirm, before pulling her one more time in the opposite direction. "C'mon, we have to find Piet."

"Who was back there?" Hally asked as they ran.

"No one," the boy responded. There wasn't enough time to get a better answer.

They ran shielded with invisibility, to the other side of the building, dealing with the guards they found on their way, the alarm still blaring loudly. There was supposed to be another set of cells, where Lukai assumed Piet was being held.

Not long after, Pam appeared, she was tired and sweaty from running around.

Hally pulled her against the wall and made her invisible as well, losing all the guards and doctors for good.

"Do you know where we're going?" the Asian girl asked Lukai.

"Yes," he assured for the third time.

The three of them walked slowly and close together. Turning to Pam to get them through the walls and doors that were on their way.

It took them fifteen minutes until they made it to the cell block.

As a tsunami, a wave of guards flooded the hallway. Before any of them reacted, they were separated by the crowd, Hally on one side and Lukai and Pam on the other.

Hally fought trying to keep the invisibility, but it was like trying to run another meter after running a marathon, she couldn't keep all of them hidden.

"Here she is!" a guard exclaimed. He grabbed her neck and pinned her against the wall.

Hally moved her knife around, but the guard grabbed it and threw it away before she did any damage. He was stronger and bigger, and she was too tired.

She tried to kick him, unsuccessfully, her lungs each second burning harder in search of oxygen.

"Ahhh!" Lukai yelled from her right. The guard loosened his grip.

Hally fell to the ground, breathing. Lukai punched the guard on his nose and Pam sunk his feet and hands into the ground.

The rest of the uniforms formed a circle around them.

"Here," Lukai handed Hally's knife and helped her to her feet.

"Nowhere to go," a guard mocked.

"Maybe for you," Pam replied. "Hold on tight," she grabbed their shoulders and pushed them through the metal door, inside a cell.

"Piet!" Hally exclaimed happily; she didn't have to see to know that tall figure was Piet.

"Guys!" he responded with a smile.

The kids ran to him and hugged him.

He was sitting in a chair, his hands and ankles restrained, and his arm connected to a hanging bag. Hally moved her hand through his arm and through the chord that took liquid to a plastic bag.

"What happened to you?" she asked.

"What happened to *you*?" he asked as Pam loosened up the ropes on his feet and hands.

"I'm blind," Hally said.

"Since when?"

"Now. Took the wrong pill. Tell you the story later," Hally summarized. "What are they doing to you?"

Piet stood up, taking the cord out from his arm.

"They were taking blood from me."

"Why?" Lukai asked. "We have penicillin in our system, any bacteria experiment won't work."

"Maybe they're just a bunch of crazy bloodthirsty monsters," Pam babbled.

"Or they found a way to replicate some ability using our blood," Hally theorized.

"Anyway, nothing good," Lukai said, reaching for the bag. "Can you turn this into a stone?" he asked Piet.

Piet touched it.

Lukai laid the rock on the floor and poured a blaring light on it. Suddenly there was nothing left but ashes.

"Good try," Tanner's voice came from the roof (actually from a couple of speakers that were on the roof). "But four teens are not going to beat a full team of the brightest minds in the world."

"They're barging in," Hally said. As the words came out of her mouth, the door started to open. The four of them raced to keep it closed.

Portal. We just have to figure out how to make a portal.

Hally closed her eyes and breathed, she had to focus.

"Hally, this wouldn't be a bad moment for a portal!" Piet exclaimed.

"I know!" she replied, this was harder than she had ever expected.

"Halls"

"Shut up!" she shushed Lukai.

"There's no way out," Tanner laughed.

"Ahhhh!" Hally yelled and stepped up front, leaving Pam, Lukai and Piet fighting alone to keep the door closed.

Hally extended her arms, her palms facing the floor. She relaxed herself, let everything from around her drain out, every noise and every person. And she found it, the power.

"Okay I think I have it! Where do you want to go?"

"Anywhere away from here," Lukai said.

Anywhere.

Hally moved her hand as if she was turning the handle of the door and she opened it, the portal.

"Move!" she yelled to the rest and together they crossed, the portal closing behind them.

The four of them fell to the ground.

Hally moved her arms; she heard the rest moaning and exhaling out of relief. She felt the cold floor underneath her, the warm sunlight hitting her face, with her left hand she felt the edge of a soft rug. She didn't need to see to know where they were, they were in her house, her house from Flikos.

39

"HOME", BUT NOT HOME

Hally woke up to silence. She hated it. It was only a reminder that everything had changed.

More than a week had passed since she had left that same home, a week since she had woken up and her first view wasn't that same wall, a week since she hadn't seen her parents. During the past few days she had tried not to think a lot about it, as a matter of fact, she hadn't thought about it at all. But now, out of nowhere, it was all over her mind.

She stood up (her eyesight already back), made her bed and took a shower, just like she had done many times in the last years. The last thing she remembered was lying in the living room, the portal had taken so much energy she had fainted. She assumed one of the guys had taken her to her room, easily distinguished from the others.

When she came out of the shower she expected to hear the sound of Tom walking through her room, the smell of her father's cologne filling the house and the sound of the blender coming from the kitchen. None of those things came. Her parents were gone, whether to the university or back to Costa Rica, Hally had no idea. She only knew they had left in a rush, most of their things were still left there, waiting to be packed and taken.

Should I call Mom? I haven't talked to her.

No... It's better to let them think I'm still safe within Blake's custody.

She folded her used clothes; they were so dirty she was ready to burn them.

A USB fell from her pocket.

She picked it up.

"Where do you come from, little guy?"

She moved the silver object from hand to hand.

"Who uses USBs in this century?" She shook her head. "Sorry little bud, but you're going to the trash."

She was about to throw it out when that urge came over her, she needed to know what was inside.

She rushed to her old computer on her desk and plugged the thing in.

One file opened up; a shiver went down her spine. Suddenly she had that feeling that she was once again being watched by the shadows.

Hally turned around just to make sure no one had sneaked up on her and turned back to the computer.

She stared at the screen for a few minutes, making up her mind. She didn't know where that USB came from, or whether its information was real. But it was there, in front of her, and it was calling for a choice.

She took the computer, it was time to talk with the others.

Quietly, Hally walked down the stairs. She stopped and took a good look at the pictures hanging on the wall. A week ago she would have been instantly filled with a feeling of home. Now, she smiled at them, but they weren't anything more than memories. That place, those pictures, none of them felt like home anymore. Whenever she thought about home a tingle came to her hands.

Hally looked at her hands, that tingle was a portal. She gave it a thought.

Home.

Platz came to mind. The first place, the first people and the first days in years that hadn't made her feel cursed. It was right there, she just had to open the door and step into the other side.

Hally shook her head and the tingle disappeared, in its place came something new: knowledge

The voices from the kitchen grew louder.

Hally grabbed the computer closer; home would have to wait.

She took a final look at her family pictures.

"I'll see you soon Tommy, I promise I'll try."

As she reached the first floor, she smelled the French toast in the making. She walked to the kitchen where Pam, Piet and Lukai were. Pam and Lukai looked like they had taken a shower, Piet looked as if he had just woken up.

"Good morning," Hally greeted them with a soft smile as she sat beside Pam.

"You came just at the right moment," Lukai said, placing some toast in front of her.

Hally thanked him and turned to Piet.

"You can stop the faces; I can see you."

"Ahhh..." Piet sighed disappointedly.

"Your eyesight is back," Pam said, not that excited, she seemed as if she hadn't rested that well.

"Oh gosh, don't sound that happy," Hally replied sarcastically. Piet laughed. "What do you have there?" Hally asked her.

Pam laughed.

"A beautiful picture of baby Hally. You were such a chubby baby?"

Hally rolled her eyes.

"I don't have time to deal with this," she muttered to herself.

Lukai took the last plate and sat in front of her.

"How did you all sleep?" she asked.

"Mmm," Pam answered, shrugging her shoulders.

"We slept in the living room, it felt rude using a room that wasn't ours," Lukai explained.

"Whose house is this anyway?" Piet asked.

"Hally's," Lukai and Pam replied in unison.

"Didn't you see the pictures?"

Piet shrugged.

"I thought you were from Costa Rica."

"I am, but for the last few years we have been living here. Now that I think of it, not the best place we could all be. I mean this side, Flikos, it's alright, but if we move to Miso, just a few blocks away, we might find some problems with the Superiors."

The others nodded as they understood Hally's indirect way of saying to be careful and stay inside the house.

"There's something wrong, isn't there?" Lukai asked, staring at Hally. "Your eyes say something is wrong."

Hally finished chewing before she answered.

She placed her computer on the table and showed the rest what she had found.

"Turns out we weren't that lost when we were talking about why they were taking Piet's blood. They did find something in our blood. It's a protein we all share, even with places that come from an Íroes origin like Megalo Dentro," she explained.

"What does it matter?" the blond boy asked, giving his orange juice a last sip.

"According to the records the General is considering selling it."

Pam scoffed.

"Why would they want our blood? Last time I checked vampires didn't exist."

"A week ago neither did Íroes." Hally pointed at her with her fork as she spoke.

Piet slammed the table with both his hands, eyes opened double their normal size.

"Do you think vampires exist?"

Hally shrugged.

"I mean you got a girl's phone number, everything is possible," she mumbled, chewing her way through the last of her breakfast.

"Hey!"

"You got a phone number?" Pam frowned. "She must be desperate to go after a baby."

"I'M NOT A BABY," the boy exclaimed, his pale face a bright shade of red.

Pam and Hally fist bumped.

Lukai cleared his throat.

"Going back to the important things."

"The vampires?"

"Shut up Piet, drink your milk. I mean The General," Lukai turned to Hally.

"Oh yeah... She's selling it to the Superiors..."

"And?" the three kids asked.

Hally took a sip of her own glass, a sudden cold reaching her neck.

"They will try to replicate it, make it a... weapon."

There was silence.

"What are you trying to say?" Pam asked, face filled with maple syrup.

"As I see it there are two options. Actually there are more but for sake of the explanation I'll use two. The first one being we portal back to Platz, leaving all of this in Blake's hands. Not my favorite. Blake shouldn't take the risk, it's I the one with powers, I'm the Íroe. Why would I have him take the risk?"

"And the second?" Piet inquired through a mouthful.

"Well, I have a plan. It's not the perfect plan and you guys know my ideas aren't always the best. They are actually very spontaneous and sometimes not that well thought-"

"Hally," Lukai interrupted her.

"Yes?"

"What's the plan?"

"It's a few days' plan and once we are in there's no going back, no 'let's better not do it' or 'let's head back'. We portal to the outside of their city, where they are taking our blood, and camp in the forest until I get my strength back. Then go into the lab, get the samples and get out the same way. We exit the third frontier, portal back to Platz. They have very advanced technology and I'm not sure if my portals give any type of signal they can track, that's why we wait to portal outside the border. Getting in would be the easiest part, coming out without being caught and with the blood would be the harder one. And let's not mention that we'll be walking around people that would happily put us in a cage and study us for the rest of our lives."

There was another silence.

"So you want us to make a choice," Piet let out, his breakfast nowhere to be seen.

"But you already made yours," Pam said to Hally. "What is it?"

Hally shook her head.

"I'm not sure..." she admitted.

There was silence.

Hally finished the last bite of her French toast and stood up to wash her dish and glass. As she did this she turned to the rest.

"Hey, feel like you're home. Take anything you need. Just please don't make a mess, and don't go opening the windows and curtains, if the neighbors see someone here, they are going to be suspicious." Hally dried her hands.

"Where are you going?" Piet mumbled.

"For a walk," Hally answered, taking a sweater off the coat rack and heading for the back door. "I'll be back soon."

"Think about that choice..." she added and closed the door behind her, her face hidden underneath a hood.

As she was halfway the yard Lukai called from the house.

"Wait, I want to come," he said and ran to where she was. "Where are we going?" he asked when he caught up with her.

Hally continued walking.

"You'll see," she answered, she didn't mind the company at all. "You should put your hood on," she added, Lukai did so.

They walked together a while, quietly, Hally leading the way and Lukai walking by her side looking at the houses and the empty streets.

"Did you ever have problems with the Superiors?" Lukai asked, his eyes fixed on the backyards filled with toys they passed by.

The sun was up, but its heat wasn't enough to warm the kids. And despite the colorful houses, the joyous memories of the good neighbors and the distant sounds of children and cars going by, Flikos had never been more dead in Hally's eyes.

"As much as anybody else," she answered, knowing that it was a lie. "The Gang controls Miso. Well… they are trying to control it… It's a mess, that's the point."

"But have they ever really gotten into your life?" Lukai kept asking, Hally felt there was somewhere he wanted to go with the questions.

Hally forced a soft chuckle, good enough to convince him.

"I lived here. Miso is down the block, of course they were in my life. How would they not?"

"Don't be surprised, people can be incredibly ignorant." He spoke as if he was angry about something in particular but didn't dare to say it. "That's what they are good for. They see in the news the mess these psychos do. They talk about it for two days and then forget. Let me tell you, it's not so easy to forget when you're the one that suffers, the one left behind to gather up the pieces."

Hally looked at him, she hadn't known Lukai for so long now, but the way he was speaking was almost like a completely different person. An angry and revengeful person.

"Well..." Hally looked straight ahead, the same road she had taken for many years. She too had the right to feel that way, but she didn't. "Just because you yell fire it isn't going to extinguish itself. People are like that Lu, and there isn't anything one can do about it except play your part. Fight the battles you can and defeat the evil you are able to. I have the belief that there is a higher justice in life. Everything one does will be paid back sometime, every good and every bad."

Lukai frowned, still staring at the floor, shoulders tense. His eyes seemed darker, as if a shadow had fallen upon the Canadian boy.

"I wish I could afford to think like that."

"What do you think?"

"I believe in my justice, making people pay and suffer what they must so they get to know what it feels like."

Hally looked up.

"Just because you bring someone else to the ground it isn't going to make it any softer."

"If you say so," Lukai muttered under his breath as if he was sad that that was Hally's answer. "Wait, we are going to Miso? Why are we going in that direction? Isn't it dangerous?" he asked, his kind eyes back, the usual smirk on, his freckles scattered on his face, the shadow completely gone.

"A little bit," Hally said confused and chuckled at Lukai's reaction, he was back to the same guy she had dealt with the last few days.

"Then why are we going there?" Lukai asked. "You, ma'am, have a problem with dangerous places."

Hally laughed.

"There's this shelter I used to help with. I never said goodbye or explained why I wasn't coming back, so... And I also want to see how things are going."

Lukai nodded as he understood.

"Before we reach it, I have a question," Hally said to him.

"Ask away."

"When we were running in the Lab and I couldn't see, we stopped. Why did we stop?"

"What do you mean?'

"When we were coming from the security room."

"Ohh," he froze as if he was thinking of an answer.

"I felt there was someone there," Hally added.

"It was no one, just a doctor looking the other way," Lukai said.

"Okay."

Hally continued walking in silence staring at the ground, but she had felt it, Lukai's heartbeat pounding faster. He was lying.

"Look, that's the shelter," she said, pointing to the cement building at the end of the street.

"Oh," the boy let out.

It wasn't a pretty building at all. It was half destroyed. Not well taken care of. And it sure looked a little abandoned.

Hally laughed and tugged Lukai.

"Come, inside is where the magic is." She pulled him to the back wall, where she started to climb.

"Wait!" he called her confused. "What are you doing?"

"I'm going to go inside," Hally replied, already a meter above the ground.

"You do know most buildings have a door, right?"

"Oh really? I had no idea! You're a genius," she sassed back. "This building's door is on the other side, which is techni-cally Miso, a place where I can't go because: A, I am Latin and the Superiors from Miso don't really like us. B, now I'm also an Íroe. And C, they're usually guarding the doors," she responded as she reached the top.

Lukai stared from the ground.

"Come," she called him once more with a smile.

Lukai smiled; he couldn't believe it. He started to climb, a sloppy uncertain climb.

"See, this is why you're the group's spy," he said with short breath.

"Because you lost your agility?"

He smiled.

"I was going to say that it was because you were the one that likes to sneak into places, but I guess that's also right."

Hally helped him onto the roof and gave him a few seconds to recover. There was no one on the roof, no one guarding. No one up front either.

"I'm gonna guess climbing isn't your sport."

Lukai sighed.

"This is far from baseball," he said.

Hally choked on a chuckle.

"Why is baseball so funny?"

"You wouldn't understand."

Lukai rolled his eyes.

"What now?"

Hally couldn't help smiling. She walked to the left corner, where the loose skylight waited for her.

Followed and observed by Lukai, Hally moved it away.

"Oh gosh!" Lukai exclaimed. "You're crazy!"

"Life is crazy, I'm just catching up. Take it or leave it," Hally responded before stepping onto the cupboard and carefully jumping to the empty lab table.

"Get down here," she said once on the ground.

Lukai looked through the hole at the cupboard and the table.

"I'm gonna get killed by following you," he muttered between his teeth and followed Hally's steps.

He stepped at the cupboard and then, not as careful as Hally, he jumped to the table, almost missing it by a centimeter.

"Are you okay?" Hally asked.

"Yeah," he babbled, stepping down the table. "Just please tell me there is no more climbing."

"Not for now."

Lukai let out a relieved sigh.

Hally had to resist the need to get her white coat, she wasn't there as a doctor.

She crossed the heavy doors; she was greeted by ten empty beds. Ten names. Ten periods.

"No…" she whispered.

She stared at the place, Rory and Lisa down by the little kids giving out blankets. Jess by the older folks, all of them too busy to notice her.

A spark of color caught her eye. She turned, bright on the wall, a red hand had been painted.

Hally got chills only by looking at it, what had happened there in the last days?

She looked once again at the beds. She walked to the closest one and grabbed the paper, in it it was written: 'Milo Mane.'

"Milo..." she sobbed, a knot forming in her stomach.

Lukai placed his hand on her shoulder.

"What's wrong?" he asked.

"He's dead," Hally she babbled between her teeth. Suddenly her mind filled with the memories of the last time he had seen her. She couldn't help but wonder if he had managed to finish up all the sunflower seeds. He probably had, he loved them.

"Friend of yours?"

Hally nodded, the words gathering at the base of her throat. She couldn't let them out without releasing tears as well.

"It's you," a voice quivered.

Hally looked up. An old lady, dressed in nothing but a dirty nightgown, white hair a mess, bandages around her arm and head, looked back at her. She stumbled a few steps on her bare feet until she leaned on the closest bed for support.

"It is you," she proclaimed.

Hally stared at the lady; she didn't recognize her.

The lady stumbled another few steps until she reached the young girl. She grabbed her hands, her long white cold fingers wrapping around Hally's.

"My mother told me the stories," she gloated. "I never thought I'd see one of them in real life. *Junak!*" She turned to the open room. "*Junak* right in front of my eyes!" she exclaimed.

Suddenly all the patients directed their attention to the newcomers, from the little ones to the oldest ones.

"We don't have to be afraid anymore!" A man cheered from his bed, one of his legs missing. "*Junaks* are here!"

Several joined his cheers.

"No, no, no. We aren't *Junak*," Hally stopped them before they got their hopes up.

The old lady squeezed her hands and touched her ring, her silver ring.

"Of course you are." She gave her a bow, a deep respectful bow.

The man without a leg grabbed onto the wall and stood up. He too bowed.

Another joined them, and then another.

Hally's heart skipped a beat. Who did these people think she was?

Jess ran from the end of the room.

"Hally," he greeted her and pushed her back through the doors.

Hally looked over her shoulder, more people joined the bowing.

"What was that?" Lukai asked.

Jess' eyes were glued on Hally, his hair was messier than usual, his eye bags darker than what she remembered.

"They think you are-"

"*Junak*, a hero," Hally finished his sentence, her mouth stayed open and her eyes widened.

Jess studied her.

"Are you?" He shook his head. "Of course you are."

"You aren't gonna start bowing, are you Jess?" Hally asked.

Jess tittered.

"I'm just happy you finally found out what it was. I always knew you were a different breed."

"Gee, thank you."

"I mean it."

Those three words felt like a pit in Hally's stomach.

She got the courage to ask.

"What happened here?"

Jess looked at the floor.

"Ty finished his initiation... After that, things just went downhill." He sighed.

"The Superiors, they...," he made a small pause, "are acting weird. Some of the rumors say they found a 'Champion' I think. Anyhow, the easterners have backed away scared. And the Gang is taking more risks than ever. They have been acting outrageously, more refugees than usual. The initiations are now taking place at the station, breaking free the prisoners. Maxwell is going nuts... Barbara went down there..."

Hally looked down at the paper she had grabbed.

"Milo?"

"Buried. A sunflower between his hands."

Hally looked up.

"Not a rose?"

"No, with his last breath he requested a sunflower."

Hally had to make an extra effort to keep the tears away.

"You aren't here to stay, are you?" Jess asked.

Hally looked over his shoulder, through the small glass pane of the doors. If she had been there, she would've been able to save Milo.

"I don't know."

"Go," Jess declared.

"What?"

"Go," he repeated. "The world needs a hero."

"But the refuge needs a Hally."

The doctor placed his hand on her shoulder.

"What was the last thing I told you?"

"To run and never come back."

"Why aren't you listening to me?"

Hally grinned.

"I never did."

"Then do it today... We'll be fine. We'll keep fighting. You go out there and do your job."

Hally eyes met the ground.

"You," Jess turned to Lukai. "Who are you?"

"I'm Lukai," the Canadian boy responded.

"Pleasure to meet you Lukai, now can you make sure this one doesn't do anything stupid?"

Lukai shook his head.

"I doubt anybody is capable of that."

Jess chortled; he was right.

"Then, can you make sure she doesn't do anything stupid alone?"

Lukai smiled, proud.

"That I can do."

"Good..." He turned again to Hally.

Their eyes met.

"Go," he begged.

Hally nodded, for the first time the words seemed to come from a hundred mouths.

The back door flung open.

"I made my choice," Hally announced.

Piet came in from the living room, Pam lifted her eyes from a drawing, Lukai sat in a stool. The three of them looked at the Latin girl, waiting for her answer.

"I'm going for the blood," she declared firmly.

Lukai stood up; his freckles gathered in the middle of his face.

"When do we leave?"

Hally shook her head.

"I don't want you to come only because you feel forced to," she replied.

"I'm also a Guardian of Kinds, responsibility has been laid on my shoulders and I'm not about to ignore it. You aren't forcing anything," Lukai assured.

Piet took a deep breath.

"Let me shower and I'm also in."

Pam rolled her eyes.

"I guess I don't have anything more interesting to do," she muttered. "Perhaps a suicidal mission, why not?"

Hally looked at them, out of the many decisions she had made in her life this was one she knew she wasn't going to regret.

Lukai straightened.

"Then we rest today, take some time to build a detailed plan and leave tonight."

The others agreed.

"The sooner the better, you said it yourself, they are considering selling the blood. If we don't get it soon, we might be too late," Pam said as she resumed her drawing: four heroes.

40

ANOTHER CHANCE

"One more chance, that's all you're going to get!" James yelled at the kids.

Tom nodded. It was a new day with new opportunities.

He wasn't sad, or angry, or hurt, not anymore. The only thing he could remember from the day before were those feelings, although he never remembered the reason. He had come to the conclusion that it wasn't that important or he would have never forgotten.

"And we all know what you're going to get if you don't pull this one off," James continued.

They were finally setting out on their mission for the 'last' part of the portal for James. After this job they were going to be 'discontinued', exactly the word James had used, until they found where the fourth piece was.

Tom had actually spoken to James about this, he was worried that he wouldn't be able to achieve his goal of getting the four pieces. James had immediately smiled at him and told him not to worry, that would no longer be a weight on *his* shoulders as it would be another's job. Tom had smiled back as James had left.

"Why are you smiling?" Isla had asked him.

Tom looked at her, keeping a smile. He was happy.

Isla didn't share the emotion at all. She frowned. Her still-swollen nose didn't help her in the least.

"I'm not sure," Tom had said.

Isla glared at him.

"If I was you I wouldn't keep that smile. He's going to replace us," she had said.

"Great," Tom had replied. "We're being promoted!"

"No. I heard The Company isn't happy with us."

"Why wouldn't they be happy?" Tom had asked with a smile.

"Because Ayala and I refused to give a 'good' performance and you were so drunk that you couldn't even tell a bird from a leaf."

Tom let his jaw drop, acting offended. Then he let out a laugh, it was a joke. He hadn't been drunk, at least he didn't remember it.

"How are you not seeing the problems in all of this?" Isla had asked desperately.

Tom had shrugged his shoulders.

"Whatever makes the Superiors the happiest makes me happy. Then we can all be happy."

Isla had scoffed.

"Get your head in the right place. This is the last mission. They are going to kill us after it. And then go for the rest of the Íroes."

For a fraction of a second Tom felt those words were important, like they meant something, and he had to remember them.

He smiled, happiness soaring from deep inside, they weren't important.

"How good for them," he had said back.

Isla turned; she was scared. Tom saw a few tears in her eyes, almost as if she lost hope. How weird.

"What have they done to you?" Isla had whispered to herself.

Tom had looked at her, he didn't understand what she meant.

The third object was called Stémma and it was at the very center of a labyrinth. Well, that was the name that James and the other purple cloaks had used. Based on what Tom and the girls had heard it was a library that had been built into a labyrinth. Talk about the riddle of knowledge.

There was a big problem though, as expected. The library belonged to the Guarders, the Northern Guarders. It wasn't in their territory, that's why they could get in there. Nevertheless, the library had traps set to make sure that something like what the Superiors were planning never happened. And just in case the kids thought about going to the Guarders for help, James had set explosives around the place. Either they got the crown in the allowed time, or they were blown into pieces.

None of it made sense to Tom, as if they were talking a different language.

He watched as the cloaks got on the plane. He observed Isla and Ayala pushed behind, being kicked into the ground and even spit on. The smile never wore off. It was a good day, it was sunny, and the wind carried a delicious smell from the cafeteria. What else could he ask for?

He sat on his seat, across from the girls, the jet wasn't big enough for them to be separated. He watched the clouds moving by. They all had shapes: a hat, a bunny, a house, a lake.

"Drink!" Ulyssa's voice snapped. A shiver went down his spine.

"Wake up!" Aina whispered beside him.

Tom rubbed the back of his neck, dazed, and rubbed his eyes.

His smile started to turn on and off. He remembered the last time he had been on a jet; he had been bleeding and he had cried his eyes out. He remembered he didn't want to be there. He remembered he had been scared and hurt.

He focused on his surroundings, at the purple cloaks, the guns, the looks of hatred, James. For the first time in the day, they scared him.

They landed; rain poured out the small window.

"Wrists," a guard said.

Tom looked up, confused, his mind still a hurricane.

The guard grabbed Tom's wrists by force and unlocked his handcuffs.

Like a tsunami the rest of the memories flooded. He remembered what was going on, where he was. He remembered the Gang, Elowen, Platz, the field trip... And more importantly, he remembered James, and everything he had done.

The smile faded, completely.

"Off you go," a guard said.

Tom stood up and walked behind Isla and Ayala just to be stopped by a tapping on his shoulder.

Tom turned around; it was James.

"A toast?" he offered him a glass with a brown liquid, keeping one for himself.

Tom studied the glass and then James. He knew it really wasn't a question. But what did he have to lose? He was already doomed.

"I'll have to respectfully deny it."

"Of course," James said, keeping his forced smile, his white teeth showing like a threat.

Tom walked after Isla and Ayala; the purple cloaks escorting them. The three of them moved through the rain. It was too dark to see how the library looked from outside, only the small lights by the walls, the bombs lights, being visible.

Together they walked through the enormous wooden doors.

"Good luck," Beatrice taunted. "You're going to need it."

The doors were locked behind them. One final time, leaving the kids to survive on their own. Their death was just a matter of time.

The library was an actual labyrinth filled with many traps, some so dangerous that made the kids think twice about what kind of people the Northern Guarders were.

The roof was tall, taller than what could be considered normal. Every single centimeter, the floor, the walls, and the furniture, was made of a dark brown shiny wood, the place reeking of a forest-like smell. The architecture was ingeniously planned, every wall, every window, and every shelf designed to play with sound. A whisper couldn't be heard through the books but the falling rain on the roof echoed.

Ayala pulled at the doors.

"They're locked."

"We leave here with the piece or none at all," Tom mimicked James.

"Nice to see you were finally paying some attention," Isla snapped, she was angrier than usual at him.

"We could get it, and give it to the Guarders," Ayala proposed.

Tom stared at the many shelf-created-paths, and obstacles: the holes, tricks, spikes, axes...

"Either way we'll have to get Stemma, but it doesn't seem possible."

Isla walked to the closest path, she took a step, nothing happened.

"Don't say that. We'll make it," she said.

"Whoa, you're being positive."

Isla chortled.

"I've been on the verge of death so many times the last few days thatI said screw it, let's do an Ayala."

Tom chuckled, perhaps he should consider that as well.

"I'm not trying to ruin the moment but," Ayala pointed at the watch on her wrist, "time's slipping."

Tom sighed.

"Let's get to work." He studied the paths.

"We should split up. I'll take the left, Ayala center and Isla the right side."

"You're supposed to mention yourself last," Isla corrected him.

Tom turned to her.

"Your nose is still swollen," he blurted before he thought twice.

Isla scoffed and crossed her arms.

Ayala touched the closest spear, part of a trap, the dangerous object didn't move.

"What about the traps? Wouldn't it be safer if we walked together?"

"The aisles are too narrow, walking together would only increase the possibilities of falling on a trap."

"Besides, I doubt the labyrinth has only one solution. The more paths we cover, the faster we can find the ones that take us to the center."

Ayala's lips formed a circle and she nodded.

"Any other questions?" Tom asked, looking at Isla. Even after all they had been through, she was still the most beautiful human being he'd seen.

Isla didn't bother to look back and responded with silence.

"So, we'll meet in the center," Ayala said. She nodded goodbye to the others and stepped in.

Tom readjusted his backpack and followed her example, taking a different path.

The first thing that captured Tom's attention weren't the books, the dying flowers hidden between the shelves, or the smell of men's cologne and clove. What tickled his curiosity were the decoys everywhere. At the entrance the traps seemed barbaric, even psychotic, meant to scare even the bravest of warriors. But the deeper he walked, the closer he went to the center, the stupider they became. Changing so obviously towards the end that even a blind person would be able to tell them apart.

Tom remembered all the time he had spent in libraries. He'd learned so many things from books. He'd learn history, languages, strategy, math, music, art... How many of those things have been useful in the last few days? He had to ask himself, if he knew how little they would matter now, would he still be willing to study them? Was that really the life he wanted? A month before he would have argued knowledge had no equal, now he didn't know who he wanted to be, much less what he wanted to get.

He kept walking by, free of any fear towards the obvious traps, calling the girls' names from time to time to make sure they were okay.

As he moved through a book aisle, jumping over and dodging anything suspicious, he found an enormous wooden sign. Right there, high on the wall, it read: 'Men only'.

He tittered, suddenly it made sense. The smell, the traps, the books... The Northern Guarders were the oldest boy club ever.

"Thomas!" Isla screamed.

"Yes?"

Tom's heart raced.

"Tom!" she called again.

Tom relaxed; it wasn't a bad scream.

"Yes?" he replied louder.

"We found the center," Ayala announced.

"Wait for me," Tom asked and left the big sign to reunite with the girls.

The center of the labyrinth was a circle formed by bookcases. Among the shelves were the most important copies, tales, laws, and traditions Tom couldn't help but want to read. In the very center as a spotlight, or the heart, there was a book pedestal, on top of which laid Stémma.

Stémma was by far the prettiest of all the objects the kids had had to find. It was all made of shiny, pure, beautiful silver. Its metal was formed with carvings of sunflowers, its centers made of diamonds and the petals of gold.

"So marvelous," Tom let out as he gasped from afar.

"Are we supposed to just take it? No security?" Ayala asked.

"The Northern Guarders may be arrogant enough to not put traps in the last aisles. But it would be too negligent to not put some kind of safety on this pedestal," Tom replied.

"What would you say the trigger actually is?" Isla asked.

Tom looked at the pedestal and walked around it. He wasn't good in mysteries; he was good in numbers.

"I mean, it could be a weight thing, which means..."

"I appreciate the possible explanation, but I know what it means," Isla interrupted him. "Ayala, please help me look for a thick book."

"Like this one?" Ayala asked, showing Isla a thick brown book with silver lines.

"I believe that one would be too-"

"Tom's right. Too heavy. Try finding a book a pinch smaller than that," Isla asked.

"Found this," Ayala said later, this time a book a little bit smaller than the last one.

"Perfect," Isla smiled.

She threw a few seeds on the ground and made vines grow into two thick green arms. With precision and patience, she picked up the book and moved it to the pedestal. As no one dared breathe, then in a split second the crown was in her grasp and the book on the pedestal.

Tom gawked at her.

"Stop looking at me."

"Sorry."

Isla lowered the vines and took the crown.

"Impeccable," Tom whispered.

He shouldn't have said that. He shouldn't have said anything.

The whole library shook, the floor cracked. The books fell from the bookshelves and Tom's face filled with shock.

"What's happening?" Ayala cried, wrapping her arms around a shelf for support.

"Add a book!" Tom yelled over the falling books. "Add some weight."

Isla moved her vines, which she had been using up to that point to keep herself in balance. She grabbed a book, if that's what you could call it, it was barely ten pages. She tried to place it over the bigger book. Before she had done so another book jumped off the shelf and hit it, making both fly through the air aimed at Tom's face.

Tom threw himself to the floor.

He lifted his head, the mess just getting worse.

A tingle came to his fingers, there were electric currents underneath the floor. He focused. The weird buzz and floor cracks weren't coming from the pedestal, it was a malfunction of the entire security system.

Tom smiled; he knew how to fix it. He raised his arm into the air. This time it was easy, the electricity was there, waiting for him, he didn't have to beg it to help.

He punched the floor, small sparks and currents shot in every direction.

The hold thing stopped. The buzz. The cracks. The machine. Everything was suddenly replaced by silence.

"Well, that was an experience," Ayala confessed, there was no sarcasm in her comment, but it wasn't genuine either.

Isla looked at Tom as if ready to forgive him. She didn't manage to do it.

"Time to finish this."

She picked Stémma off the ground. Then she pulled the drone out of her backpack. Carefully she placed Stémma inside the small metallic box, she pressed the green button just like James had asked them to do.

With a gentle buzz the robot lifted into the air. It moved a few meters getting its bearings, and then lifted into a window on the wall in search of its owner, nothing was going to stop it.

"Shall we give our escape another try," Isla whispered.

"Ummm. Tom? Isla?" Ayala called. "I don't think time is supposed to go that fast." She showed her watch, the same watch that controlled the bombs outside.

Where they had had more than an hour left, a minute earlier it had quickly turned into thirty minutes and time continued decreasing, supernaturally fast.

"Wait, what? It doesn't make sense," Tom asked himself, looking at the clock.

Isla pulled his ear.

"DON'T YOU SEE IT! HE WANTS US DEAD!" she screamed and ran. "We have to get out of here!"

Ayala and Tom copied her lead, each through the same path they had used before, this time fighting against the fallen books and the traps to reach the entrance before the library exploded.

Tom ran, every turn, jump, obstacle memorized from the first time. He ran past the sign, the windows, axes, knives, decoys. He crossed the last third. The path narrowed, the books became newer, the smell of clove disappeared.

A scream echoed through the walls.

"Isla!" Ayala cried. "Help me! HELP ME!"

Tom turned.

The sound came from behind, far behind, the opposite side from the door.

"Help!" Ayala cried in her high-pitched voice, piercing Tom's ears and cracking the windows.

The boy froze, not because of the obstacles, or because of the bombs, or the screams, but because he recognized the books he had by his sides. He was close, one corner away from the entrance. He was almost out of there.

"Please!"

Tom ran, far from the entrance to Ayala. They had worked together so far; it wouldn't matter if they didn't finish together as well.

The path seemed to become narrower while Tom ran through it.

He turned a corner.

"Tom?" Isla exclaimed, her green eyes wide open.

Tom stared back at her, she seemed shocked to see him run towards Ayala.

Ayala cried once more.

"We are on our way!" Tom yelled back.

Together, the two ran through the place, jumping over piles of fallen books and avoiding decoys until they reached where the screams came.

All they saw was the blood.

Ayala hadn't been careful, or she had had bad luck, either way she was now paying the price. Her foot had stepped on the wrong tile and now it was caught in a bear trap. The metallic teeth going through her leg.

"Ayala!" Isla exclaimed when she saw her.

"Just get me out of here, please," Ayala cried, nothing but tears in her eyes, blood flooding her clothes, staining the pages of the fallen books.

"Isla help me, with your vines," Tom exclaimed.

She didn't have to hear it twice. The green thick plants crawled like serpents and wrapped around the metal.

The three of them fought against it, for a while it seemed they were losing.

"Pull harder" Isla yelled.

In the end they were Íroes and they were stronger than the metal.

"Ahhhhh!" Ayala yelled as she pulled her leg out. Her foot or what was left of it was useless, for now.

"You're gonna be fine," Isla assured her, giving her a hug

"None of us are gonna be," Ayala showed her the time, there was a minute left.

Fifty-nine seconds.

Fifty-eight seconds.

Tom's mind went blank. He looked up, they were too far from the doors now. What were they going to do?

Forty-five seconds.

Isla, by his side, focused. The fear left her eyes, maybe not her heart, but her eyes.

Forty-seconds.

She poured a circle of seeds around them, some of them falling into Ayala's blood.

Thirty seconds.

She extended her arms and trees started to grow, not vines, but trees. Big trunks and fat branches forming a protective shield around them.

Twenty seconds.

"Isla! It's too much!" Tom cried; they hadn't been trained for such powers.

Isla growled as she fell on her knees.

"Nothing is too much to save you guys!"

Ten seconds.

She screamed as she finished the sphere, it *was* too much power, but she pulled it off. The last branches fell together.

One second.

41

GETTING IN

When Hally woke up for the sixth time she was in a car, and she promised never again to put her ideas into a plan.

And after she'd accidentally portaled them into a small village in North France, where they were not only near one of the strongest Superiors gangs, but where they were trapped for a few hours. And then again, this time near the city, as in-the-middle-of-the-forest-outside-the–city near, the rest had promised never to trust her portals again.

"Where do I go now?" Lukai asked Pam who was sitting in the copilot's seat, a map wide open on her lap.

"Left!"

"Right!" Piet corrected her from the backseat.

"Which way?" Lukai asked again.

"Left!"

"Right!"

"Who has the map?" Pam snapped at Piet.

"Mistakenly you! You don't even know how to read it!"

"Hey!"

"Which way!"

"Left!"

"Right!"

"Straight," Hally muttered, her eyes barely open.

"Hally!" Piet exclaimed.

"Hally?" Lukai asked from the front.

"Straight, just go straight," Hally muttered again.

"No. Go left!"

"Right!"

They came to the exit. Lukai continued straight.

"You listened to her?" Pam slapped Lukai's arm. "She's barely awake!"

"I know!" Lukai exclaimed. "But we have followed *your* instructions for hours, and we're still lost."

"Hey!"

"Ay callate," Hally mumbled. "Remind me to never... to never... to never... Ay, I forgot the word. To never... go in the car with you!"

"You mean *drive* with us?" Piet asked.

"Exactly!" Hally cheered. "Drive, that was the word," she sat up. Her neck hurt from the weird position she was sleeping in and she was already getting dizzy from the car movement.

She opened the window wide and let the cold air hit her face. Outside all she could see was forest on either side and a really long road heading north and south.

"You really are one to complain. You left us in France!" Pam exclaimed.

"Hey! That was days ago."

"Yesterday," Piet corrected.

"And you have no idea of where we are right now," Hally continued.

"And you do?" Lukai asked.

"I don't, but I know where we'll be if we head north."

Lukai and Pam looked back at her confused.

Hally grabbed Lukai's head and turned it to the front.

"Eyes on the road," she said before pushing her head to the front. "Here you have the road on the map. The city is north. This road takes only two directions. Sun's that way, it means north is there." She pointed up front. "We keep going until eventually we find it. See, it isn't that hard. Seriously! What did you learn in school?"

"Drawing."

"Flirting."

"Baseball."

"This is why our future generations are doomed."

"Hey!"

"How come you just wake up and get to correct us?" Pam asked herself.

"Because she's right," Lukai let out, he had started to slow down as one more car was waiting in line to go through the tall, beige wall. They had made it to the city.

"Okay let's get our story straight," Lukai said. "We come from the international boarding school of Spain," Lukai pulled a bag from under his seat and took several fake documents Madame Rosemary had packed. "I'm Max, Pam is Melissa, Piet is Peter, and Hally is Samantha. If they ask us, we are going to take a picture with the big chemistry statue-"

"I never agreed with being a nerd," Pam complained.

"And later we're going to have lunch at the science cafe, which is also known for its tourism. See you don't really have to be a nerd," Lukai continued.

Pam growled quietly; she wasn't convinced.

"So we are tourists doing touristy things," Hally recalled.

"Exactly!" Lukai stated, then he turned his head. "Besides, how are you feeling?"

Hally shrugged her shoulders, she was a little bit dizzy and still half asleep, but her powers felt normal, and she had to pee.

"I'm OK," she declared, that was the best answer.

"You sure? Don't want some chips or something?"

"Well now that you mention it, I could have some of those," Hally admitted.

With a little help from Piet, the French chips bag was gone long before they reached the Wall.

The Wall became bigger every single meter they got closer. At first Hally had thought of it as a mere decoration, a visual aid. The closer they got the more she realized that she was wrong.

Police officers in weird uniforms patrolled the area. Up on the wall, beside the road, walking through the cars, rifles by their side, cameras looking in every direction. It made sense that people came to escape from the Superiors. This was the safest city in the world. Unless of course you were an Íroe.

They reached the front of the line rather quickly and were asked to step out of the car. Each of them was taken to a different corner by a different soldier.

"Language?" asked the uniformed guy with white hair.

"English or Spanish," Hally said, she could see Lukai talking to another uniformed guy with the corner of her eyes and she could feel Pam's and Piet's lips moving behind her, she had to be sure their answers were the same.

"Where are you coming from?" the uniformed guy asked, he had a strong accent.

"We're from a Spanish boarding school," Hally answered.

"What's the name of the boarding school?"

"Internado Espanol Internacional." That had been the same answer as Piet's.

The guy wrote the answers in their tablet.

"Why are you here?"

"They want to take a picture with a statue. I just want to eat at the science cafe."

The guy nodded, wrote the new information and left.

Hally looked around confused, what was she supposed to do now?

She turned to her right and glanced at Lukai. Lukai shrugged his shoulders.

The uniform guy returned a few minutes later and asked the same questions. Hally gave the same answers, just for him to leave and come back one more time and ask the same questions.

"You're allowed to go, just wait for the car to be checked," the uniform guy finally said the third time and left Hally free.

Hally joined the rest.

Although it all felt very suspicious, the kids had done as asked without complaining, something a little bit harder for some, more than the others (I mean for Pam who had an actual obsession with complaining).

"I almost gave it away, I forgot what we came here for," Piet muttered.

"It wouldn't have really mattered. When answers are too rigid, too similar, it's easier to assume they were rehearsed. Besides, there's always a person in a group of friends that has no idea what is going on," Hally said. "You're that one."

Piet scoffed.

"Hola guapo," a young girl called from a car a couple of lanes down and winked.

Piet turned to Hally.

"What does *guapo* mean?"

"Idiot."

"Ah."

"What are you frowning about, don't you have a girl already?" Hally asked.

He looked up with that stupid, love smitten face. He pulled a piece of paper from his pocket.

"You're right, I'm gonna call her."

Lukai stared at him.

"You still have her number?"

"Yes."

"We've been kidnapped, sold, almost experimented on, lost in France. And you STILL HAVE HER NUMBER?"

Piet shrugged.

"What can I say? I have my priorities straight."

He walked away, to the public phone by the road.

"No Piet. Come back! This is serious," Pam called after him.

"It'll be five minutes," he claimed from afar. "Just tell them I had to pee."

An alarm rang from one of the further lanes.

The gray dressed guards appeared, out of nowhere, like ghosts. They acted like robots, nothing stopped them. Their uniforms, a dark shade of gray, covered with armor. In their hands, ready to be used, all of them held a gun.

"What's happening?" Hally asked Lukai.

"I don't know," Lukai admitted and the three of them watched horrendously.

The soldiers walked to a family, a few lanes down from where the kids stood. The family, a tall cowboy looking guy with a brunette girl (wife) holding a bunch of blankets, most likely a baby, stood by a red car.

The soldiers marched to the guy and smashed his head into the car. The wife screamed. The soldiers smashed the guy's head again. This time the girl pushed the soldiers away; two other soldiers grabbed her back and ripped the baby from her arms.

That's when the true yelling started, the girl screaming for the soldiers to give her baby back, the other soldiers screaming for the guy to answer their questions, and the baby shrieking.

The rest of the lanes kept working, all the cars going through unbothered.

"That's not right," Hally mumbled, giving a step forward.

Lukai grabbed her hand.

"Wait until the soldiers leave. You'll do no good if you end up on their bad side," he said to her.

Hally reluctantly stayed back; she knew he was right.

The soldier kept asking the guy questions, occasionally hitting his face into the ground, or kicking him. Meanwhile others destroyed the interior of the car looking for something, or just out of fun. The rest mocked the mother, playing around as if they were going to drop the baby while she was held off.

"How can this happen? Aren't there laws against this?" Lukai asked.

"Yeah, but they might as well not exist in places like this. Laws are always bought, they're a bluff for the people to think there's some kind of justice. And they don't apply to the ones that enforce them," Pam answered.

No one said anything.

In the other lane a new soldier arrived, wearing the same uniform as the rest except for the golden ribbon across his chest. He was in control.

Instantly the others froze and stood firm.

Two soldiers, the ones that had been destroying the car talked to him and the golden ribbon guy slapped one of them. He yelled at all of them, and the soldiers looked at the floor and took orders. There was nothing wrong with that family, they were to leave them alone.

Hally waited for every soldier to leave before running to them.

"Hally!" Lukai called her.

"I'll be back in a second, just tell them I had to pee," she said without turning around.

"That's my line," Piet argued from the phone.

The view from up close was worse than the one she had had before. The car was a disaster, a true disaster. The girl was crying her eyes out and trying to calm her baby, and the guy wasn't moving on the ground.

Hally moved closer to the Mom.

"No! Stay away. Stay away!" she screamed.

"No ma'am. I'm here to help."

"No!"

"Really, I'm here to help," Hally repeated, and she grabbed the Mom's shoulders. "Look at me. Look at me," she repeated quietly with a kind voice when she didn't do it the first time.

The Mom's eyes met Hally's.

"Do you have a favorite song?"

She nodded faintly.

"What I see," she answered.

Hally smiled at her.

"I know how it goes, it's one of my favorites too. Sing with me. I see lightning..."

"I hear thunder..."

"Something stirring..."

"Six feet under." The girl gulped.

"You're doing great, keep singing. I'll take a look at your husband." The girl nodded without stopping the song.

The husband, fortunately, was conscious.

Hally kneeled beside him. She looked around, and when she was sure no one was looking, she called her medic bag. She pulled a small flashlight and looked at the man's eyes, the brain was reacting normally.

"Sir what's your name?"

"Mitchell Gordon."

"Where does it hurt Mr. Gordon?" Hally asked him.

"Aren't you a little too young to be a doctor?"

"Depends on where you are, but I'm not here as a doctor, I'm more like an EMT."

"I believe you're still too young," the guy said.

Hally chortled.

"Does your head hurt?"

"It does a little bit," he said, showing Hally the left side of his head where his forehead met his hair. It was thoroughly bruised, bleeding.

Hally pulled a cotton cloth and some alcohol and cleaned the wound.

"Is it bad that it is bleeding so much?" Mr. Gordon asked.

"Well, it really isn't bleeding that much, and it doesn't look like a very bad cut. But if I were you, I would go to the hospital and make sure you don't have a bad concussion."

Mr. Gordon gave a sad chuckle.

"I never liked hospitals," he said. "And I don't think the hospitals near this place will accept me," he added.

Hally understood what he was saying, Superiors ruled the places around, and they hated anyone who didn't fit their idea of prefect.

She finished attending to the man's wounds the best she could with the little time, and she helped him get to his feet. Before leaving she looked at them.

"I'll advise you to turn your car around and head to the east, the Superiors have little to no power over there."

"We were trying to go inside the city for shelter. Things are getting uglier," the girl said.

Hally shook her head. The city might not have been under the Superiors control, but she knew The General was just as bad.

"Don't do it. Trust me, I have a hunch that things in here are about to get a little tense."

The couple looked at Hally in search of more answers; she added nothing else. They would have to drive a little bit, but they would survive.

"Hally!" Lukai called her from their car.

She took a second look at the car, the husband and the crying baby. If that was what these people did when they suspected someone, what were they going to do when they found someone who was actually guilty? What would they do if they found out who they were?

She turned, Pam was laughing at something, Piet was playing with his hair as he talked on the phone and Lukai was looking at her, his kind eyes smiling at her.

A tear came to her eye, she knew what she had to do. They had so much to live for. So much to accomplish.

She walked back to them.

"Come with me," she called Pam and Lukai.

"What's happening?" Pam asked as she followed.

Hally didn't answer. She walked to the phone. Piet looked up.

"We'll talk later," he hung up. "What's going on?" he asked.

"We have no idea," Lukai replied.

Hally continued walking to the convenience store at the side of the street, it was closed. She kept walking to the backside; the rest followed her.

"Hally," Lukai begged. "Talk to us."

She stopped at the door, as she expected it, there was a little storage room in the back.

"I've got a feeling," she managed to say.

"About what?" Piet asked. "About what's inside?"

Hally nodded.

Piet turned and opened the door. He looked inside. Pam and Lukai joined him.

"I'm sorry," Hally said, a tear rolling down her cheeks.

Pam turned.

"What are yo-"

Her words were stopped by the needle in her neck. She fell gently into the ground, beside Lukai and Piet.

Hally lowered her hands; it was a mild sedative. They would wake up in a couple hours, maybe even a day.

She looked at their unconscious bodies. Piet snored.

Another tear fell down her cheek.

She moved the bodies inside the storage room and locked the door.

They'll be so mad when they wake up.

But they'll be alive.

Hally nodded. When she was younger, she used to run for her school team. One day she had pulled her knee and hadn't been able to run anymore. At first, she'd believed it was a punishment, then she'd understood that it was the way of the world to force her to sit down and read for the first time. She felt like that day all over again.

When she'd seen the car, all the blood, she knew it was time. It was time to stop running and start fighting. Blake had known it, Madame Rosemary too and even Lukai. This was what she was meant to do, to fight. And if that was how she was supposed to die, she'd do it. But she couldn't let them all walk into that danger without stopping them.

She returned to the lane where a confused guard waited by the car.

"And your friends?"

"There was a family emergency. It'll be me. Only me."

The guard handed her an approval slip.

"I hope you have a nice visit, miss. Enjoy the city."

Hally thanked him. She stepped in the car and drove in alone.

42

THE CAB DRIVE

The city wasn't much different from all other cities. There were shops, people, houses, restaurants... Only the gray clothed soldiers, patrolling, their guns ready at their waist attracted all the attention. They walked firmly; their expressions looked as if they'd just tasted a bitter candy. Hally would have laughed if it wasn't for the small jar with a powder hanging from their belt.

Hally turned on the radio, without the others the car was just too quiet. Behind, a dark car followed her. She drove slowly, trying to make sense of the French map Pam had gotten.

"They'll be fine, better than in here," she kept repeating.

Soon she found the cafe. She parked the car up front and walked in.

She laughed as soon as she crossed the door, it was horrible. Small, crowded, nerdy.

Pam would've complained.

And Lukai would've said something about the food that would've taken her back to the raisin topic.

And then Piet would've asked for something to eat.

She shook her head, she had to focus on what she was doing.

Hally walked up to the counter, where there was a young girl.

"Hi, excuse me," she said.

"Hello, with what may I help you today?" the girl asked with a smile.

"I know this will sound really weird but, do you have a back door? I'm new here, an intern. This is my first time on the job. And I was supposed to be there ten minutes ago, but the street is closed and there are these weird, gray suited soldiers and..."

"Girl," the waitress stopped Hally. "Totally get you. Come," she said and took her behind the counter and through a metallic door.

"Here," she opened the door, they were on the other side of the building.

"Thank you," Hally said to the girl, the black car would have to do better to follow her.

"With pleasure. Good luck on your first day," the girl said.

"Thanks, I think I'm going to need it," Hally responded.

She looked at the street. If she wanted in, she needed information. What better source to get information than the citizens? And who's more likely to speak than a cab driver?

Finding the cab wasn't very hard. Neither was starting a conversation with the cab driver.

"How long have you been in the city?" Hally asked the driver, Landon.

He was a mid-fifties man. His light blue eyes filled with kindness and his long curls made a mess. His face was filled with freckles. Her heart had stopped the first time she saw him, remembering Lukai's unconscious face.

I did what I had to do.

"A little bit longer than a decade and a half," he responded nicely as he turned to the left.

My age.

"That's a long time," Hally chuckled. "Why did you come here?"

Landon shrugged his shoulders with a smile.

"It was a new opportunity, they needed workers, and I needed a job."

She looked at the ring in his hand.

So, he's married.

He has a sticker from a school on the windshield.

He studies?

No. High School.

Which means, kids.

He's a family man.

He must have a picture around somewhere.

Discreetly Hally looked around for a picture, she had asked the driver to take her to the closest restaurant to the frontier as she was 'meeting a friend there'. This meant the drive was long, but not endless. She had to hurry.

There was no picture, at least not visible. Her eyes fell to the visor in front of her.

"If you don't mind, I'm going to use your mirror," Hally said to Landon.

"Of course, go ahead, miss."

Hally pulled down the visor, there it was. As she looked in the mirror, or pretended to, the picture stayed there. It was a young woman, around her late twenties. She had a lab coat, blond hair and a set of beautiful clear blue eyes. She had to be his daughter.

She could work inside the third frontier.

As she closed the visor she made the picture fall.

"Oh," she said, bending over to pick it up from the ground. "I know it's none of my business, but what a lovely picture."

Landon looked at the picture in Hally's hands and smiled, there was joy on his mouth, sadness in his eyes.

"That's Madelaine, my daughter, she was always very photogenic like her mom," he laughed, his heart didn't.

"Is she a scientist?"

"Yes, she *was* a scientist. She passed away three years ago; a heart attack came out of nowhere. She died working," he said.

Hally's intention to get information faded and she shared the pain in his words.

"I'm so sorry," she mumbled, she had no idea of what else to say. "Did she work around here?"

"Oh yes she did," Landon declared proudly, he turned to the left. "She was the brains of the family. Smarter than all the other students in the university and most teachers. Even at her job, smarter than her colleagues at her building in the Inner City, not something she would ever admit," he chuckled.

"Let me guess, chemist?" she asked, looking at Landon.

Landon looked at her for a second and laughed.

"Oh my, how much did she hate chemistry," he answered. "She was a physicist, loved math with all her soul."

He talked about her with such love and the brightest smile, Hally just knew he really did miss her. She couldn't even start to think about the pain a parent would have when losing their kids, like losing a part of themselves.

"She was the chief physicist of the whole building," he continued. "Let me just show you," he said, reaching for the glove compartment and taking another picture from inside. "Look at that," he gave her the photo.

There were three buildings, the biggest being the one in the middle. They look elegant, beautiful and professional.

"My little girl," Landon said pointing at the left building, it seemed to be made out of several shapes like circles, spheres and squares. "She was the boss of this whole building. My daughter! Born in poverty. With barely enough resources to make it to university and with nothing more than an old computer and a half-used notebook, that I got when she was twelve. She looked me dead in the eye and said, 'dad I'm going to work there'. 'Really?' I asked her. 'Yes, and I will not only work there, but I will be in charge. I'll be the boss.' And she did. She worked her back off. She was like a tornado, not letting anything stop her until she reached the top."

Landon's voice cracked.

"I'm just glad she made her dream come true before she passed," he added.

Hally looked at the picture, the buildings all had doors painted in a different color.

"What are the colors about?"

Landon laughed.

"Each color is a faculty. Red for biology. Lemon green for Chemistry. And yellow for Physics. She despised yellow!"

"Even more so than chemistry?" Hally asked.

Landon thought about it for a second.

"I think both things might have been in rough battle to become the most hated," he chuckled.

"At least it was just a door," Hally let out.

Landon tittered.

"That's what Madelaine wished, but the colors represent everything. The trucks of the building were yellow, the badges were yellow, the chairs were yellow, the envelopes were yellow. She even complained that inside her officer there were yellow roses all around," he laughed. "Of course, I never saw them... Some days I just wished I could see her on the job, doing what she loved so much."

"You never visited the office?" Hally asked.

He shook his head.

"It's something most tourists don't understand. No one can go inside the Inner City, just workers, no one else. Not even cabs!" He laughed at his own joke.

"What about you, miss?" he then asked. "Got any dream you wish to aspire to?"

Hally looked at the cars in front of them and smiled.

"I would like to become a doctor someday," she answered, leaving out the part that she also wanted to change the world, to make a difference. She wanted to become a hero.

She also left out the part that she had to survive the next couple of days to really have a chance, she felt it was a little bit of a mood killer.

Landon looked at Hally.

"Go for it, miss. I never scam people, I never do. And I hate lies. So, you must believe me when I say that there is light inside you, young lady. You're like a star, you glow with your own light. Don't let the world try to dim you, because it will. And when anyone calls you out for being bright, and listen carefully to this one, be brighter. Be like that tornado, that leaves no one and nothing stop them."

Hally smiled, fighting to keep the tears inside her eyes.

She looked at Landon.

"Thank you, I needed to hear that."

Sometimes all it takes is *one* person to believe in us.

It was not until that moment that Hally knew. She might not have the best training, or an army with her, but after all she was an Íroe. It was in her blood. She was finally able to put her keychain pack in her pocket, all her fear was gone, courage in her veins like blood.

"We're here," Landon said, pulling aside, in front of a pizzeria.

Hally looked at the pizzeria and let out a quiet sigh. She pulled some dollars out of her pocket and paid Landon.

Then she grabbed the two pictures and handed them to him.

Landon took a picture of the Inner City.

"You can keep this one," he said.

"Seriously?" Hally asked, it felt bad taking it from him, even though it could be useful.

"Yes, I look at the buildings any time from this side of the frontier. Who knows when you'll come back. I want you to have it, so you always remember my daughter, and how, if *she* was able to achieve her life mission, you can too," he said with a smile.

Hally took the picture.

"Thank you so much for the ride," she thanked him and got out of the car.

"No, thank *you*," he declared. "You reminded me of the heart my daughter had. A good one."

The cab drove away.

Hally dried her eyes.

"Are you okay?" a girl passing on the street asked her.

"I am," Hally answered, for the first time in a while it wasn't a lie. She was ready to take on the world.

43

ALONE

Tom froze, the world moved in slow motion. He kept staring at the zero on the clock, expecting to feel the heat of the explosion around him. Nothing happened.

He just wanted to be home, he wanted to be safe. He was tired of all that life filled with danger and incalculable possibilities. He wanted to be home, not Tirabia. He wanted Costa Rica, where he knew the place, and the place knew him. Where everything was easier and much less complex. Where there weren't Superiors or Guarders, or powers, or anything of that sort. He wanted to turn back time to when he was the best, because all he could give was his brain and he always gave five hundred percent of it. He wanted to forget the last week, where he had to deal with those powers, those stupid powers.

"Tom!" Isla exclaimed, one of her vines smacking Tom's leg faintly. "Help me!" she begged holding Ayala's unconscious head.

Tom hurried and helped set her on the ground, Isla herself looked as if she was about to faint, face pale, legs trembling.

Tom looked up at the protective shield. It was a masterpiece but in the case of the explosion he had no idea how useful it would have been; however, now it was another obstacle. The three of them had to get out of there, before the bombs decided they would work and blow them apart.

Ayala was unconscious, still bleeding, and even if she were to wake up she wouldn't be able to walk, at all. Isla had used too much power, she couldn't risk using more and losing them forever or worse, faint beside Ayala. And they still had to find a way out of the tree sphere and out the labyrinth.

Isla pulled Tom's sleeve faintly.

"Pick her up," she struggled to say. "Get out of here." She shoved Ayala his way. The bandages of her arms stained with blood, some hers and some Ayala's

"What...? What are you doing?" Tom exclaimed at her.

"I'm helping you guys get out of here," she whispered, her eyes closed heavily.

Tom shook his head.

"No. No! You can't do it!"

Isla opened her green eyes, they pierced into Tom's soul.

"Do. Not. Tell me what I can or I can not do!" she exclaimed at him, she still had enough strength to get angry. "I've spent my whole life hearing 'you can't do that' or 'you better do other things, you're not strong'. But you know what? I *am* strong enough. And whether you or my mom believes it or not it's not going to change the fact that I *can* do-"

"But I can't!" Tom yelled at her. It wasn't the fact that he couldn't leave one of them behind. Or the fact he was three words away from a complete meltdown. Isla might have been strong enough to push herself over the limit, but he wasn't.

"I'm not capable of doing this!" He continued. "I'm no hero, I have never been. I have tried so hard to convince myself that these are my things and I'm the best, but the truth is I'm not. I don't even understand what has happened on the last day. Now I know I'm never going to be the best, not in this. I'm not like you, or Ayala, or even Hally."

Isla stared at him and said nothing.

She stood up, carefully and in a sloppy way holding on to a tree.

"I can't make you believe otherwise, neither can anyone else. The set of ideas you have in your mind won't be moved or changed by anyone that isn't you. That's why I won't even bother arguing with you. You might not be the best, but for today, you'll have to be enough." She raised her arms.

She tensed her fingers. Sweat drops coming from her forehead. The biggest tree started to move, losing its natural shape, bending to Isla's will.

Tom looked at the tree moving, disappointed

At least by now he had learned the lesson. It could be James, or Blake, or on the bad side, the Guarders, who came looking for a champion. He wasn't the one they were looking for. And so, he stood there, looking at the lovely thick brown tree twist, accepting his fate. He was destined for failure.

The tree stopped. Tom turned around just in time to watch Isla fall to the ground.

He ran to her and placed his fingers on her wrist, slow but steady he felt a pulse. She was alive, but extremely exhausted. She was out of the game.

Tom stood up and took several steps back, watching the whole scene. They were still trapped within the tree circle, nowhere to go. Ayala was still losing blood, her foot every single time looking less appealing. Her skin was turning a weird purple. He didn't have to be a doctor to know she was dying.

He looked at the bodies of the two girls' unconscious, and he started crying, tears pouring down his face. He was just a kid. It didn't matter how 'prepared' he had gotten. He was fifteen! He didn't know what to do. He didn't know how to act if he ever got kidnapped and forced to steal things. He didn't know how to act if someone wanted to kill him. He didn't know how to act when a bunch of drunk teenagers tried to drown him. He didn't know how to act when the guilt started to eat away at him. He didn't know how to act when he saw a friend bleeding away. He wasn't prepared for any of it. He was just a kid.

"What would Hally do?" he asked himself.

"If you need to cry, cry. It's okay to do it. But don't let it engulf your life. At one point you need to dry the tears, pull yourself up and keep fighting. It's like you fell and hit your knee, it may hurt, really hurt. And you might have to take some seconds or minutes to stay on the ground and let yourself deal with the pain. But at the end you must stand up again, clean the dirt off and keep going. If you never pull yourself together, you'll stay there for the rest of your life and never move again," Hally's voice echoed in his mind.

Tom raised his head and dried his tears with his shirt. He pulled himself up, it was up to him.

With some tears still escaping his eyes and a sniffle here and there. He cut away a strap of the backpack and tied it above Ayala's knee to slow down the bleeding.

Then he moved the girls as gently as he could and he made a barricade with the backpacks and branches to hide the bodies, that way they would be safe.

When they were tucked away, he placed his hand on the floor, he could feel the energy moving through a couple of meters underneath. It was solar power, not that strong, but it would have to do.

He moved to the tree and put his hand in the center. He wiped the last tear from his cheek. It was time.

From his feet the electricity rose; the electricity going up his body. He moved it up to his hand, he could barely feel it. That wasn't going to be enough. He pulled more electricity from the ground and then some more. Soon the slight touches were no longer a tingle; it was a burn. He growled from the pain, but he needed more.

When the pain was more than he could handle he set it free.

He was pushed backwards; into the barricade of branches and bags he had just constructed.

When the dust came down and the resting energy continued its course Tom looked at the tree. The vast majority was no longer there, instead there was a hole big enough for five Tom's to fit through at the same time.

He couldn't keep himself from letting out a sigh of relief and a really light chuckle.

"Tom one, tree zero."

Moving the branches and the backpacks aside he took the girls one by one to the other side. He took Ayala first, her face closer to looking like a giant bruise, by the minute. Then Isla.

He managed to get them all to the doors quickly. A strong smell reached his nose, gasoline. He felt a cold sensation hit his stomach. It was true, James had been trying to kill them, erase them.

He slapped his cheeks; the powers had left him sleepy. The goal now was to get away, the three of them. And maybe, just maybe, they could get their old lives back. The one that many would call boring but made Tom feel safe.

The lonely boy pushed against the doors; they were locked. He looked at the sides, he would have to use the windows. He tried opening one, and then another, none of them gave in. He turned to the bookcases.

"It'll have to do," he whispered.

He grabbed the biggest book and threw it against the glass. It shattered. He took his sweater off and used it to clean the remaining shards. Then one by one he got the girls outside and placed them against the wall.

The rain still poured hard and cold, beyond the library, in the forest, nothing but darkness greeted him. No one was going to rescue them, they were truly, utterly, alone.

Tom looked at Isla, he had to wake her up. He returned inside and searched for a bottle of oil used to keep the books in good shape.

He found it and smelled it; it was strong enough. He went back out and placed it underneath Isla's nose. It took several tries, partially because at first Tom let the bottle underneath her nose for two seconds, scared that it would do her any damage. Then he got a little bit more confident, and desperate, and he left the bottle there.

After the fifth try Isla finally woke up, coughing.

Tom helped her sit up and let her breathe.

As she recomposed, he went back in. If they wanted to get somewhere they needed some light.

He climbed one of the bookcases by the entry, struggling. He carefully grabbed a sweater around his hand to prevent burns and took two light bulbs off the roof.

He went back outside.

"You got us out," Isla mumbled proudly. Her eyes were getting their shine back, the bruises losing their color by the second.

Tom half smiled at her, he felt proud, no doubt. Yet it was being overpowered by the shame of the fear he constantly had.

"I did," Tom managed to say, whether he was sad or tired from it, Isla couldn't understand.

Tom took the light bulbs in his hands and looked at them. He could feel the electricity the library was using, he just needed some of it. He easily pulled some from the ground and led it through his legs up to his hands and the bulbs. They lit up, brighter than what they did back at their old place.

"Stay right here. I'll be a sec."

Isla chuckled.

"Sure, as if I can stand up on my own and start running."

Tom stared at her.

"Now I do know you're not feeling right. You just made another joke."

Isla smiled. She truly was beautiful.

Tom walked around the building, maybe there was something he could use. The building was surrounded by blue, fake bushes. Within the bushes there were cables. Carefully, Tom followed the cables, they were attached to small explosives. He estimated hundreds of explosives around the whole building. There was just one issue with them, they were all fake, just meant to frighten.

Soon he was back to where he had started, at the front. Isla was still sitting beside the door, trying to catch her breath.

Tom continued his walk and checked the door. He hadn't paid much attention to it beforehand. Maybe he should have. The door had a trap system, made to be opened up with a specialized key. If forced open it stayed locked.

"What's that look on your face?" Isla asked him.

The facial tone was back, she was getting better.

"The more I look into it, it doesn't seem like..." he was about to say that James and the Superiors had actually left them to die. Maybe the kids had just been a little too scared and they had started to read in things out of nowhere, after all James had no actual motive for something like that.

"It doesn't seem like what?" Isla asked.

"It doesn't seem like we should stay here any longer," Tom replied, he had to leave the Superiors behind, they had left *him* behind.

They had to find a way back to their homes. That was a fact, the rest were simple extras.

"You're absolutely correct," Isla said. She pushed herself up. "Where are we going to walk to?" she asked, looking at the dark woods.

"North."

"I'll go ahead and dare to ask how are you sure?"

"The Northern Guarders are the best option we have."

Isla shook her head.

"I just hope for them not to be as bad mannered as the last Guarders we met."

"Me too," he managed to say.

He helped her up to her feet and picked up Ayala while holding a lightbulb in his hand.

They moved through the forest. Isla carried the compass, Tom the light. They walked. And when they were tired, they continued walking. When they felt they were lost they continued walking. When the night just became darker. When the light flickered or Isla stumbled, they continued walking. In the same direction and with the same determination.

For hours they walked, with nothing more than silence besides the cold, wetness, and fear. Tom knew that a forest was quiet only when a predator was close, and for some reason he knew they weren't the predators.

"Just keep going, we're closer than before," was the phrase that they kept repeating to one another.

By the fifth hour the light started to flicker until it was completely gone. Just like their hopes.

Alone, the two kids felt the world around them fall. Isla had wrapped Ayala's leg with some healing plants, and she had stuffed another bunch of leaves into her mouth. That, apparently, was the only thing that had kept the kind girl barely breathing. Tom felt her cold body against his arms, he wished there was something he could do to save her.

I have to admit, they tried, they really did try, that was the only thing Tom knew how to do. Yet without light they kept walking in circles, falling to the ground and smacking their faces into trees. That's when it started to sink into Tom's head, they were going to die. There wasn't another solution.

And so, as a matter of magic, a fragile, small light appeared in front of them. Far away, very far away, in the mountains.

Tom looked at it, it was faint, and it was real, they were getting somewhere.

"A light can mean-"

Another flying light interrupted Isla.

Tom followed it with his eyes.

He gasped.

It was an arrow on fire, directed to them. They were under attack.

44

NO MORE RUNNING

S oon it was raining, a horrible and dangerous rain of arrows on fire.

Tom ran for cover behind the biggest tree he could find. At least the fire replaced the light bulbs.

He pushed Ayala against the tree, pressing her arms against her stomach to keep her from getting burned. Tens of arrows fell beside them, the fire eating anything that surrounded it.

He watched it spread throughout the dried leaves on the ground, burning every leaf of grass and every flower on its way.

The light made Tom able to see Ayala, she was blue. Her eyes were half open, her skin was cold.

"No, no, no."

He tried to check her pulse and her breathing, the shaking and the fear didn't let him find it.

He looked at his sides.

"ISLA!" he screamed; she was nowhere to be seen. "ISLA!" he called her again, no answer came. He was alone.

"I'm done...," he said and gently set Ayala's body against the tree, her hands and legs as close as to her, to keep her from the fire.

Tom accepted his fate. He had been fighting it, maybe even a little bit too much. He had tried to find opportunities where they didn't exist. Now finally he stepped away, he was going to die, and he couldn't do anything about it.

He closed his eyes for a second, his heart broken. He just wished for another second to tell his mother that he loved her. Just one more second to tell his dad he was going to eat his food. One more second to tell May that all this time he just missed her and should have called more often. One more second to give Hally a thank you. One more second to tell Ayala and Isla he was sorry.

The second never came, just more arrows and more smoke to decide Tom's fate.

Tom stepped away from the tree, it was his time, and he accepted it.

45

THE LAST FRONTIER.
THE LAST MISSION?

Hally waited until dark to cross the second frontier. Exactly one minute before the twelve-hour shift ended, she showed up at the frontier. She was greeted by a clearly overworked twenty-year-old. The guy had immense bags under his eyes and couldn't keep himself from yawing every five words.

She made sure to use a soothing voice in a whispering way. She was nice to him and spoke slowly and calmly. As a consequence, the worker didn't even mind asking anything and when she handed her papers, he didn't even look at them before handing them back and letting her through.

The town after the second frontier was much more exclusive to residents. There were less shops and more houses. She could have slept, rested a little before trying for the third frontier. She couldn't bring herself to do it.

In its place she decided to roam the streets like a lost child. She soon realized it had been the best and the worst decision she could have taken. On one hand, there was no one and she didn't have to deal with people, much less guards. On the other, the streets were so quiet, so lonely and dark that it made her skin crawl. All she could imagine was the Shadower back at Platz. It's pointy teeth and sharp claws. Her brain didn't seem to care that she now had incredible powers, fear was still fear.

She moved carefully, yet freely, through the whole place, only finding two houses with the lights still on. She tried to get as close to the frontier as possible. As she got closer she got she decided to use her invisibility and eventually found a building that she climbed. From the roof she observed. The Inner City was bright, every light turned on. And the buildings... they were gorgeous.

The third frontier was significantly smaller than the two others, composed of two lanes. The workers surely weren't asleep in this one. As a matter of fact, Hally wasn't even sure those were normal workers. They look more like trained assassins, not only because of the complete military uniform and the guns at their side.

She stopped focusing on the actual entrance, there was no way she was going through that.

Along the frontier there was something like an electromagnetic invisible fence. Hally could feel it, better said it was what she didn't feel that made her feel it. She couldn't feel anything on the other side. Any leaf, bird, building, or car, it was like they didn't exist.

So, no powers inside?

No... I think it just works keeping things from going through it.

Hally climbed down the building, she would have to find a way to make a hole in that fence and make it through it. With Pam it would've been easier.

When she was far from the frontier, she found an alley and made herself visible, ninety-nine percent of the people were asleep, she wasn't going to risk being seen using her power by the one percent.

She walked with no place in mind, she would have to try in the morning. She wished for Lukai and his plans, or Piet and his warmth, even Pam and her company, but once again she was alone.

By half past 3 am, Hally continued walking. She had long passed the family side of the neighborhood, and now she was on the side that looked more like government owned. There she found a parking lot filled with trucks and vans.

She laughed when she saw it. Now she understood the hatred Madelaine had for the yellow, it was ugly and that's saying little. All the vans and trucks were completely painted, there were some red, some lemon green and some with that horrible mustard yellow. They seemed to be in storage, which meant they were well taken care of, not in use.

She looked at the vans from outside for a second before her curiosity took over. Soon she entered the parking lot protected by her invisibility.

She focused on the vans. The trailers looked like normal trailers with colors. The vans however did show that they were used for not so average things. She peeked inside the windows and tried to open several, they were all closed.

She was looking at a red van with its window slightly open when she heard something. She turned around and saw a figure walking around the vans like she was.

Hide!

She felt the need to give herself a much-deserved facepalm.

I'm invisible.

Hally moved after the figure to see what it was doing until she caught up to its face. Then she went ahead to make herself visible and quickly moved directly behind him.

"Lukai?"

"Ah!" Lukai jumped. "Hally!"

"Hi."

"Hi," he said back, trying to catch his breath.

"What are you doing here?" she asked.

"You mean what I'm doing here after you sedated me and locked me in a storage room. Helping you of course, I wasn't going to leave you alone in all of this."

Hally looked at him.

"You're not mad?"

He shrugged.

"I get why you did it. I'm only angry that I didn't think of it first. What are *you* doing here? I expected you to be finding a way into the Inner City."

"That's exactly what I'm doing, something in these vans could get me through the frontier," Hally answered, still confused. "How did you get out? Where are Piet and Pam?"

Lukai looked at her and smiled. There was something weird about it.

"It was half open. Piet and Pam decided to stay out. I was walking, looking for you, when I ended up here," he said. "Something in this place called my attention."

Hally's smile faded. He was lying, his heart said so.

"Really?" she asked.

"Yes, I guess maybe it was the colors," he replied.

Hally put a hand behind her back and called upon one of her knives, something was off. This was the second time he acted this way.

"You're lying," Hally said, it was better if they went straight to the point.

Lukai's eyes darkened a single sentence written on them, 'why did you have to find out'.

"Are you with the Superiors?" she continued.

Lukai scoffed.

"With the Superiors? You have to be kidding me!"

He took a step forward.

The grip on her knife tightened.

"Don't move," Hally threatened him.

"Hally... I can explain," Lukai assured her.

"Then go ahead, explain. You're working with somebody, who is it?"

Lukai didn't answer.

Hally laughed; her heart broken.

"Gosh! I can't believe it! Since when? Since you got on that bus? Have you been playing us?"

"No! Of course not!"

"Then since when? Did you alert the Superiors on the field trip? Is it your fault we separated from the rest? Are we just merchandise?" Hally's voice was one step from breaking.

"No-"

"Wait! It was you who told Tanner about the Shadower. About MY fear of the Shadower!"

Lukai blinked, perplexed. It had been him.

"Is all of this why you have gone above and beyond to get along with us? With me? To find out our weaknesses and exploit them?"

Hally waited for the answer, it never came.

"I can't believe it!" she cried. "And I was stupid enough to..." She couldn't even bring herself to say it.

"It's hard to explain-"

Her gaze hardened.

"What are you doing here?"

"Hally, I can't tell you."

"What are you doing in this place, right now? And where are Piet and Pam?"

Lukai licked his lips.

"Pam and Piet are safe, still asleep from the thing you gave them. I was smart enough to know you'd do something like that and took something beforehand. And I'm here looking for something for someone," he admitted.

"For whom? And what? Is it a doctor from the Lab?"

"That's all I can say," Lukai shrugged his shoulders.

"It is from the Lab! You do understand that we are going against those same people at this same moment. This is a battle!"

"Hally there are about five sides in this war."

"And every single side is wrong!"

"That's why I'm picking the one that ensures me they'll give them what they deserve!"

"Are you doing this out of revenge?"

Lukai looked at Hally, he wanted to tell her. He couldn't.

"It's not like that."

"Then explain."

Lukai took a deep breath.

"I'm the same person that you have known for the last week. The team, Pam, Piet, you and me, there hasn't been a moment where it was faked. I just have something else to do."

"Something else to do?" Hally asked. "What the heck does that mean?"

Her voice echoed through the cold night air.

"Hey! Don't act like that. It's not like you don't have secrets," Lukai scoffed.

"Secrets? What are you even talking about?"

"I don't know. The Gang. That scar on your right arm. The anxiety. It's obvious you know things you are not telling us. It's obvious you too want people to pay."

Hally forced a laugh.

"Those 'secrets' you talk about, aren't secrets. Those are memories. Memories that I have fought to keep locked up. Memories *I* have the right to keep private!"

Lukai crossed his arms.

"We are not gonna get anywhere like this." He came closer.

Hally pulled her knife from her back

Lukai's sword appeared at his side immediately.

"Put down your sword," Hally ordered.

"You pulled your knife first."

"You lied first."

Lukai took another step forward.

"Don't get closer!"

Hally lifted her hand, ready to push Lukai against the trucks.

"Hally," Lukai called, he knew he stood no chance if a fight broke out, not with Hally's powers.

"Lower your sword." She was no longer asking.

"I would never hurt you, you know that."

"I don't know anything at this point. You're working for The General!"

"That's not true!"

"The General. A scientist. Tanner. What do I care? They are all the same, just like you are. You must be proud. Huh? You tricked the spy. You got away with it. But it's okay, anyway it's my fault. You can't be betrayed unless you trust someone."

Hally fought the tears back; she had learned that lesson before. Why had she ignored it?

"We can still work together," Lukai replied.

"Oh really? How's that going to work?"

"We still need to get the blood off their hands."

Hally looked at him.

"Is that what your boss wants?"

"Yes."

I might need him.

He's a traitor.

Hally sighed. She called off her dagger and it disappeared. Lukai followed suit.

"We're getting that blood, and we're destroying it. Then we're getting out of this city, and I want you gone. Whatever it is you are doing, whoever's dirty job, I'm not going to let you drag the rest of us into it. Because whatever it is, if it has to do with one of them, it will only end badly."

"Hally, you don't know what you're talking about."

"Maybe not. Maybe I do. But that's the condition. We put an end to all this, and you are gone like the wind. You are out of the Guardian of Kinds, out of Platz, out of all our lives, and you get to continue your side hustle. When that moment arrives, you're going to tell everybody that you don't think this is the life for you and you're going back to your family."

"Why?"

"Because Piet, Pam, Tom… All of them have enough on their plates as it is. They don't need this feeling of betrayal–"

"Hally I never meant –"

"If you don't agree with this, we can solve it another way. But you know you can't win, not against me. I'm far more powerful than you are."

Lukai's eyes met the floor. He was thinking.

"Deal?"

"Deal," he muttered.

"And if for a second you do anything that looks like it's going to jeopardize the mission or hurt Piet and Pam, you're done. You hear me?"

"Loud and clear."

Hally looked at the star filled sky. How had she ended up like that?

"Halls I just want to say–"

"I don't want to hear it," Hally interrupted him.

"Why?"

"I'm used to manipulating words to get myself out of situations, why do you think?"

Hally didn't wait for an answer, she returned to what she had been doing before, figuring out how to get through the third frontier, getting the blood, saving lives.

She moved closer to the van and looked inside, it felt dangerous to turn her back like that to Lukai.

Hally shook her head; she couldn't let her feelings get into that one. There was blood that could take many lives, it was her job to change that.

The window was slightly open. Hally looked through it, on the other side she could see the lock on the driver door. It was way too far away to reach it with her hand.

She focused on the lock and silenced the world around her. The lock started to move slowly but steady. Before unlocking it fell.

Hally let out a growl.

She tried again.

The lock started to move again. It moved little by little until it was unlocked.

The outside noise returned to Hally's brain, and she smiled to herself.

"Want any help?"

The smile faded.

She ignored Lukai and walked to the driver's side of the van. Lukai followed her.

"Halls?" Lukai asked again. She still didn't respond. "Aren't we supposed to work together?"

He reached for her arm to call her attention.

"Don't touch me," she hissed, moving her arm away from him. "I said we put an end to all of this. If to do so you can help, do it. If not, stay out of the way."

She opened the door and went into the van.

Lukai jumped inside right behind her.

"What are we looking for?"

Hally glared at him in silence.

"I know, something to get through the third frontier," Lukai replied.

Hally continued her search.

I should have used the knife.

Hally dropped the papers she was looking at.

Lukai rushed to pick them from the floor and help her, but Hally took them first.

"Halls…," he said. "I'm sorry, really sorry. About all of this. There's much going on you wouldn't understand"

That wasn't a lie.

Hally turned, studied his eyes.

"You made two mistakes. First, don't *ever* talk about something you don't really know about or even understand. Yes, I have secrets. Events in my life, people I met and things I have been through that my family doesn't even know about. All of them are past mistakes, past wounds and past lessons I *have* learned. And sure, maybe I have a lot of stuff with which I haven't dealt with, but I don't let those things get in the way of how I behave or act now. So don't come now and shove it into my face as if I was some kind of secret villain, because I'm not. And second, I understand that you're doing what you believe to be the best thing. But I can't work with someone that lies to my face and withholds information like you're doing. However we *are* going to get that blood, and we are going to focus on that. Until then we are not teammates, nor coworkers, nor classmates, nor friends. We are allies, which means we get along because we can't afford not to do so, and we tolerate each other even if we don't want to so we don't become enemies. Do you understand?"

Lukai looked at Hally, there was something broken in his eyes.

"Yes..." he muttered, filled with sadness.

"Perfect," Hally said, trying to hide the same sadness.

It broke her. For a few days she thought she had found the friends she had looked so much for. And for that time, she had thought Lukai was that friend Blake had advised her to have, that friend in which she could really count on.

I guess nothing can be perfect.

Lukai turned around and started looking around the van, his head down like a puppy that had just been yelled at.

"We just keep looking then," he said quietly.

"There's no need," Hally replied, she turned to him and punched him in the nose.

Lukai stumbled back, hands on his bloody nose.

"What-?"

"I already have an idea, and there's no way I'm letting you ruin it."

Lukai looked up.

He held his hands up.

Hally formed a shield; the light didn't get anywhere close to her.

She called another needle to her hand, it appeared.

"I'm sorry, Lukai," she lifted a finger and pressed him against the van, keeping him from moving. "I'm sorry I was going to fall with the same rock twice."

Lukai fought against Hally's invisible force.

She stepped closer and punched the needle in his thigh. Slowly he closed his eyes.

"And just in case you try it again," Hally said as she took a roll of duct tape from the front of the van.

Hally left Lukai comfortable and safe behind another van. When the sun got up, she found a public bathroom and cleaned herself up. Then she got herself a disposable phone and managed to manipulate an ID she found in the van to suit her.

Before leaving she took a final look at Lukai, despite who he'd work for, he had still been her friend. She thought of Piet and Pam. And then of Tom, Ayala and Isla. She did this for them, so they could have a safe life.

Hally smiled; Lukai had been right about something. If she was going down, she was going down with chaos.

She stepped into her van. New dark clothes on, her knives by her side. The official Inner City uniform on top and her ID ready.

She turned the van on, the engine was quiet. In her mind she thanked her grandpa for teaching her how to drive.

Hally took a final deep breath and started moving. She was going to the frontier.

As she drove, she grabbed the burner and dialed. There were two rings before they picked up.

"Aló?" Gia's voice came like a melody from the phone.

Hally's heart broke in pieces.

"Aló?" she repeated.

"Hi Mom, it's me Hally," Hally answered with a couple of tears flooding her eyes.

"Hally!" Gia said with joy. "Are you okay honey? How have you been? Where's Tom?"

Hally chuckled.

"We're okay Mom. Tom's not here right now but I'll tell him to call you. It has been a really tiring week and the signal is terrible. That's why I'm just calling. We're living in this beautiful place called Platz, learning every day. I can move things with my mind!"

Gia laughed.

"Really?"

"Yes," Hally said, the happiness in her voice was real. "Food is amazing too, but not as good as Grandma's. Make sure to tell her I said that when you see her again. When are you moving to Costa Rica?"

"In about two weeks, we're fine though. The university is quite comfy."

"Is Dad there?" Hally asked.

"No honey, he's working."

Hally had to pull the phone away to keep her mom from hearing the sobbing. All she wanted was a goodbye.

She calmed down.

"Well, tell him I love him when you see him. And I love you too Mom. I just felt I had to say it since we haven't talked for a while. And please tell May congratulations on her graduation when you see her, I wish I could have gone. And don't forget to tell Grandma and Grandpa I miss them."

"What's with all the messages?" Gia chuckled; she knew her children perfectly.

"It's just that the signal sucks up here, I have no idea when I'll be able to call you again," Hally said, her calm tone convincing her mom. She wished she could tell her all the things she loved about her and give her thanks for everything, that would make her worry more.

"It's alright," Gia assured her, "I'll tell them. But first talk to me, I want details of your new life. I only know what Blake has told me."

Hally smiled, she wanted to keep talking with her mom for hours. The frontier was in front of her.

"I would love to. But I have to go now."

"Ah," Gia sighed, disappointed. "I understand. Don't take too long to call again. And when we are settled back in Costa Rica make sure to ask Blake permission for you and Tom to come and stay for a while."

"Love you."

"Love you too, can't wait to see you again," Gia added.

The call ended.

Hally's eyes filled with even more tears. She was scared about the idea of never seeing her family again, but this was what she needed to do.

As she pulled up to the frontier, she wiped her face and readied her words.

When she got there, she rolled the window down and what the officer saw was a serious worker.

"ID," the officer asked.

Hally showed him her card.

"Aren't you on the night team?" the officer asked, looking at the van.

"I am," Hally said as if she was tired. She yawned. "They needed someone, and I can use the extra pay."

The officer laughed.

"I do the same every time," he returned the ID without passing it through the computer. "Have a nice day."

Hally took the ID.

"You too," she said and drove in.

She was now inside the Inner City, and she knew she might not make it out.

46

GETTING RID OF
BLOOD IS A HARD JOB

The place was packed with people. Half of them were scientists and workers and the other half were soldiers and officers. Of the soldiers most of them looked to be part of the Superiors, they were there as buyers.

Hally drove the van to the back and parked it between two other red vans just like hers. She walked around the biology building until she found a dark lonely corner out of the camera's field. There she ditched the worker uniform and turned invisible.

Getting in was easy. The different soldiers were continuously getting in and out of the building leaving the doors wide open long enough for her to walk in, the same approach worked to sneak in and out rooms. She just had to be patient and sufficiently quiet.

The first floor of the red building was a big, elegant dining room. There, a group of scientists ate and talked with a lady and a young man. The whole room had more soldiers than the rest of the building. That was where they were conducting the business deal. Hally didn't have to be a genius to know it.

The room was a simple glass walled meeting room. The scientists had nothing, but their coats and their IDs marked with a big red twenty. And the lady, who Hally recognized to be a politician, whom the outside soldiers kept referring to as Ms. Duckstein, didn't yet have the blood. She only had the young man who seemed her personal escort, the same soldiers from outside referred to him as Atonal. Funny name if you asked the Latin girl.

Hally got on an elevator following a scientist and got to the second floor, a floor which she searched through and still found no hint of where the blood was.

She continued on to the third floor and the fourth floor, this is when she realized, the higher the floor the more classified things it held. By the tenth floor it finally moved from normal biology studies to dangerous and extravagant research. On the seventeenth floor she found the whole floor dedicated to a memory loss serum. They were calling it Ph200, and it was to be sold to armies to use in wars and with soldiers, so that secret ops would actually stay secret ops.

"We should be starting trials in a few weeks," she heard a scientist say.

Hally didn't stop to look at it for long, she quietly grabbed a jar and slipped it into her pocket.

She went up all the way to the nineteenth floor and still found nothing. So, she went back and waited inside the elevator for a while for someone to come in and press the number twenty, the last floor. No one came, so she got down and made her way up the stairs.

Finally, she got to the last floor. This had to be it. She wondered if Lukai had woken up.

This last floor was empty, as dead as the streets she had roamed earlier.

Unlike the prior floors, this one had no doors or individual labs. It was one big room.

She moved through the open floor and its weirdness. She went by the cages with tarantulas, in front of the jars with dark ash like Unicorn Powder, until she reached the very end of it. There, perhaps the start of the world's most dangerous weapons, in a supermarket-like-fridge, categorized and sealed, was the blood. How comical her life had become! She couldn't help but chuckle. All resulting from her efforts for that?

It was time to end it.

A lot of things had led her there. A lot of changes. A lot of problems. A lot of pain and fear. But she'd gotten there with power. A power no one else held. And although there was a lot to learn about that aspect, Hally knew one thing for sure. She was no weapon, and no one was going to use her like that.

She focused on the keypad by the glass door, she didn't have the key.

She lifted her hand; she could feel the tiny parts between the pieces of glass that made the doors. She pulled the tiny parts apart.

The glass door exploded in a million pieces, stretching all the way to the end of the room. Nowhere close to Hally.

Chemicals in hand and a smile on her face, Hally pulled the red bags and poured chemical after chemical into them.

"You're going to need to find someone else, Tanner. Someone else's blood to suck in, vampire."

Soon 'blood' wouldn't define what was inside those bags.

"And just in case..." She pulled out a lighter and set fire to them.

Hally smiled; the job was done.

She watched the bags burning, the fire forming beautiful colors as it burned the chemicals.

She took a step back, peace ruled her.

Her eyes fell on a set of papers on a desk beside her. She frowned. She lifted them and read them, word after word getting worse than what she could have ever imagined.

"What the heck?"

They were a research proposal for human experiments. Atrocities I won't dare write about.

Hally looked around, suddenly she noticed more and more papers around, each worse than the last.

Anger rose through her and before she knew it, she was adding everything to her list, the fire growing like a storm. She grabbed the papers, opened the spider cages, and smashed the computers. They weren't going to use anyone else like a weapon either.

"My job here is done," she said proudly when she stepped inside the elevator again, chaos, the only thing left behind.

The elevator door closed. Hally sighed; she could go home now. She imagined herself back at the beach with the rest of the kids. Tom by his side. She would have a great time telling him about her adventures, he would probably scold her for some of them.

Hally smiled; she couldn't wait to see her brother.

The elevator stopped midway, an emergency alarm and a red light followed.

"No, no, no." She was so close, too close to give up. They couldn't get her.

Hally lifted her hands, the door opened. The elevator had stopped right in between the floors, close enough to give her space to get out. She climbed her way onto the floor.

The hallway blazed with the same red light. There were no scientists to be seen, they knew what had to be done during those situations unlike Hally.

"Hally Black, thank you for coming!" Tanner taunted through the speakers on the wall along the alarm.

Hally tightened her fist by her sides as she kept moving, she was still invisible, she still had some hope.

"We're going to get you," Tanner added.

Hally moved opening door after door, where the heck were the stairs!

"You thought you could come without us knowing? How rude! Seems after all we'll get our blood."

You wish

Boom!

An explosion came from above her head. Hally smiled; the fire she'd started had finally reached the gas tanks.

"YOU BLEW A HOLE IN MY BUILDING! THAT'S IT!"

Her laugh soon changed.

From the walls, just by the speakers, clouds of black dust burst into the air, then into Hally's lungs.

A burning feeling came from inside Hally's head. Her lungs burned, her stomach turning. Whatever that powder was, it was certainly not made to breathe in.

Hally covered her mouth with her sleeve, it didn't make much difference, the powder had already done its effect.

She managed to open one last door before falling to her knees. Where the heck were the stairs!

Hally looked up; her eyes were watering.

"Like it? This is how it was meant to end!" Tanner roared.

Hally called her medical bag and looked through it. She found an energy pill, this time the correct one, and she pushed it down her throat. Her stomach sent it back up. She grabbed the pill again and pushed it inside her throat one more time.

She felt the hard rock-like sensation going inside of her, the pain lightened. It wasn't enough.

Hally forced herself off the ground, she fell again, gasping for air. She knew it now; she wasn't invisible anymore.

"There you are!" Tanner laughed.

Another explosion came, this time stronger.

The room was filled with smoke. It was a mess. The dust had doubled. The fire had spread, everything was getting destroyed. And the burning in her head had returned, this time stronger than before.

"I'm going to enjoy this!"

Hally lifted her head. Was this how she was going to end? Listening to Tanner's horrid voice?

At the end of the hallway a door opened, Lukai came in.

"Hally!" Lukai exclaimed.

Cockroach

As he breathed the powder, he too started to feel its effects, it was noticeable in his eyes. Still, he walked in and pulled her to her feet.

Hally tried to push him away, she was too weak.

Lukai tightened his grip, and soon they were in a different elevator, a working one, far from the dust, smoke and fire.

Hally coughed. Her lungs welcomed the fresh air and her stomach settled.

"Are you okay?" Lukai asked.

Hally pushed him away; his nose was swollen from her punch.

"How did you get here so fast?"

"Did the same as you," he pulled an ID from his pockets.

"I don't need you saving me," she replied. "It doesn't mean I don't thank you," she added.

Lukai smiled.

"See, I'm not the bad guy."

Hally took a deep breath, the blood was gone, burned. No one was going to use it for a weapon. The job was done! They could finally go back to Platz and relax.

The door of the elevator opened; they were back on the first floor. Outside Tanner waited, beside him stood ten soldiers, guns pointing at Hally.

She looked at them, they were all backed up against the walls.

Chaos. She chuckled. She certainly wasn't weak enough not to cause a scene.

A soldier came towards her, he swung his fist. She ducked, knife in hand and a clean slice on his leg as an answer.

Two more came, she pushed them against the roof. And then she turned to the man himself. Tanner.

Hally called a second knife.

"Get closer and I'll kill him," he threatened.

Hally looked at the frightened Lukai inside Tanner's grip. His throat white underneath the knife.

She hesitated. She could leave him there, betray him the way he had done. Would that be right? The answer came naturally.

Hally put her hands up, the knives vanished. She was powerful, yet her mind was still too foggy to take the risk. Her wrists soon met the horrid handcuffs, her powers gone.

Tanner smiled.

"Good job boy," Tanner said to Lukai, releasing him with a pat on his back.

Lukai looked at Hally.

Not the bad guy?

"Hally, I promise you-"

Hally didn't even bother looking at him, he was a traitor. And she had fallen for it, twice.

Soldiers came in and grabbed her by her arms.

"Please just trust me…" Lukai exclaimed at her as she was pulled away.

The soldiers took Hally into the fancy dining room on the first floor and sat her down in front of Ms. Duckstein and the scientists.

The place was quiet, all eyes fixed on her.

"Please bring food for the young lady," Tanner said as he stepped in, behind him came Lukai. No handcuffs on his wrists.

A rush of anger flooded her veins.

Not working with Tanner, huh?

A waiter came in and put a plate in front of Hally.

Hally looked at Tanner.

"You may eat," he told her.

"Sure," she responded sarcastically and held up her tied hands.

Tanner signaled a soldier who walked by and untied the handcuffs, leaving her with two Unicorn Powder bracelets that still didn't allow her to use her powers but allowed her to move her hands freely.

The room was quiet. Tanner stared, waiting for her to eat.

Hally grabbed the plastic spoon and grabbed the plate closely. She was about to take a bite when she smashed the whole thing into the ground. Eggs spread into the nice white rug and pieces of ceramic falling everywhere.

A soldier moved towards her. Tanner stopped him.

Hally looked at Tanner directly in the eyes.

"That's not lady-like," he said.

"Neither is it gentlemanly to kidnap a fifteen-year-old to sell her blood, yet you do it," Hally responded.

Ms. Duckstein laughed; she was a really, ugly lady.

"The girl's right perhaps. I should take her," she said.

Tanner turned to Ms. Duckstein.

"Just wait a second, I have a deal that will work for the both of us."

"What would that be?" Atonal asked, the young man didn't look so young in his uniform.

"I'll take her, get enough blood for my studies, maybe some more research, and then give her back to you. Then you and your group can use her as you wish for your little stupid quests."

"They are not stupid quests!" Atonal exclaimed standing up.

"Shh, calm down," Ms. Duckstein told him, and he sat down grabbing his side, he was hurt. "I already have three of these specimens you call Íroes with me, why would I want another one?"

Hally looked perplexed at Ms. Duckstein.

"The Superiors have Íroes?" she asked, chills covering her arms.

"Ohh yes," Atonal said, annoyed. "They have this new 'champion' that plays with lightning."

Tom.

"Atonal!" Ms. Duckstein scolded him. "Don't overshare information! Today we are trying to make a deal with these scientists. Let's not forget they have been our enemies for a long time."

"That's what we are trying to do," Tanner said to her. "With the Íroes finally here we can join forces, against the FSC and The General, but especially against the Guarders."

That would certainly start a lot of trouble.

Hally hid her hands beneath the table and called for a knife. A small one appeared in her hand. She started quietly tapping her bracelets.

Ms. Duckstein looked at Tanner.

"You still haven't told me, why would I want another one?"

Tanner gave a step closer to Hally. She looked at him with contempt, if he dared to touch her, she would bite his hand off.

Tanner understood the message, he stayed where he was.

"This is no ordinary Íroe," Lukai intervened. "She's a Magister," he added and looked at Tanner.

Tanner nodded in approval; Lukai was allowed to speak.

"What does that mean?" Ms. Duckstein asked.

"It means she is stronger and more powerful than you could have ever imagined. She's still learning but with proper instruction she can become the most dangerous creature in history, destroying cities without moving a finger," Lukai added.

Hally felt anger inside of her, how could he really be a traitor?

She tapped her bracelets once again until the plastic gave in. The powder started to fall into the rug. Little by little she got her powers back.

"With her the Superiors could have more power than the whole world together," Lukai finished.

"She also has teleportation powers, easily she could get all of you inside Platz. Or she can get the lost piece of the portal you have been looking for so badly. I saw it with my own eyes, she has it," Lukai added when he noticed the woman wasn't convinced.

Ms. Duckstein looked at Hally, new interest growing in her face.

It's time, we have to get out of here.

Hally hurried the powder out of the bracelet and made a hole in the other.

"How much money are you asking for?" Ms. Duckstein asked. A soldier handed her a case filled with bills. "I assume you're going to want something as a proof that we'll keep our side of the deal."

Tanner gave a malicious smile at Hally that read 'you're not getting away this time' and turned to Ms. Duckstein.

"The price we had talked about, from the start," he said.

"Alright, I believe we have a deal," she responded. The soldier handed the bag of money to Tanner. Her ugly face was filled by an even uglier smile.

Tanner turned to the scientists.

"Get her ready for the experiments and tests and–" he said.

Hally made a retching sound.

Everyone stopped.

"Sorry, excuse me."

She repeated the action adding some coughs.

The scientists looked at each other. Even Lukai stared at her confused.

Hally hit the bracelets against her legs trying to get the last of the powder off. She calculated that she still had some of the energy pill in her system, she would need all of her powers to be able to escape from there.

She made the sound again.

"Stop that!" Tanner exclaimed at her.

Hally felt the last of the powder fall into the rug. Her powers rose from her stomach.

She looked up at him.

"Your shoes are untied," she said. Tanner looked at his feet.

Hally stood up, an invisible force coming out of her like a wave. The scientists and soldiers were smashed against the glass walls, unable to move or reach their guns. Tanner, Lukai, Atonal and Ms. Duckstein were crushed between the wooden table and the wall.

Hally pressed the table against their bodies.

"I'm getting the portal piece!" Ms. Duckstein yelled angrily. "Atonal!"

Atonal tried to move. Hally pressed the table even harder.

"Hally-" Lukai started to say, she pressed so hard she started to hear their difficult breathing.

She called her bag and from it she took out the golden ball.

"You want this?" she asked Ms. Duckstein. "James wants this?" she asked again.

"Yes!" Atonal muttered.

Hally looked at it in her hand. It disappeared. She felt the fatigue striking, she fought it off.

"It's gone. Portaled. To anywhere on this planet. And the only person who knows where it is, it's me. You're never getting to Platz," Hally said to Ms. Duckstein.

"I'm getting it one way or another. I'll torture you until you talk!" Ms. Duckstein yelled.

"I'll never do so," Hally responded confidently.

"Then I'll torture your parents, grandparents, siblings, friends, teachers. We'll see how many people you watch suffer and die before talking," she replied.

Hally's confidence faded.

No one is dying. I'm not letting it.

"Good luck," Hally said to Ms. Duckstein. "I won't be able to talk about something I can't remember," she pulled a small jar from her pocket. "Recognize this, Tanner. It's yours, a memory wiper. Cheers." She brought the jar to her mouth.

"No!" Tanner and Ms. Duckstien yelled.

"Stop," Atonal yelled.

"Hally!" Lukai begged.

The cold liquid went down her throat. It tasted terrible, worse that she could have imagined. At first if burned, then it made her dizzy, and finally she started to lose her grip with her powers. The energy pill was done, and the serum was working.

Everyone dropped to the floor. Hally no longer controlled the room.

The soldiers hurried for their guns.

"Guns!" Lukai alerted her before the first shot was fired.

Hally formed a thin and weak shield around her.

It was too late, she looked at her stomach, a bullet had gone through.

It didn't hurt surprisingly; she was far too tired to notice the pain.

She fell to the ground; Lukai ran towards her. She pushed him away.

"Hally!" Lukai said to her, he sounded panicked.

Hally looked at him. She didn't like him; she couldn't remember why.

Her vision blurred.

Explosions filled the place. Before Hally realized there was a young girl beating the bad people, at least she thought those were the bad people, she didn't quite remember. The girl was followed by another one, Asian and very angry and a blond boy who looked really young.

"What is going on?" Hally managed to mutter to herself before her eyes closed.

47

BACK

"No!" a voice said from the dark.

A figure came out of nowhere and pushed Tom to the ground behind another tree covering him from the arrows.

"What are you doing?" the figure asked as it rose up.

Tom looked at his face illuminated by the fire. It was Blake.

"I was accepting my fate," Tom admitted.

Blake looked at him, his heart broken.

"You're not going to die. Not now and not like this," he said before pulling him close and giving him a hug. "You're safe Tom, we got you."

Tom felt his face against Blake's warm body. He wasn't used to hugs, but he liked that one.

"Isla! And Ayala!" Tom exclaimed as Blake stepped backwards.

"Isla's safe," Blake replied. "I found her a minute ago. Where's Ayala?"

Tom pointed at the tree beside them. Ayala's body remained moveless against the tree.

Blake's heart sank.

"Is she...?" The words didn't make it out.

"I'm afraid I don't know."

Blake looked at Ayala and then to Tom.

"Stay behind this tree, I'm going to get her out first," Blake said.

Tom nodded and Blake moved to the other tree. He ran rapidly avoiding the continuous, oncoming arrows. He carefully picked her up and disappeared in the dark.

Tom looked around; more arrows came. He moved closer to the tree until there was no place to do so. The fire grew out of control. He panicked. The smoke rose, screening his eyesight. The heat got closer. Where was Blake? He had said he wasn't going to die...

Before the fire got to him, a pair of hands pulled him from behind the tree and pulled him away into the forest, away from the fire.

Tom sighed.

"I must thank you-" Tom let out.

"It was my pleasure," James said, his wicked teeth showing across his face.

Tom's heart stopped. Wrong brother.

"I- I-" he muttered; he found no words.

"Relax champion, I don't come here to kill you. You have done a good job, I just want you to remember which is the right side when this war starts," James said.

He took Tom's hand and handed his golden pin.

"You'll know when to call me." He went into the dark.

Tom looked at his hand, his pin just like he remembered it.

"Tom!" Blake called him desperately from the dark.

"Here!" Tom replied putting the pin in his pocket.

"Tom!" Blake called again.

Tom ran toward the sound. Until he found the source.

Blake looked at him, there was a big fire separating the two of them.

"Stay there," Blake said with determination in his eyes.

He took off his coat and looked at the rising fire as nothing. He backed away a few steps and ran towards it. He jumped.

He made it to the other side.

"How are we getting through the fire?" Tom asked Blake.

The fire continued, now it was impossible to jump over it. The smoke burned Tom's eyes and throat.

"Don't worry. I'm getting you out of here," Blake promised.

Tom coughed, his way of saying please.

Blake grabbed his arm and pulled him into the forest. He turned here and there, apparently random. Several times their path was interrupted by fire.

Eventually they made it into a valley. In the center of it there was a helicopter showered by the moon's light.

Blake ran towards it and helped him in. There, Ayala already had medicine bags hanging from her arms. Beside her, Isla sat elegantly.

"Put on the seatbelts," Blake ordered as he jumped inside.

Tom looked around; everything was going too fast for him.

"Seatbelt," Isla repeated.

"Oh yeah," Tom blurted out. He tied the straps across his chest.

"I'll dare ask who will fly the helicopter?" Isla asked over the fire still sending smoke up their noses.

"I will," Blake gloated, and the engine started.

Tom fell asleep on the ride. When he woke up, they were reaching the ground, and his hand was wrapped around the pin in his pocket. He knew he had dreamed something about it, he couldn't remember what exactly.

The engine stopped. They were back. They were in Platz. But somehow it wasn't the same one they had left. All the colors Tom had worshiped, dead. All the beauty, stolen.

They were met by a doctor, a friend of Blake that owed him a favor. With the help of Blake they took Ayala off the helicopter and rushed her inside Center into an improvised infirmary.

Tom and Isla were met by Beira and Bobby, who could care less about the ash and hugged them.

"We're so happy you're here," Beira sobbed.

Both were taken inside. Beira helped them get upstairs and get themselves cleaned up. She made sure to talk to them calmly and quietly, she didn't ask any questions.

For most of the time Tom was lost in his thoughts, especially when he showered. He had no idea how to process the last few days. The good thing was that he was back at Platz. Right? That's what he wanted?

Soon he was informed that Hally was also missing. She wasn't with the Superiors though. That brought some peace to his soul, at least she wasn't in the inferno he'd been through.

After getting themselves clean Bobby met Isla and Tom with a plate full of food.

"Thank you," Isla said.

Tom looked at the food, he had been so hungry lately that he wasn't able to feel hunger anymore.

"Drink this," Bobby gave him a glass. Tom wrapped his fingers around it.

For a second he was back fighting against Atonal, striking him in the stomach. James at his table, proud.

He stood up, spilling water everywhere. Heart pounding, chills falling down his neck.

"I'm so sorry," he apologized over and over again.

Beira walked around the table and put her hand on his shoulder.

"It's alright, it's no problem. I'll clean it up," she assured him. "You continue eating. What would you like to drink?" she asked.

Tom shook his head.

"No… no… I don't want to drink anything," he replied.

Beira opened her mouth. Then she closed it, she had given it a second thought.

"Okay," she accepted and went to the kitchen to get some napkins.

Tom sat back down, his hands shaking.

"Don't worry Tom, I make messes all the time. It'll dry up," Bobby assured him.

Tom looked at Isla in front of him, she had barely touched her food. She was lost in her thoughts and even had an elbow on the table.

His memory was hazy, large parts missing, only the ugly ones persisted. Yet he knew he'd made a lot of mistakes that had caused pain to Isla and Ayala. Somehow, he knew those weren't going to be as easy to clean up like spilled pineapple juice.

After eating, the doctor came and looked at Isla and Tom, he too made an effort to minimize the number of questions. It was hard with the wounds.

When he took a look at Isla's arms, at the horrible cuts James had so maliciously inflicted, Tom saw something die inside him. Bobby started to cry, and Beira had to take him outside. Blake just stood there, blaming himself.

"What did he do to you?" he asked.

"Whatever it took for us to comply," Isla responded

Isla got a few stitches and some shots. Then the doctor gave her a nutrient bag. Isla tried her best to act as she would have a week earlier, at times she was successful, at others she just couldn't. Whenever the doctor touched her arms, she flinched.

Tom himself didn't get any stitches. His cuts were healed and the bullet hole as well, however he had several infections and his blood tested for weird components. The doctor gave him a few shots as well and nutrients, just like Isla. Tom sat and listened to him talk with Blake. Isla and he were going to be okay. Ayala would have to fight the poisoning, and she could lose her leg. Blake just nodded.

As soon as the doctor left Isla excused herself to her room quietly. Blake stayed with Tom. Tom explained to him what had happened, he avoided many details, and with them many memories.

Blake sat there, providing all the time Tom needed and listened to him.

When the night came, he was offered another plate of food that he refused. And just like Isla he excused himself and went to his room. Before entering he turned in the hallway and knocked on the girl's door.

"Come in," Isla responded.

Tom opened the door and poked his head.

Isla was sitting in her bed; she had been crying. Beside her, Ayala was tucked in her own, medical machines plugged around and in her.

"I just wanted to see if everything was alright," he said.

Isla stared at him.

"Everything is not alright," she mumbled, pointing at Ayala and then at herself. "They messed us up. We'll make it through hopefully," she told herself and took a deep breath.

Tom nodded.

"Okay," he awkwardly answered and backed away.

"Tom!" Isla called him.

"Yes?" he asked, poking his head back in.

"Everything you did, it wasn't your fault. Blake said the pills they gave us in the mornings, those, messed with our heads."

Tom nodded again not knowing what to say.

"Just for you to know," she added.

"Thanks, good night," Tom replied and went back to his room, he couldn't remember ever getting a pill.

Tom woke up and stared at the ceiling. His heart racing and his whole-body trembling. For a second he imagined Roberts at the front of his cells, James waiting with his cane to hit him. Then he remembered, he was in Platz. The noise that woke him up repeated. Those were voices. A lot of them.

He took a sweater as fast as he could and ran down the stairs.

Were those the Superiors? Were they there to kill them? No, that didn't make any sense. James could have just killed him in the forest. Why hadn't he?

He ran to the entrance of the Center.

He saw the reason for the noise. There were the other missing kids. Blake and Beira ran past Tom to greet them. Tom stayed there for a second.

They were talking to each other, Beira and Blake making sure that everyone was alright.

Tom looked at the kids, Pepper, Piet and Pam were being squeezed by Bobby's hugs. Lukai was talking with Blake.

He studied them. Some cheers. Some laughs. Some tears.

He only cared about one thing.

"Where's my sister?"

EPILOGUE

I t was raining, dirt turned to mud. A black car awaited. Inside it James played with his cane, it had been a long time since he'd met him.

Another car came from the darkness.

"It's time sir," a soldier told James.

James grabbed a hold of his cane and combed his hair.

He opened the door. His brand-new shoes met the ground. He walked into the rain.

From the other car a door opened, and a figure came out, sending down a shiver through James' spine. Yes, even he was scared of *him*.

James put both his hands on his cane.

"James," the figure said.

"Sir," James saluted.

"I don't have much time, speak fast."

James swallowed hard.

"The boy is on our side."

The figure took a rock out of his pocket and moved it around his fingers.

"Are you sure?"

James nodded.

The rock flew by James' head into the car, leaving a permanent mark.

"Speak!"

"So- sorry, sir. I am- sure," James muttered.

"Then why am I here? I have things to do!"

"I need to know how to proceed, sir. What does the Company want me to do?"

The figure sighed.

"Have I taught you nothing?"

James didn't respond.

"Is the boy really on our side?"

"Yes, sir. I made sure of that myself, sir."

The figure smiled.

"And the portal?"

James' voice trembled.

"The last piece is lost. And the girl is... missing."

"Ahh!" Another rock flew by James' head.

"What should I do now sir?"

"If the boy is on our side, then not all is lost. Look for the piece. Alter the gangs. Double the violence and fear. We need them to be focused on their problems. Start fights and battles. We need a war."

"A war between who, sir?"

"Everyone, every single person that stands against a gang will be considered a Guarder and they will have free rein to kill them. Eventually the governments will have to deal with their people killing each other and we'll get what we want."

"Which is, sir?"

"Power. Real power, James."

James smiled; he liked the sound of that.

"What should we do about the girl then, sir?"

"Leave her. The General and her scientist are going crazy looking for her. They need her, and better, they want her.

The girl is far stronger than the boy and a real Íroe, eventually she won't be able to take it and she'll come out to play the hero. The government will then find her, and they will shatter her into pieces. Once she is broken, we can reconstruct her the way we want."

There was silence, the rain soaking both gentlemen's clothing.

"Would that be all, sir?" James asked.

"No. Prepare your men."

"What for exactly, sir?"

The figure turned to James.

"Can't you smell it?"

James didn't smell anything.

"I'm afraid not, sir."

The figure laughed.

"It's the air before battle, soon the only smell left will be blood."

Hally woke up. She was met by the face of an old lady, fierce blue eyes looking back at her.

"Hello," the lady said.

"Hi..." Hally muttered back confused.

The lady took a step backward, giving Hally enough space to

sit up. She was in a pretty room, yellow walls, big windows, vanilla scented.

Hally grabbed her stomach, it hurt.

"Can you tell me who you are?" the lady asked.

Hally looked at her, her face was filled with freckles.

"I'm Hally Black Sols," she replied.

The lady's eyes opened wide.

She looked at her shocked. That wasn't the answer she was expecting.

"What can you tell me about the Íroes?"

Hally hesitated to give the answer.

"You can trust me," the lady assured her.

She seems fine.

"They are people that are born natural heroes who gain powers. I'm a Magister, one of the five types," she said.

"She's okay?" a voice asked behind the lady.

Hally looked. By the door there was an older girl with bright blond hair.

"We can tell Tom and Blake, they'll be ecstatic!" the girl continued with a smile.

The older lady turned to her.

"I suppose," she answered, more like a question than a statement.

Hally stared at them.

"Before you do that, I have some questions," she said, getting their attention. "Where am I? Who are you? And who's Tom?"

ACKNOWLEDGMENTS

As I write this, I find it interesting that the word used to describe this segment is *acknowledgments.* In my native language it would usually be called "agradecimientos," which translated would be something similar to "giving thanks". Yet, I like the English version better, because the next names I will mention are not just people that I thank, but people I would love every reader to acknowledge and to know, deeply, that it is because of them that they are able to hold this book.

Firstly, I would love to acknowledge God. It is because of faith that I live. It is because of faith that I first picked a pen. And I am very honest when I say that it is because of faith that Hally and Tom exist. I would love to acknowledge my parents as well. My mom is and will always be my biggest fan, my role model and if you ever wonder whom I thought of when I dedicated this book to all heroes out, she is the first that came to mind. On the other hand, my dad will always be my first reader, and nothing can beat that, for he picked a book even when he doesn't like reading just because it had my name on it and for that I am eternally thankful. I love you both, for ever and ever. I am eternally grateful for believing in me even when I couldn't. And for teaching me to never be afraid of flying. This is for you.

I would love to acknowledge my sister, even though she never reads my books, she's still there and I love her. And it's impossible to finish this book without mentioning my biggest friend, Lilo, my dog. Perhaps for some, it is insane to thank a dog, but only she has dared to sit by my side every single afternoon and never judge a word (although she doesn't know how to read). Oh, I can't forget Don Jean. There are teachers out there that stand and talk but never teach. And there are others out there that teach even when they are quiet. If you ever wonder how I became the person I am today, just know that this guy played a big part and that he has done such a good job in every class that his work can even be seen through the words that tell this story.

I want to acknowledge my grandparents, Abuelito and Mom. Thank you for everything.

And I can't forget the people that have helped this book... Don Allan Tépper, Johanna Vega, George Parr, Karla Herrera and Wendy Hernández.

Finally, I want to acknowledge everybody that went out their way just to ask: "Hey, how's the second book coming?" Many days I didn't know what to answer, but today I can say: *It is going well, very well.*

ABOUT THE AUTHOR

Ivonne Quesada Carazo, known as Ivo Q.C, is a talented Costa Rican writer whose passion for reading manifested itself from an early age. In 2020, Ivo begins her wonderful journey into the world of writing and in 2023, at just 15 years old, she publishes her first novel, *La última oportunidad*. Currently, Ivo studies and dedicates her time to inspire other young people, sharing her experiences and promoting their passion for writing and following their dreams.